Praise for Lisa Wingate's
Accent Novels

Beyond Summer

"*Beyond Summer* is beyond good. It's great! Lisa Wingate's tale of three women from disparate backgrounds and how they join together to survive corporate greed is a cautionary tale for our times. But it is also a story of women's love for each other and their families and the consequence of that love. Out of hardship comes growth and out of desperation, friendship, and out of unasked prayers come answers."
—Sandra Dallas, author of *Prayers for Sale* and *Whiter Than Snow*

The Summer Kitchen

"As always, Wingate's stories are uplifting . . . dealing with matters like friendship, grace, and the power to make a difference in others' lives."
—*The Beaumont Enterprise* (TX)

"The consistently engaging and popular Wingate delivers a warmhearted and genuinely inspirational story of tragedy and hope." —*Booklist*

"An entertaining inspirational family drama. . . . Fans will enjoy this fine tale of a family bonded by need and love, but also seeking actualization from loved ones and especially their selves." —Genre Go Round Reviews

A Month of Summer

"With her signature gentle spiritualism, Wingate sheds light on the toll that aging and disease take on families as she launches a new series with broad appeal."
—*Booklist*

"*A Month of Summer*, with characters we love and plot twists that surprise us, teaches us that it's never too late to open our hearts." —*Southern Lady*

continued . . .

Written by today's freshest new talents and selected by New American Library, NAL Accent novels touch on subjects close to a woman's heart, from friendship to family to finding our place in the world. The Conversation Guides included in each book are intended to enrich the individual reading experience, as well as encourage us to explore these topics together—because books, and life, are meant for sharing.

Visit us online at www.penguin.com.

A Thousand Voices

"Wingate paints a riveting picture of the Choctaw Nation as one woman searches for the family she never knew. Heartfelt and revealing, Wingate's latest proves that she's a rising star in the world of women's fiction." —*Romantic Times* (Top Pick)

"A delightful, heart-wrenching story written in first person with captivating characters, *A Thousand Voices* is sensitively told and masterfully written. It will capture the imagination of readers from the first page . . . not to be missed . . . a perfect 10." —Romance Reviews Today

"Lisa Wingate provides a warm character study of a fully developed individual seeking her roots." —*Midwest Book Review*

Drenched in Light

"Heartfelt and moving, enriched by characters drawn with compassion and warmth." —Jennifer Chiaverini

"Another winner." —*Booklist*

The Language of Sycamores

"Heartfelt, honest, and entirely entertaining . . . this poignant story will touch your heart from the first page to the last." —Kristin Hannah

"An excellent storyteller who knows how to draw readers in quickly and keep them turning the pages, laughing one minute and grabbing for a tissue the next." —*Lubbock Avalanche-Journal*

"Wingate presents another one of her positive and uplifting books . . . tales in the midst of turmoil that are inspirational without being preachy." —*Booklist*

Good Hope Road

"A novel bursting with joy amidst crisis: small-town life is painted with scope and detail in the capable hands of a writer who understands longing, grief, and the landscape of a woman's heart." —Adriana Trigiani

"Wingate has written a genuinely heartwarming story about how a sense of possibility can be awakened in the aftermath of a tragedy to bring a community together and demonstrate the true American spirit." —*Booklist*

Tending Roses

"A story at once gentle and powerful about the very old and the very young, and about the young woman who loves them all. Richly emotional and spiritual, *Tending Roses* affected me from the first page." —Luanne Rice

"You can't put it down without . . . taking a good look at your own life and how misplaced priorities might have led to missed opportunities. *Tending Roses* is an excellent read for any season, a celebration of the power of love." —*El Paso Times*

Praise for Lisa Wingate's "Texas Hill Country" Series

Over the Moon at the Big Lizard Diner

"A beautifully crafted and insightfully drawn page-turner . . . this is storytelling at its best." —Julie Cannon

"A warmhearted tale of love and longing, grits and cowboys, horse psychology and dinosaur tracks." —Claire Cook

"Wingate lets her magical Texas setting and idiosyncratic supporting characters shine." —*Kirkus Reviews*

Lone Star Café

"A charmingly nostalgic treat. . . . Wingate handles the book's strong spiritual element deftly, creating a novel that is sweetly inspirational but not saccharine." —*Publishers Weekly*

"Lisa Wingate is making a national name for herself as an excellent storyteller. Her novels . . . are upbeat and refreshingly wholesome." —*Abilene Reporter-News*

"Leaves you feeling like you've danced the two-step across Texas." —Jodi Thomas

Texas Cooking

"Lisa Wingate writes with depth and warmth, joy and wit." —Debbie Macomber

"*Texas Cooking* . . . will have readers drooling for the next installment . . . [a] beautifully written mix of comedy, drama, cooking, and journalism." —*The Dallas Morning News*

"Takes the reader on a delightful journey into the most secret places of every woman's heart." —Catherine Anderson

"The story is a treasure. You will be swept along, refreshed, and amused. . . . Give yourself a treat and read this tender, unusual story." —Dorothy Garlock

Other Novels by Lisa Wingate

The Blue Sky Hill Series

A Month of Summer

The Summer Kitchen

The Tending Roses Series

Tending Roses

Good Hope Road

The Language of Sycamores

Drenched in Light

A Thousand Voices

The Texas Hill Country Trilogy

Texas Cooking

Lone Star Café

Over the Moon at the Big Lizard Diner

Beyond Summer

Lisa Wingate

NAL ACCENT
Published by New American Library, a division of
Penguin Group (USA) Inc., 375 Hudson Street,
New York, New York 10014, USA
Penguin Group (Canada), 90 Eglinton Avenue East, Suite 700, Toronto,
Ontario M4P 2Y3, Canada (a division of Pearson Penguin Canada Inc.)
Penguin Books Ltd., 80 Strand, London WC2R 0RL, England
Penguin Ireland, 25 St. Stephen's Green, Dublin 2,
Ireland (a division of Penguin Books Ltd.)
Penguin Group (Australia), 250 Camberwell Road, Camberwell, Victoria 3124,
Australia (a division of Pearson Australia Group Pty. Ltd.)
Penguin Books India Pvt. Ltd., 11 Community Centre, Panchsheel Park,
New Delhi - 110 017, India
Penguin Group (NZ), 67 Apollo Drive, Rosedale, North Shore 0632,
New Zealand (a division of Pearson New Zealand Ltd.)
Penguin Books (South Africa) (Pty.) Ltd., 24 Sturdee Avenue,
Rosebank, Johannesburg 2196, South Africa

Penguin Books Ltd., Registered Offices:
80 Strand, London WC2R 0RL, England

First published by New American Library,
a division of Penguin Group (USA) Inc.

First Printing, July 2010
10 9 8 7 6 5 4 3 2 1

 REGISTERED TRADEMARK—MARCA REGISTRADA

LIBRARY OF CONGRESS CATALOGING-IN-PUBLICATION DATA:

Wingate, Lisa.
  Beyond summer/Lisa Wingate.
    p. cm.
  ISBN 978-0-451-23001-0
  1. Young women—Fiction. 2. Real estate business—Fiction. 3. Self-realization in women—Fiction.
4. Dallas (Tex.)—Fiction. I. Title.
  PS3573.I53165B49 2010
  813'.54—dc22   2010009216

Set in Adobe Garamond
Designed by Alissa Amell

Printed in the United States of America

To Ed
for being a friend,
an encourager,
and an inspiration.
And to Teresa
for being my head loon
and a crazy long-distance gal pal
who sees the humor in everything
and reminds me to laugh at life.

$\mathcal{A}$cknowledgments

As is the case with many stories, *Beyond Summer* grew from a combination of fact, fiction, a sprinkling of whimsy, and with the help of some generous and wonderful people. For that help, and for the friendships that grew and deepened during the researching and writing of this book, I am truly grateful. First and foremost, my thanks go once again to the amazing volunteers who run the Gospel Café, which inspired the Summer Kitchen in the story. My working with you and spending time at the café has given reality to the people of the Blue Sky Hill neighborhood. In particular, thanks to Sherry for being a supportive writer friend, Marsha for your welcoming smiles and warm hugs during my café visits, the volunteer crews for laughter and chatter in the kitchen, and Paula for helping with research for Sesay's character. To Daisy, Kathy, and Mandy, thanks for a wonderful lunch in Salado and for patiently answering dozens of real estate questions. An enormous measure of gratitude goes to special friends, Jennifer Magers for eagle-eyed proofreading, Ed Stevens for technical help with book videos on the Lisa Wingate YouTube channel, and Teresa Loman for being the Head Loon of the Lisa Wingate Facebook group and the best online scrapbook designer ever. The three of you are the best friends a writer could ask for.

On the print and paper side of things, my heartfelt gratitude goes to the smart, talented people at New American Library, and in particular to my editor, Ellen Edwards. Thanks also to my agent at Sterling Lord

Literistic, Claudia Cross. As always, my undying gratitude also goes out to all the booksellers and media personnel who have shown such devotion to the previous books in the Blue Sky Hill series, *A Month of Summer* and *The Summer Kitchen*.

My thanks also go to the many readers who shared the books with friends, took time to send letters of encouragement, and asked for a sequel to the final book in the Tending Roses series, *A Thousand Voices*. While *Beyond Summer* isn't exactly a sequel, you will discover a few old friends living on Blue Sky Hill, and you'll finally find out what happened to Dell and Jace. Lastly, thanks to all the readers and friends far and near, who have encouraged me along the way. There are no words to express how much your letters, notes, and e-mails mean to me. You inspire me, you encourage me, you make me believe in the power of story. What a gift I've been given in each of you. I hope this story repays that gift in some small measure.

Beyond
Summer

Chapter 1

Tam Lambert

It's strange, what you look past in a normal day—the big picture you don't see, while you're busy focusing on all the little things that seem to matter in the moment. Good hair, an outfit that looks just right, a green light ahead when you're in a hurry to make an appointment, a short line at Starbucks, a straight shot down the fairway in a game of golf, a smile from a cute guy in the parking lot. You rub your life like Aladdin's lamp, and magic floats out in little clouds. It works time after time after time. You never stop to consider that there could be a day when a charmed life isn't charmed anymore. At that point, the wishes become prayers, and you hope against hope that God will take up where the wishing lamp left off.

The summer I turned eighteen became the summer of unanswered prayers. I was hoping that, since the lease was up on the hand-me-down MINI Cooper I'd been driving, there was a new car in the works for my birthday—a combination getting-ready-for-college and welcome-to-adulthood present. And maybe a surprise party—something Hawaiian themed, out on the patio, with floating tiki torches in the pool, grass skirts and coconut bras, and a caterer filling the cabana with fruit baskets carved out of watermelons, perfect for early July. Instead, I got a phone call letting me know that my stepmother had rammed her Escalade into the front doors of the Baby

Bundles upscale resale shop while delivering a load of gently worn or still-had-tags-on-them kiddie clothes. The accident wasn't her fault. It was the stilettos that did it.

Such things are to be expected from a thirty-four-year-old woman who takes the kids to playgroup in high heels, studies future plastic surgery options, and shortens her name to Barbie, because she looks like a life-size version of the doll. If the nickname fits, then wear designer shoes with it, was generally Barbie's theory.

The emergency phone call was from the nanny. She wanted me to know she was off work in fifteen minutes, and if someone didn't show up at home before then, she'd be leaving *los niños* with *la tía loca*—the crazy aunt.

The crazy aunt, Aunt Lute, was part of my summer of unanswered prayers, which made sense, considering that Aunt Lute claimed not one prayer in her life had ever been answered the way she wanted. She'd pause after she said that, and contemplate the deeper meanings, her eyes the violet-gray of an iris bloom drying in the sun. Then she'd punctuate the sentence in one of two ways. Either, *The best things in life hide around the blind corners*, or, *Watch out for small favors, Tamara Lee*. The first was an invitation, the second a warning. One ended with a wild laugh, the other with tears pooling in the corners of her eyes and fanning into the wrinkles, like twin rivers flowing into estuaries before being lost in the ocean.

It was impossible to know which one of those assessments of life she really subscribed to. But then, that was Aunt Lute. Crazy as a March hare, which was how she ended up living above our garage after being evicted from a house stacked floor to ceiling with stuff that was fit only for the trash. In a family prone to burning the candle at both ends and dying young, Aunt Lute was a record setter at seventy, and the only old person I'd ever been around for any amount of time. Not that Aunt Lute was your typical old person. She didn't bake cookies, or tell family stories, or knit afghans. After having spent her life working a mindless factory job and caring for a now-deceased handicapped brother, she seemed to have traded her real past for several dozen fantasy lives she made up as she went along. My father, fifteen years her junior, was her only financially stable relative, and probably the one person with a place big enough to put the crazy aunt at one end and still stand to live in the other.

I didn't mind Aunt Lute's being there, really. I did my best not to be home, and aside from that, there was the fact that Aunt Lute's presence irritated my stepmother. Aunt Lute's memory wasn't good, in terms of the recent past, so half the time she didn't have a clue who Barbie was, which drove Barbie nuts. The four blond-haired in vitro munchkins running around the place were a complete mystery to Aunt Lute, as well. It was news to her that my real mother was off in Ecuador with a mission group led by our ex-pastor, and my father had a thirty-four-year-old wife with a ticking-like-a-time-bomb biological clock that had so far resulted in Mark and Daniel, then Landon, and finally baby Jewel, who was just now getting old enough to cast worried looks at *la tía loca*.

Tempting as it was to pretend I hadn't gotten the nanny's phone call, so as to continue with the golf lesson I didn't really want to take, I couldn't quite convince myself to do it. Leaving the Fearsome Foursome home with Aunt Lute amounted to child endangerment in any number of ways. Considering that even the nanny couldn't handle them—the kids *or* Aunt Lute—there was no telling what might happen in the time it could take for a tow truck to extricate Barbara's SUV from the jaws of Baby Bundles, and then bring her, and what remained of the vehicle, home. Left to their own devices, the Four would tear the house down brick by brick, then throw the bricks at one another, while Aunt Lute stood in the backyard in her artist's smock, painting pictures of the sky, or wandered the house tipping all the framed art slightly off square, or sat in her room pecking away on her typewriter, composing memoirs of fantastical events that had never happened.

My bugging out of the lesson ticked off the golf coach, of course. He was the best money could buy, and not accustomed to such utter disregard. He told me I needed to get my priorities straight. "You want to keep that college scholarship, you've got to put in the time," he said, and then he went on to lecture me about competition, and how not everyone was fortunate enough to get a University of Texas golf scholarship, and how my father had most certainly called in every favor he'd ever been owed, and blah, blah, blah. Meanwhile, my fifteen nanny minutes were ticking away like the countdown on a detonator. "It's the flippin' University of Texas," Coach reiterated, and he gave me a narrow-eyed look that more or less indicated I was a slacker. "Talent's not enough. Hard work beats talent when talent doesn't work hard, Lambert. Considering your father's reputation on the football field, you'd think you'd know that. Your dad wasn't the biggest guy in the NFL or the one with the most natural talent, but he gave it everything he had. That's what made him a great quarterback. You might . . ."

More nanny minutes rushed by while he lectured me about responsibility and the debt I owed my coaches, my father, Highland Park, and the golf club. Now probably wasn't the time to tell him I was still trying to figure out how to confess to the world that the golf scholarship to UT was my father's dream, not mine. Since Barbie's brat pack was too young for collegiate sports, I was, athletically speaking, the family's only hope, at least until the munchkins got older. But what I really wanted to do was take a year off and spend it bumming around the youth hostels of Europe with my best friend, Emity. Em's parents didn't think there was a thing wrong with postponing college in order to discover the world.

When Coach came up for air, I told him about Barbie, and the fender-bender, and the stilettos. Coach had seen Barbie chasing one of the Four down the fairway at our last tournament, so I guess he got a pretty accurate picture. He laughed so hard he had to yank off his hat and fan himself to keep from passing out. When you're a fifty-five-year-old man who'll never be able to afford a thirty-four-year-old wife, it probably feels good to know someone else's sugar baby just wrecked the Escalade.

He was still laughing when I grabbed my bag and headed for the parking lot. No doubt the Barbie story was about to become lively conversation at the pro shop.

By the time I got home, the nanny was standing in the driveway with her tote bag in one hand and Jewel dangling under her arm like a chubby-cheeked Beanie Baby. I got the nanny rundown in ten words or less, in a mixture of two languages: The oldest three kids were locked in the backyard play area, the baby needed a diaper change, and *la tía loca* . . . Leaving the sentence unfinished, the nanny rolled her eyes heavenward and flipped her hand in a motion like a bird taking flight. Then she shoved the baby into my hands and snorted so hard I felt spray on my arm.

Hiking her tote bag onto her shoulder, the nanny told me to remind my father that she hadn't been paid in three weeks; then she hurried to her vehicle, glancing nervously back at the house, like a horror-movie actress escaping the lair of alien possession. Only when she'd reached her car and planted one foot inside did she bother to tell me that Barbie had called, and that sometime during the fender-bender excitement, Barbie had felt like she was *sueño*, as in passing

out, and the shop owner had taken her to *el doctor*. I was stuck with
the brat pack until whenever Barbie felt better, or my father came
home from his office, which was usually sometime around midnight,
after he figured the Four had finally worn down and lost consciousness on the furniture somewhere.

No wonder the nanny was peeling away from the curb like an
Indy driver leaving the pit. She was scared to death of being stuck in
the insane asylum all night.

Whimpering, Jewel stretched her chubby arms toward the retreat-
ing nannymobile, as if she didn't want to be marooned here without
a responsible adult. No doubt even a seven-month-old could tell I
was in no way qualified to take charge. Aside from that, I had plans
tonight, which hardly included acting as zookeeper for a bunch of
rug rats. Sometimes life could be seriously unfair.

I went inside, put Jewel in the high chair with some Cheerios, and
started calling everyone I could think of—Barbara's friends, everyone
on the Barbie babysitter list, the teacher from Mark and Daniel's preschool, the lady who kept the nursery at church, even a couple of my
old schoolmates who were desperate for some money their parents
didn't know about. Nobody wanted to come over and take on the
sibs. Around our neighborhood, the Four were legendary, which was
saying something, considering that our neighborhood specialized in
highly indulged showcase kids, and made no apologies for it.

Through the French doors, I watched the three boys while I
opened yet another address book, looking for anybody else I could
call to take over. The book was old—from the bottom of the stack.
There were entries in my mother's handwriting—friends, old coaches
and dance teachers, the PTO president from seven years ago. My
mother was vice president then. It seemed strange that you could be
vice president of the PTO one year, and heading off to Ecuador with

a mission group the next. But that was my mother. When she was into something, she went all the way. My mother was *The Purpose Driven Life* in a good pair of running shoes.

Outside, Mark and Daniel were using the climbing rope to scale the wavy yellow slide on the playscape. They knew they weren't allowed to do that. The rope, in fact, was supposed to be wrapped around the beam overhead and tied there, so they couldn't get it down. The last time they rope-scaled the slide, Daniel had ended up in the emergency room getting four stitches in his curly blond head.

I stood at the door, trying to decide whether to grab Jewel and take her with me, or leave her where she was while I went out to save lives in the play yard. Jewel was almost through pushing Cheerios off the tray and watching them bounce across the tile. She had a bored, tired look that said, *Look out. I'm gonna blow.* When Jewel got wound up, she could literally scream and wail for hours, and nothing would stop her. The pediatrician said she had some digestive issues. My father said she took after Barbie, but he didn't say that within earshot of Barb, of course.

Outside, Daniel was halfway up the slide. Mark and Landon had picked it up from the bottom and were shaking it, either giving Daniel a ride or trying to knock him off. With the brat pack, there was a thin line between good clean fun and murderous intent. If I'd ever acted like that when I was little, my mother would have put me in the time-out chair until my rear end took on its shape, but since I'd been an only child, there wasn't much incentive for me to compete in any way.

Yanking open the French door, I hollered, "Cut it out!" The boys, of course, ignored me completely and shook the slide harder. In the high chair, Jewel jerked her head up, looked around the kitchen, and let out a wail.

Daniel stumbled sideways on the slide, caught himself on one foot, and teetered there, clinging to the rope. My body tensed as I waited for him to swing through the air, careening toward the nearest solid object. He'd end up in the emergency room right next to his mother.

"Cut. It. Out! Get down!" I screamed out the door, but it didn't do any good. The sibs were used to Barbara hollering, nannies yelling, the white noise of one another, and Aunt Lute occasionally popping in with an outburst unrelated to anything. Loud sounds and sudden displays of emotion meant absolutely nothing to them.

I heard Aunt Lute's squeaky pink house shoes come down the stairs and cross the living room as I was trying to undo some new plastic thing that was holding the screen door closed—Barbara's latest attempt at child safety. As the Four had grown in size and dexterity, efforts to keep them locked either inside or outside had turned my father's house into a Fort Knox of the latest kid containment devices.

Perfume and pink chiffon floated by as Aunt Lute shuffle-squeaked into the kitchen, where Jewel was howling like a banshee and trying to push her way out of the high chair. Aunt Lute passed by on her way to the sink, seemingly oblivious.

"Can you get her?" I snapped, grabbing the screen door with both hands and throwing my weight against the child lock. "Aunt Lute, can you get her?" Glancing over my shoulder, I took in Aunt Lute's weird combination of fluffy pink housecoat, slippers, and a poufy bathing cap that looked like something from *I Love Lucy*.

Calmly filling her glass, she swiveled my way. "Whose is she?" It was impossible to tell whether Aunt Lute was asking a question or making a point, as in, *Whose problem is the screaming baby? Certainly not mine.*

Which was exactly how *I* felt about it. However, blood was about

to be drawn in the backyard, and I really didn't want that on my conscience. Technically, those were my father's children, flesh of my flesh,
even if my father rarely crossed paths with them.

"Barbara wrecked the Escalade again." Yanking a jelly-covered
butter knife off a plate on the counter, I prepared to commit mayhem on the child lock. It was either kick down the screen door, or let
Mark and Landon assassinate Daniel. He was hanging on to the rope
and the slide now, tossing out threats and preschool potty words in a
growl-shriek that sounded remarkably like my stepmother's.

"Barbie had to go to the . . ." I paused to wedge the knife into the
plastic lock in an attempt to pop it loose. ". . . stupid . . . doctor." If it
didn't give in the next thirty seconds, and Jewel didn't shut up, I was
going to go crazy. I really was. Tomorrow, no matter what, I wasn't
coming home. I was telling everyone I had a late lesson, and then
I was spending the night someplace else. Anyplace. Anywhere that
wasn't a flippin' nuthouse for munchkins.

I smelled Aunt Lute's perfume, and a whisper of chiffon tickled my arm. "This way," she said nonchalantly, then slipped a finger
around the jelly knife and pressed some mysterious, invisible switch.
The plastic security loop popped loose so suddenly it shot across the
room.

I slid the door open and ran across the yard, pointing the drippy
jelly knife at the boys like a weapon. "Cut it out! Right now! Mark!
Landon!" They were unfazed, of course, and kept shaking the slide
right up until I got to the playscape and started grabbing little body
parts. I got Daniel first, because he was the one in mortal danger.
Yanking him off the rope, I stuck him on the platform above the
slide, then went after Mark, since sending his twin brother to the
hospital had probably been his idea.

Mark dropped his side of the slide and ran. The slide fell, knocked

Landon down, and landed on his leg. Landon let out a howl. On the playscape, Daniel seized a plastic bat and ran down the slide, pinching Landon's leg and causing him to scream bloody murder. Daniel hit the ground running and went after Mark with the bat, hollering, "Doo-doo, dookie poop face! I'monna mop you!" Mark tripped over Barbie's cat, the cat squalled, and Daniel caught up, then whacked both his brother and the cat with his weapon of choice. The cat screeched, retreated, and ran for her life, looking for a hole in the play area fence.

Dragging Landon from under the slide, I set him on his feet, swiveled toward the other boys, and yelled, "Cut it out!" Again.

The pool gate alarm went off. I wanted to scream right along with it.

From the corner of my eye, I caught Aunt Lute's pink housecoat fluttering against the iron gate. When I turned to look, she was entering the water in her swimsuit and bathing cap, the squeaky pink slippers still on her feet. She held Jewel in one arm. Naked. My mind flashed to a picture of *la tía loca* drowning the baby. "Aunt Lute, wait!"

The bloodcurdling tone of my voice attracted the boys' attention. All three froze instantly, looked at the pool, then ran to the play yard fence, grabbed the iron bars, and stuck their faces through, suddenly captivated.

"Why'za Jewee swim?" Landon babbled, his three-year-old voice suddenly sweet and inquisitive, and his blue eyes wide beneath fluffy blond curls.

In the pool, Jewel gurgled happily and kicked her feet as Aunt Lute dipped into the water just enough to cover the baby's legs, then bounced up again.

"Why'za Jewee swim?" Landon repeated. He followed me through the play yard gate and across the lawn, while the other boys stood at the fence, fascinated by the sight of *la tía loca* and the baby. In the pool, the diaphanous puffs of pink fabric on Aunt Lute's bathing cap caught the late-afternoon light, giving her a sunny rose-colored halo as she bounced up and down with the baby, both of them giggling.

I remained cautiously silent until I'd made it to the pool fence, just in case *la tía loca* had completely lost it this time, in which case I'd need to dive in and rescue the baby. Opening the pool gate, I held Landon off and stepped inside by myself. "Aunt Lute, what are you doing?"

She bounced in a semicircle until she was facing me. Her violet eyes were bright in this light, reflecting long rays of evening sun. "Come on in. The water is lovely." Fanning a hand across the surface, she altered the shape of the light, causing it to bend and dance. Jewel babbled and flapped her arms in appreciation, then wanted to touch the water herself. Aunt Lute leaned her over so that Jewel could reach. Holding my breath, I moved a step closer to the edge.

"Aunt Lute, I think we'd better get out of the pool," I suggested cautiously. "Barbara's not home." Once upon a time, I would have gladly gone in for a swim, but I hadn't been in the pool during day-light hours since the twins got old enough to walk. After that point, I couldn't go into the pool, or anywhere else, without them hanging all over me. Taking a swim meant getting stuck with babysitting duty while Barbie took advantage of the time to bleach her roots, or ar-range her shoes, or whatever else was pressing on her agenda. It was easier to go swim at Emity's house.

Aunt Lute smiled and bounced Jewel up and down in the water again. "Everyone can come in." She nodded toward Landon, and then the terrible twosome hanging on the play yard fence. "Let's all go for a swim."

Well, this is it, I thought. La tía loca *has finally snapped. She's lost it completely.* Squatting down, I reached over the water. "Here, I'll take the baby inside."

Aunt Lute's gaze lifted slowly, locked onto mine in a way that would have seemed entirely lucid, if not for the fluffy hat, the pink slippers, and the naked baby. "Let's have a swim," she repeated. "It will be good for them."

I shook my head, trying to figure out how to get the baby away from Aunt Lute without jumping into the water and getting my golf togs all wet. If I got wet, I'd have to change clothes, and there was no telling what the sibs would be into while I was up in my room. "They don't have suits on. I'm not even sure where their suits are." *Barbara probably took them to the resale shop so she could buy new ones.*

The corners of Aunt Lute's mouth twitched upward, forming half-moon wrinkles under her sunlit eyes. "Let them swim in their shorts. We'll hang the clothing over the fence when we're finished."

"Barbara'll have a cow." The boys were wearing some kind of matching Baby Gap stuff that looked like it'd never even been washed before.

Aunt Lute checked the yard. "I don't see any *Barbara*."

I laughed, and *la tía loca* nodded, smiling slyly. Every once in a while, I had the feeling that Aunt Lute was a fox in a sheepskin, not nearly as out to lunch as she pretended to be.

"The water tires them out," she said. "They become so exhausted"—pausing, she yawned and stretched her free arm—"they can't help falling asleep. Just like little angels."

All of a sudden, Aunt Lute and I were on the same wavelength, and her point was as clear as the water in the pool. The Four were at their best when they were asleep—their puffs of curly blond hair like rays of curving light against the pillow, their cheeks red, and their lips pursed into tiny Cupid's bows.

"Come on, guys. We're going swimming," I said, and headed out the pool gate to spring Mark and Daniel from the play yard. Landon trotted along behind me, and when we retrieved the twins, everyone was so happy about going swimming that nobody smacked, bit, or pushed anybody on the way across the yard.

I stripped off the boys' shirts, put water wings on Landon's arms, grabbed a swim diaper for the baby, and the pool party commenced. Aunt Lute showed the boys a few maneuvers she'd learned in some imaginary life as a synchronized swimmer in Vegas. The twins could swim like fish, so they weren't too bad at the aquabatics. It kept them entertained, anyway, and by the time we dragged everyone out of the pool well after dark, the sibs were so tired they barely made it through peanut-butter-and-jelly sandwiches before passing out in front of a Disney movie. I carried the boys to their beds, and then put the baby in her crib. At the bottom of the stairs, Aunt Lute and I gave each other a high five.

"Glorious evening," she pronounced. "Princess Stephanie loved to swim, as well. She had beautiful golden hair, and the softest brown eyes, just like yours." Making a motion to illustrate flowing locks, Aunt Lute smiled, then turned away and headed for the bonus room over the garage, her wet slippers leaving twin slug trails on the tile.

No telling who Princess Stephanie was.

"Good night, Aunt Lute," I called after her.

"Good night, Princess." She finger-waved over her shoulder as she disappeared around the corner, adding, "I've some dry underwear in the laundry room."

Still contemplating the weirdness that was Aunt Lute, I cleaned up the sandwich crusts on the bar, then went to the living room, turned off the Disney movie, and flipped through the cable channels.

My father was on channel forty-three in one of his "We take

shabby homes" commercials. He was wearing a cheesy Superman suit, and his favorite advertising partner and former second-string fullback, Randy Boone, was dressed as Superboy with dreadlocks. They were rescuing some lady from back taxes she couldn't afford on a house that needed costly repairs. My father gave her a market estimate and made her a purchase offer in twenty-four hours or less. And solved all her problems. Behind them, the house changed in an instant, going from shabby blue with a weed-filled yard to a bright, clean Householders yellow. Another derelict property rehabilitated by Householders, television magic, and my dad's superpowers, as easy as one, two, three.

From outside, the glow of headlights panned into the front room, traveling from one end to the other as a car rounded the circle drive on the way to the garage. I changed the TV channel in case it was my father pulling in.

Lately, he hated those commercials.

Chapter 2

Sesay

They are interesting to watch—the people. They move in the same patterns each day, but some things are always different. Their clothes change. The clothes whisper as they pass, telling the stories of the people. I can hear them, because I remain very still and listen the right way. My grandfather taught me long ago, as we walked far across the burned country the soldiers had left behind, all the way to the shore. He told me of the story children, and how they became scattered over the world. Then he put me on a boat with my auntie, and let me go.

The boat was old, and it was packed body-to-body, and the waves pushed over it, but there wasn't water enough to drink. Auntie died on the boat, but I did not. I came here, to a new place. I think I am from Haiti. I think I am the boat people, but I cannot say for certain. I can tell many stories much better than I can tell my own. I think most people are this way.

Sometimes I share the stories with the storyteller. I go into her shop, where the sign says *Book Basket*. I know this, although I cannot read it. The storyteller will trade a book for a good story, and sometimes she will trade a doughnut, as well. I come early, while there may yet be a doughnut in the bag on her shop counter. Sometimes I share an old story, and sometimes I tell the stories the clothes have told me about the people. Today, there is another yellow house on Red Bird

Lane. It was pink, but they've painted it yellow. There are four others like it on the same street.

I tell this to MJ at the Book Basket, and she is not pleased. "Householders!" She snorts, her nostrils going wide. "They'll have control of the whole neighborhood before long. Tear it down and put up more stinking condos." Her eyes get hard as hearth coals then, and her lips pull back, showing her teeth white against coffee-bean skin. Her skin is dark like mine, but much prettier. She has beautiful teeth, as well. White like linen. I think it must be wonderful to have lovely teeth. But mine are not, so I hold my smile on the inside.

"It was pink—the house," I say, and MJ nods.

"I know that place," she replies. "It belonged to the woman who started the Summer Kitchen in the church. Her uncle built that house a long time ago." She points across the road to the old white church. I know the Summer Kitchen, of course. I go there for lunch some days. MJ tells stories to the children after the meal, and I think one day I may help her, if I have a mind to.

"A woman should not sell the house her family built," I tell MJ, and I think of my father's home. My mind must stretch very hard to go there. "Not to the yellow-house people."

MJ frowns again and pushes long, thin braids over her shoulder. Three of them have fallen forward. Most often she keeps them wrapped in a turban, but not today. Today she wears her hair down, and I know why. I can hear the man working in the back portion of her building. She sells that space to him—the big area that was once for repairing automobiles—but as far as I can see, he never comes into the store to talk to her. He keeps to himself, as do I.

"SandraKaye didn't want to let go of the house," MJ tells me. "Her mother sold it out from under her, oh . . . a couple months ago. Just before you came to the neighborhood, I guess. SandraKaye wanted to run the Summer Kitchen there, but after the house sold, she had to move the free lunch café to the church building instead."

"It's bad to have a mother like that, a selfish mother," I say. I cannot remember my own mother well, but I have a good feeling when I imagine her. I see her on the veranda of my father's big house. She opens her arms, and calls to me, and smiles. I think it must have been very hard for her to send me away with my grandfather when the soldiers came to take my father's house.

"Yes, it is," MJ agrees, and her eyes tell me a bit more about her. She understands what I have said about mothers.

The man in back makes a noise. He drops something metal— most probably a can of paint—and it echoes through the vast, empty space there. MJ turns an ear to it.

"People moved into the new yellow house this morning," I say. "A young woman, and a man, and two little boys. They look like him." I point toward the door, so she will know I speak of the man in back. His hair is long and dark, and he ties it with a leather thong when he works on a painting. He looks like the Indian chiefs on the old television shows at the Broadberry Mission down the road. "He went to the house and helped to carry in the heavy furniture. I saw him there."

"Hmmm . . ." MJ's eyes dart toward another metal sound. "I'll have to ask him about it." But I know she won't. She never disturbs the painting man. The artist. He is an artist, truly. Like the ones who painted the pictures that hung on my father's walls.

"It's bad that they have moved in there," I tell MJ. "They are nice people. I can tell. And they are friends of his." I indicate the man again, the painter. Through the small square of glass in the door, I can see the top of his head, his dark hair flowing long and loose today, like a horse's forelock. "He should not allow his friends to move into a yellow house. A Householders house." Perhaps he is not aware that those houses tell a bad story; as far as I can see, the man does not often go around the neighborhood. He paints here, and then goes to the place where he lives, a few blocks away on Blue Sky Hill, where the mansion homes are. His home is not a mansion. It is atop someone else's garage.

"I'll warn him about it," MJ replies. Both MJ and I know what happens to people in those yellow houses. "I hope they haven't signed anything."

I back away from the counter, because the talk of signing papers weaves my stomach tight, like a basket drying in the sun. People make you sign a paper so they can take away your soul. I know this.

I go to the front of the store and quickly pick out a book from the many stacked on the shelves. "I will take this one today," I say, and hold it up. I like the picture on the front.

MJ nods. "They're starting another evening class at the church. Three nights a week." She adjusts the pad of paper on her desk and pretends to be searching for a pencil, so as not to look at me. She knows I cannot read the book. The class at the church will be about reading, of course. She has told me before.

"I like this book," I say, and give her a little smile. One that doesn't show my teeth. When the book has pictures, you do not need to read the words to hear the story.

MJ holds up the white bag that has been waiting on her desk. "Don't forget your doughnut, Sesay."

I come back to the counter and pinch the bag between my fingers, then tuck it into the pocket of my big brown coat. I haven't taken it off this morning, but I will when I go outside. It is hot here, even in the mornings. "Remind me to tell you about the children of Story Mouse," I say to her. "I was thinking of that today."

"I will." She looks at me with interest, which causes me to like her even more. Most people cannot see me. Outside, I am invisible for hours at a time.

The man drops something in the back room again, and MJ looks away.

"Warn him about the yellow house," I tell her.

"I will," she answers. "Have a good day, Sesay." She waves as I go out the door. I allow myself the real kind of smile, once my back is turned. I am invisible now, anyway.

Because no one can see me, I sit under the tree by the fence to eat my doughnut and look at my book. From there, I can watch through the big garage door into the place where the Indian chief is working. He is painting something large—just beginning it with a thick brush, in bold shapes of brown and green. He leaves white space that looks like mountains as he lays the colors on the canvas. He does not know I am watching him, as I often do. I like to see the picture take life.

It tells a story, and stories are something I keep. I am a storyteller, like my grandfather.

Chapter 3

Shasta Reid-Williams

If you drove by it on the street, it wouldn't stand out much. It was just a little house, like all the rest on the block. Maybe it was in better shape than a lot of places on Red Bird Lane. It had actual flowers in the flower beds—not just dandelions, Bermuda crawlers, and thistles, but plants somebody planted. The windows weren't plastered with tinfoil and old sheets, and the place had a fresh coat of paint, even if it was road-stripe yellow. There were a couple more homes down the street painted the same ugly color, like a highway department truck had lost a fifty-gallon barrel of paint, and the neighbors found it and divvied it up. Nobody'd do their house in neon yellow unless the paint was free.

"It's our signature color," the salesman had said when Cody made some rude joke about the paint job, while we were looking at the house. "Sort of like a calling card. It lets people know we're working in the neighborhood, cleaning up these old places, and helping young families like yours step off the rental roller coaster with no down payment. Why throw away your hard-earned money when you can be the master of your very own castle. Am I right?" He sounded like the commercial that came on, like, every half hour during the daytime soaps, and late at night on the stations that showed stuff like fishing shows and car chop jobs, stuff only Cody would watch.

It was the commercials that first gave me the idea. After catching them about a bazillion times while we were stuck in an apartment where I couldn't let the kids go outside because there were lowlifes around and police sirens going off all the time, one of the House-holders commercials mentioned the Blue Sky Hill area, and I knew it was a sign from God. Blue Sky Hill was close enough to where Cody needed to be for his training with the Dallas Police Academy, and Terence Clay lived there. He was a distant cousin of Cody's, and the only person we knew in Dallas. Even if he was an artist, and, well, kind of weird, he was Choctaw, like a lot of folks from back home—like Cody and me. Whether they know each other real well or not, Choctaw folk stick together, especially once they get out into the real world, outside Pushmataha County, where members of the Tribe are thick as gnats on a bull's back. Here in Dallas, as far as I could tell, there was us and Terence, which made us family.

The Householders commercial said no money down, and you didn't even have to have great credit. I started to think, *Maybe we really can get a house. A real house. The kind that doesn't have wheels on it.* Back home in Hugo, Oklahoma, we'd moved out of a rental house and bought a trailer, but it wasn't really like owning our own place.

The trailer was set up out behind Cody's parents' barn, and even with no lot rent, we got so upside down on the payments, we made a deal to let the trailer go back to the bank when we moved to Dallas so Cody could get in with the DPD.

After I saw the Householders commercials, I started to think about our possibilities. We'd been planning to hold off the house hunting until after Cody got his big graduation bonus for finishing the police academy, but with a no-money-down loan, it seemed like we could do it now. We figured it all up, and even with payments on our new-used pickup, and what we still owed on old debts, and credit card payments, we could swing it. We drove out to Blue Sky Hill, surprised Cody's cousin, and found our house. The Householders program made it all so easy, you'd have to be an idiot to keep wasting your money on rent.

All of a sudden, everything was perfect, and there we were, standing on the curb of our first honest-to-gosh house, with all the furniture moved in, and the papers tucked away in the footlocker Cody bought at an army buddy's yard sale. Home at last.

"We did it," I told Cody, and put my arm around him while Benjamin and Tyler ran across the yard and slipped under the porch behind an oleander bush on the corner. They'd found that spot while we were moving the furniture in, and they had big plans to make a fort there.

"I guess we did." Cody didn't sound as happy as I wanted him to be. Houses aren't such a big deal to a guy, I guess.

"It's ours. Our first real house."

Underneath my arm, his ribs expanded and deflated in a big ol' sigh. He was all muscle now. For months, he'd been jogging and doing extra push-ups with the kids sitting on his back so he'd be in shape for the DPD physical fitness requirements. "Guess so."

I looked up at him, and I could see our house, tiny like the pictures in a locket, reflected in the dark centers of his eyes. "Try not to sound so excited about it." It was just like him to be all macho about everything and spoil the fun. It was like he thought that's how the man of the family oughta act—just like his daddy, who was the manager at the lumber mill back home, and about as much fun as having a cavity drilled.

"I'm excited." Cody spat out the words with his lips in a tight, straight line.

"Yeah, sure. You sound real excited."

He went stiff under my arm and shifted away a little so our sides weren't touching anymore. "I said I'm excited."

"Well, could you show it a little bit?" The complaint snapped out sharp as a rubber band popping, and then I was sorry. I didn't want us to fight, especially not today. "You don't have to be all police business here, you know. This is home. This is *our place*. You can just be my Cody-boy."

Back in high school, Cody was the biggest goof-off there was. He was always doing something stupid to get a laugh, which drove me nuts. I wanted him to act more grown-up so Mama and my brother would like him better. Now that Cody was all about being the serious, frowny-faced Dallas police gonna-be, I missed the fun guy.

"Sorry." He pasted on a big, stupid smile, and leaned so close to my face that his eyes were meeting in the middle. "This better?"

I giggled, of course. He knew I would. "You're such a fart." Grabbing his chin, I squeezed hard, then pushed his face away.

"I know." He grinned again, and we stood looking at the house some more.

"I wish Mama could see the place." As soon as I said it, I knew I shoulda kept my mouth shut. Bringing up my mother would only throw a wet blanket on our big day.

Cody's face went straight. "I don't think you wanna know what your mother'd say about this. She's still griping because we let the trailer go back to the bank, remember?"

I nodded, and I didn't mention Mama again. She was mad at Cody and me for leaving Hugo and moving to Dallas in the first place, and if she knew we'd jumped into buying a house before Cody was even through the academy, that would just be one more thing for her to rise up on her hind legs about. She'd give me a great big financial speech, and tell me we didn't have any business taking on a

house loan until we'd paid off every single credit card, and saved up
an emergency fund, and blah, blah, blah. Just thinking about it made
me queasy, and I was queasy enough already.

"We've gotta do something about that oleander bush," I said,
when the boys squirmed out from under the porch and took off for
the backyard. "Take it out, I guess."

Cody pulled back and squinted at me. "Why? It looks good there.
I bet it's been there forever."

I took in the plant, thinking that it most likely had been there a
long time. Branches had grown through the porch railing and all in
the lattice underneath, so that it seemed like part of the house. The
first time we came to look at the place, I'd caught the sweet smell of it
the minute we got out of the car. It was sad to think of killing it.

"They're poisonous," I said.

"What are?"

"Oleander bushes. They're poisonous."

Cody's chin jerked, and he spit out that little "Khhh!" sound I
couldn't stand. Like I was making it up or something. "My mom had
those all over the yard, and none of us got poisoned."

"Well, you guys probably didn't happen to eat any of it, Cody." I
hated it when he acted like he was Mr. Big Daddy who knew everything, and I was the little nincompoop who got pregnant right out
of high school.

"So we'll tell the boys not to eat it." His shoulders went up and
down, like it was that simple. Just tell kids not to do something, and
they wouldn't. Where'd he been for the last five years of Benjamin's
life, and the last three years of Tyler's? Oh, yeah—hanging out at the
deer blind with his daddy, or out four-wheeling and fishing with the
guys he worked with at the county sheriff's department. He didn't
have a clue what it was like to be home with the boys all the time.

Whenever Cody was supposed to babysit, his mama was right there to do all the work, and Cody sneaked off to the backyard with the bird dogs, or ended up in the barn doing some project for his daddy.

"You have to baby-proof everything when you've got kids around, Cody. They try stuff out when you're not looking."

He snorted softly. "They're not babies. It's not like they walk around picking junk up and putting it in their mouths."

Heat crawled over my back and made a muscle go spastic at the base of my spine. I reached around to rub out the cramp. What with getting the furniture into the house and then taking the boys down to Chuck E. Cheese to celebrate, this was feeling like a long day. I wanted to go inside, curl up on one of the mattresses still on the floor, and go to sleep, but there was lots to get done yet. "You never know what they'll do. It's not worth having a poisonous bush in the yard."

Cody stuck his arms out and posed like he was a sci-fi robot about to take on the bush with his death ray. "Evil Plant of Death. Must destroy."

"That's not funny, Cody." He was only putting on the goofy act to get me off his case. If I left it up to him, that bush would still be there six months from now, but the freezer would be stocked with fish fillets, as soon as he found a place to drop a line in the water. "I don't want that plant there, okay?"

"The boys aren't gonna eat the plant."

"I mean it. I'll chop it down myself if I have to." Cody gave me a weird look, and I knew he was trying to figure out why I was pushing so hard. I couldn't exactly tell him it wasn't the boys I was worried about. It was the new baby. The one that would be showing up in about eight months, give or take. Cody didn't know about the baby, and I hadn't figured out how to tell him without starting a meltdown. Telling Mama the next time I talked to her would be even worse.

She'd have a conniption so big you'd be able to see it hanging in the sky over southeastern Oklahoma, like a wall cloud.

Cody lowered his death-ray fist and gave me his confused look, like there was some ridiculous woman thing going on in my head. He crossed his arms over his chest. "What the heck is wrong with you all the sudden? I thought we were celebrating the new house. Happy-happy, remember? Havin' a good time."

"There's nothing wrong with me." *When you tell him, you have to make it sound like you got pregnant on accident. If he thinks you did it on purpose, he'll be so mad, he'll never get over it.* "I just want you to help do things with the house. You can't spend all your time either at the academy, or crashed out on the sofa, or looking for someplace to fish. We have to get the house ready."

An eyebrow hung low over one dark eye. "Ready for what?"

The baby. Our baby girl. "Just the kids and stuff. It's an old house. There's things that aren't safe for kids in an old house—like plugs, and we need to check for lead paint, and take care of the cords on the blinds, and put batteries in the smoke detectors, and things like that." *Maybe you should just go ahead and tell him. Right now, while he's happy, and his mind's on the house.*

He'll never believe you didn't do this on purpose. He'll know, and he'll know why you did it, too. . . .

"You watch too much TV." He tipped his head toward the sound of the boys playing in the backyard. Tyler was squealing, and Benjamin was hollering something about Pokémon. Any minute now, they'd be in a fight. "*I* grew up in an old house." Lifting his arms, he turned his hands palms up, as in, *And look at the wonderfulness of me.*

"Yeah," I said, smirking at him. He could be such a smart-aleck. "Exactly."

He smacked himself in the chest and coughed out a breath like I'd taken a shot at him and he was catching the arrow where it went in. Not likely, since Cody was tough as leather and just about as easy to make a dent in. "Oh-ho! That's it. Them's fightin' words."

The next thing I knew, he'd scooped me up and tossed me over his shoulder.

"Cody, put me down!" I squealed, but of course he wouldn't, and with him two hundred pounds of muscle now, I didn't have a prayer of making him do anything. He twirled me in a circle, and I watched the grass, and the pecan tree, and the yellow house, and the brush along the creek next door, and the slide in the little kiddie park across the creek, all blend together into a swirl of color. I saw the oleander bush, and Tyler running around the corner of the house, his stocky legs pumping hard, his head a dark, fuzzy burr, like his daddy's. He skidded to a stop and crossed his arms over his chest, just like someone else I knew.

"Daddy, pud-a-Mama-down!" he ordered, shaking a finger at us. Then I couldn't see him anymore, because Cody spun me around and scooped up Tyler in his free arm, and we were bouncing along together, laughing.

I heard Benjamin come around the corner and complain, "Dad-deee!" Grabbing my arm, Benji tried to pull me free, headfirst.

Cody stumbled sideways, and the thick smell of oleander filled my nose. I felt the leaves brush my arm.

"Oh, no!" Cody cried out. "It's . . . it's . . . the evil Bush of Death!" He staggered backward, gasped his last, then collapsed to the ground just a few inches short of making a pancake of our oldest kid. The three of us landed in a pig pile, Benjamin jumped on top, and we rolled around, laughing and tickling and wrestling in the dried-up crust of last year's oleander leaves. When the craziness died down, I turned onto my back, and Cody lay beside me, and we just stayed there, looking up at the corner of the house, and the pecan branches overhead, and the clear, blue summer sky. Our little piece of sky. Over our trees. Over our house.

The house that was worth everything it took to get here.

Next door, a window blind pulled back, and then fell into place again. Whoever the neighbors were, if they were watching, they probably thought we were nuts.

Chapter 4

Tam Lambert

It wasn't the first time Barbie had wrecked the Escalade. It was just the first time I'd seen my father cry about it.

All of a sudden, I wished I hadn't started the morning by trapping him in the game room and going off about my getting stuck with the Fearsome Foursome after Barbie's fender-bender. It was just that I'd been ready to behead someone since last night, when I learned that Barbie wasn't at the hospital, but with her massage therapist, Fawn, drinking wine and trying to recover from the trauma of crashing into the Baby Bundles. When she did come home, Barbie brought Fawn with her, and they uncorked a bottle of wine in our kitchen, so I couldn't say what I wanted to. Barbie knew that, of course. She wasn't always as blond as she looked. Sometimes she actually thought things through. She had a little bruise on her cheek where she'd hit the steering wheel, and Fawn helped ice it while Barbie droned on about what a blessing it was that the kids weren't in the car when it *went crazy*. Somehow, the wreck had become largely the fault of the vehicle, which was now sitting in the driveway with the front end crumpled on one side, and the grille hanging in pieces.

I left the kitchen, so as not to kick off World War III, and went up to my room and vented to Emity in a text message. *Gonna bite someone's head off tomorrow*, I said before we signed off. *Europe's not even far enough away. So sick of this.*

LOL, Emity ended. *Spare the innocent children, K?*

I sent her back a laugh, then went to bed. I dreamed about *la tía loca*. She was swimming in an Olympic-size pool with the sibs. They were wearing matching pink bathing caps with puffs of chiffon and furry pink slippers. The fur expanded underwater, so that their legs looked like Q-tips with pink ends as their feet fanned the water, sending strange currents swirling toward the surface. They were performing synchronized swimming maneuvers. Even the baby. The team made a pyramid with their legs, and Jewel was on top, holding an inner tube that looked like a giant Cheerio.

I actually woke up in a good mood, but halfway down the stairs, I caught the lingering scent of incense from Fawn's visit last night, and I was mad all over again. I caught my dad in the game room and told him exactly how I felt about Barbara stopping off for a winefest and a whinefest with Fawn, while I was stuck home babysitting. "I can't handle them. The nanny can't even handle them. I didn't ask you guys to have a bunch of kids no one wants to take care of."

It crept into my consciousness that my father hadn't moved or responded in any way, and that possibly he wasn't even listening to me, but I was on a roll. I stabbed a finger toward the upstairs, where Barbie, blissfully asleep as usual, knew that the nanny would arrive at seven to wake up the sibs. After the morning tantrums and breakfast were taken care of, Barbie would descend below stairs to tackle the dressing and hair combing, thus bringing the pack to the level of cuteness required for playgroup dropoff at church. "I'm sick of everything being about Barbara. I'm sick of not being able to come home without her dumping kids on me. I'm sick of . . ."

The light from the window caught my father's face suddenly, and there was moisture sparkling in his eyes. I'd never seen him cry. Even at my grandparents' funerals, and the day my parents told me they were splitting up, my father had been as steady as Lincoln at the Memorial—stoic and thoughtful, with a pale patina of regret, as if he'd studied the mask that should be worn at such times. By watching, you could tell how he was *supposed* to feel, but not how he really *did* feel. He was a mystery, a cipher, but then, that was nothing new. His lack of accessibility, as my mother referred to it, was one of the reasons she left. She needed depth, meaning, connection. Being married to him was a starvation of the soul she could no longer endure, after twelve years. She was ready to spread her wings and fly, to do something that mattered, to be fulfilled.

I couldn't really blame her. Even at eleven years old, I understood what she meant. It was painful to know that we didn't fit into the larger equation, but I could relate to what she was saying. Before she was someone's mom, someone's wife, she was *someone*. She was a journalist working her way up through local news, which was how she met my father. Now she wanted to be someone again.

I wondered what she would think if she could see my father now, his hand clutched over the surgically implanted hairline that my mother thought was ridiculous, his fingers tightening into the skin of his forehead, his lips forming a thin line, trembling. His eyes were turned toward the window, two blue pools draining down his cheeks, where the skin was smooth and free of sun damage, thanks to the laser treatments at Barbie's favorite spa. The skin-care package was a Christmas present, to let him know Barbie was thinking of his well-being.

My mother had responded with an Internet laugh when I told her about it. *LOL. Guess she just realized he's over fifty. . . .*

"Dad?" I whispered. The ground shifted under my feet, and I tried to catch my balance. Maybe something had happened to Barbie overnight—some sort of weird aftereffect of the accident. "Dad? What's the matter?"

He sat unmoving until finally his lips parted, letting out a long draft of air. Trembling fingers combed his hair—the fuzzy part on top that didn't look quite natural, and then the real stuff toward the back. He clutched it for a moment before his fist dropped into his lap. "You might hear some things today, Tam. At the country club, or just . . . around. You might hear some things. Don't worry, all right? Just go about your normal day, and . . ." His eyes slowly fell closed, and his head swayed as if he were falling asleep midsentence. When he looked up again, moisture clung to his lashes, turning them dark. They were thick, like the boys'. "It's just a normal Thursday."

An uncomfortable sensation crawled underneath my golf shirt, turned my neck hot and itchy. "It's Friday," I whispered.

"Right . . ." he muttered. "Friday." His gaze slid back and forth across the fireplace, as if he were searching for something in the squares of white marble. "Almost the weekend. Nobody does business on the weekend." Chewing his bottom lip, he nodded, still scanning the wall, the darkness in his face easing slightly. "Nobody does business on the weekend."

Crossing my arms over my chest, I shifted from one foot to the other, uncomfortable, uncertain. Something was wrong. This man heaped in the chair, babbling nonsense, his cheeks wet with tears, was not my father. My father was strong, silent, always on the cell phone, wrapped up in negotiations to take a partial interest in some business deal, in return for attaching his name to it. Anything attached to Paul "the Postman" Lambert's name and face was golden, even fifteen years after his playing career was over. My father was larger than life in every possible way.

"Dad, what's the matter?" Maybe Barbie had stormed out again. Maybe they'd had a fight about the Escalade. "You're scaring me." Surely he knew that Barbie wouldn't really leave. Where could she go? Her family, whom she didn't speak to anyway, lived in some backwater town in Louisiana, and none of her spa girls or her mothers'-day-out friends would take on Barbie and the Four.

Maybe my father's meltdown was work-related—some deal gone wrong. He'd be on the cell phone like crazy for a day or two, and then this weird, weepy mood would blow over.

Would he really sit in the game room and shed tears about work?

Shaking his head, he cupped his fingers over his lips again. I heard the nanny coming in the kitchen door. In a few minutes, she'd start rousting the twins, and then the house would descend into the usual chaos. "You might as well tell me," I said. "If it's going around at the club, you know I'll hear it. Whatever it is, I can handle it." *An affair. It's probably an affair. Somebody strayed, and now word's out. It'll be a big scandal at church.* "I'm not a child anymore."

"No," he murmured, his eyes falling closed again. "It's just business. These things get blown out of proportion."

"Ohhh-kay, but what . . ."

The nanny walked by in the hall, and we waited for her to pass. "*Hola*," she called; then a string of Spanish drifted behind her as she continued down the hall.

"She wants you to know you forgot to leave her check out last week. Counting this week, you're three weeks behind."

He nodded again. "I need to go talk to Barbara." Pushing himself out of the chair, he stood up and left the room. Overhead, dull thumps shook the ceiling, followed by the crash of something hitting the wall, then bansheelike howling. The sibs were awake.

I hurried to the kitchen to grab a bottle of water and a breakfast square, and make my escape before the Four moved downstairs. Outside, Aunt Lute was sitting in a reclining chair by the pool, her legs crossed yoga-style and her arms held out with her index fingers touching her thumbs, so that she looked like one of those goddess statues from India. The only thing missing was six more arms and a headdress. She was wearing white spandex exercise clothes with a Bahamas logo on the front. It looked like something out of Barbie's closet—not a good choice for a seventy-year-old woman. Loose, wrinkled skin hung out everywhere, folded and bunched like yesterday's laundry.

Stuffing my breakfast in an empty Whole Foods bag, I ran upstairs, grabbed my golf shoes and a string top with a cute pleated miniskirt for later, plus a jacket for the clubhouse—maybe I'd ask Emity to meet me for lunch, and then we could hang out at the pool and talk about Europe. She'd be upset that I hadn't told my dad about our plans yet, but today clearly wasn't the day to bring it up.

Stuffing everything in a gym bag, I checked myself in the mirror—not too bad. I'd be a mess by the time I left the course anyway. The main thing now was to get out the door before one of the sibs decided to stow away in my vehicle. For them, escaping the house and hiding in one of the cars was the coup de grâce of nanny pranks.

Landon was standing at the top of the stairway rubbing his eyes, naked except for his Spider-Man undies. His little body was bony and brown and potbellied, so that he looked like a poster child for a Feed the Children campaign. His hair, which had dried in soft, wavy curls after last night's swim, framed his face as he yawned, swayed on his feet, and held out his arms like he was waiting for a hug.

Squatting on the top stair, I reached for him, and he looped his arms around my neck, then nestled under my chin. The sibs could melt you when they wanted to. "Hey, buddy," I whispered, because Mark and Daniel's bedroom door was open, and I didn't want them to hear me. The boys were never all in a good mood at once. "What's the matter?" I could hear the nanny in the twins' room, which meant Landon had gotten out of bed on his own this morning. "Go lie back down for a bit. Esmeralda will be there in a minute. I have to head out to the club." If I didn't show up on time to play eighteen this morning, after having left the lesson yesterday, Coach would give me more than just a lecture.

Landon shook his head, the cottony tips of his hair tickling my neck and chin. I tried to stand up, but his arms tightened around my neck so that he rose with me, then looped his legs over the top of the gym bag.

"Landon, I've got to go."

He held on like a spider monkey clinging to a branch in a stiff wind. The circle around my neck tightened until I was choking, the strap of the gym bag cutting into my collarbone.

"Landon, quit it, now. I said I have to . . ."

He sniffled, and I felt moisture on my skin. *What in the world . . .*

Something slammed against the master bedroom door at the end of the hall, and Landon jerked in my arms, his body quivering. The muffled sound of Barbie yelling drifted forth, followed by the deeper tone of my father raising his voice in response, both of them trying to be heard at once. Something metallic collided with the door, then spilled what sounded like marbles onto the floor. They click-clacked against the tile and clattered around the room.

The argument continued. I wanted to move close enough to make out the words, solve the mystery my father had created downstairs, but Landon trembled in my arms, whimpered softly, and suddenly I knew why he was up before the nanny call. His room was right next to the master suite.

Slipping a hand into his hair, I started down the stairs, my stomach clenching and tears prickling my throat. I knew what it was like to wake up with your parents eviscerating each other on the other side of the wall. "Hey, buddy, it's all right," I whispered, and kissed the downy hair over his ear. "Big people fight sometimes just like you guys do. It doesn't mean anything." The irony of that statement struck me as I reached the downstairs landing. *Big people fight just like you guys do. . . .*

No wonder the boys acted the way they did. Nothing here was like it was supposed to be. Nothing was right, or normal, or secure. Even the kids could feel the ground constantly shifting.

In the living room, I pried Landon off, set him on the sofa, then turned on a Disney movie. "I've gotta go, bud-pud. Just sit here and watch your movie until Esmeralda comes down, okay?"

Landon didn't answer. He was already zoning out to the opening credits of *Toy Story*. Something thumped so hard upstairs, it rattled the chandelier overhead. Landon didn't even notice. He wiped his cheeks and curled into a ball in the corner of the sofa, his blue eyes dull and unfocused. I tossed a fuzzy *101 Dalmatians* blanket over him, and he snuggled it against his chin.

Via the baby monitor on the end table, Jewel let out a wail. Mark or Daniel hollered something from the top of the stairs. A mystery object hit the floor. Landon tugged the blanket up higher, pulling it off his legs. There was a bruise on his thigh from the slide collapse last night.

The back door opened, and Aunt Lute stepped in, her face serene, a faint smile on her lips, as if the commotion in the house were of no concern to her.

"Aunt Lute, can you watch Landon?" I asked, and then headed for my car without waiting for an answer. I was out of the garage before the long hand on my watch could slide past another minute. My cell rang while I was on the way to the club, and it was Emity, of course. "*Hola, chica,*" she said, and after the bizarre morning at home, the cheerfulness in her voice seemed out of place. "*Buenos días.*"

"No foreign languages today, all right?" For a while now, Emity and I had been working on conversational French, Spanish, and Italian, so we'd be ready for Europe.

"Whoa, what's wrong with you?"

"Sorry. Weird day on Wisteria Lane. You know Barbie."

"Word's around about her taking out the Baby Bundle." Emity hitched a breath, and I could tell she was ready to get the dish on last night.

Normally, I would have been totally into spending the drive dealing out the Barbie details, but I couldn't get past the picture of my father crumpled in the chair, crying in the morning light. It made the Barbie blunder seem anything but funny. "I don't know what's going on. My dad was sitting in the living room crying this morning. Crying. Can you believe that? When I left, they were having a massive fight upstairs."

"Whoa," Em breathed. "What about?"

"No idea. Have you heard anything? Like, from your mom?" Emity's mom was head of the Coffeetime Club at our church, Forest Lane Fellowship, so she more or less heard everything. Aside from that, my mother and Em's mom had been friends since Em and I were in diapers together, so she'd scoop the dirt on my dad's new wife any chance she got.

"Nothing, except she took out the Baby Bundle with the Escalade. I heard she got her heel hooked under the gas pedal and couldn't get to the brake. Your dad's probably ticked about that."

"Yeah, I guess. The Escalade's still drivable, so it could be worse." But there was a queasy swirl in my stomach that wouldn't go away— as if I'd eaten something bad, and it was coming back to haunt me. "It was just weird. He said I might hear stuff at the club, and I shouldn't listen to it. What kind of stuff, you know?"

Emity thought for a minute. "I guess about the big wreck."

"I guess," I muttered. "Hey, Em, I've got to go. I'm at the club. Come meet me for lunch at the Club Grill, 'kay? See if your mom knows anything . . . about Barbie, or whatever, all right?"

Em answered in Spanish, and then we signed off. I went into the clubhouse feeling like there was a bomb hidden somewhere, and I was just waiting for it to explode. All morning long, I heard it ticking in my ear. My eighteen holes with Coach were uneventful. Not good, not bad. He thought I was a little off, but other than the blips in my swing, there was no indication that today was anything but normal.

In the clubhouse after lunch, the manager politely pointed out that our tab from last month hadn't been paid yet. I told him I'd remind my dad. "I think everything just autodrafts from the checking account," I said, and instantly the argument with Barbie started making sense. She'd probably run the household account dry again, and autodrafts were bouncing all over town. No wonder Dad was ticked.

Emity and I blew the afternoon at the mall, and then I headed back to the club to play another eighteen, while Emity went to her cousin's birthday dinner.

The nanny called just as I was setting up on the second tee. She was yelling in Spanish so loud and so fast, I couldn't understand anything she was saying. In the background, Barbie was screaming at someone, the sibs were running wild, and a man was trying to speak above the fray. The male voice was not my father's.

"Esmeralda! Esmeralda!" I hollered into the phone, but the line went dead. When I redialed, no one answered. I gunned the golf cart back to the clubhouse, left my clubs and everything else with the attendant, and ran for my car.

Horrible possibilities raced through my mind, and the few miles from the club to the house seemed endless. When I pulled into the driveway, a sheriff's department car was leaving our curb, the nanny was standing in the doorway trying to keep Mark and Daniel from escaping onto the front walk, and Barbie was kneeling on the front lawn, clutching a piece of paper in one hand and a cell phone in the other. As I stepped from my car, she pushed to her feet and staggered toward me, her eyes rimmed with mascara tears, her hands shaking. "It's . . . it's not true. It's a mistake. . . . I can't . . . I can't find him, though. He. . . ."

She reached toward me, and I stepped away. "Barbie? What are you talking about? Who? Who's missing?" Panic exploded like a scatter bomb inside me, and I looked toward the door, counted the faces pressed around the nanny. Where was Landon? "Who can't you find? Barbie! Who?"

Barbie staggered backward, her heels sinking into the sod. "I tried to call. I tried to call so he could talk . . . the sheriff."

"The sheriff . . . what? Barbie, who's missing? Who?"

Shaking her head, she held out the paper, stumbled sideways. "It's not true. It's . . . It's a mistake. I tried to call Paul. I tried to call."

"Dad?" I reached for the paper. "You tried to call Dad?" I

pinched the paper between my fingers, pulled on it, but Barbie held tight. "Let go!" I snapped, then yanked it away. The sheet fluttered in my hand. I straightened it out, scanned the boldface line of print at the top.

Twenty-four-hour Notice of Eviction . . .

Chapter 5

Sesay

The reverend father at the Crossings Church has talked longer than usual today. His voice is deep, and his face is a smooth, even brown, like a palm leaf when it dries. I know the word for his color of skin. It is far back in my memory. *Mulatto*, my father would have called him, and pushed air through his teeth and spit on the ground. But here, no one says the word, or spits on it. Here at Crossings Church, the people are so many shades of color that no one seems to notice, except me. I only see it because my father taught me to see when I was very young, and the lessons taught to the young grow deep roots.

I would never spit on the reverend father, of course. Michael, he calls himself. I am happy enough to sit here under the highway crossing and listen while he tells stories from his book, the Bible. The book is small, and brown, and he can read from it for a long time one day, and then more the next. He reads and reads, while the people sit stacked on the cement slope, their heads nodding forward, their clothing and blankets whispering in the breeze as they pass the time. They gaze out into the dusty lot, where the Glory Wagon is preparing something that smells good. The scent paints the back of my throat with water, and I look at the Glory Wagon, too. The Glory Wagon comes with Michael, and after you have listened to him tell what Father God wants to say, then the people in the Glory Wagon will give you something good in a paper bowl. It is only on certain days. Sometimes I pass by the bridge and see no Michael, and no Glory Wagon, and no paper bowls. I am learning the way of it, as you must when you come to a new place. The street people will help you, if you know how to ask.

Today, the men under the bridge are restless. They want to move on to the meal. I like the stories, though. I put them in my mind, but some of them are difficult to remember. I do not believe Michael keeps them all in his little brown book. There is not enough room in there for the pictures to tell so many stories. I think Michael must have many brown books with many different Father God stories, but all the books look the same. I think it is a trick he plays.

When he finishes, Michael prays over all of us. I watch him stand in the light filtering through the concrete piers, and hold his hands toward the sky, and call down a blessing. For a moment, everything is far away. I remember a building with no walls. I am a little girl on a blanket, and the sun is pushing through the roof in tiny pinpoints of heat, sending down shafts of light that dance in the dust from the floor. I have caught a piece of light in my hand, and I want to show it to someone. Another child. A younger one. There are brothers and sisters and cousins all around me. They have their eyes closed, as Father speaks a prayer over us, but I am looking at the sunbeams. For a moment now, my mind can see my brothers and sisters and cousins, their feet bare and brown in the dust, the tiny straws of sunlight falling over the braids in their hair. But then they fade, as they always do. I do not know what became of them when the soldiers broke down the gates of my father's house. When my mother found me hiding beneath Father's desk, no one was with her. She held my hand, and we ran through the house alone, into the darkness. . . .

There is movement all around me, and I am under the bridge again. Michael has finished his prayer, and everyone is walking toward the Glory Wagon—men and women, and a family with children alongside. Some of the men limp, some weave and stagger, and some just walk, as do I. Michael smiles at me as I come close. "Hello, Sesay," he says, and points to the pocket on the front of my pack. It is clear, and you can see through it to know what is inside. "I see you've got another book."

"I see you have one, as well," I tell him, and he laughs.

"It's the same book," he answers. "Same old Bible."

I blow a sound through my teeth, so he knows I am not such a fool as some of these people. "I like the story in this one."

"I figured you would." He looks down at the book, lifts it, and shows it the way a mother would display a favorite child.

"I have heard that story before—about the giant," I tell him, and for a moment, I see a man's hand, whirling as if he's holding a bit of leather, a slingshot that will throw the rock to kill a giant. It is a white man's hand, so I know it is not my grandfather's. "Somewhere . . . my ears caught that story. . . ." Like so many rememberings, this one is a tiny scrap, like a bit of paper with the hand drawn on it. Nothing else is attached. There is only the hand floating in my mind. I watch it for a moment. "Is there a picture of the giant? In your book?" Perhaps if I see the picture, the memory will come back with it.

"No pictures in this book," he says. "Just the words."

"Father God could send pictures," I point out, and look at the book again. "And then you would not need so many words."

Michael laughs. "I never thought of it that way." Lowering the book to his side, he turns toward the Glory Wagon, and we begin to walk. "I'll look for a picture of Goliath and bring it to you, if I can. You going to be at the Broadberry Mission tonight?" In the evenings,

Michael speaks at the mission, eight streets west, where the roads tangle together like snakes in a dance.

"Perhaps," I tell him. "I saw a new family on Red Bird, beside the park. The house once was pink, but now it is yellow." I want to watch the family more, to listen for their story, but I also know that when new people unpack, they put out boxes, and often the boxes have things in them that I can use—a bit of string, a can of paint, a china plate that has broken in the move.

Michael curls his lip like a growling dog when I mention the yellow houses. His hand goes tense on the Bible, and tight muscles shoot up his arms like cords of rope twisting. I am reminded that he is a young man. He has the anger of the young, but he fights against it. Sighing, he looks down at the sidewalk and shakes his head. He weighs the Bible in his hand. "Householders," he murmurs, but does not say anything more.

"The family may be putting out boxes by now," I tell him. "Boxes with things left in them."

Michael narrows an eye and it twinkles at me. "Sounds like you've got important business. Guess I should stop holding you up then, shouldn't I?" We reach the end of the line at the Glory Wagon, and he moves to take a place behind the table. Most days, he gives the spoons and greets everyone as they pass. He knows the names of so many people, even the newer ones like me. Some answer to the names and some do not. Today, a young girl with red hair gives out the spoons and bowls. She smiles, but she is not certain she should look anyone in the eye. She sets the bowls and spoons on the table, so no one will touch her.

Michael takes my spoon from her and keeps it just out of my reach. "You have anything for me?" he asks.

I have been waiting for the question. "Of course." I pretend to search the pockets of my pack, but that is only for show. I am wearing my green pants with the pockets, like the ones the army men have. The thing Michael is waiting for is there, and I know it. When I finally take it out, he gasps with anticipation.

"It's wonderful," he says, watching as the little red fish dangles from a loop of orange thread. The thread was tangled in the fence near the school, and the fish I carved from a bit of pecan wood that was floating in a puddle in the ditch where the children play beside the white apartments. I know how to find the story in a bit of wood. My grandfather taught me.

"It's just a little thing," I tell him, but the fish is good. I rubbed it against the paint on the curb to give it the red color. I saw fish like it in the ocean, after my grandfather put me on the boat. Auntie showed the fish to me, and she told me to watch them. When I looked up again, the shore was far away, and my grandfather was as tiny as the little wooden fish, now dangling from the orange string.

"It's very nice," Michael decides, and I am pleased.

"I can carve a good fish." For just a moment, I feel taller, and then I realize that I am smiling, and my teeth are not pretty. "It is equal to a bowl and a spoon."

Michael nods. "It certainly is." He pockets the fish and hands a bowl and spoon to me. The red-haired girl chews her lip, and I can see what she is thinking. The bowls and spoons don't cost. But she does not know me. She does not know that I pay my own way. When you pay your own way, no one can own you.

I feel inside my pocket again. There's still a turtle and a bird in there. I will have need of both yet today.

I go through the line and have my bowl filled, and then I'm off. I can walk and eat at the same time. If I arrive at the Summer Kitchen to help clean the dishes, the woman there will pack a sandwich and chips for me to have for supper, and I'll have no need of going to the mission tonight.

My bowl is soon empty, so I slip it into a trash bin and wipe my face and walk down the block toward the white church, where the Summer Kitchen is in the squatty building beside the chapel. The line stretches out the door, so I know I have arrived too early to wash dishes. At the Book Basket, the sign is turned to the side that means the door will be locked, so I move to the tree and stand there to watch the Indian chief, instead. The big doors on his part of the building are open, and I can hear music. The soft, clear tune of a flute draws me closer as if I am a snake, charmed from a basket. I walk to the corner and look in, then come nearer. I do not see the Indian chief, but it would be no matter if I did. I am invisible to him.

The big room where he works is empty. He has been painting on the large canvas again—broad, angry strokes that make a picture of a warrior on horseback, galloping. The white spaces yesterday have become mountains today.

There are splatters of paint by the door. Blue and green, still glistening wet. I look around for the chief again, and then I slip inside just far enough. I reach into my pocket, take out the turtle and the bird, push my finger into the paint, and color the turtle green and the bird blue. These are the right colors for them, and now both are finished. This is good, because I will need one for my sandwich from the Summer Kitchen.

The other is for the family in the new yellow house.

Chapter 6

Shasta Reid-Williams

Something weird happens when you're from a big family, and all your life, y'all have been bouncing off one another like mixed nuts in a can. Even when you finally break out, you can still hear all the relatives talking in your head. I never really counted on that when Cody and I moved to Dallas. I had it pictured that once we were in the city, and Cody was finally on with the police department, we'd get all settled in, and I'd finally feel like a grown-up adult, like I really was almost twenty-four years old. After being married five years and having two (and a quarter) kids, it seemed like it oughta be time.

But all I could hear the first day I was alone in our little yellow house was my mother whispering in my ear. I lay down on the mattress in the boys' room just long enough to get them to take a nap, and Mama pointed out right away that the ceiling had a big spot in the middle where the plaster dipped like a bubble about to burst. Someone'd painted over it, but it was there. Big cracks fanned out from it like spider legs, and ran down the walls. Lying on a mattress on the floor, I couldn't miss it.

How could you even walk into the room and not see it? the invisible Mama in my head wanted to know. Nana Jo Reid was right beside her, making a *tsk-tsk* through her teeth, and saying, *That'll cost a bun-*

*dle to fix. You'll have to chip the plaster off way down to the edge, Shasta
Marie. There'll be plaster everyplace.*

Cody's mom was one step behind the other two with her nose in
the air, saying, *It smells like mold in here. Black mold, most likely. It'll
ruin the boys' lungs. For heaven's sake, Shasta, you can't raise the boys in
a house full of mold. What were you thinking?*

My heart started racing, and I clamped my hands over my ears to
shut them up. It didn't work. I should've known it wouldn't. Cody's
mom just kept on comparing our house to the one Cody's sister,
Randi, just built on ten acres off the back side of the folks' place.
Randi's house had a porch all the way across the front and around
one side, a bay window in the kitchen, a whirlpool master bath, and
ceramic tile all through. I could of described every square inch of it by
heart, I'd heard about it so many times. Randi did things just right—
college degree up at East Central in Ardmore, big wedding with a
huge white tent and the whole deal, good job doing accounting at the
headquarters of the Tribe. If you're from southeastern Oklahoma and
you're Choctaw, that's what you do: get whatever education you're
gonna get, then take a good job with the Choctaw Nation, the school
district, or the highway department, build a nice house, live the good
life. Cody's sister did it. My brother did it. My cousins did it. Everybody with half a brain did it.

If you haven't got half a brain, you fall for somebody in high
school, get pregnant and married, get pregnant again and buy a dumb,
overpriced trailer house you'll be paying on for the next twenty years;
then you run up some credit card bills to put new furniture in it. Finally at some point you realize that really was stupid, and you've got
to do something drastic if you're ever gonna dig your way out.

"This is *our* house," I whispered, staring out the window into
the backyard, where roses and crape myrtles grew around the edges,

and a gorgeous stand of hollyhocks made a big square in the middle, and pecan trees were so huge you couldn't reach both arms all the way around them. Randi's new place didn't have anything as incredible as those trees. "This is *our* place. *Ours*." My voice echoed off the walls, and Benjamin twitched on the mattress; then Tyler rolled over and pushed his fist up into his mouth. I sat looking at them for a minute, watching Tyler smack his lips in his sleep, and the tips of Benji's black, burr-cut hair touching the sunlight on the pillow, and I thought, *Randi doesn't have anything like them. She doesn't have anything as great as my boys.*

I got up and left the room, because there was stuff I needed to do while the kids were down for their nap—wash out the kitchen cabinets and unpack all the dishes, for one thing. After the big celebration at Chuck E. Cheese's yesterday, we needed to start cooking at home. Our first supper in our new place. I'd have to think of something special. Something that wouldn't cost much. Between buying the new truck, and moving into the house, and paying to get the electricity, the cable, and the water turned on, the checkbook was thin as a banker's smile. There wasn't money left for anything else. Luckily, someone nearby had Wi-Fi, and it wasn't password protected, so we could connect up with Cody's old laptop and use the Internet for free. Altogether, we had two hundred and forty-eight dollars left to make it for the month, which would be tight, but we could do it. Back home, we'd come through the month with less money than that lots of times.

The cell phone rang in the kitchen, while I was walking down the hall noticing that the light fixture there was old and pretty, but it was hanging out of the ceiling a couple inches, like the bolts were coming loose. The wires above it looked dusty and ragged. While I passed by, the mind-Mama pointed out that it'd probably burn the house down.

When I got to the kitchen and picked up the phone, my brother's number was on the screen. Jace never called out of the blue. He was probably doing recon for Mama. I had the weird feeling I used to get back in high school when I was someplace I wasn't supposed to be, and she'd ring my cell, and I knew I'd gotten caught. My friends always thought I did something to give away all our secret plans, but they didn't know my mama. She raised Jace and me by herself after my daddy took off, and at the same time, she finished up her nursing degree and moved all the way up in the hospital until she was a shift supervisor. My mama was like Superwoman, complete with X-ray vision, radar ears, and a nose that was into everything, all the time.

I set the phone to one side and let the call roll to voice mail. Later on, after the stuff was unpacked in the kitchen, and Cody was home from the academy, and we'd finished a nice first meal in our new house, I'd give Mama a call.

Or maybe tomorrow.

Or next week . . .

Maybe I'd just e-mail her and Jace and tell them that Cody was taking the phone to work with him every day. That way, we wouldn't need to actually have a conversation.

"You're so lame," I muttered to myself, but then I went to the back door and stood looking out into the yard, and I felt better. This place was just right for us, and if we would of waited two weeks or two months to look for a house, this one would of been gone. Like the guy from Householders said, deals as good as this didn't come along every day, especially with no money down and no closing costs. I'd never get Mama to see that, of course. She'd just say we shouldn't've gotten ourselves any deeper in debt.

I went back to the kitchen and started on the boxes. Cody'd plugged in an old radio he found stuffed in the back of the hall closet, and I turned it on and let the music fill the kitchen and spill through the doors into the dining room and the utility room on the back end and the living room in the front. Even that felt like a serious victory. In the apartment, the walls were paper thin, and I couldn't put the boys down for a nap without my noise or someone else's waking them up. But here on Red Bird Lane, it was quiet, and I could dance in the kitchen without bothering somebody.

I danced all through the house while I was unpacking the boxes, just because I could. I caught a case of what we folks in the Reid family call the flappy happys. I felt so good, every once in a while I just had to stop and flap my hands in the air and squeal.

The phone rang again, and it was my fave long-distance girlfriend, Dell, so I picked up. "Guess what I'm doing?" I said.

"Ummm . . ." was the only answer she came up with. Dell knew that with me, *Guess what I'm doing* usually had an answer that would scare most people. "I don't have a clue . . . what?"

"Guess." Dell was such a stick-in-the-mud sometimes. She was, like, the most serious-minded person I knew. I liked her, but in the three years we'd been friends, I'd never, ever seen her do one single thing that was the least bit spontaneous. I guess I could of learned something from that. Dell was in music school at Juilliard, and I was . . . well, pregnant again.

"I wouldn't even know where to start guessing," she said.

"You are *so* not fun," I complained, and then it seemed like I'd hurt her feelings, so I went ahead and spilled the beans. "I just picked up a big stack of boxes, and I'm carrying them . . ." I stretched out the sentence, giving the play-by-play while I headed to the front door. ". . . across the living room . . . out the door . . . over the porch . . . down the steps . . . across the . . . *my* yard. . . ."

"Oh, my gosh, you got a house!" Dell squealed. "Already? Three weeks ago you were just trying to figure out how to get Cody to *think* about a house."

Was that really just three weeks ago? "Well, you know us. We don't think for long. We just jump right in." If I said that to my mother or one of my aunts, they would of tried to hammer some sense into me, but Dell never judged anybody. She wasn't like everyone back home, who thought that just because you were smart in high school, you had to go make some big-deal life to impress everyone. Dell understood why I wanted my own family and my own place. "I caught a TV commercial talking about these Householders deals, and they mentioned the Blue Sky Hill area, and I knew it was a sign."

"Blue Sky Hill?" Dell chopped off the last word like she was holding her breath on it. I'd kind of expected her to react like that.

"Yeah, guess who helped us move in?" She didn't answer, but I didn't wait for her to, either. "Your biological daddy-o. Mr. Terence Clay. We just looked him up when we drove over here to hunt houses. He was actually kinda helpful about it. He showed us around the neighborhood. Our house is, like, five or six blocks from his house, and his studio is, like, right around the corner from here in the back end of what used to be a gas station, but there's some kind of used bookstore in the front part. You'd think a guy who's had art in the Amon Carter Museum and his face on *D* magazine would have a fancier office than that, but that's where he works—in this big old garage building with the doors open and no air-conditioning."

"You *called* him?" Dell was about a half mile behind me. Most people are.

"Yeah, I figured, why not? We don't know anybody else in Dallas. He's from Pushmataha County; we're from Pushmataha County. He's Choctaw; we're Choctaw. Him and Cody are cousins way back. You've got to network where you can, right? If it wasn't for him, we wouldn't've found this house. They'd just finished the paint job on it, and there wasn't even a sign up yet."

"*I* don't even call him."

"Maybe you ought to. He's not a bad guy." Dell had found out about her biological dad, like, three years ago, and in all that time, all she'd done was trade a few e-mails and send him a card at Christmas. If my daddy left a door wide open, wanting to be in touch with me, I'd of been through it so fast the hinges would of been swinging like the front of a saloon. "Terence came over and helped us move in. I said that already, didn't I? He just showed up. He's kind of . . . quiet, like he doesn't say much about anything, but he's nice. He let me put my pottery stuff in his studio. He said it could stay there for how-ever long we needed—until we were ready for it, which'll be a while. There's a ton to do on this house, and, of course, Cody's gone, and if he's not gone, he's studying or crashed out. You know who's going to be the one unpacking all this junk, and kid-proofing all the plugs, and tying up all the cords on the window blinds? Me. Yesterday, I showed Cody this big old oleander bush by the porch, and, so I'm, like, telling him those are poisonous, and we've got to rip it out be-cause of the kids, and he's, like, 'Well, duh, just tell them not to eat it.' Like you can count on little kids to do what you say, and . . ."

It hit me that I was standing on the curb holding the boxes and blabbering on, and Dell wasn't making a sound on her end. I had the feeling that always came right before my mama would say, *Shasta Marie, don't you ever think?*

Maybe getting in touch with the biological dad your friend hadn't really warmed up to in three years wasn't such a good idea.

Since someone had to say something, I went with the obvious. "You're not mad at me, are you?" Dropping the boxes on the curb, I started back toward the house.

Dell had to think about how to answer . . . which isn't usually a good sign. "No . . . it's just . . . I'm in shock. I didn't think you'd . . . be . . . living right around the corner from Terence. It's kind of weird."

I felt my face going hot, which for me is saying something, because I don't embarrass easy. "Oh, geez, I'm sorry. I stepped in it, didn't I? You know how I am. It didn't even cross my mind how you'd feel about it. I just . . ."

"It's all right," Dell said, and I caught my breath. "I really just called to tell you I'm coming to town. I didn't think you'd be living down the road from my . . . from Terence, that's all. I was kind of thinking of getting in touch with him while I'm in Dallas, but I guess now I'll have to."

"You're coming to town? When? Why?"

"August. There's a symposium on Native American studies, and I'm coming for the music sessions as part of one of my Juilliard classes. Then I'm driving up to Oklahoma. There's some research I want to do for a presentation about Choctaw flute-making traditions. It's a multimedia thing, so I'm combining photos and recordings of traditional Native American flute music. Your brother's going to hook me up with some flute makers and flute players around Push County. He came up here a couple weeks ago and helped me lay out the whole project."

"He did?" Getting my brother to travel someplace outside southeastern Oklahoma practically took an act of Congress. Jace was rooted in the hometown like a stump. He and Dell had kept up a weird long-distance thing for the past three years, but both of them were too busy with their own lives to do anything serious about it. They were always saying they were just friends. *Just friends*, my rear. If I was in love with somebody, I'd admit it and quit wasting time,

but then, that was me. "Awesome," I said, then looked at the house
and thought, *Oh, shoot.* Dell's symposium meant that, like it or not,
the family reality was gonna come crashing down on our little yellow
house. As soon as Dell saw the place, my brother'd know about it, and
then when she got to Oklahoma, everyone else would know, too.

Once Mama and Cody's folks heard, they'd hit the road and head
for Dallas to see what kind of a mess we'd dug ourselves into now. I
had until sometime next month to get this place in shape. "What day
did you say you were coming?"

"The sixth of August. Is that okay? Will you be there?"

The sixth . . . I had four weeks and a few days to make the house
look respectable, get the boys signed up for Head Start and kinder-
garten at their new school, put safety caps on the plugs, get locks on
the cabinets, and cut down the oleander. Maybe Cody's mom didn't
care if her kids ate oleander leaves, but my mother would be all over
it like mayflies on a streetlight.

My stomach rolled over, and I rubbed it while I crossed the porch.
By next month, I'd be having morning sickness like crazy. Not much
chance Mama would miss that . . .

"Is something wrong?" Dell's voice was like a fuzzy little puppy
hopping around the dust devil of a dogfight. I couldn't even hear her,
at first.

"Huh? No . . . why?"

"You're quiet all of a sudden."

"I was just thinking." *The bubble in the ceiling, the hanging-down
light fixture, the oleander bush, check the backyard fence for holes, put
the safety things on the hot-water faucets, paint everything, hang pictures
so the place looks homey, fix the cracks around the window frames, repair
the bathroom tile, weed the flower beds, scrape the dried paint off the
window glass, maybe put something cute on the boys' walls. Maybe get*

them some new sheets. Something colorful. No, Mama will notice they're
new. She'll think you're out blowing money again. . . .

"You never get quiet."

"Thanks a lot." If she could of heard the inside of my head, she
wouldn't've thought it was *quiet.* The panic voice was so loud in
there, I couldn't hear myself think. Mama was gonna have a fit about
the burglar bars on the windows and the front door. She'd think we'd
bought into the worst neighborhood ever. She'd never believe that just
a few blocks away, upscale new condos were going in, and in a year
or two, these neighborhoods would be the place to be for people who
didn't want a long commute into Dallas. "Listen, whenever you talk
to Jace again, don't mention anything about the house, all right?"

"All right." Dell sounded suspicious. "Are you sure you're okay?
You don't sound normal."

"I don't feel so good this morning. Too much Chuck E. Cheese's
last night, I think." I couldn't exactly start telling friends about the
pregnancy until I'd figured out a way to let Cody in on it. Actually,
I didn't want to tell anybody. The picture of that news spreading
through the family made the house situation seem like a little side
story. *News flash, Shasta's pregnant again. It's the end of the world!*

Dell chuckled. "Well, listen, I'd better go. I have to get to re-
hearsal." I pictured her skipping off to Juilliard with her violin in
hand, sunlight bouncing off her dark hair and slipping around her
skinny body in the cute latest-thing clothes her adopted parents could
afford to buy for her, and I felt like a loser. A stupid, stretch-marked,
tired loser trying to make something good out of a dumpy little house
nobody would be impressed with anyway. They'd all think buying
this house was one more dumb move in a line of dumb moves. Typical Shasta stuff.

I said good-bye to Dell and headed inside, but the house didn't feel the same. I saw all the things wrong with it again, and even though I was unpacking boxes as fast as I could and carrying the trash out to the curb, I felt like I wasn't getting anywhere. I was in the middle of a mess, and I always would be.

No one in my family would ever understand the house, or the pregnancy. They'd never get it that, now that we had health insurance, Cody had his mind set on a vasectomy, and even though Benjamin and Tyler were perfect, I didn't want to go through the rest of my life without a baby girl. I wanted a daughter, and Cody wouldn't even talk about it, and I had to do something before it was too late.

"It'll be all right," I whispered, cupping my hands around the baby that wasn't even big enough to see yet, though I could picture her already. "We'll figure it out."

By the time the boys woke up, I was so busy unpacking, I pretty much forgot to worry about the house. There was a mountain of empty boxes and paper in the living room, and the place looked like a tornado'd blown through. Once the boys found the mess, they went wild, tearing around, climbing in and out of boxes, shredding up paper and throwing it at each other. For a while, I just sank down in a chair and let them do it. My clothes were plastered to my skin with sweat, and my body felt like one of those pieces of deer meat Nana Jo used to beat to death with her spiky metal meat-tenderizing hammer.

My eyes tugged closed as Benji stuck his brother in a box and shut the lid. "Don't hurt him." Just about the time I got the words out, Benji tipped the box over and Tyler hit his head, and the game went from fun to dangerous. "All right, you guys, quit." I checked the clock, hoping that by some miracle it would be time for Cody to come home, and he could play with the boys. But, of course, it was only three in the afternoon, which meant we had hours to go yet before Cody, or our pickup truck, got back.

Pulling myself out of the chair, I groaned and whimpered, rescued Tyler from the box, then stopped him from kicking his brother. "All right, we don't kick," I said, and Ty stomped his feet, crossed his arms, and poked his bottom lip out at me, his eyes squinting up, the dark centers disappearing behind round cheeks. Sometimes that kid looked and acted so much like Cody, it was unbelievable. "And we don't give Mommy the pokey lip either," I told him. "I'll tell you guys what. Let's see how fast we can put all the paper in the boxes, and then y'all can help Mommy carry this stuff out front, and then, when we get all that done, we'll go out in the backyard and play awhile, okay?"

Of course, the only part the boys heard was, *Go outside and play.* They headed for the back door like someone'd shot them out of a gun barrel.

"Wait a minute!" I hollered, and they stopped in the doorway. "We have to clean up the stuff in the living room first."

"You said we can play outside!" Benji argued, sticking out his chin. In the three months since we'd moved to Dallas, he'd really started to grow an attitude.

"I said, after we finish picking up all the trash in the living room and hauling out the empty boxes, then we can go out and play. Do you see trash in the living room? Because I do."

Benjamin gave me the death-ray look, then locked his arms and sat down right there in the doorway.

"If Daddy was here, he'd bust your rear," I told him, but Benji knew better. He knew that Cody'd probably be out in the backyard with them, while the boxes stayed in the living room, stacked floor to ceiling. "But since he's not, you just go ahead and put on a big ol' pout. I'm gonna sit here, and we'll all just pout." I didn't wait for him to answer; I just got on with the pouting, like the child psychology lady on MommyTime said to.

Benji came out of the doorway first, and inched his way into the room. He leaned around the chair and checked out my pout lip. "Mommy?" His voice was quiet, like the whole thing sort of scared him.

"Don't bug me. I'm busy pouting." The corners of my lips twitched up, and I worked hard to pull them down.

Benji moved closer, and Ty was right behind him. "I no wanna pout." Ty touched my knee to shake me out of it.

"I do," I said. "Come on, let's just sit here and pout, and not fill those boxes. Let's see who can pout the best."

Benji blinked, his eyes flying wide in a way that said, *Mom's lost her mind!*

Ty stomped a foot. "I no wanna! I wanna put da papew box-es." A spray of spit covered my leg as he worked hard on the last word.

"C'mon, Mom," Benji added, one eyebrow squeezing down low over his eye.

I sighed and hauled myself out of the chair like they were waaaay too much trouble. "Well, oh-kay."

Within minutes, we were all stuffing paper like Santa's elves. Once we were done, we hauled the junk to the curb, and then we gave each other high fives. I wished all the people back home who thought I couldn't handle my own kids could of seen it.

In the backyard, the boys found a little patch of dirt beside the storage shed by the fence, and they settled in to build cities and roads, while I explored the yard. In the bright afternoon light, it seemed bigger than last night. The old white picket fence across the back and the flower beds along the sides made the place a picture postcard. Overhead, the pecan branches swayed lazily, and dragonflies buzzed back and forth from the creek next door, where the edge of our property sloped downward. Near the middle of the yard, the tall, square flower bed of hollyhocks wasn't really a flower bed, but the foundation from an old building—something small like a storage shed. I made an opening in the hollyhocks and stepped through, and it was like I was in a hidden room with a rock floor and living walls. There was a little iron table in the center, with three chairs. Just the right number. Sitting in one of the chairs, I looked around at the room. It felt like someone had just been there having a picnic.

When I came out, Benji was alone in the sandbox. I scanned the yard, and my heart skipped a beat. "Benjamin, where's Tyler?" Benji was busy playing and didn't answer at first. "Benjamin, where's your brother?" I hurried around the shed, looked behind it and on the other side. Benji sat back on his heels, his head twisting while he checked bushes.

He lifted both shoulders.

My heart jumped in my throat like a jackrabbit. "Benji, that's not funny. He was just here with you."

Benji pushed against the ground and got to his feet. He followed as I ran around the side of the house by the driveway and checked the gate. Closed. There wasn't any way Tyler could undo the latch by himself. I turned, half tripping over Benji, half pushing him out of the way.

"Tyler!" I hollered. "Ty-llller!"

I rounded the house again, and suddenly there he was, coming from the little slice of yard on the west end. His arm was stretched high in front, something blue dangling from his fingers. I felt it brush my shoulder as I slid to my knees and hugged him. "Don't do that," I breathed. "Ty, you have to stay with your brother. What were you doing over there?"

Stepping back, he smiled and held out his prize. He'd made a little fist over a loop of string with something blue swinging from the end.

Lifting my hand, I held it still, leaned close, took in the tiny, carved bluebird in my palm. Its neck was stretched out, its wings raised, like it'd been frozen just before taking flight.

"Where'd you find this, baby?" The old owners must've left a few treasures behind, other than the garden table. "Where'd you get it?"

Dropping the bird into my hand, Tyler pointed toward the narrow strip of yard hidden on the other side of the house. "Da lady gimme."

"Lady?" I repeated. "What lady?"

"Da green-pans lady." He reached down and patted the knees of his pants. "Da green-pans lady."

"Green pants? What lady?" I whispered, the hairs prickling on the back of my neck. Standing up, I moved a few steps to the side, looked around the corner of the house.

No one was there.

Chapter 7

Tam Lambert

They say that during the crash of 1929, prominent men who'd suffered sudden reversals of fortune climbed onto window ledges and plummeted to their deaths. My father's version of jumping from a high-rise was booking a one-way ticket to Mexico. He fled the country just before the feds raided the corporate offices of Rosburten, where Dad had a posh corner office and the misleading title of chief operating officer. In reality, my father was the public face and pitchman for Rosburten's holdings, and the friend and international fishing companion of the company's flamboyant CEO, Ross Burten. My father's association with Rosburten Corp. had added a glow of celebrity and an air of likability to the company, which helped to bring in big investors for planned real estate projects involving revitalization of decaying neighborhoods, construction of low-income housing projects, and most recently, a sports megacomplex and theme park that, despite the company taking investors' money, appeared to have existed largely on paper.

Ross had a reputation for being able to get his projects through city hall with amazing speed, and for winning low-income housing contracts and lucrative tax credits. The problem was that Ross's magic came at a price. Apparently, he was greasing palms all the way through the process, including his own. Now Rosburten Corp. was under investigation, Ross Burten and his family had mysteriously left the country for a European vacation, and FBI investigators were having a field day, collecting files from the Rosburten building. Meanwhile, three city council members were busy denying having taken kickbacks in Ross's real estate schemes, and Rosburten Corp.'s shiny marble facade was set to tumble like a house of cards.

I watched the drama on the five-o'clock news, as did Barbie and probably everyone else in town, including the nanny, who told us she'd found a new job and wouldn't be showing up tomorrow. She didn't want anything to do with *un asunto de policía* (a police matter). And by the way, would we destroy the sticky note by the phone with her name and address on it, and any other *referencias* (references) to her around the house?

Before she'd even made it out the door, the phone started ringing. Barbie and I stared at the television and let the phone roll to voice mail. The landscaper wanted to know if he should still come tomorrow, the pool boy was now operating on a cash-only basis, Barbie's massage therapist, Fawn, assured Barb she didn't believe a word of the news report, every member of Barbara's coffee club wondered how she was doing, and the care pastor from church offered to come sit with us. The offer was halfhearted, and he was quick to hang up. He was probably busy watching the feds raid Rosburten's offices. Meanwhile, an unconfirmed source stated that my father, well-known former Dallas quarterback Paul Lambert, had reportedly flown to Mexico that morning, beyond the reach of federal investigators.

Barbie pressed herself into the corner of the sofa, her face ashen, her foot twitching like a spider's leg right after someone sprays it with a toxic chemical. Her arms were wrapped so tightly around Landon that his eyes were bugging out. The toe of her stiletto bounced Jewel's baby seat in a rhythm so rapid that Jewel's mewing babbles sounded like an engine cranking on a cold day. Barbie had watched the news report on three networks, then switched over to FOX to watch it again. Snatching the eviction notice from the coffee table, she pinched it between two French-manicured fingernails, as if she were trying to fit it into the scene on TV.

FOX News had made it all the way to the airport, tracking Dad's sudden exit from the country. In an odd twist of fate, the cabdriver who'd brought him there had once been the owner of a Householders casita—right up until the mortgage adjusted, the payment skyrocketed, and his American dream ended in a nightmare he was still paying for. If he'd realized who he was taking to the airport, he said, my father would have been leaving for Mexico in a box.

I stumbled numbly backward and landed on a bar stool as the news reports echoed against the vaulted ceiling. The television coverage was like something from a bad prime-time drama. None of it seemed real.

How could any of this be real?

Around me, everything was happening in slow motion, as if I were watching it from the vantage of the lazily spinning ceiling fans. In the kitchen, Aunt Lute paced back and forth, holding a sack of carrots and a butcher knife. The twins careened down the hallway, carrying some sort of long, plastic rods that looked like they'd been taken from the miniblinds. Someone screamed, and a large object crashed in the playroom. Barbie jerked upright on the sofa and clutched Landon more tightly. Aunt Lute plunked a cutting board down on the kitchen counter and started carving carrots into long, thin strings. Barbie lifted the remote and tried another channel.

The phone rang again. I slapped the button to turn it off. My cell chimed in my pocket. I hit the mute without taking it out. It vibrated against my leg. "Barbara, we have to do something," I said. Do what? What were we going to do? What could we do? "We can't just sit here watching the news. They're coming tomorrow to kick us out of our house."

Apparently, somewhere during the financial downslide my father had hidden from us, he'd ceased to pay for almost everything we owned, including the seven-thousand-square-foot dream home that Barbie had lovingly furnished with gaudy decorator pieces of a French provincial nature. According to the eviction papers in Barbie's hand and the information we'd been able to glean from frantic phone calls before the end of the business day, one department of the bank had proceeded with foreclosure, even while my father had been attempting to negotiate some sort of a reprieve with another department. Our home had been sold on the courthouse steps, and we were now squatters. The new owners wanted us out.

My father must have known this was a possibility. He must have felt it this morning when he was crying in the game room, yet he never said a word. How could he do this to us?

In the kitchen, Aunt Lute moved from carrots to broccoli and continued slicing, as if she hadn't a care in the world.

"Barbara," I snapped. "We've got to do something." There had to be someone we could call—someone who could straighten out this mess. My father's accountant, his lawyer . . . anyone.

I didn't even know who those people were. Other than laughing at his occasional TV commercials, I'd had no interest in my father's business dealings. I'd gone blithely along with my life, trusting him to take care of us, to provide for us. Until now.

"Stop it!" Barbie hissed, swiveling toward the kitchen. "Stop that noise!" Flailing an arm at the offending sound, she pointed a finger to Aunt Lute's butcher knife. "Stop doing that!"

Landon took advantage of the opportunity to squirm out of his mother's grasp and bolt for the playroom down the hall.

Aunt Lute lifted a brow in Barbie's direction, then picked up an apple and whacked it cleanly in half. Barbie jerked upright, her breath catching in a tiny gasp. Down the hall in the playroom, the twins were taking out the Sheetrock, by the sounds of it, but Barbie was oblivious to that.

Letting my head fall against the wall, I leaned across the bar into the kitchen. "Aunt Lute, please. We have to figure out what to do here. We have to think."

Aunt Lute tipped her chin up haughtily, cored the apple slices, then swept everything into a crystal bowl. "In the meanwhile, someone must throw bread to the birds. The natives are restless." Scooping up the bowl, she cupped it against her chest and shuffled across the kitchen without giving Barbie another look. The knife lay on the counter, glimmering atop a pile of dismembered fruit and vegetable parts, the juices running in a sticky stream along the seam in the granite, flowing downhill toward the floor. I grabbed a jelly-stained napkin and dropped it over the lazy river, stopping the flow as Aunt Lute disappeared down the hall, heading toward the mayhem in the playroom.

A moment later, the cacophony stopped, and finally everything was quiet. I turned back to Barbie. She was changing the TV channel again, as if by trying it enough times, she'd finally find one with different news on it.

"I called Paul," she muttered, holding up her cell phone, like some kind of proof that she was doing all she could. "I've called and called, but he won't answer. . . . He'll call back. He'll tell us what to do."

"He's in Mexico, Barbara." Where I had harbored something between love and ambivalence for my father, now there was a burning anger, painful and bitter. But there was also disbelief. My father was Superman. This couldn't happen to him. He wouldn't do this. "He left us."

"That's just . . . it's just something . . . something on TV," Barbie murmured. Snatching the cat from under the coffee table, she stroked it in a frenetic rhythm that matched the bouncing of her foot against the baby carrier. "He told me . . . this morning, he said I might hear some things . . . he said . . . he said not to worry. He said . . . he said he'd have it worked out . . . by tonight. He was upset about the car wreck. He told me it wouldn't have happened if I hadn't been down there getting rid of stuff the kids should still be wearing. We had a fight, but then he told me he'd take . . . he'd take care of it. . . . I shouldn't worry. . . ." Her voice quavered to a stop, like a scrap of paper coming to rest in a blind alley.

He told me that, too. He lied. "Barbie, he's gone. He left the country. Whatever's going on, he's in some serious trouble and so are we." Barbie just didn't get it, or she didn't want to. "I think we should call Uncle Boone." Uncle Boone wasn't really my uncle, but he was my father's oldest friend. Boone and Dad had been together since their football-playing days—as far back as I could remember. They starred in Householders commercials together, and my father had helped Boone's construction company win various building contracts. Other than Aunt Lute, Boone was the closest thing to family we had. "If anyone knows what's going on, Uncle Boone will. He can tell us what to do."

"Paul's going to call. We just have to . . ." Tears welled and glittered in Barbie's eyes, ready to spill over. Her lips, perfect and plump and surprisingly still wet with gloss, trembled as she looked around the room, then put down the cat and scooped Jewel out of her carrier. "He'll call."

"We can't wait," I whispered. Didn't she see that waiting for Dad to sweep in and save us was pointless? He had created this mess, and now he was powerless to fix it. For months, maybe even a year or two, or more, we must have been sinking further and further under, yet he'd never said a thing, never told Barbie to slow down on the spending, and never suggested to me that there wouldn't be any new car arriving on my birthday. He'd come and gone as if everything were normal. Only two months ago, he'd let Barbie plan a massive superhero birthday bash for the twins, complete with over two hundred guests, a petting zoo, a bounce house, a water slide, and a make-a-movie studio in the playroom. My father even wore his Householders' superhero suit for the event.

Was it really possible that, while he was hamming it up on the lawn, signing autographs for kids from preschool and playgroup, he knew that some banker was drawing up papers to kick us out of our house? Would he really have moved Aunt Lute in six months ago if he believed we might all end up on the street? Would he have kept paying for Barbie's spa days, and my private golf lessons, and the country club membership, and the twins' preschool, the nanny, and the endless supply of high-end kiddie clothes from the best boutiques in Highland Park?

"I'm calling Uncle Boone." With my mother out of touch on her mission in Central America, Uncle Boone was the only one we could turn to. "We can't just sit here and wait to see what happens tomorrow morning." My head was a swirl of words as I searched through my cell directory for his number. It was impossible to know what to say at a time like this.

Aunt Lute returned with her bowl. The doorbell rang. Barbie didn't move. Aunt Lute disappeared down the entryway. The bells chimed on the wall as she opened the door, then chimed again as she closed it and returned to the kitchen.

"It's best to avoid the front entrance," Aunt Lute advised as she rinsed her hands in the sink, then dried them on a towel while checking her purple fingernail polish. "A man out there came bearing a camera. I gave them what was left of the fruit, and he made a film of me."

"He . . . what?" Sliding off my stool, I closed the phone, then crossed the kitchen and the foyer to check the entry hall. Shadows moved outside the door, pressing close, trying to peer through the swirls of frosted glass. Someone knocked, then rang the bell incessantly.

"Hello?" A voice echoed through the wood. "This is Garth Culver with Channel Eight news."

"Don't open it," Aunt Lute whispered. "He'll think we've gone out." She winked one foggy violet eye before disappearing in the direction of the utility stairs and her room.

Backing away, I dialed Uncle Boone's number again, and this time he answered. He was on his way home from the lake with some girl giggling in the car. When I told him what had happened, his answer was a string of expletives, followed by a long sigh. "Guess the Postman got caught with his pants down this time. I told him this was gonna happen."

The girl in his car stopped giggling. I could hear her asking, "What's wrong, honey?"

What's wrong? There wasn't enough time between here and Lake Ray Hubbard to even begin to answer that question.

Within an hour, Uncle Boone was at our house, minus the girl. He forced the reporters off our lawn and back to the public domain of the sidewalk. The chimes on the doorbell finally stopped their insane ringing, and Jewel quit wailing. When Boone came in, Barbie deposited Jewel in the bouncy seat and said to no one in particular, "Take her down to the playroom. She likes to watch the boys."

I stared at Barbie, wondering what planet she was living on. Could she not hear the boys tearing down the playroom walls? Jewel wouldn't last five minutes there before someone tipped over her bouncy seat or whacked her with something. But after an hour of nonstop noise, I was willing to do almost anything to keep the baby quiet, so I picked up the carrier and went looking for Aunt Lute. I found her in her apartment over the garage, serenely reading a copy of *Lord of the Flies*.

Tucking the book cover under her chin, she smiled at me. "Have you seen this novel? It's very good."

"Aunt Lute, can you watch Jewel for a few minutes?" I stood in the doorway with the bouncer propped on my hip. Normally, the sibs were strictly forbidden from Aunt Lute's room—too many prescription bottles, tubes of oil paint, containers of solvent, and hoarded treasures she'd been unwilling to leave behind at her old house. "Uncle Boone's here. We're trying to figure out what's going on."

"Certainly," Aunt Lute agreed, smiling as if today were nothing out of the ordinary. "I'll take her downstairs again, if she requires her mother."

"Thanks," I said.

"Is there a problem?" Aunt Lute gave me a lucid look, and for the first time today I had the sense that she wasn't as unaware of our situation as she often seemed.

"I think so," I admitted, walking into the room and setting the bouncer on the coffee table in front of Aunt Lute's small sofa. "I think Dad's really in trouble."

She nodded gravely. "We lost the farm once. If a man from the bank comes, don't let the mother leave." Frowning at Jewel, she stretched out a hand, her fingers crooked and trembling as she pressed a knuckle to Jewel's foot and lifted it. "Tell her a mother must stay."

More than once over the years, I'd sat at banquets where my father was the celebrity speaker. I'd heard him blithely tell the story of my grandfather losing the family farm, and the family's downward spiral into poverty and dysfunction. *After a few months, my mother just packed her suitcase and left,* the story went. *There were seven of us, and my father worked long hours. My oldest sister, Lutia, took on the raising of us as much as she could, but Lute had to work, too, which left us with a lot of time to run the streets. Luckily for us, that first apartment in the city was right down the road from the Boys and Girls Club. . . .*

Dad's "One Thing Can Make All the Difference" speech went on to chronicle the descent into gang life of my father's eldest brother, the death of a sister in an alcohol-related teenage accident, the gang-related shooting that killed one brother and left another in a wheelchair. Even Aunt Lute, who by my father's definition had been a brilliant, creative girl, had become trapped in the shadow of the neighborhood, working a mindless factory job while caring for her father and invalid brother. Out of seven siblings, Dad was the only one who'd pried loose the grip of poverty and alcoholism and left his old life behind. He was a poster child for community intervention into the lives of struggling kids. He'd climbed from the ghetto to grab the brass ring.

Sometimes I wondered if, underneath all the hype, there was still the frightened nine-year-old boy who'd wandered the streets alone, locking the world outside, angry at everyone, until a coach at a community sports program lured him into a game of flag football and found a way in.

"Nobody's leaving," I told Aunt Lute. As much as the sibs drove me crazy, they were still my family. I knew what it felt like to have the people who were supposed to take care of you decide to move on. My father knew that feeling, too. How could he just take off for Mexico and leave us behind?

When I came back downstairs, Barbie was wrapped around Uncle Boone, her arms interlaced over his broad shoulders, her head buried against his T-shirt, her long blond hair trailing pale and golden against his coffee-and-cream skin. He was patting her shoulder with one hand and trying to dial his cell phone with the other.

I heard a crash down the hall, and one of the sibs—Daniel, I thought—let out an ear-piercing scream.

Barbie lifted her head, trembling as she wiped a mascara-stained cheek. "Can you go get him?" she whimpered.

"Why don't you?" I snapped.

"Tam . . ." Nothing irked me more than when Barbie tried to use the mom voice on me. She only did it when we were in front of people—so that she'd look like the perfect, parental stepmom, and I'd look like some teenage spoiled brat.

Right now, I didn't care. "You know what, Barbara? The boys are not my problem. You're their mother. You're not my mother, thank God, but you're *their* mother. Why don't *you* take care of them?"

Barbie's blue eyes narrowed and turned icy. She disentangled herself from Uncle Boone so she could point a long, French-manicured fingernail in my direction. "Why don't *you* stop acting like it's *your* world, and we're just living in it, Tam? Why don't you just—"

"Me?" Anger and frustration and hatred for Barbie exploded inside me like a land mine. "Me? You're the one who—"

"All right, all right. Just a minute!" Stepping out of Barbie's reach, Boone held up his hands like a referee calling time. "You two going at it ain't gonna help any." Even after years in the city, and with the big diamond stud in his ear, Uncle Boone was still as country as dirt. "Both of you siddown. We need to talk. There's a lot bigger problem here than whether the two of you like each other or not."

By the time Boone finished explaining what he already knew, and what he'd been able to piece together about my father's financial situation, Barbie was the least of my worries. The fact was that my father was embroiled in a financial scandal that was as large as Ross Burten, who, along with the company's chief financial officer, stood accused not only of bribing city officials, but also of siphoning huge amounts of investor money out of the athletic park project and various real estate developments to support lavish trips, a professional sailing team and boat, several estates and vacation homes, and Ross's $1.5 million wedding to his third wife. Unfortunately for him, his second wife had tipped off the feds.

The question now was how much my father knew, when he knew it, and whether he'd shared in the ill-gotten windfall. Burten's ex-wife, who knew my mother and had a particular disdain for middle-aged men with young replacement wives, had implicated my father along with Burten and the rest of the company's financial management.

Given my father's current financial state, and the fact that he'd fled to Mexico, the prognosis didn't look good—for him, or for us. By noon tomorrow, Barbie, the sibs, and I would be out on the street. The new owners of the house didn't want to talk to us—they just wanted us out. Immediately. Uncle Boone had already tried calling them, and they weren't budging—especially not for a homeowner facing a federal investigation.

"I told Paul he needed to come clean with it all," Uncle Boone finished. "I told him he was only gonna dig this thing so wide and deep even Superman couldn't get out."

"But he said things were fine," Barbie protested. "This morning, he said . . . he said he knew the bank account was dry, but it was all a mistake."

Uncle Boone shook his head. "He was jus' hoping he could still find a way out. He's Superman, you know? He jus' couldn't buy that it was really gonna come down and everybody'd find out what's been goin' on."

Barbie's lips trembled. The edges, normally perfect, were smeared where she'd been pinching her mouth with her fingers. "You're wrong!" She sobbed. "Paul wouldn't . . . he wouldn't do those things. You're wrong!" The rising panic in her eyes said that even she was beginning to understand the nightmare was real.

"I wish I was," Uncle Boone answered quietly. "I wish I was."

Barbie stood up abruptly. "Get out!" she hissed. "Just get out!" Spinning around, she flung a hand toward the door and disappeared down the hall, her stilettos tapping a rapid tattoo on the tile.

Uncle Boone's eyes fell closed. "Man," he whispered, slowly shaking his head. He looked toward the playroom, where the thumping had started again. Barbie was yelling at the sibs and sobbing at the same time, half ordering them to behave and half pleading with them to be quiet before she went crazy.

"What now?" I whispered. "What do we need to do?" *I could get my stuff together, load it in my car, and call Emity—tell her I need a place to stay. Her mom would let me. Maybe we could just . . . head for Europe early.*

Where would I get the money? There was nothing in my wallet but a Visa card that apparently wasn't good anymore and a debit card for the overdrawn household account.

"Pack up everything you can." Uncle Boone's voice broke into my thoughts. "The important stuff, the stuff the kids need. The stuff you don't wanna lose. I'll bring one of my construction trucks over here in the mornin'. You think you can find some boxes?"

"I guess so," I muttered, thinking, *This can't be happening. It can't. I have a golf lesson in the morning. . . .*

My head reeled, tears stinging the backs of my eyes. I wasn't going to cry. I wasn't. Barbie was the weepy, helpless one. I wasn't like her. No matter what, I wasn't like her.

"Where are we going . . . when the truck comes?"

Uncle Boone stood up. "I'll figure out somethin'. You just work on gettin' things together—the stuff you need, all the important papers, medicine, diapers . . . all that stuff." He nodded toward the ongoing commotion of Barbie yelling and the sibs destroying the toy room. "And talk some sense into her."

Chapter 8

Sesay

If I wait for the young mother to put out her boxes each day, I cannot walk to the mission before the line is too long. You can stand in it, but the rooms will be gone before you reach the door.

I am not bothered by this. I have been watching the family in the yellow house for four days now—checking their boxes. The weather is warm and dry, so nothing is ruined. If I help with cleaning at the Summer Kitchen, the woman there—her name is SandraKaye, but the children call her Mrs. Kaye—will give me a sandwich in a bag, and then Teddy, who tends the church garden, will smile shyly and offer a flower to me. I will trade a bird, or a horse, or a dolphin, if I have one in my pocket. He will laugh and hold it up to twirl in the sun. He is not a normal boy, Teddy. He is the size of a man, but he has the mind of a boy. I can never be invisible to him. He calls my name and waves each time he sees me. He leaves the lock open on the storage barn behind the church. I can sleep in there now, and I am safe for the night.

I bring Teddy good things I have found in the boxes from the new yellow house—a flowerpot that looks like a frog, the handle from a broom, and a little statue of an angel with a broken wing. He placed the angel in the garden and used the broom handle to support a tomato plant behind the church. I am still waiting to see what he will do with the frog.

Each day, MJ at the Book Basket talks about the reading class. "It'll be starting week after next, Monday, Wednesday, and Friday in the evenings," she says. "Six o'clock. There's a signup sheet in the Summer Kitchen during lunch."

"I have watched the family in the yellow house," I tell her. "In the evenings, the father comes home. The Indian chief stopped to visit them. They were eating supper."

"They're relatives—cousins of some kind. I asked him about it." MJ gives me a crooked look. "You shouldn't be hanging around looking in people's windows, Sesay," she says.

"They cannot see me," I tell her. "I found some branches they had cut from their bushes. I carved a turtle and a fish. Today, I have a fat little toad. I carved him of pecan wood." I bring out the little toad that's made of a knot of wood from their clippings, and I lay it on the counter.

"Looks like it needs a string yet," MJ notices.

"God will bring one," I say. "He leaves bits of string everywhere. For the birds."

MJ smiles and takes a roll of heavy black thread from under the counter. "You can trade me for a story. Come over to the Summer Kitchen for lunch, and you can share a story with the kids after they eat."

"I may go," I tell her, cutting the string with my knife and threading it through the toad, then tying it. Next, I cut a second one, because there's a little lying-down horse in my pocket, as well. "I think we will soon have another yellow house. Across the street from the last one. I have been watching it."

"I hope not."

"I think so. I saw the big man with the ponytail—the black man with the hair like mine. Have you seen him? His workers are busy repairing the house." When the big man and his workers fix a house, they always paint it yellow. Then new people move in. If they do not last long in the house, which usually is so, the big man comes with more workers and a large truck, and they take away what was left in the house, and then repair it for another family to come in.

"Boone," MJ grumbles. "He's nothing but a henchman for House-holders. I hope you're wrong about the house. That would make six on Red Bird, now. A few more and they'll be trying to force everyone out so they can tear the houses down and build condominiums."

Six, I think, and count the houses in my mind. "I think they will paint the house soon. Yellow." I imagine the wet paint and wonder how my horse or the fat toad would look in yellow. The horse, perhaps, I decide, but not the toad. The toad should be brown. Perhaps the Indian chief will use brown paint today. Lately, he lays a painting palette by the door, and if I go two steps into the room, I can swipe my finger across and have any color that is there. He does not see me when I come and go, even if he is inside working. "I will share a story after lunch today. For the children," I tell MJ, and then, "I am going to see the house now." If they paint the house yellow, someone new will move in, and there will be more boxes. The family in the last yellow house has fewer boxes now.

I trade for a new book, and MJ gives me my doughnut, and then I slip around the corner to eat it. The Indian chief is painting again. After a bit, he sets one palette by the door and picks up another one. He does not see me, so I slip in to rub a bit of brown on my toad. There is white, too. The Indian chief has painted a rider—a warrior on a horse. The horse is spotted white and brown like a dog. I put white on one finger and brown on another, thinking I will color my horse the same. This horse is for the Indian chief. When paint is on the floor, you can take it. It will dry up anyway. But on a palette, it would be stealing if you did not pay for it. They will cut off your hand for stealing.

"I left a brush there for you," he says, as I move two steps past the door. He says this without turning around. "It'll probably work better than your fingers. You can clean it in the cup when you're done."

I look around to see who he is speaking to, but there is no one other than me. On the chair by the palette, a brush and a small cup of liquid rest on a square of newspaper. I wipe my fingers on the newspaper, then squat beside the chair, and set down the little horse, and paint it.

I can do much better with the brush. I remember that my grandfather had brushes. He kept them in a small leather pouch. He'd made them from horsehair, and twigs, and a tiny bit of metal from a cracker tin, which he pinched into place to hold the bristles. He carved beads, and painted them, and traded them to a man who came with a donkey and a wagon. My grandfather's beads were beautiful, but they were never the valuable color. *Too many red beads*, the man would say. *Everyone has red beads today, but I suppose I'll take them anyway.* Then he would do the favor of taking the beads. The next time he came, there would be too many blue beads, or green, or carved ones painted to look like birds or fish. You could never know ahead of time which beads were too many.

I finish the spotted horse and paint brown on the toad. Just a bit of green around his eyes, and black for the eyeballs, and a few spots on his back. He looks very fine with so many colors. A big, fat toad. I hold him in the palm of my hand and turn him 'round, and I know where I have seen him before. He was sitting on the window ledge of the little house that isn't really a house at all. It has been made from the back of a large truck, but there is a window in it. I remember it now, as if I were there again, though many years have passed since I saw that house. It was a lifetime ago.

In my memory, I am tired from the boat, and burned from the

sun, and the room is crowded with people sitting on the floor. The door opens, and the light pours in, and from the corner of my eye, I see a man come, but I am watching the little toad. Grandfather once told me that a good, fat toad is a blessing.

The man walks through the room, and he looks around, and people watch him without moving their heads. *Those two, and that one*, he says. Then I feel him standing close to me. *And this one*, he says, and someone touches my arm. The hand pulls me up, and I land on my feet. *No parents with her? Does she speak any English?* he asks, and another man, the man who has brought us here from the boat in the dark of night, answers him. There are no parents with me. Auntie is somewhere in the ocean. I look out the window, and the toad hops away, taking his blessing with him. . . .

The memory feels painful, then. I lower the painted toad away from my face and cut off the memory like a fruit with a worm in it, going rotten on the tree. It will spoil the crop, if you let it.

I stand and wash the brush in the cup. The Indian chief has moved to the corner. His back strains as he stretches canvas over a frame.

"You can keep the brush," he says.

I do not answer, but I leave the little brown-and-white horse, and I tuck the brush into my pack as I walk down Red Bird Lane to see about the house that will soon be yellow.

Something is happening down the street. I stop in the trees by the edge of the creek to watch. The house remains faded blue, like a winter sky, but the building trailers are gone. There is a big truck in the driveway.

The house isn't being painted today.

Someone is moving into it.

Chapter 9

Shasta Reid-Williams

It didn't take Tyler long to notice there was a moving van across the street. His things-with-wheels radar went off the minute the truck rumbled up Red Bird. He wrapped his hands around the burglar bars on the front door, like a little jailbird trying to break out. "See da tuck! See da tuck! Got a ooh-hawl!"

I pulled my paint roller away from the wall long enough to look out the front window. A construction crew had been working over there for days, but now it looked like someone was moving in. "It's not a U-Haul, Ty." To Tyler, everything was an ooh-hawl, ever since we rented one to move our stuff from Oklahoma. Carrying boxes up and down the U-Haul ramp and riding in the truck was a bigger thrill than Chuck E. Cheese's, and after that he was a U-Haul man for life. "That's some other kind of moving van."

"Unna go see!" Ty cheered, clapping his hands, then reaching through the bars.

"No, baby." Sitting back on my heels, I swiped my forehead with the back of my arm. It was seriously hot in the house with the windows and the front door open. The sooner I could finish painting this wall and get the place aired out, the better. I still had major caulking work to do on the trim, and the rest of the living room to paint, but at least this was a start.

"I unna go-ohhh," Ty complained, stretching out the words as he plunked down on his butt in the doorway.

"Mommy's got work to do." I was almost as whiny as Ty. I was hot and tired, my hair needed to be washed, and after a week of non-stop unpacking, painting, cleaning, window scraping, and trying to camouflage old termite damage no one'd told us about, I was sick of the house and everything in it. The boys were just plain sick of being stuck inside. In a whole week, they'd barely gotten to play in the yard, and we'd never made it next door to the park. Even though Cody was sure Ty's "green-pants lady" was made up, like an imaginary friend, it creeped me out to let the boys be in the yard by themselves. I couldn't get over the feeling that someone might be watching them. Little wooden animals kept turning up in strange places, for one thing. Each time, they were in out-of-the-way spots—hanging on the back-yard fence, underneath the oleander bush, strung in the roses by the porch, tangled in the iris bed by the mailbox, on the window ledge outside the boys' room, swinging from a tree branch by the creek between our yard and the park.

It always seemed like it was possible that those things had been there all along, and we'd just never noticed them—like last year's Easter eggs that turn up all of a sudden. Finding them was the thrill of the day for Benji and Ty, but their talk about the green-pants lady and their going on about seeing her in the trees by the creek made me feel like someone was stalking our house—watching my kids, and leaving behind little totems. Worse yet, the boys could describe the green-pants lady in pretty good detail. She looked like a cross between a Hobbit and Whoopi Goldberg, as near as I could figure. Benjamin drew her with big feet and long, gray coils of hair.

Other than the let's-pretend green-pants lady and the construction crew across the street, our part of Red Bird was quiet as an undertaker's parlor most of the time. A few of the neighbors came and went from their houses, but they weren't friendly, and the old lady next door peeked out her windows at us when she thought we wouldn't see. One evening after supper, I heard some kids over in the park, squealing and playing and talking in Spanish. Cody wasn't thrilled that we had neighbors that *talked Mexican*. I told him not to be such a redneck.

Maybe whoever was moving in across the street had kids. . . .

Setting the paint roller in the tray, I stood up, stretched my back, and looked at the newly red wall. I wasn't even sure why I'd gotten it in my head to paint one wall of the living room red. I saw it on a home makeover show one night, and the next thing I knew, I was grabbing the keys and heading down to Walmart to get some red paint. On the show, they hung some family heirlooms in shadow boxes on the red wall. We had Cody's granddaddy's chaps and a hand-woven saddle blanket, and a Choctaw baby quilt my Nana Jo made, and a rawhide quirt, some woven blankets that'd been in the family, and a few other things in a trunk Cody'd brought from Hugo. I could picture it all looking real classy on the wall, impressing Dell, and eventually Mama and Jace, when they came for a visit.

But now I wasn't even sure the red wall looked any good at all. Cody'd probably have a heart attack. He'd say there was nothing wrong with the off-white paint that was on there before. He'd probably notice the way the sun coming in the window bounced off the new coat of semigloss, making crooked lines that showed the places where the seams in the drywall were bubbled up.

"Maybe we can just let people come visit after dark," I muttered, standing at the door with Tyler. "What's going on over there, Ty? You see any people?" I touched his hair, and it was plastered to his head with sweat. The sun hit the boys' room this time of day, and it was probably hotter than a firecracker. If I didn't finish painting and turn on the air conditioner by the time Cody got home, he'd moan about it. I couldn't exactly tell him that since I was pregnant and probably shouldn't be painting anyway, I had to keep the place opened up, so there wouldn't be fumes.

"'Ere's a people!" Ty pointed to a big black guy with a ponytail of long braids. He was single-handedly unloading a mattress from the truck. I'd seen the guy there before, while the construction crew was working. He usually had a hard hat and a clipboard, like he was the crew boss. Maybe he actually owned that house and was gonna live there.

"Huh . . ." I muttered. He looked like a guy with money—Nike Shock shoes, a big gold chain around his neck, some kind of a tight-fitting bodybuilder T-shirt, and a massive diamond stud in his ear. That thing was so big it was catching the sun like a Morse code mirror.

It crossed my mind that Benji was being awfully quiet in the bedroom. "Ty, what's Benji doing?"

Ty jerked his shoulders up and down, still watching the truck.

"Is he playing with his toy cars?"

"Him talk da gween-pans wady."

The muscles in my back pulled tight like elastic. "What do you mean. . . . ? You mean she's in the house?" I swiveled toward the hall, a creepy feeling prickling over my skin, leaving behind goose bumps. There was no way anyone could get into the house. . . .

Nobody real, anyway . . .

"In da window."

"In the window? What?" Fear sizzled through me like the electricity from a bad electrical socket. The window in the boys' room was open, but there was a screen on it, and the burglar bars were locked.

Benjamin was safe . . . wasn't he? "Benji?" I called, heading down the hall. "Benjamin?"

He didn't answer, and I started running, my footsteps echoing against the bare walls and rattling the stacks of needing-to-be-hung family photos. "Benjamin, you answer me! Benja . . ." I skidded around the corner, sneakers squealing, and there was my big boy, sitting in the little cubby under the bay window. He was reading a book, the sun falling softly over his dark head and turning his skin the velvet tan of a fawn's hide. My heart settled back into my chest, and I squatted down beside the window seat, brushing a hand over his hair. "Benjamin, why didn't you answer Mommy? You scared me. I didn't hear you back here."

"I was readin' this book." Blinking, he wiggled away. "It's about a family of mouses. About the mouse lady and her babies. She's got a bunch. They gotta go all over the world and tell some stories to all the people."

"Hmmm . . . storytelling mice, huh?" I repeated, sitting back on my heels. Even though Benji couldn't read yet, he had a great imagination. He made up all kinds of things. The book in his hands was a takeoff from a Disney movie with mouse characters. "Where'd we get *The Rescuers*? I don't remember buying that."

"Huh-uh. It's Lady Mouse, Mama." Scooting his rear toward me, he held up the book so I could read the title page. "See?"

The Rescuers. "Okay, and what's Lady Mouse about, Benji?" If Cody's parents had been sitting on the window seat, they would of been making Benji sound out the real title, whether he wanted to or not. Being a slacker mom had its advantages sometimes. I was okay with letting him call the book whatever he wanted. Probably, he was using *The Rescuers* book to tell me a tale he'd learned in Head Start class back home, or maybe my Nana Jo had told him the mouse story, sometime. Nana Jo was always sharing old Choctaw stories with the boys.

"About Lady Mouse." He lifted his free hand palm up, as in, *Duh*.

"What does Lady Mouse do in the book?"

His finger touched the girl mouse on the page—Bianca, who was looking rather stylish in her mink coat, hat, and muff. "She tells some stories. She made different clothes for all her kids."

"How come she made different clothes for all her kids?"

Benji snorted, rolling his eyes. "So they wouldn't be nekked." He giggled, and I laughed along.

"I guess that makes sense."

"And 'cause they gotta have pretty clothes. All kinds'a different clothes."

"Really? That's cool. Who's this mean lady here?" I pointed to Madame Medusa, the evil villainess in the movie.

Shrugging, Benji turned the page. "I dunno. A mean lady, I guess. She don't want the Mouses to tell the little girl no stories."

"I guess not." I rested my chin on my hand, watching him look at the pages and think about the pictures, and I had one of those mom moments when all I could do was look at my little guy and feel wonder settling over me. Only five years old, and he was already turning into his own little person. Learning things. Growing.

Tipping up the cover, I looked at the book again. "Where'd we get this, anyway?" Between the gifts Cody's mom bought the kids, what my mom gave them, and the hand-me-downs from older cousins, I was always coming across stuff I didn't know we had.

"She brung it."

"Who did?"

Benji looked out the window. "The green-pants lady."

"Ohhh, the green-pants lady." Guess we'd finally solved the mystery of the green-pants lady. She came from the same place as Lady Mouse—Benji's imagination. A book couldn't just morph through burglar bars and a screen and appear in his room. "Was she here just now?"

He shot me a low-browed glance, like he knew I didn't believe him. "Uh-huh."

"And she brought you a book this time instead of a little animal?"

"Uh-huh. She gots a little toad, but she can't gimme it yet. She's gotta turn it yellow. She just remembered, brown ones're bad luck."

Sometimes, when you were a parent, you had to just sit back and wonder how in the world a little brain came up with things. "Wow, that's kinda bad news for toads, isn't it? Most of them are brown."

"Mah-ommm!" Benji could tell I wasn't buying the green-pants-lady-bad-luck-toad story.

I rubbed his hair. "Sorry, buddy. But some things are just pretend, all right? Like the green-pants lady and the talking mice. There's nothing wrong with pretending things, but you shouldn't scare—"

"It's not pretend!" he insisted, his hands flipping into the air, then slapping down. "The lady brung it."

I laid my fingers over his and held them in his lap, wishing I hadn't started the argument. Now I'd have to finish it. "Benji, no lady can make a book just appear in your room. That kind of stuff is in our imaginations, which is fine, but it's not the same as real things. One's real, and one's just pretend. Understand?"

Benjamin nodded, and I let out a sigh. What a relief. For once, he was going to take my word for it. Usually with Benji, arguments got settled with a million questions and a minimeltdown. He was as hardheaded as his daddy.

"Okay," I said. "You go on and read your book. I'm gonna get back to my painting." I started to stand up, but Benji held on to my hand. Twisting his knees under himself, he scooted toward the window, pulling me with him. I watched him turn the book sideways and slip it through the bottom corner of the screen, where the netting hung loose.

"She brung it like this." His voice was a whisper that slid over my skin, raising a prickle of goose bumps as he passed the book through the burglar bars, then brought it back in again.

A shiver ran across my shoulders, and I leaned close to the window, pressed my nose to the screen, looked both ways. The moving crew across the street was unloading some seriously nice furniture that totally didn't belong in our neighborhood, but otherwise Red Bird Lane was deserted. Sunny and quiet. Peaceful.

Chapter 10

Tam Lambert

You see the features on *48 Hours* and *Oprah*—stories of normal families living in nice homes one day, then just a few days, a week, a month later, they're in a camping trailer, or a car, or a tent. On the news reports, their expressions are numb, bewildered, ashamed. You watch with morbid fascination—the way you'd turn to look at a car wreck you pass on the highway. You can't help yourself. Deep inside, there's a pang of empathy that tells you it could be you, but you don't really believe it. It fades as soon as the scene disappears from view. That could never be you.

You don't ponder it more deeply, because it's too hard to think about. It means you don't really have control over your own life. Control is an illusion, a skin-deep reality you sell yourself, until all of the illusions are stripped away. It really is possible to be the family on the news. It can happen quicker than you think.

If it hadn't been for Uncle Boone, we would have ended up on the curb with nowhere to go, but after a week of living with him, the kids trashing his condo and breaking expensive electronics equipment, even he was ready to ship us off. Boone needed his space back, and we couldn't leave the sum total of our remaining worldly possessions stacked in his construction truck. He needed that back, too. Considering he'd just figured out that all the money he'd invested with

Rosburten was gone, the fact that he'd offered to move us to a little house he was refitting for Householders was remarkably generous.

"I can hold off finishin' that house for a while," he'd said. "Won't be anything happening with Householders till they decide what to do with Rosburten and all the companies it owns." The muscles in his arms tightened, and he cursed Ross Burten under his breath.

Barbie's only reaction had been to open her cell phone and send text message number 1,004 to my father, hoping he would miraculously reappear and solve our dilemma.

"How are we going to get out of here without the media following us?" I'd asked. For the past week, we'd been virtual prisoners in Uncle Boone's gated condo complex.

He'd thought about it for a moment. "I'll go out the front with the truck, and y'all can head out the service gate in the alley after a while. I'll drive around and stop off at a few construction sites till they figure I'm not worth followin'. Ain't nobody gonna look for y'all in that neighborhood."

In that neighborhood, or the way he'd said it, stuck in my mind, flapping in and out of my consciousness as we packed up our suitcases, the sibs' toys, and the cat, piled everything into what was left of Barbie's Escalade, sneaked out the back gate like convicts, and headed across town. Since the hand-me-down MINI Cooper I'd been driving had already gone back to the bank, I didn't have much choice but to make the trip.

When we exited the interstate, the pit of my stomach was swirling like a ten-jet Jacuzzi. The neighborhood didn't look so bad, at first. On the corner by the highway, a new Walmart and some fairly upscale shopping centers seemed acceptably similar to home. Within a few blocks, we passed some recently built condo complexes. Looking down the streets, I could see old mansions that perhaps needed face-lifts, but weren't bad. We could live in a place like that—at least for now.

The streets passed by, but Barbara didn't turn. She picked up the map Boone had drawn for her and gave it a worried glance, then looked for landmarks as we drove along. The new construction stopped abruptly, and the neighborhood went downhill. Fast. We crossed under another highway overpass, and I glanced into the rafters. There were sleeping bags, and cardboard, and pieces of clothing tucked under the girders. A man in a ragged overcoat sat on the grass by the guardrail, blankly watching the traffic pass. I looked away and hit the door locks. Barbie jumped at the sound, her eyes wide, blue circles surrounded by bloodshot white.

Neither of us said anything. In the back, the sibs were quiet, as if even they were scared of the neighborhood. Barbara set down the map. I twisted sideways and looked at it. Unfortunately, we were on the right road. A few more blocks and we'd get to Red Bird Lane, where Boone and his construction crew were unloading our belongings.

Turning to the window, I picked up my cell and started to text Emity—something like, *SOS, come get me. You won't believe this. . . .*

Emity wouldn't answer. She'd been grounded from her cell— grounded from everything—and all of a sudden her mom had decided Em needed to visit her grandparents in Galveston, instead of going to Europe this summer. Our trip was off. Like everyone else we knew, Emity's father was in the Rosburten loop. Those investors my father had solicited were now figuring out that Ross Burten had been living the high life on their money, using the income from new investors to pay dividends to old investors. Now that the feds had broken open the scheme, it was also clear that many of Ross's perks and lavish vacations had been extended to our family, and that my father had received large bonuses, over and above his quite healthy salary.

Whether my father had actually been aware of Ross's misdealings or not, he was now a pariah—a symbol of the sort of executive greed that had infected corporate America. Like everyone else we knew, Em's parents didn't want anything to do with us.

We passed a dumpy-looking convenience store and a crumbling strip mall with bars on the windows and men hanging around the parking lot. Across the street, a dirty white apartment complex looked like government housing. A pair of empty plastic bags floated from the Dumpster and rolled down the sidewalk like tumbleweeds, chasing our car, then racing ahead before blowing into a drainage ditch, where kids were playing in puddles of slimy green water.

Ahead, a used bookstore with colored glass bottles hanging in a tree and little wooden totem poles for porch posts seemed like something out of Fortune-tellers-R-Us. Opposite the bookstore stood a white wooden church where a line of people stretched out the side door, around the corner, and all the way to the street. A homeless man with a shopping cart was moving into position at the end.

"What're they doin'?" Mark asked from the backseat, pressing a hand against the window and stretching in his booster seat.

Barbie didn't answer.

"I think they're getting something to eat." The realization was dawning on me as I said it.

"How come?" Mark's question was innocent, his bewilderment obvious.

"They're hungry, I guess," I told him, and he leaned closer to the window, like a zoo patron looking through the aquarium glass.

"How come?" When the sibs weren't fighting, they were inquisitive enough to make your head spin.

"I wanna see." Daniel grabbed Mark's shoulders and tried to push him out of the way.

"Stop-pit!" Mark squealed, twisting to shake Daniel off. "Mom-eeee!"

Barbie hung a right so fast that Daniel's head collided with Mark's elbow, Mark's head bumped the window, and in the cargo area, the cat carrier rolled over. Both boys screamed, and the cat growled and hissed. The noise woke Landon, and jostled Jewel in the third seat, and the car was filled with wailing, pulling of hair, and gnashing of teeth.

"Be quiet!" Barbie's voice was lost in the din. "Quiet! Now! Stop it! I can't stand this!" Hands shaking, she grabbed a folded Dallas map and threw it blindly into the backseat. It skimmed Daniel's head and hit Aunt Lute in the third seat.

Aunt Lute jerked upright, blinked drowsily, and said, "Good heavens! Did you see the horses go by?"

With the exception of the baby, everyone in the car fell silent and looked at Aunt Lute. She went on talking. "All colors. Black and bay, dapple gray. All the pretty little horsies." She sucked in a breath, her eyes wide. "Did you see them go by? Look." She pointed toward the window, and Mark, Landon, and Daniel sniffled back tears, pushing closer to the glass to look for horses. Aunt Lute slipped the pacifier into Jewel's mouth, and the car was quiet again, except for the cat growling unhappily. We drifted along, idling because Barbie had taken her foot off the gas pedal after turning onto a residential street. Her mouth hung open, her face going pale beneath the fading spa tan.

I had a bad feeling we were on Red Bird Lane. The nameplate on a crooked mailbox confirmed it: VASQUEZ, 202 RED BIRD. Three houses farther down, past a small creek and a thick line of trees, Uncle

Boone's truck was parked in a driveway. Barbie let the car roll across the bridge and come to a stop at the curb. Her hands were shaking so badly, she couldn't shift the vehicle into park.

"Here." Grabbing the gearshift, I slipped it out of gear.

"This can't be . . ." she murmured, and for once, we were on the same wavelength. The house was as bad as the rest of the neighborhood. Old, small, sealed with window bars and a cage across the front door that, in spite of the decorative iron at the corners, looked like the entrance to a prison cell.

Barbie yanked open the door and stepped out as Uncle Boone appeared from inside the house with a stack of moving pads tucked under his arm. Setting them in the back of the truck, he met Barbie at the curb. I didn't have to hear them to know what she was saying. The body language and Barbie flailing a hand toward the house made it crystal clear. She was telling him he was nuts. Half of me wanted to get out of the car, grab Barbie by the ponytail, smack her like you would one of those hysterical women in a movie, and say, *Wake up! If you alienate Uncle Boone, we won't have anybody.*

The other half wanted to stand right beside her, screaming at him. How could we stay in a place that had bars on the windows—where there were soup lines and homeless people just down the road, where we were only a few blocks from what looked like the projects?

I wanted to call Emity's house, let the phone ring and ring and ring—keep calling until someone answered, and I could say, *You have to let me come stay with you. I don't have anywhere to go. This isn't my fault. I didn't do anything wrong. . . .*

Opening the cell phone, I flipped through the directory, thought about it; then I closed the phone again, dropped it into my lap, tried to mold my thoughts into something that made sense. I couldn't call now. Not with everyone in the car, and the cat squalling in the back. As soon as I could get a minute alone, I'd do it. Em's mom was my mother's friend—at least, they had been friends. If she knew how desperate I was, she'd have to help me. *Just until I can get in touch with my mom*, I'd tell her. But so far, I hadn't even tried to contact Mom. Deep inside I couldn't give up hoping that Dad would come through, and everything would work out, and my mother would never have to know what shape we were in. I didn't want to end up living in a mission in Ecuador with my mother and our ex-pastor's group of volunteers. It wasn't like Mom was going to give up her new life just for me.

"Oh, I see one!" Landon whispered, oblivious to the moaning cat. I adjusted the rearview mirror, so I could watch him. "A bw-ack one!"

"I see him, too! A lovely black stallion." Aunt Lute cheered, and they watched an imaginary horse trot by. "My, he's fine. Can you tell if he has white feet or brown?"

Landon squinted. "White foots."

"All four?"

"I fink so."

Aunt Lute tapped Daniel on the shoulder and pointed. "Isn't he glorious with his four white feet? What do you think he's doing?"

"Eatin' a flower."

"Oh, yes, eating a flower. What color flower? What sort? I can't quite tell from here."

Mark pointed to the irises by the mailbox across the street. "Blue, like them."

"Blue, truly!" Aunt Lute agreed, touching Jewel's cheek with a fingertip and letting the baby's fist curl around hers. "Do you see the horse? Do you think we could ride him?"

Underneath her pacifier, Jewel made a noise that sounded like a horsie snort.

"Very good," Aunt Lute cheered. "Wonderful! Princess Anya could make the most wonderful horse sounds. Of course, she spent far too much time in the stable. The king didn't like it one bit. . . ." Aunt Lute went on with a story that was a weird cross between *Sleeping Beauty* and *Jack and the Beanstalk*. In her version, Jack traded a horse for the magic beans, and the king gave the horse to his daughter as a birthday gift. Eventually, when Jack climbed the beanstalk, the castle was surrounded by thorns and the princess fell into a deep sleep.

Watching the sibs in the mirror, all three of them wide-eyed, I felt a tug in some inconvenient place between my lungs and my heart. I knew why I hadn't gotten in touch with my mother, or called to beg Emity's mom to let me into their house. The sibs needed me here. They couldn't understand what was happening, but they knew something . . . everything was wrong, and they were powerless to set it right. Someone had to look out for them.

I watched in the side mirror as Barbie rammed her hands onto her hips, her chin jutting forward while she ranted about the house. By the front door, Uncle Boone's moving men had stopped working to take in the show.

Barbie's voice pressed through the glass, drowning out the sounds of the sibs and Aunt Lute talking about invisible horses, and the cat mewing. Outside, Barbie was alternately cussing out both my father and Uncle Boone, then breaking down and sobbing. "I can't stay here! I can't handle this!" She waved toward the vehicle, the house. Us. "I can't!"

Uncle Boone attempted to calm her, then yelled at his crew to get back to work, as if he knew he needed to finish this project and be out of here before Barbie imploded and left a black hole on the sidewalk.

He reached into his pocket, fished out some money, and slapped it into Barbie's hand. This was becoming a familiar gesture, since we had almost no operating cash. My father's bank accounts were dry, and with a twenty-four-hour eviction notice hanging over our heads as we had evacuated our house, we'd had no choice but to leave behind things that could have been sold for cash. There was no easy way to transport heavy, ornate imported wardrobes and dressers, custom playhouses and yard toys, and the gigantic gilded billiard table Barbie had ordered for my father on his fiftieth birthday. There wasn't any time to sell them in place, and undoubtedly no one from Highland Park would have bought our leftovers, anyway. Small items that could have been converted into funds—Barbie's stash of custom jewelry, the collection of foreign gold coins that hung in Dad's office, a set of valuable antique pistols, some autographed memorabilia from guys he'd played football with—had disappeared from the house in the past months. My father had told Barbie he was taking those things to a safe-deposit box, but he must have sold them. She'd never suspected a thing.

Heat flooded my cheeks as I watched Uncle Boone hand over the money, then force a key ring into Barbie's palm and fold her fingers around it. He probably couldn't afford to be doing all this for us. Considering what he'd lost in Rosburten and the fact that construction had slowed everywhere, he was strapped. I'd heard him on the phone yesterday talking to someone about unloading his boat. Quick. The *Touchback* was his favorite pastime, man toy, and chick magnet. He and Dad had often disappeared for days at a time, headed out to fishing tournaments that were mostly an excuse for Boone to escape his ex-wife, and my father to enjoy some peace and quiet away from our home-based romper-zoo.

There was no way Uncle Boone would be letting go of the boat unless things were bad. He was probably sorry he'd ever answered the phone when I called the day the Rosburten news broke.

My body felt limp, and I let my head fall back against the seat. I wanted to crawl off to some dark place and hide from everybody. This couldn't be my life. This couldn't be happening.

Tears pressed my eyes, blurring the line of tiny homes on Red Bird Lane. I blinked hard, trying to push them away. Uncle Boone was headed toward the house again, and Barbie was following him, shouting, her heels clicking against the sidewalk, rapid-fire.

I looked in the driver's-side mirror, still hanging cockeyed from Barbie's Baby Bundles wreck. A woman was standing in the bushes by the yellow house across the street, her body hunched over, her shoulders humped with a coat or a backpack. She was little more than a shadow, standing and watching, her camo green pants and a tattered gray button-up shirt making her nearly invisible among the leaves. Her skin was dark like the shadows. Long, gray dreadlocks swirled over her shoulders and seemed to twine around her like vines encircling a branch. A muted patch of sunlight fell across her face as she lifted her chin and turned her gaze slowly from Barbie's tirade to me. She met my eyes, and I felt the pull of her gaze, or her presence, as if she were about to say something, and I was sitting on edge, waiting for the words.

One of the sibs kicked the back door, and the mirror vibrated with the impact, creating a blur of sunlight, and leaves, and shadow, out of focus, like a photograph taken while the camera was moving.

When the mirror stilled again, the woman was gone. I swiveled in my seat, checking the line of foliage beside the yellow house. No one was there—just the trees rustling slightly in the wind, and the underbrush fluttering, and a thick stand of cattails swaying along the creek.

Barbie was pacing the sidewalk, her arms stiff at her sides and her fists clenched. Uncle Boone followed behind her, still trying to convince her to accept reality.

This place. This tiny blue house with the prison bars was our reality now, whether we wanted to face it or not. When you fall from the top to the bottom, there's no soft place to land.

Chapter II

Sesay

The boys in the yellow house are watching the man and the woman argue across the street. I hope it does not frighten them. The yellow-house boys are kind, and I like to visit them. Their skin is the color of cedar underneath the bark, where the red streaks hide. Cedar is good wood, strong and sweet-smelling, and it dries hard, so the things you carve from it are good. I have given the boys cedar names—Root and Berry. They have other names, of course, but I do not know them. They look for me now, when they come outside. Their mother looks for me, too, but I will not let her see me. When the mother sees you, she pulls her children away and hurries them down the street, and says, "Don't talk to people like her!" In these years of wandering—ten years, I think, but perhaps it is more—I have learned that people do not want me near their houses or their children. They want me to go somewhere else.

I love the little children. I birthed four babies of my own, and my arms yearn for them at night when my dreaming mind drifts into the past. They were *his* children, but he took each away when they were small. *This is America. Here, children belong to their fathers*, he said. *You wouldn't want them working in the cane fields anyway, would you, Sesay? I can give them a good life.* Then he drove away through the sugarcane, and I knew I must not follow. If you go past the end of the fields, his men will call the police, and the police will take you away and put you on a boat. *Here in this country*, they tell the laborers, *you can't just go wherever you want. You have to do your work, because you owe for your food and the bed you sleep in. What? Do you think all of this is free?*

Sometimes, when *he* came, I saw little faces in his car. They had gray eyes. Mulatto eyes. His eyes. I watched them, an ache blooming in my arms and my breast. I gave names to them, but they never knew those names. This is why I want to be near the children now. I yearn for my own, even though years have gone by and they are grown by now.

The little boy in the yellow house gave a toy animal to me when I handed my book to him. We traded. Now my book is his, and I have a white rabbit in my pack. I will carve a similar one and bring it to him when I come to his window again, but just now, I should go. The angry woman screams at the man across the street, and the sound beats a hammer in my chest. I worry that someone will call the police.

I walk on to the Summer Kitchen. On the way, I try to think of a story to go along with the toy rabbit. A rabbit story. I'm certain I must have one. I have traded stories with many people as I've wandered. I trade stories at the Broadberry Mission, as well. Now there are so many people at the mission—not only men and old women, like me, but also families. Some of them have come from yellow houses, such as the one in which Root and Berry live. Now the families live at the mission.

I watch the mothers at the mission reading books to their children. They will let you listen to their stories, if you do not touch the children. One of them told the story of a boy rabbit, a little one. He is a bad little fellow, this rabbit, and he turns against his mother's wishes, and sneaks into the field of the *patrón*. The man, McGregor, chases him with a pitchfork, and as he runs away, he loses his new mitten. Peter. The rabbit's name is Peter Rabbit. I have decided that he is sneaking into the field after sugarcane. I am not certain whether he is a cottontail or one of the short-eared muck rabbits that live in the cane fields, because I could not see the pictures when the mother was reading the story. You must keep a distance from the families at the mission.

I think Peter is a muck rabbit, because he is a crafty fellow, but when I tell his story, I will show the toy rabbit in my pack.

I pull out the little rabbit and rub it close to my face. It is soft, like the pelts that hung by the dozens on the sides of the workers' quarters when the cane fields were burned in the winter, and the rabbits ran. There was food for the taking, then, but the sound was terrible, and the air thick with smoke and blood and screams.

This little white rabbit does not smell like smoke. He smells like a child—like soap and soft powder. I am glad that I gave the book in exchange for him. I can trade a story for another book at the Book Basket, but the rabbit is something to keep. MJ will ask what happened to the last book, but I won't tell her. If I told her, she would say, *Sesay, you mustn't be hanging around people's windows.*

The line is still forming when I reach the Summer Kitchen. Some people are eating on the porch already, and the children dash around, and bounce basketballs, and run on the lawn playing soccer while their parents wait for the lunches. Some days, the line stretches off the porch, down the sidewalk, and around the corner. Mostly, the men from the mission do not come down here. It is farther than they prefer to walk. But the families come. They need a way to pass the afternoon, now that the children are away from school. At the Summer Kitchen, they eat and the children hear a story, and then play until the kitchen closes in the afternoon, and finally Pastor Al locks the doors, and Teddy tucks the toys and balls into the shed.

I do not like to come when the line is still growing. It's too many people so close together. You would not want someone to look at you too carefully. They might know you have run away from the cane fields. *There's no place you can hide where the* patrón *won't find you*, the men tell you in the cane fields. *There's no point running away.*

But so far, I have done well. I have been wise. I never stay long in one place. He has not found me in these many years. I have come far from the cane farm, and I hope it is distance enough, but still I must be careful. I must be watchful, so that the police cannot put me on a boat, where I will end up in the ocean, my body sinking slowly beneath the surface, like Auntie's.

In the Summer Kitchen, no one can come and go without being noticed. I know this much already. The young girl with the long blond hair—her name is Cass—waves at me and smiles, and says, "Hi, Sesay! You're early today. Are you going to help with the story-telling in a while? MJ said you might." This girl likes stories. I think she will be a storyteller one day. She stops cleaning the tables and comes to listen when MJ sits and tells stories to the children.

"I have a story today," I tell her, and her lips spread into a wide smile that puts lights in her eyes. She is beautiful, this one. She moves as if the world is laid out before her like a banquet. She goes around the kitchen with fast, sure steps that bounce her hair like a shimmering ribbon. I try to remember who I was when I was at her number of years—twelve, she has told me she is. I was living in *his* house then, caring for the little girl in the wheelchair. The girl was my friend, and I was a companion to her, and this was the work I did for *him*, to pay for my bed and my food. The girl and I dreamed of adventures we would enjoy someday. We saw pictures in books, and made plans, and there was a light in me. Then the girl sickened and died, and *he* put me in the car and drove me to the sugarcane fields to cook for the cane cutters. It was all that was left for me to do to pay my way, as the girl did not need me any longer. *If you don't pay your way, the police will put you back on the boat*, he told me.

I can hear him in my mind yet. I can feel that day, if I let myself, as if it is yesterday.

Deep in the cane fields, all the light died. It died in his silent, dark room with the large metal desk, where he told me to write my name on the paper, so I would not have to go away on the boat. The sun left the one small window, and he took away the last of the light in me; then he walked me outside to Olani, and told her to give me easy work in the kitchen, as I was good to his daughter.

Olani was not bad to me. She was just indifferent. She told me I thought too much of myself. I was no one special anymore. She told me that before he lay with me, he lay with her, and when I grew old, he would leave me alone. She laughed and said by then I'd better make sure I knew how to cook.

I push that day away like a bad smell creeping up my nose. Here in this kitchen, the Summer Kitchen, they call out my name when I come to the counter. The woman who oversees the cooking here, Mrs. Kaye, greets me and smiles, even though she looks tired, her hair hanging in wet, red strings around her face. They have been at work for hours now, preparing lunch and then serving it. "We have some spaghetti left, or beef noodles," she tells me. "Which would you like, Sesay?"

I think for a moment. It feels strange, having choices. I lean over the counter and look into the pans. "This one," I say, because I am not certain which is which. "Thank you most kindly." This is what would have been said in the house with the girl in the wheelchair.

Thank you most kindly. I know this is the proper way, because in the house, as in my father's big house when I was young, everything was very proper.

"You're very welcome," Mrs. Kaye says, and while she scrapes the contents of the pan onto my plate, she adds, "I have a batch of dish towels going into the wash. If you're staying around for cleanup, I could launder something for you while you're here."

"I would very much like to wash these," I say, and look down at my shirt and green pants. I have not stayed at the mission for days, and my clothes are soiled. They smell very bad, I think.

"Go on back," she tells me, and nods toward the hallway behind the counter. "I'll keep your plate for you."

"Thank you most kindly," I say, and then carry my pack around the counter and down the hall to the bathroom. A woman with a young child has just finished in there. Their hair is wet, and I know their clothes will be in the washer, as well. It will not be full of dish towels. It will largely be filled with clothes. Later, I will help Mrs. Kaye hang them on the line outside, where their owners can find them.

"Shut the lid and turn on the machine when you're done," Mrs. Kaye calls to me, and I tell her I will.

I wash and change, and then stand in front of the sink. There is no mirror—only a frame with words in it. I have no way of knowing what it says. Someone has painted a flower next to the words, a rose. I think the words must be about roses.

When I come back to the kitchen, I've changed into a long red dress I traded for at the mission store. The dress is loose and comfortable, like the ones my auntie wore when I was young. At the counter, the food line is still moving, but the used dishes have become piled, and Mrs. Kaye is trying to wash them while Cass and the other women serve the food. I step behind the sink, even though Mrs. Kaye tells me to sit down and eat. She has saved my plate for me.

"I will," I say. "Later." We move through the dishes. I scrub and she dries them. She admires how quickly I can do this. I am *way ahead of her*, she says. I tell her, in my lifetime I have washed enough dishes to fill this room. She laughs as if she does not believe this is so.

"We're starting another evening reading class here," she tells me.

I hear the children gathering on the porch. MJ has come over from the Book Basket. "I have a story to tell today," I say.

Mrs. Kaye whisks a hand at me, as if I am a fly. "Go ahead. I'll tuck your plate in the warmer and finish these dishes. We're caught up now, anyway."

I take the rabbit from my pack and hurry to the door. My reflection walks toward me in the glass. For a moment, I can only stop and look at it. That isn't me. That is an old woman.

I remind her not to smile when she tells the story of the rabbit, Peter. An old woman like that does not have beautiful teeth. She should not smile.

I don't feel like an old woman.

I open the door, and the children cry out for a story, and I know I am smiling. "I have a story," I say, and they want to know what it is about. I hold up the little rabbit. "This is the story of Peter, the rabbit, who lived with his mother deep in the cattails alongside the sugarcane field. . . ."

Chapter 12

Shasta Reid-Williams

The moving scene across the street was about to come to an explosive conclusion, I could tell. The woman had already gotten in her car and taken off once. Now she was back, and she and the guy were arguing some more. I couldn't help myself—I put down my paint roller again and went to the boys' bedroom, where there was a better view. Benji and Ty crawled up onto the window seat with me, to watch.

That woman was seriously out of place in the neighborhood—super-high-heeled shoes, a chest rounder than anybody gets naturally, tanning-bed skin. She was dressed in a tight T-shirt and shorts—the matching kind that come from a high-dollar department store.

The man wasn't arguing with her, really, just standing there letting her bombard him with words. Finally, he held her by both shoulders, said something to her, and turned her toward the car. Behind the tinted windows I saw the head of someone not very tall, with curly hair. There was at least one kid in there. . . .

Slipping her fingers under her sunglasses, the woman wiped her cheeks, then walked around to the back of the car, her spike heels wobbling. The man followed her, then waited while she opened the back hatch. He staggered backward a step, looking surprised when she shoved a pet carrier into his hands and slammed the hatch.

Apparently, he was getting the cat. Inside the carrier it hissed and snarled, the sound echoing through the neighborhood so that it felt like we were extras in a cross between *Desperate Housewives* and *Nightmare on Elm Street*.

Stalking back to the driver's door, the blonde swiveled in our direction, and I jerked away from the window, taking the boys with me.

The mouse book toppled to the floor, and Ty picked it up and looked at it like he'd never seen it before. "We ga a book!" he cheered, holding it up.

Benji took a step closer. "It's mine."

Ty's face instantly pruned up. "I want da book."

I took the book away and set it behind me, trying to stop a fight before it could start up. Benji and Ty could pick a fight over anything. "All right, you two. We've got a whole shelf full of books and they're everybody's to share. They're not Benji's and they're not Ty's, okay?"

Benji stomped a foot, leaning toward the book. "It's mine. The green-pants lady brung it. She gave it to *me*."

I caught a breath, let it out, thinking, *Patience, patience*. Squatting down, I took Benji's hands in mine. "Benjamin, I want you to listen to me. I want both of you to listen, all right?" I waited for them to nod and look straight at me. "I don't want to hear *any* more stuff about the green-pants lady, all right? Not *one* more *thing*. Period. I don't want you making up or telling any more stories about her, you understand? Making stuff up and acting like it's true is the same as lying. When you do that, Daddy and I don't know what to believe. If you ever do see, like, a real person around here, *not* make-believe like the green-pants lady, then you need to holler for us right away. You don't talk to anybody, and if they've got something for you, you don't take it. We don't take anything from strangers without asking Mommy first, all right?"

Benjamin ducked his head, trying to shuck the lecture like water off a duck. "Stranger danger. Like in Mrs. Hampy's class."

Thank goodness for Mrs. Hampy's Head Start, back in Hugo. "Exactly. No more talking about the green-pants lady, all right? Not one more word." Both boys nodded. "Now go find your shoes, okay? We're gonna run over and get you guys signed up for school, since Daddy caught a ride and left us the truck today. On the way home, we'll buy some cookie dough and make some cookies to take over to the new neighbors, 'kay?" Really, I should of been finishing up the painting first, but right now, even though I'd probably end up looking like an idiot for sticking my nose in, I wanted to know what was going on across the street.

I had a wicked case of curiosity.

By the time I got everyone's shoes on, gathered the boys' shot records and school papers, and made it to the pickup, the blonde was back in her Escalade. She didn't even turn her car around—just peeled out and headed down Red Bird, driving like a maniac.

While I was backing out, I took an unofficial survey of the stuff being unloaded from the moving van. Whoever they were, they had seriously nice things—heavy white wood furniture with gold leaf around the edges, a huge flat-screen TV, an entertainment center that was big enough to take up half our living room, a crib from the fancy baby store. The kind of crib every mom dreams about, but not every mom gets. I could picture our baby daughter asleep on the lacy sheets, sunlight filtering through the canopy, turning pink and falling on her skin. Maybe, by the time my baby came, they'd be interested in selling that thing. . . .

People who could afford stuff like that didn't have yard sales, though. They gave their castoffs to charity. If I asked about the crib, I'd look like the welfare redneck neighbor.

The guy with the big ponytail of braids noticed me staring, so I took my foot off the brake and let the truck roll down the street. Crossing the bridge, I checked out the tree lines and the park. Everything was quiet. No sign of any mysterious green-pants lady delivering books and wooden animals up and down the street.

"Cut it out already, Shasta," I muttered to myself, and Benji looked at me in the rearview. The green-pants lady had to be in his imagination. He could of had a dream about someone passing a book through the window screen and thought it was real. At least now he and Ty both knew they needed to quit making up stories about her.

At the corner of Red Bird and Vista, there was a break in traffic, which I figured meant today was my lucky day. Turning left onto Vista took an act of Congress most times. I let off the brake and pulled out, and the next thing I knew, the blonde in the Escalade appeared from out of nowhere and swerved around me. She just about took off my bumper, and forced me to hit the shoulder by the parking lot of the white church. Inside the Escalade, heads rocked like Weebles, then snapped back into place as the car zoomed off down the street.

"Geez," I muttered, my foot shivering on the brake as the Escalade raced on, the car darting in and out of traffic, going way too fast. I reached for my cell phone to call the police—not the best way to make friends with the new neighbors, but there were kids in that car, and she was going to kill somebody, driving like that. Then I remembered that I didn't have the cell phone today. Since Cody'd left us the truck, he'd taken the phone so he could communicate with his ride.

If she wrecks that car with kids in it, it'll be just as much your fault as anybody's, for not doing anything about it. Before I even thought about it, which is usually how I do things, I'd whipped the truck into the church parking lot, pulled up to the office on the back of the sanctuary, barreled through the door, and panted out to the surprised guy on the other side, "I need to call the police. I just about got run over by a lady in a gold Escalade. She had a fight with her husband, boyfriend, whoever, and she has kids in the car. She's gonna get somebody killed."

The guy in the office, who looked like he belonged in an episode of *Little House on the Prairie*, dialed the phone and handed it to me. He waited, a little confused, while I stood in the doorway, keeping an eye on Benji and Ty as the 911 operator asked me what seemed like a million questions. By the time she was finally done, my head had stopped whirling. I caught my breath as I handed the phone back to what I now figured was the pastor.

"Thanks," I muttered, pressing a hand against my stomach, because all of a sudden acid was gurgling up my throat. My head swirled again, and tiny sparks danced in front of my eyes. My skin went cold and clammy. *I won't throw up, I won't throw up.* This pregnancy was getting to the queasiness point sooner than usual.

"You all right?" the pastor asked, slipping a hand under my elbow—to catch me, I guessed.

"Yeah, I'm . . . ohhh, I'm . . . Is there a bath . . . a bathroom here?" I tasted breakfast in my throat. My body was going haywire.

"Right through that door, in the back of the fellowship hall," he answered, pointing. "You need help?"

I shook my head, swallowing hard. "Can you," I choked out, pressing one hand over my mouth, and pointing toward Benji and Ty and the car with the other. "Can you watch them . . . ?" I took off through the office, busted through the swinging door into the dark hallway behind the sanctuary, and made it to the bathroom just in time. It was the men's bathroom, but I didn't care.

When I'd pulled myself together and made it back to the parking lot, the pastor was standing by my car window, handing each of the boys a kids' bulletin with a coloring picture on it, and a little box of crayons. "Better?" he asked, giving me a doubtful glance. I probably looked awful.

"Yes," I said, and thanked him for watching the boys. "A little morning sickness, I think."

"Ohhh." He gave me an understanding smile, and right then I realized I'd just blurted out the big secret I hadn't even told Cody yet. Oops.

I took a step toward my car. "So, listen, thanks for the phone . . . and the bathroom . . . and the help."

"Don't feel like you have to run off." He followed me around to the driver's side. "There's still time to grab lunch over in the Summer Kitchen before they finish cleaning everything up. Spaghetti or beef noodles today. Anyone's welcome."

For about a half a second, I was offended. I'd seen the people gathered on the other side of the building, and it was obvious that the Summer Kitchen was some kind of charity lunch program. Did we really look like we needed free food? "Oh . . . well . . . thanks, but we're headed off to the school to get these guys signed up for kinder-garten and Head Start this fall."

"New to the neighborhood, huh?" The preacher gave the boys an interested look.

"Just moved here last week. Over on Red Bird."

His round cheeks squeezed his eyes into slits as he smiled. "Well, glad to have you." He stuck his hand out to shake mine. "Pastor Al. Stop by and see us anytime. We've got lunch provided by the Summer Kitchen Monday through Friday, and after lunch, there's story time and recreation for the kiddos. We'll have an adult reading class start-ing in the evenings soon, Mondays, Wednesdays, and Fridays."

Geez, did I look like I was hungry and illiterate? "Yeah, okay. Thanks." When you're young, and not white, and you've got a couple kids already, people assume you're, like, a welfare case.

"We're always looking for volunteers."

Volunteers . . . All of a sudden I felt much better. Volunteer? Me? "I'll think about that."

"Wonderful!" Rocking back on his heels, he clapped his hands and rubbed them together. "Always happy to get some new fish in the net." Grinning, he held up his necktie, which was printed with fishing rods and bobbers. "Sorry. Old fisherman's joke, from an old fisherman. But it doubles as a pastor joke—two for one. We've got nursery for the kiddos during the reading classes, too. Free child care."

"Those are the magic words," I answered, and he chuckled.

"Always good to see new families moving into the neighborhood. Wasn't so long ago it looked like this old church might die off for lack of interest. Neighborhood gets ragged, you know, and places go downhill, congregation gets old and tired, and the church turns quiet and sleepy." With a loving glance over his shoulder, he took in the building like he was a painter looking at his masterwork. "Nobody falling asleep around here these days, I'll tell you. With the Summer Kitchen open now, and the evening reading, GED, and English-language classes, we're a happening joint. No reason for anybody to sit around the house and be lonely in this neighborhood these days."

I had the weird feeling he'd read my mind. With Cody gone so much, and all the little problems with the house, and being pregnant, I felt like I needed somebody to talk to. I couldn't even call Mama, because talking to her or my brother or anyone back home would just remind me that I was keeping some big secrets, and I was doing that because I didn't want anybody telling me I'd gone and done something stupid again. I needed a friend here, but it probably wouldn't do any good to talk to the preacher, because preachers are like mothers—they think it's their duty to tell you the things you don't want to hear.

"Well, I'll sure give it some thought," I said finally.

"Door's always open." A siren blared up the road, and Pastor Al turned an ear to it. "Hope they've apprehended your maniac driver. Done too many car wreck funerals in my day, that's for sure."

"I hope they did, too."

"You come volunteer with us." He grabbed the handle and opened the car door for me. "Anyone who'd jump on a wild driver knows how to take control of a situation. You've got *tutor* written all over you. I can tell it."

"Thanks," I said, then got in my car and headed off toward the boys' new elementary school, thinking, *I've got* tutor *written all over me?* It felt good to hear that. Back home, all I ever heard was what a bunch of wasted potential I was.

I could teach somebody to read. I really could. In high school, I was smart. During my study hall period, the principal used to send me down to the elementary school to help kids with their homework. In southeastern Oklahoma, some kids grew up so far back in the sticks, you needed a four-wheeler or a mule to get to their houses. Those houses were more likely to have a meth lab in the kitchen or a marijuana patch out back than they were to have books around. I loved when those kids finally realized that reading a story was something awesome. *You're good with these kids*, the principal used to tell me. *They need to see that it's okay for a young woman to be smart. That there's more to life than having babies young and going to work for the pulpwood companies. . . .*

The high school principal talking in my head was hard to take. I'd ended up doing everything he told me not to do. The whole laundry list. All of a sudden, my happy feeling came sinking down like a balloon deflating. It settled over my shoulders and started to weigh on me, getting heavier by the minute. I didn't even want to go sign the boys up for school. I wanted to go home, and flop down on the sofa, and sleep off the blues the way my daddy used to sleep off a hangover, back before he moved off and left us.

The truth was that no matter how hard I tried, I never got it right. Everything I did was stupid and wrong, and here in Dallas, things were worse than ever. I didn't have any friends, and neither did the boys. I missed my family, and I missed home. I'd thought getting a house would make everything better, but it wasn't better.

When this baby comes, you'll be all alone with it. There won't be anyone to help you. The idea went through my mind like a sudden thunderbolt, and then the rain started falling. The next thing I knew, I was turning the car around and heading back home.

"Where goin', Mommy?" Ty asked, and I couldn't even answer. The lump in my throat was about to burst. I wanted to hit the highway, start driving toward Oklahoma, and not stop until I got there.

"Mommy?" Benji whispered, stretching as far as he could in his seat belt. "Are you cryin'?"

I swallowed hard, sniffed, and shook my head. Above the church parking lot, the marquee read,

---

THE SUMMER KITCHEN

LUNCH, STORY TIME, GAMES 11:30
EVENING ADULT READING AND GED CLASSES,
ENROLLMENT OPEN
TUTORS WANTED

Tutors wanted. I read it twice.

In the churchyard, a group of kids was sitting under a tree, listening to a woman talk. Her hands flapped wildly, making her long red muumuu swirl around her high-top tennis shoes. She twirled in a circle, and then ran around the tree, like someone was chasing her. When she reached the sidewalk, she froze, and the children froze with her. The only movement came from her long, gray-black dreadlocks, swirling like the snakes in Medusa's hair. Watching her, I almost missed a perfectly good gap in traffic. Something about that woman was weirdly interesting. . . .

In the backseat, the boys were as fascinated as I was.

"Is a lady!" Ty cheered, weirdly excited. "What her do?"

"They have story time over there after lunch," I answered, then stopped watching the storyteller and gunned it across to Red Bird. "She's reading the kids a book, I think."

Twisting in his seat, Benji strained to watch through the back window.

"Is a wed-dwess lady!" Ty observed.

"Yeah," I said. "I guess she is a red-dress lady." Why the boys had this strange new thing about naming people by their clothes, I had no idea, but story time did look interesting, and at least the red-dress lady, unlike the green-pants lady, was a real person. Maybe if the boys had someone real to talk about, they'd quit making up imaginary people.

Whenever I finally finished getting the house in shape, maybe I'd bring the boys back here, after all. It couldn't hurt. The church was close enough for us to walk. We needed something to do on days Cody had the car. Maybe we'd even take a little break and try it tomorrow, or the next day. Just for lunch. Just for a little while.

No reason for anybody to sit around the house and be lonely in this neighborhood these days.

I was lonely here.

When I pulled into our driveway, the old lady next door was out by her mailbox. *Speaking of lonely people.* Even though there wasn't twenty feet between our houses, I'd only caught sight of her a couple times, when she was peeking out her window at us, or coming and going in her car. I'd knocked on her door once, thinking I'd try to be friendly. She hadn't answered, even though the TV was on, and I knew she was in there. Today, she was watching me with her arms folded, frowning. Definitely not any friendlier than usual.

"Who's that?" she asked, jerking her chin toward the moving van across the street as I got out of the car.

"New neighbors, I think." I took few steps closer, thinking, *Maybe she's actually nicer than she seems. . . .*

"Mmm," she muttered, squinting at the blue house. Her lips fused together, pleating in a single frown line.

"They had kind of a commotion over there earlier." Usually I could talk to a tree, but this lady was hard to like.

"I saw," she said. Nothing else, just, *I saw.*

I thought about getting the boys out of the car. There was always the chance that she liked kids.

She turned back toward her house, then stopped and looked across the street again. "Two of you in one week."

"What?"

"Two in one week," she grumbled, shaking her head.

I felt my cheeks go hot, and I wasn't even sure why. "Two of what?"

"Householders." She snorted, and walked off without saying another word.

Chapter 13

Tam Lambert

Barbie sped down the block, turned left instead of right, and drove three blocks in the wrong direction before whipping around the corner, catching the curb, and bouncing the rear end of the car onto one tire momentarily. After missing the highway ramp, she hung a U-turn so fast she cut off a guy in a rusty pickup truck, and he honked and gave her the finger. Changing lanes, she nearly clipped someone else.

"Mommy, no!" Mark screamed. He had destroyed enough toy cars to know what happened when two vehicles ran into each other. Aside from that, Barbie let the kids watch the news, and cop shows, and old episodes of *CHiPs*, so they knew all about police chases and the mangled results of driving disasters. Car Chase and Car Wreck were two of their favorite make believe games.

"Be quiet!" Barbie snapped, her voice vibrating through the car in an ear-piercing shriek. "Shut up! Just shut up!" Her fingers kneaded the wheel as she darted in and out of traffic.

Mark sniffled and let out the kind of long whine that usually preceded a tantrum.

"Don't you start *crying*," Barbie hissed through clenched teeth.

Mark responded with a loud wail, then grabbed a Happy Meal

toy from the seat and threw it toward the front. It hit Barbie's arm, bounced off, and landed on the floor.

"That's it!" Growling in her throat like an animal about to bite, Barbie leaned over and fished for the projectile. "You want to see what that feels like? Do you?" The Escalade swerved across the center line into oncoming traffic before Barbie grabbed the Happy Meal toy and steered the vehicle into the correct lane as an oncoming garbage truck laid on the horn.

"Barbara, stop it!" I tried to reach for the wheel.

"Look ahead!" Aunt Lute cried as all three of the boys descended into tears and Jewel let out a wail in the backseat.

Lowering the window, Barbie pitched the toy out. "You want to see how it feels?" Her voice was ragged, between a desperate scream and a sob. "You want to see how it feels?" Opening the console, she grabbed one of the kids' DVDs and threw it out the window. "It's like this!" She pitched another. "And this, and this!"

"Pull over!" I screamed, reaching for the steering wheel again. "Pull over, now!"

Barbie whipped into a McDonald's parking lot, then hit the brakes and threw the car into park all at once. The vehicle was still vibrating when she dropped the last DVD, buried her face in her hands, and began to sob.

My heart pounded in my throat as I leaned over, turned off the ignition, and tucked the keys into my pocket. Barbie would be getting those back over my dead body. I collapsed in my seat, my throat burning and too dry to form words.

A police cruiser pulled into the parking lot and stopped behind our vehicle.

"Barbie." I forced her name past the pulsating lump in my throat.

"There's a police car outside." *Thank God*, part of me said. *Thank God somebody's here.* Then a myriad of terrible possibilities ran through my mind. If Barbie ended up in jail, what in the world would happen to the sibs?

The officer tapped on the window, but Barbie ignored it. I hit the button to lower the glass.

"Everything all right here?" The officer leaned closer to the window, taking in the whimpering kids, the sobbing driver, Aunt Lute, and then me.

"We've been lost," Aunt Lute piped up, unbuckling her belt and leaning over the second seat. "Terribly so. It upset the children."

Squinting at Barbie, the officer pursed his lips skeptically. "I had a complaint called in about reckless driving. The vehicle matched this description. You know anything about that?"

Barbie shook her head, wiped her eyes, and patted her cheeks. "I'm fine. I'm fine. I just . . ." Closing her eyes momentarily, she took a page out of Aunt Lute's book. ". . . got lost. I don't know this neighborhood."

Backing away from the door, the officer asked Barbie to step out of the car.

"I'm all right now," she insisted, and he requested that she step out of the car anyway.

"I haven't done anything!" Her voice quavered with a haughty combination of anger and tears.

The officer braced his hands on his gun belt. "Ma'am, if you're refusing to comply, I'll have to remove you from the vehicle forcibly."

Barbie unlocked the door and lifted the handle, and the officer took another step backward, as if even he were reluctant to get involved with whatever was going on in our vehicle.

Barbie stepped out, and the conversation took on the usual Barbie drama. Within minutes, she was in an epic meltdown like nothing I'd ever seen in my life. She paced the parking lot, babbling incomprehensibly about the Baby Bundles wreck, my father, the eviction from our old house, and the blistering descent of the past week, while the cop followed behind her, trying to calm her down and keep her still. Staggering over a storm grate, she twisted her ankle, then yanked her foot free, pulled off her stilettos, and threw them at the car, screaming, "Homeless people! He thinks we're going to live in a house with homeless people lined up. Just lined up!" She raked her fingers over her hair, creating so much static that the top of her head looked like an upside-down haystack. "But we've got bars! We've got bars. That'll keep them out. Bars on the house, and he thinks I'd live in a place like that! I'm not an idiot. I have . . . I have friends. I have . . ."

Tipping his hat back, the officer scratched his receding hairline and gave the Escalade a look that said he wished we'd landed on some planet other than his.

Inside McDonald's, a growing audience stood plastered against the glass, watching Barbie's performance, and in the backseat of our car, the sibs had just realized we'd, quite conveniently, stopped at a McDonald's with a playscape out front. They wanted to go inside and enjoy the facilities.

The officer tapped the passenger-side window, and I rolled it down. "Is there someone I can call for you?" he asked, monitoring Barbie's rant from the corner of his eye.

"Someone?" I repeated, thinking, *No, there's no one. Not a soul in the world.*

"A friend, a relative, a clergy member?" he suggested, clearly hoping to turn us over to a higher authority, or any authority, actually.

"No, sir." Both of us watched as Barbie kicked the car tire with her bare foot, then roared in pain. "We're all right, I promise," I said, trying to mollify the situation before we ended up in state custody. "She's always like this. Well . . . not quite like this, but it's been a bad day. She'll calm down once we're home."

He slowly folded his ticket pad with what would have been our ticket still in it. "Are you a licensed driver?"

"Yes, sir. I'm sevent . . . eighteen." I realized my birthday had passed without my even noticing. The luau and the new car I'd been expecting seemed light-years away now.

Tucking his pen in his pocket, the officer gave Barbie a worried look, then turned back to me. "All right. I want all of you to go inside, cool off, and calm down for a while. Then I want you to drive. If I see her behind the wheel again, I'm taking her straight downtown."

"Yes, sir."

"Is she on any medications?"

"No, sir." That was probably a lie. In the past week, Barbie had made short work of a bottle of Xanax, as well as a smattering of herbal stuff provided to her by her only remaining friend, Fawn. "This is just her. She's high-maintenance. You should see her when she breaks a nail."

Shaking his head, he pulled his hat into place and backed off. The police procedure manual probably didn't have a recommendation on what kind of social services to call for a hysterical, stiletto-throwing woman having a really bad day in the McDonald's parking lot.

"All right." He pointed a stern finger at me. "Take a little break until everyone's got it together; then head on home. Safely."

"Yes, sir."

His police radio beckoned, and he took advantage of the opportunity to hurry off and engage a problem that could be solved.

I climbed out, retrieved Barbie's shoes, shoved them into her stomach so hard she coughed out a breath, and said, "Here. Good

job, Barbara. You just about managed to get us taken to jail." I pictured Barbie under incarceration and the sibs and me stuck in some
kind of emergency shelter, and a shiver went down my spine. There
were worse places than the blue house with the burglar bars. Much
worse.

Barbie stood on the sidewalk with her shoes dangling loosely in
her hands as I unloaded the sibs and herded them, along with Aunt
Lute, toward the restaurant. "For heaven's sake, Barbie, get a grip!"
I growled out, waving at the officer as he circled the parking lot and
drove off.

Inside McDonald's, the sibs and Aunt Lute headed for the play
yard, trailed by the curious stares of restaurant patrons. Stifling a sob,
Barbie dashed toward the restroom, a hand over her face. I didn't
try to stop her. Locking herself in the bathroom was one of Barbie's
favorite tricks. It drove my father nuts. Undoubtedly, we were going
to be in McDonald's for a while—however long it took Barbie to get
her head together and realize that the blue house around the corner
was the only place we had to go.

At least the sibs were happy in the meantime. Within moments
of our arrival, Aunt Lute had them convinced the playscape was a
castle, and they'd forgotten all about the mama drama. Meanwhile,
Barbie's emotional surrender to reality slowly progressed, first in the
bathroom and then in the play area. While Jewel dozed in her carrier,
Barbie stared out the window, her eyes tracking the passing cars, flicking from one to the next as if she were waiting for a solution to drive
by. Every so often, she fished her cell phone from her purse, thumbed
through her contacts, dialed up a number, then either waited while
no one answered or, occasionally, had short conversations with ex-
friends whose discomfort echoed through the phone. Everyone Barbie knew was suddenly on the way out of town, had company in the

guest room, or felt it was better not to get involved. Even Fawn was "putting new carpet" in her apartment, but she did promise to come take Barbie "out for a mocha later in the week and talk about everything." Listening in from the next table, I almost felt sorry for Barbie. She was finding out that nobody cared.

Eventually, the twins lost interest in employing the playscape for its intended use, and began running around the enclosure like overwound toy trucks, making engine noises and bumping into the walls and other kids. When Landon fell asleep on the lower deck, they made a game of bombing their sleeping brother with balls from the ball pit. The only other mom in the place gathered her kids, sent a dirty look our way, and left. A few minutes later, the manager came in and gave us the boot. "You can't stay there. This is a restaurant, not a day care." He studied us while chewing his lip, then shook his head and walked away.

I felt sick to my stomach. "Barbara, we have to go."

She didn't answer. She just picked up her cell phone and started thumbing through her contacts again.

I walked over and scooped Landon off the floor, then told the twins to put on their shoes. They ignored me, of course, and disappeared into the maze of brightly colored tunnels overhead. Landon sagged in my arms like a rag doll, his hair tickling my chin, his feet bumping my thighs as I turned back to Barbie and Aunt Lute. "We need to go. *Now.*"

Aunt Lute slid to the edge of the seat and unfolded herself to a standing position, then walked to the edge of the playscape. Linking her hands behind her back, she bent forward and began walking back and forth in front of the slide as if she were searching for something on the floor. The boys stopped to watch from the playscape balcony. Mark asked what she was doing.

"I think they've left tracks," she told him.

"What tracks?"

"The leopards," was Aunt Lute's answer. "I think they've left tracks." She moved slowly toward the door, still trailing the leopards. Mark and Daniel slid down the slide and fell into line behind her.

"We mustn't forget the little pea," Aunt Lute pointed out, touching Jewel's face and grabbing the car keys I'd set on the table, then heading out the door. The noise of the boys' departure caused Jewel to whimper. Barbie gave the sound a dull look, then dialed another number on her phone.

"Barbara!" I snapped, my voice reverberating in the glass enclosure. "We're leaving."

"Ssshhh!" she hissed, waiting for someone to answer the phone.

"Barbara!"

"I'm trying!" she shrieked.

Landon jerked in my arms, his head sliding off my shoulder. "No, you're not," I spat. "You're not trying. You're not doing anything, Barbara. You're just . . . sitting there."

She flicked a narrow glare my way. "I'm trying to call someone. I'm trying to find a place."

Before I even knew what I was doing, I'd reached out and knocked the phone from her hand. It slid across the table and bounced off the red padded seat. Landon flopped backward, and I caught him, tucking his head under my chin. "No one's going to answer. Nobody's going to take care of us. We have to take care of ourselves."

"Shut up!" Barbie rose to her feet. Fingernails sinking into her hair, she paced a few steps away, closing her eyes and keeping her back turned the way she often did when the sibs were out of control. "Stop it! I can't think when you're doing that!"

Outside, Aunt Lute was getting in the car with the boys. Mark and Daniel had slipped in through the driver's door, and Aunt Lute was right behind them. Getting into the driver's seat. The scary part was that she had the keys.

"We're leaving." I scooped the baby seat off the table, carried it to Barbie, and shoved it into her arms. "Here's your kid. You have four, remember? Why don't you start taking care of them? They can't sit in McDonald's all day, Barbara." For just an instant, Barbie looked hurt, and I felt a twisted sense of satisfaction.

Barbie's eyes—azure blue because of the contacts—glittered with a watercolor wash of tears. She looked lost and afraid, completely uncertain of what to do or where to go. Even her helplessness gave me a perverse sense of satisfaction. Now she knew how I'd felt for the past seven years. Ever since my mother left and then Barbie moved in, I'd been living in a place where I didn't belong, where no one wanted me. *Now you know what it's like*, I thought, and the anger inside me took on shape. Barbie's shape. If it weren't for her—her idiotic plastic surgeries, the huge house, the trips, the jewelry, the thousand-dollar shoes, the in vitros, all the stuff for the kids—my father wouldn't have ended up in this mess. He was just trying to make her happy, but there was no making Barbara happy. She always wanted more. More money, more things, more kids. More of my father. She needed, wanted, demanded everything.

I wouldn't let her use me like she'd used him. As soon as I got her settled in the house, I'd find a way to get out—out of Dallas, away from her, away from this mess. I'd leave for college, leave all this behind, get out on my own.

Out on my own. The truth was I'd never been on my own. I had no idea who was going to pay for college now. I didn't even know what kind of bills I'd be racking up each month. The charges were supposed to come in online, to be paid for from my father's account.

My debit card would be reloaded with cash each month. That was all I knew. It was all I'd wanted to know. I wasn't prepared to take on the financial responsibilities of college on my own. Even if I could find a job that would work around classes, I'd never make enough money to pay for tuition at UT and living expenses. The golf scholarship was just a drop in the bucket compared to the total cost. In reality, I wasn't any more prepared for life than Barbara was.

"Let's go," I whispered, the truth leaving behind a bitter taste. "Let's just go."

I started toward the door, Barbara's high heels clicking after me, her footfalls heavy with the weight of the baby carrier. When we reached the car, Aunt Lute was trying to figure out which of Barbara's handful of keys would turn on the ignition.

"She's not driving," Barbie snapped as she yanked open the back door and hip-butted Jewel's carrier into the seat, then climbed onto the running board to lift Jewel into the third row.

"Shut up, Barbie," I bit out. Right now, Aunt Lute was probably the most stable of the three of us.

"There goes the fuzz." Aunt Lute swirled her hand in the air, indicating a police siren blaring somewhere in the distance. "Watch out. They could be headed right for us." The direct look she aimed at Barbie seemed entirely lucid, and in spite of everything, a laugh tickled the back of my throat, forcing out a puff of air.

"Here, Aunt Lute," I said, shifting Landon to my other hip so I could take the keys. "I've got it. Don't worry. I won't let Barbara drive."

Aunt Lute's eyes met mine, and she nodded with satisfaction as she turned over the keys, then vacated the driver's seat, circled the car, and climbed into her space in the back. After the arduous process of getting the boys buckled in, we drove away with the left front tire making a strange rattling noise, Aunt Lute peering through the window at the leopard tracks, and Barbie slouched in the passenger seat with her head in her hands.

The closer I got to Red Bird Lane, the more I wanted to turn around and drive the other way. The homeless woman with the dreadlocks was standing on the corner when we reached the intersection. Her gaze captured me, stole my thoughts as the car slowed. I was conscious of the blinker ticking out a steady rhythm, demanding *turn, turn, turn, turn,* the rattling tire causing the steering wheel to vibrate in my hand, pulling the car left instead of right, resisting the curve. I felt my hands moving on the wheel, one over the other, forcing the vehicle to make the corner, but my mind was on the woman.

Her gaze followed as we passed, her head swiveling. When I looked at her in the mirror, she was still watching, her loose red cotton dress swirling around her in the breeze of our wake, outlining a slim, stooped figure with legs that bowed outward and shoulders curving into her neck, forming a slight hump.

"Watch where you're going!" Barbie shrieked as we rolled toward our new address. At the blue house, Uncle Boone had disappeared, along with the moving truck.

The message was clear.

We were on our own now.

Chapter 14

Sesay

Now there are more boys to go along with Root and Berry. There are three. Three more. The new boys have skin as pale and smooth as milk, hair the color of cane straw, and eyes as blue as water. Their faces are worried and sad. They do not laugh and smile as Root and Berry do. In the house, the women yell, while the baby cries, and cries, and cries. I can hear their voices outside the window. The walls of this house are as thin as the Indian chief's canvases, stretched on a frame.

"We can't just go out and buy curtains, Barbara!" says the young woman. She is beautiful, with hair like the boys' but eyes the color of fresh earth. Both of the younger women are beautiful. I wonder at the fact that the man has left them here. What man would leave such beautiful women alone? The world is not safe for a woman when her face is young and lovely.

The baby's cries cause me to remember my babies. *A cane field is no place for a baby,* he said, and he took them away to his house, to his wife whose crippled daughter had died, who could no longer carry a child of her own. *What would you do with a baby all day long while you work? Set it in the mud and let the alligators carry it away?* I knew he was saying the best thing. I must work, after all, to pay for my food and my bed, but I begged him to take me back to his house so I could work near the babies. He only laughed and said it was a silly notion. *You work where I tell you to work*, he told me. *You're lucky I keep you on—lucky I keep the police from taking you away and sending you home in a boat. This is America. You don't do what you're told, I can have you shipped off in a heartbeat.*

I gave him my babies. I did the best thing, and my heart split open, and for a long time there was not one beautiful thing in the world. Everything was gray and cold.

Now I hear the baby inside the blue house, and I want to slip through the walls and pick it up, so it will not cry. Inside the house, the women continue to yell, their words whipping quick and sharp like the cane cutters' long knives.

"I'm not living here! You don't know who's out there. You don't know who might be skulking around." The voice quavers, high and thin.

I shrink closer to the wall, listening.

"Reality check, Barbara." The younger woman's voice is steady, filled with venom, heavy with anger. "We don't have the money for anyplace else. The car payments are three months behind. If we don't come up with thirty-five hundred dollars, they're going to repossess the Escalade. Then what do we do—sit around and look at the curtains? If we sell your ring and the laptop, and whatever else we can find that's worth cash, between that and the money Uncle Boone gave us, we can catch up the car payments, and buy some groceries, and make it for a month or two until we figure out what to do."

"I'm not selling my ring in some . . . some . . . pawnshop. We can just . . . just ask Boone to—"

"Get real, will you? Wake up! Uncle Boone's tapped out. He's sick of us. He's sick of this whole thing. Why do you think he's not here right now? We're lucky he moved our stuff and gave us a place to live."

"Pfff! A place to live. We're in this dump while he's—"

"Shut up. Just shut up. He didn't have to do *anything* for us. He could have kicked us out on the street."

"It's not fair. It's not . . ." The words melt into a sob, a long, low moan of grief, like a woman giving birth to a child she doesn't want. "Paul's coming back. He'll . . . he'll straighten this out . . . fix it. He'll be . . ."

"You know what, Barbara? Maybe it isn't everyone's job to take care of you. Maybe for once, you're just going to have to figure out how to take care of yourself. Maybe you need to worry about how you're going to feed your kids, instead of sitting there calling someone to bail us out."

Silence stretches between them, then the tap of shoes crossing the floor, and then the young woman's voice, but softer this time. "Here. Give it to me. I'll go find some pawnshops tomorrow and sell it."

The shoes run away. The sound disappears across the house. The young woman picks up the baby and rocks it, talks softly until the room is quiet.

At the back of the house, a door opens and closes. I slip into the shadows of the creek, move through the brush until I can see who's come into the yard. The boys with water-colored eyes are there. They come through the doorway quietly, carefully, so that no one hears them. A gray cat follows them down the steps. I wait to find out if anyone else will come, but there are only the boys. I let them see me, and they stand watching from a distance. "Do you know the story of Peter, the little muck rabbit?" I ask, and I take the soft white rabbit from my pack. They move closer to see. They shake their heads, and so I begin to tell them the story. Their eyes are wide and so beautiful, but they are afraid to come too close. They do not know me as the boys across the street do.

From inside, a woman's voice calls out. It is the old woman, the one I have guessed is the grandmother. She calls for the boys, but they do not answer. I step back into the trees so she will not see me. "Boys!" Her voice echoes from the house. "Where have my boys gone? Are they hiding in a box? Are they hiding under the table?"

The boys look at one another and giggle, their faces wickedly pleased. They are playing a game with the old woman, just as I once played with my mother.

The smallest boy comes to the fence. He twines his fingers through it. He is not afraid of me. "Where you how-sh?" He points over his shoulder at the house, so I will understand him.

"Here," I say, and wave a hand toward the trees, the street, the white church on the corner, the mission. "I live everywhere, like the little muck rabbit."

"I got nudder how-sh," he says. "Got swim-pool, backet-ball game, swing shet, foosball . . ." He goes on, but I cannot understand many of the words.

I have the little toad on a string in my pocket. I have repainted him with my brush. He is a blue toad now. I pull him out, check to see that there is no one coming out the door, and then I let the little toad hop over the fence. The boy slaps his hands together, catching it. I slip deeper into the brush, and he cannot see me when he looks again.

"There you are!" The old woman comes to the door now. "I see you out there, but you'd better run on inside before the Crocodile Queen finds you. She'll eat you up for being in the yard."

The boys squeal and bolt toward the doorway, checking over their shoulders, as if they think I could be the Crocodile Queen. When they are gone, I move back to the side of the house, where there is no fence. The mother of the children is there in the window. She stands with her forehead pressed to the glass and her eyes staring upward, but not seeing. Tears seep down her cheeks, like rain.

I wonder, how can a mother cry while her children, such beautiful children, play? With your children at your feet, how can there be sadness? I think that if my children were near me, I would only have room for joy.

The little boy from the fence comes into the room, and he presses between her and the window. Tugging at her shirt, he raises his hand and opens it. The blue toad is inside, floating like a dot of water on his palm, beautiful like his eyes.

She lays a hand on his head, her fingers sinking into the straw curls of his hair. She pulls him close; then her face tightens with pain. Pushing him away, she leans against the glass again and raises her arms to shield her face. He watches her, then turns and leaves. Somewhere in the house, his brothers are yelling and making loud noises, and the baby cries again. The woman moves away from the window with an angry face.

A noise across the street catches my ear. A door closing. I shift the leaves aside so as to see. Root and Berry are coming out the door with their mother. Each carries a red plate with plastic wrapping and a ribbon tied on top. They dash toward the street as their mother closes the door, and she warns them not to go past the sidewalk alone. They stop at the edge to wait, the plates tipping in their hands.

"Don't spill the cookies!" the mother scolds, but they are not listening. But for the wrapping, the cookies would have spilled already.

I wonder where they are going. Perhaps to the church. Sometimes women bring plates with cakes and cookies to the Summer Kitchen.

Lunch is long over today, but perhaps they will leave them for tomorrow. If they do, I will go there again for lunch. I will have one of Root and Berry's cookies.

They search the trees along the creek as they wait for their mother, and I know they are looking for me. I poke my head above the leaves, and they see me and wave. Then I vanish again. I watch them come across the street with their mother. I hide like Peter Rabbit in the cane field. Once across the street, the boys run ahead.

They are taking the cookies to the blue house.

Chapter 15

Shasta Reid-Williams

It didn't take long to figure out that the new neighbors were strange. When we rang the bell, an old lady wearing a pink shower hat, a swimsuit, and a filmy bathrobe came to the door and opened the burglar bars. She caught me scoping out her swimming gear, and said, "We were just about to enjoy the water."

Considering that backyard pools in this neighborhood were about as likely as icicles in July, that didn't make any sense. "Uhhhh . . . We . . . ummm . . . brought you some cookies," I muttered. "We live across the street. Just moved in last week."

She took the cookies and smiled. "Oh, lovely! Crumpets."

We all stood there for about a half a sec, having one of those awkward silences, and then something inside the house crashed and broke, two little boys hollered potty words at each other, a baby cried, a kid screamed so high the fillings in my teeth rattled, and some lady screeched, "Leave things alone! Do you see what you've done?" Then I heard laughing and what sounded like a herd of wild buffalo running through the house. Something toppled—a stack of boxes maybe—and a million tiny pieces of plastic hit the floor and scattered. LEGOs, just guessing. We had some wild times in our house, but nothing like what was going on in this place. A door slammed, and the mom roared like she was going to kill the first kid she could catch.

Benji's eyes got wide, and him and Ty slid behind me. Ty's arm slipped around my knee, and I tried to decide whether to say something, or act like I couldn't hear the commotion.

The lady in the bathrobe didn't even flinch. She pushed the burglar bars partway closed, just as calm as can be, and said, "Please accept our gratitude for the lovely crumpets. I believe we'd best be heading for the water now." Pushing the bars closed far enough that only her face was sticking out, she whispered, "The natives are restless." The boys peeked around my legs, watching the door slowly swing shut as she disappeared into the house, her pink robe floating behind her. The knob latched just as a kid inside screamed so high and so loud it probably shattered windows for a half mile.

"Whoa," I muttered, and Benji agreed.

"Whoa," he whispered. I grabbed the boys' hands and we hustled back over to our side of the street. For the rest of the afternoon, I painted the red wall, caulked trim, and watched the blue house. No one came in or out. While the boys were napping, I went outside and hung around the front lawn, digging up dandelions, and . . . well . . . snooping. By the time Cody came home, I was ready to trade theories about the new neighbors, but Cody showed up tired and in a bad mood and down about the academy. The physical side of the program was no problem for him, but the bookwork side was eating his lunch. Even after spending two nights at a study group with guys from his class, he'd botched a test on juvenile law. Somehow, that was my fault, because the boys were noisy and wouldn't leave him alone in the evenings. On top of that, he'd checked the bank account on the way home, and we were down to a hundred and sixty bucks until his next paycheck. He blamed it on the money I'd spent on the house, but the truth was, it was just as much his fault for grabbing convenience store food every day instead of taking something from home.

"You can take a sandwich, Cody," I told him. "It's not like we can quit working on the house. We've got to have it ready before Dell comes, and things need to be safe for the boys, besides."

Right about then, he sprang it on me that a buddy of his could get him a couple weeks' work doing a second-shift job at a parking garage downtown. All Cody'd have to do would be sit in the booth and take money. It was quiet there, and he could study his academy stuff, and pick up a few extra bucks at the same time.

"Why don't you come watch the kids, and I'll go get a job in the evenings?" I shot back.

He rolled his eyes like I was an idiot. "Yeah, right. And how am I gonna study with Benji and Ty climbing all over me? If I don't do something, I'm not gonna make it through the bookwork. This isn't the Push County sheriff's department, Shasta. The academy's tough. The parking garage job'll help us out all the way around. It's perfect."

"Perfect for you," I grumbled, but I knew his mind was already made up. Unless I threw a fit, he was gonna take that job.

He moped around for the next two evenings, grouching at the kids and slamming his books down whenever anybody made any noise, and pretty soon we were all on one another's nerves. On top of stewing about what it'd be like to be stuck home by myself every evening, I was watching the blue house and wondering if I oughta turn the neighbors in for child abuse. The more time that went by without the kids across the street showing up outside, the more my mind invented twisted possibilities, like something you'd read in one of those cheap paperback thrillers.

I pounced on Cody the minute he hit the front porch on the third day. "I think we should call somebody about those people in the blue house. Sometimes you can hear the kids screaming from all the way across the street," I told him, and he rolled his eyes, letting me know he didn't want to talk, or work on the house, or keep the boys busy tonight. He just wanted to sit in front of the TV with a blank look on his face, or stick his nose in a book.

I'd put up with the silent treatment for three days now, and I was sick of it, so I followed him into the living room, even though I knew it'd probably start another fight. "All right, geez, take the stupid job if you want to." I was surprised to hear those words come out of my mouth, but right now I'd of sent him off to a job cleaning sewers, if someone offered it.

He looked as shocked as I was, and then for a half a sec, he looked like he felt guilty. "It's just for a few weeks. What'd you say about the people in the blue house?" All of a sudden he wanted to talk. Amazing how nice he could be when he got what he wanted.

"This morning, one of the kids was screaming so loud, he might as well of been on our front porch."

He crossed the room and parked himself on the sofa. "Our kids are loud. It doesn't make us child beaters."

"I'm just saying, maybe if you went over there . . . like, with your academy T-shirt on, just, like, to say hi. Maybe you could get a look at the kids and make sure they're all right. Normal people don't keep their kids locked in the house, Cody."

Rubbing his eyes, he picked up the remote, probably hoping he could turn me off with it. "You watch too much TV."

That crawled all over me like fire ants, and I was mad before I even knew what was happening. "You know what, Cody? I haven't turned on the TV in days. I've been working on the house, which is more than I can say for you. Dell's coming the first week of August, and once she makes it up to Oklahoma, Mama and everybody's gonna know we went and bought a house, and then they'll show up here to see what we've gotten ourselves into this time, and the place'll still be looking like junk."

"Junk!" Cody's good mood went right out the window. He smacked the remote down on the coffee table, so that we could end up having to buy a new one along with everything else we needed. "I'm working my butt off to pay for this place. I thought once we moved out of the apartment, you were gonna stop griping all the time."

"I thought *you* were gonna help me with the house, instead of going and getting some stupid night job!" My whole body hurt from climbing ladders, hauling boxes, regrouting tile, pushing furniture around so I could fix the scratches in the dining room floor, and trying to repair the window weights in windows that hadn't been opened since, like, before air-conditioning was invented. And I'd been dodging phone calls from home forever, and lying in e-mails, because once we actually talked, they'd want to chat with the boys, and the boys would spill about the house, and the family back home would go ballistic, thinking we were on the downward debt spiral again. On top of that, I was pregnant and starting to feel sick in the mornings, and I kept thinking I'd tell Cody once things were settled in the house, but the house bills and the house projects kept piling up, including a leak under the bathroom faucet I hadn't even told him about. My next big job was to get on the Internet and figure out how to do plumbing.

The pregnant part of me popped to the surface, and the next thing I knew, I was crying like the front row at a funeral, sobbing out words that ran together in a stream of blabber. "You just don't listen to . . . I'm stuck here all day in this house, and . . . and . . . you don't . . . you just want to sit there with your face, with your face plastered-in-a-book-and-your-stupid-job-is-all-you . . . you don't even care if the house looks like junk, and Benji batted the Nerf ball over the fence today, and there's poison ivy in the creek, and we can't go, and nobody mows it, and that stupid oleander bush is . . . is dangerous, and . . ." The meltdown was so total, I couldn't even put together a whole thought that made sense. I wanted to run out the door and get in the car, start driving, and never come back.

Cody swung his leg around and dragged himself off the couch, throwing his hands in the air like a suspect trying to keep from getting shot. "All right. All right, already, I'm off the couch. Geez, cut out the waterworks. I'll put in a bunch of time on the house this weekend, I promise."

Even though he was giving in, I felt like I was sinking inside. When Benji and Ty were on the way, I cried over stupid things like peanut butter, Cody's socks on the bathroom floor, an extra ten dollars on the electric bill. You name it, I cried about it. If Cody'd been paying attention, he would of figured out by now that I was pregnant again. I wanted him to. I wanted it to just dawn on him, instead of me having to make a big announcement. My mother always said men only think about what suits them—like how to get a car running, or how to trade in an old lawn mower for a new .22 rifle, or how to leave behind a wife and kids for the skinny little girl at the bank.

Of course, considering my daddy, Mama didn't have a real high opinion of men. She couldn't ever accept that Cody and me might be different—that Cody was the type of guy who'd get up in the middle of the night to rescue a friend stuck on the side of the road, or put his last five dollars in the collection plate at church. He was doing everything he could to get through the police academy so he could give his family a better life.

All of a sudden, I felt guilty for chewing on him. I didn't want to fight. I didn't want to end up like my mama and daddy.

"Sorry," I whispered. "I'm just tired."

"Don't work so hard," he said, like it was that simple; then he took a drink of his Dr Pepper and set it back on the table.

"I *have* to work hard. It's not like I can keep Mama away forever. I don't want the family to see this house until it's done. You know they don't think we can make our own life here. They just want to see us tuck tail and run home, so we can live under their thumbs forever."

Cody frowned like he'd just bitten into something with a bad taste. "Who cares what your mom thinks? She doesn't have a choice in it. That's why we moved down here, right? To get everyone off our backs and out of our business."

"We can't keep *your* mom and dad away forever, either," I pointed out, and Cody swallowed hard.

"Yeah," he muttered. "I'm gonna go work on the yard."

Something in the bushes outside caught my eye just as Cody walked past me on his way to the kitchen. He turned like he saw it, too.

"What was that?" I asked.

Cody shrugged. "The wind, I guess."

"I swear somebody's out there sometimes." Chill bumps ran over my shoulders and made me shudder.

Cody's sour look came back. "Don't start up about the green-pants lady again, all right? Nobody's out there."

I rubbed my hands up and down my arms and checked the window. "Wait, wait, Cody, wait!" The door was opening across the street. "Someone's coming out of the blue house. Look, look, look!"

Stopping in the doorway, Cody rolled a glance back over his shoulder. "Wooo, call in the National Guard."

"I haven't seen anybody come out of there in *three days*. Not since the morning after they moved in. The girl went somewhere for a little while, and then she came back, and since then, nothing. Oh, look, it's the girl. Oh, oh, and the lady."

Cody pinched his T-shirt between his fingers and pulled the fabric over his mouth. "Dispatch, dispatch, this is Williams. Ten-sixty-six on a girl and a lady in the driveway on Red Bird. I need backup. Repeat, need backup. Have a girl and a lady. Repeat, girl and a lady."

"You're such a jerk," I said, but I couldn't help laughing. Cody could always make me laugh. "You think that's her daughter? Because that lady doesn't look old enough—"

"I don't *know*." Which translated to, *I couldn't care less.*

"Well, come look and see what you think."

"I'm not going to come look."

"No, really, Cody, she's . . . Oh, my gosh, wait. I think they've got a flat tire on their car." I was vaguely aware that I was hopping up and down in the doorway, and if the neighbors looked over here, they'd think I was a loony tune. "Come look."

Cody wandered back across the room, huffing out a big breath, like I was on his nerves. I could tell that, considering a car was involved now, he was more interested.

Across the street, the woman and the girl were squatted down beside the tire.

"Yup, looks like a flat," Cody agreed. "I'm gonna head on out and mow."

"Don't you *dare*." Snapping a hand out, I caught his shirt. "Go over there and see if they need help."

"They've probably got it under control."

I smacked him in the stomach, because I knew he was just messing with me. No way Cody would go mow the yard while there were a couple women across the street with a flat tire. "Come on, Cody, do they look like they know how to change a tire?"

"They don't even look like they know what neighborhood they're in."

"There's no man over there, either. Just those two, the three boys that were tearing the house down the other day, a baby, and the grandmother I gave the cookies to. Not exactly sure, but I think she's nuts."

"Was she wearing green pants?"

"Cod-eee!"

He rested his hands on my shoulders. "So, we've got two blondes, a crazy lady, three wild boys, and a baby?"

"Yes . . . right. And a cat." The women were opening the back of the Escalade now—looking for tools, I guessed.

"Sounds like a knock-knock joke. Knock-knock. Who's there? Two blondes, three wild boys, a grandma, and a baby . . ."

"Cod-eee."

"And we're getting involved why?" he asked, but he was laughing, and before he went out the door, he glanced back at me and winked, his eyes glittering like shiny black beads. When Cody looked at me like that, I totally remembered why I fell for him in high school. He could be so cute when he wanted to.

The boys came out of their bedroom while he was jogging across the street. "Where Daddy go?" Ty wanted to know.

"Daddy's going to see if the people over there need help with their flat tire."

"The weirdo people?" Benji asked.

"Benji! That's not nice! You don't call people weird."

Benjamin looked up at me with his eyebrows pinched in his forehead, as in, *I got that from you.*

The three of us stood watching through the glass while Cody introduced himself to the neighbors. Both women backed a few steps away, like they were scared of him. Only the younger one shook his hand. They talked about the tire for a minute; then Cody went around to the hatch to look for the jack and lug wrench. The older blonde went back in the house and the younger one stayed with Cody. A minute later, the crazy grandma came out, carrying the baby girl. Two of the boys followed her.

Ty perked up. "There'sa boys!"

"I wanna go," Benji chimed in.

"You guys grab your shoes." After watching these people for days, I was dying to get up close and personal—do a little private investigation, so to speak.

Walking across the street, I started to think maybe I should of minded my own business. The girl looked like the type who'd go around with her nose in the air. She was dressed like one of those models giving a preview of cute summer looks on the morning show. Her T-shirt had some kind of designer label on it, and she was wearing a short, pleated skirt, kneesocks, and tennis shoes, her legs long and smooth, a light caramel color—the kind of tan you paid for, not the kind you were born with, like mine. She looked young and hip.

The closer I got, the more disgustingly cute she was. I had a mental flash of how I probably looked—old Hugo football T-shirt that used to be Cody's, jeans with holes in the knees and red paint dribbled down one leg, a sloppy ponytail with pieces of straight black hair flying in the wind. All of a sudden I felt like somebody's frumpy old mommy.

"It's Annah Mon-nanna!" Ty pointed at the girl, his body jittering as we stepped over the curb.

I felt even worse, if that was possible. "She's not Hannah Montana," I whispered out the side of my mouth. Although, come to think of it, she did look like Hannah. "And, Benji, no calling anybody weird, you hear me?" I muttered as we started up the driveway. Hannah was still occupied with Cody and the tire, but the crazy lady and the boys saw us coming. The boys slid around behind their grandma and hid in the folds of her bright-colored Hawaiian dress. She had some kind of scarf wrapped and twisted on her head, so that she looked like the Chiquita banana lady. "Greetings." She held up a hand.

"Hi," I answered. "We met the other day. We live across the street. The cookies . . . we dropped off . . . cookies?" I looked toward the house, and a bedsheet that was tacked over one of the windows flipped back into place, which meant someone was watching us from inside. I introduced the boys, and the baby girl reached toward me, trying to push out of her grandma's arms. The grandmother handed her off like it was an everyday thing to give a baby to someone you didn't even know.

The baby smiled, and babbled at me, and looked up at me with big blue eyes. I bounced her on my hip and talked nonsense, and she gave me a smile that was toothless, except for the bottom two in the center. In about two and a half seconds, I was in love. Baby love. She smelled like Johnson's shampoo and powder, and that smell pulled at me like nothing else could. I missed having a baby in the house. I missed having someone who needed me and thought I was the center of the universe. The boys were already starting to find their own lives, but a baby girl would always be mine. As she grew up, we'd do all the special things mothers and daughters do.

My mind hopscotched forward, and I wanted to go home right away and tell Cody about the baby and have him be as excited as I was.

Cody looked up from the tire and saw me with the baby and frowned. I heard that squelching sound they use in the movies when somebody's daydream rewinds like an old reel-to-reel tape. He stood up from the car, and the teenage girl in the short skirt stood up with him.

"I need to go grab a few tools to bend that fender out," Cody said. "That's what's rubbing your tire. If you leave it that way, it'll ruin the spare, too. The tire shop might be able to fix that, or else put a used one on the rim for you."

The girl shaded her eyes so she could look at him. She was almost as tall as Cody was, but for a guy, Cody wasn't tall. Just five-nine. "Oh . . . okay. How much does that cost?"

I heard that rewind sound in my head again. *How much does that cost?* Probably not near as much as that way-cute outfit she had on.

"Not too much—ten, twenty bucks, depending," Cody answered. "I go by a shop on my way to work. I could drop it off for you tomor-row." No way Cody would of been bending over backward to drop off a tire for someone who didn't look like Hannah Montana. I felt a little pinch of jealousy.

"Oh, that would be so great," she breathed, not seeming flirty, really, just like she was used to people doing favors for her. Cody jogged off toward our house. Some snarky part of me said, *All right, now he's being too nice to the cute girl.*

I peeked around the grandmother and introduced myself, so Hannah would know Cody was attached. "I'm Shasta. I live across the street."

Her eyes flashed wide when she saw that I had the baby. "Tam." She moved closer and shook my hand, then reached for the baby, but the baby hung on to me and started whining.

The grandmother chuckled, then leaned close to the girl and whispered, "She looks like the nanny—the little Spanish one. Jewel thinks she's found Esmeralda."

The girl, Tam, turned white, then pink. "Aunt Lute," she gasped between her teeth, then glanced at me and mumbled, "I'm sorry."

"It's all right," I told her. "I love babies; babies love me. These are my guys, Benjamin and Tyler."

Tam bent down and said hi to Benji and Ty, and they were star-struck. This girl was the closest thing to Paris Hilton they'd ever seen. "I guess you've met Mark, and Daniel, and Jewel. And Aunt Lute."

"A little," I answered. "We were glad to see some kids across the street. The boys'd love to get together and play sometime."

Tam shifted from one foot to the other, her gaze flicking toward the house. "I'll have to ask my stepmom. . . ." I had a feeling that was an excuse to brush me off. The conversation ran out then. Cody came back, and Hannah wandered to the car to watch him finish changing the tire. I stood playing with the baby girl and letting the boys get acquainted until Cody was finished. The boys helped him gather his tools, and he handed them off to Benji and Ty, then picked up the flat tire to carry it across the street.

"Look what I've got," I said, and turned the baby girl around so Cody could see her. "One of the little pink kind. How cute is she?"

He gave me a narrow glance on his way past. "Don't get any ideas." He didn't even look at the baby, just headed back across the street with Benji and Ty behind him.

The girl in the fashion-model skirt gave me a curious look, and I felt myself blushing. "Guess I should give her back now," I said, feeling like an idiot. My husband could be nice enough to her, and all he could say to me was, *Don't get any ideas.* "So . . . ummm . . . let me know if y'all ever want to get the boys together to play."

She gave me an uncomfortable look, and I could tell she wasn't gonna be calling anytime soon for any playdates.

Of course she wouldn't.

I looked too much like the little Spanish nanny.

Chapter 16

Tam Lambert

The morning after the flat tire, Fawn came by to, as she put it, "get Barb out of the house for a while." After days cooped up together, while Barbie ranted with Fawn on the phone or mellowed herself with Xanax and wandered off to the bedroom to sleep, I didn't even complain about Barbie leaving me stuck with the kids and Aunt Lute. Barbie hadn't been taking care of them, anyway, other than to occasionally bring one or two into the bedroom with her and curl up in a fetal position for a group nap.

Suddenly, I couldn't imagine what I'd thought was so bad about our old life—why I'd found reasons to complain about the chaos in the luxurious home with the nanny and the endless supply of toys. Life here felt like a reprimand from God—a slap in the face meant to show me how ungrateful I'd been. Life could be so much worse. It *was* worse. The house was so small, we were stacked on top of one another. The television wouldn't work because there was no cable, the kids were bouncing off walls and boxes, and furnishings sat piled like toys created on the wrong scale for a dollhouse. Aunt Lute paced the house day and night, disturbed by the fact that her scrapbooks, painting supplies, and stashes of hoarded treasures were piled in boxes on the porch.

After Barbie took off with Fawn, Aunt Lute decided to unpack some of her materials. She left an easel and palette in the living room, and the sibs promptly knocked it down. Paint splattered everywhere, and Jewel picked that moment to figure out that she could do the seal-flop across the room. While I was in the kitchen cooking hot dogs, and Aunt Lute was on the front porch unpacking more supplies, the living room became a finger-paint masterpiece of handprints and footprints and baby slug trails.

When I saw what they'd done, I sank down in the doorway and cried. Every part of me wanted to run away, but there wasn't anywhere to go. We had one vehicle, currently with no spare tire, and a limited supply of pawnshop cash. The proceeds from Barbie's ring had been enough to catch up on the car payments, and we had money left to live on for a few months, but there wasn't anything extra to spend on luxuries like cable TV and trips to McDonald's. If the sibs were left to their own devices for a millisecond, they wreaked havoc either by accident or on purpose as a form of passive-aggressive protest over their lost toys, lost house, lost dad. Lost everything. They had no way of understanding what was happening, and as far as they could reason, their only recourse was to act out until life went back to normal.

Aunt Lute came in the front door and discovered the paint, and me crying about it. "Ssshhh," she whispered. "I think I've seen a pride of lions nearby." Motioning to the boys, she tiptoed across the room, leading them out the back door in a colorful, yet from my perspective blurry, parade of paint-spattered clothing, hair, and limbs.

Pushing the moisture from my eyes, I rescued Jewel from the floor, read the label on a tube of paint to make sure it was nontoxic, then bathed Jewel in our one tiny bathtub and dressed her again. Through the window, I could see Aunt Lute stripping the boys to their underwear and hosing them down to get the paint off. In the context of the past week, it hardly even seemed like a strange thing to do.

The boys reentered the house half-naked, wet, and shivering, little streams of water dripping from their underpants and running down their legs. I heard Aunt Lute mopping the floor in the living room while I fished for clothes from the laundry pile and gave them to the twins, then dug out a top and shorts for Landon.

Something caught my eye outside as I was pulling his T-shirt over his head. The mom from across the street, Shasta, was heading down the sidewalk with her sons. They were laughing and pointing at birds in the trees, strolling like subjects from a greeting-card photo. Her long, dark hair swung across her hips as she stopped to show the boys a squirrel running on an electric line overhead.

Yanking Landon's T-shirt into place, I picked him up, grabbed Jewel, and ran to the overstuffed bedroom at the end of the hall, where the three boys were sharing two single beds, because that was all that would fit. Daniel and Mark were sitting on a bed, their faces long and somber, as if even they realized they'd pushed things past the breaking point. Perhaps they were afraid Aunt Lute would take them outside and douse them with the garden hose again, because they shrank into the corner as I came in the door. They were wrapped in the covers, shivering still, their arms covered with goose bumps.

"Come on," I said. "You two follow right behind me, and I mean *right* behind me. If anybody steps anywhere I didn't step first, there's going to be *serious* trouble, understand? I mean it. I'm sick of you guys not doing anything I tell you. I swear, if you two don't cut it out, I'm going to walk out the door and not come back." Threats probably weren't the most mature way to deal with kids, but at the moment, I meant it. I was teetering on the edge of a place I didn't want to go, struggling to abide by the still, small voice of conscience warning me that if I left, something terrible would happen.

The boys cooperated as if they walked in single-file lines every day of the week. Usually, getting the sibs from one place to another was like herding ferrets, but today, they obediently took long steps behind me, so that their feet landed in my tracks. "We're going over to the park," I told Aunt Lute, as we tiptoed through the living room, avoiding smears of paint.

Aunt Lute was down on her knees scrubbing daubs off the floor. "It's only a small mess," she said without looking up. "Just a bit of paint. Red and blue and brown, like the birds of spring." Sitting back on her heels, she studied the spatters and handprints dotting the white walls. "Acrylic washes so easily. God must paint in oils. His birds never fade in the rain. Have you noticed?"

As usual, it was impossible to tell whether Aunt Lute was talking to me or just talking.

"I'm taking the kids over to the park," I repeated. "If I don't get out of here for a while, I'm just going to . . . lose it, okay?"

"What if you can't find it again?" Aunt Lute leaned over to pull something from between the cushions on the sofa. "Oh, look, another one of these." She drew out a string with a tiny wooden animal on it. "A little brown bear."

"'S mine," Daniel offered, and stretched out his hand, opening and closing his fingers. "I finded it."

Aunt Lute leaned over and swung the bear toward Daniel's hand, once, twice, three times until his fingers closed over it.

I hurried the sibs out the door, then headed across the yard carrying Jewel, with the boys following neatly behind me. Shasta had already made it to the bridge with her kids. The three of them were leaning over the railing, looking at the creek below. She glanced over her shoulder and waved as we reached the street.

Landon broke rank and dashed ahead to join the neighbor boys. Mark and Daniel moved more timidly, and Shasta stepped aside, pointing out the minnows in the shallow water below. "See them swimming down there? Benji and Ty brought some bread to give the fish a little snack. Share your bread, guys. Give everybody a little bit."

I watched the sibs politely take small pieces of bread from the neighbor boys. Jewel stretched in my arms, wanting some, too. "Are you headed to the park?" I asked. "We have *got* to get out of that house for a while, before somebody, probably me, goes nuts. The kids just smeared paint all over the living room, and my stepmother's, like, AWOL again, and . . ." The next thing I knew, I was blathering on. By the time I finished, Shasta probably thought I was a complete lunatic. "I'm sorry. I just . . . it's just . . . been a really bad . . . few days, and . . ." Emotion gathered in my throat, and for a horrifying moment, I was close to dissolving into tears. I swallowed hard, trying to gather myself together. "I just . . . I saw you and I thought maybe . . . you were headed down to the park."

Shasta's forehead lowered. Clearly, she was wondering why the sudden change of heart. When she'd asked about playdates before, I'd intentionally put her off, knowing Barbie would never agree to it.

"Oh, well, we're not . . ." She stopped, her gaze flicking toward the park. She had beautiful eyes, dark like those of the foreign girl who sat next to me in English class last year. I never bothered to speak to the girl, to ask what country she was from, or what her name was. I just snorted impatiently at her thickly accented English, wrinkled my nose at her strange, spicy scent, and thought she was actually very pretty, but she'd be so much prettier without that hijab wrapped over her head and fastened under her chin.

Now those casual thoughts from high school seemed pointless, immature, and idiotic. Who was I to judge anybody?

Yet I couldn't help thinking that Shasta looked even younger today, with her hair loose around her face. Not much older than me—way too young to have a five-year-old. Without consciously thinking about it, I categorized her with a long list of tags—*Minority, low socioeconomic, possible high school dropout, teen bride, teen mom, hick, not my type of person, nothing like me . . .*

The list pricked my conscience, as much for how easily it came as for its content. Tagging people, judging them according to my mental catalog, was as natural as breathing—an unconscious by-product of having grown up in a neighborhood, a school, a community that had *high standards*.

Barbie wasn't the only reason I'd put Shasta off about playdates. The truth was that even though she was friendly and beautiful, and her husband had saved us from the flat tire, and she had it together with her kids much more than Barbie did, this girl wasn't up to *my* standards.

The look on her face said she could tell that. She was reading me like a book, and she'd slapped a few labels on me, too. *Snob, brat, spoiled little rich girl . . .*

The funny thing was that none of those labels fit anymore. I didn't know who or what I was, but the spoiled, self-possessed girl who'd trotted the high school halls like she owned the world had been given a wake-up call in the most painful way.

Shasta tossed her hair over her shoulder, motioning down the street, seeming uncomfortable. "Well . . . ummm . . . actually, we were headed someplace else."

"Oh," I muttered, turning my attention to the boys, because

the situation was suddenly awkward, and tears were building in my throat again. I felt lonely, and lost, and I needed someone to talk to. "Well, that's all right. I mean, maybe another time." Stepping back to peer around the overhanging trees, I considered taking the kids to the park by myself. The idea sent an uncomfortable sensation sliding over my shoulders, causing a tiny shudder. Just down the street, homeless people stood in a soup line outside the white church. What if they got the urge to come sleep it off in the park after lunch?

On the other hand, the idea of going back to the blue house was almost unbearable.

From the corner of my eye, I could see Shasta watching me, trying to decide what to say next. "Well . . . ummm . . . actually, we were headed to the church on the corner. The little white one?"

I blinked hard, broadcasting shock before I could consider how she'd take it. No doubt my face said, *The place with the soup line?*

Along the bridge railing, the boys were laughing and talking as if they'd known one another forever. For them, there was no socioeconomic gap.

Shasta crossed her arms uncomfortably, digging the toe of her tennis shoe into the dirt at the curb. "You're welcome to come with us," she offered halfheartedly. "They told me they have a story time and games for kids there every day after lunch." She rushed the words out, seeming as nervous as I was. "And they were looking for volunteers to sign up as tutors for a reading class they're starting three nights a week. I figured maybe I'd do that. Cody's gonna be doing a little extra night work, which leaves me stuck with no car all day and all evening, and, well, I just need to get out and do something, you know?" Her eyes met mine, and I nodded.

"I can *so* relate," I admitted. Labels or no labels, there wasn't an inch of space between us right now.

Shasta's face opened, and she grinned, her expression precocious as she leaned a little closer to me. "And, for this literacy thing at night, I hear they have *free child care*." She cast a glance at the boys, and I understood everything that was being said without being said. "Come down there with us," she pressed, touching my arm. "You know, check it out and stuff. The kids would have fun playing the games."

I thought about the soup line winding from the old church like a slowly moving snake, and air hitched in my chest. Not so long ago, our church youth pastor had made plans for us to do a poverty simulation with some church that met under an overpass and served homeless people. We were supposed to give up everything that belonged to us and live for twenty-four hours the way those people did—sleeping at the mission, eating in a soup line. I signed up to go along, because I didn't want to look bad compared to everyone else, but the truth was that I didn't want to participate. I couldn't imagine what it would be like, stuck in that part of town, surrounded by derelicts, by society's castoffs, and I really wasn't interested in finding out. It seemed to me that, if we wanted to do some good, we could have a car wash or a garage sale to raise money for homeless people.

I told Dad about the trip, and he couldn't see any point in "exposing yourself to those realities." He sent me back to the youth pastor with a donation and a warning—while my father appreciated the youth pastor's zeal, he needed to be more judicious about his methods. We were just kids, after all, and some things you didn't have to experience in order to understand them.

"You know, I'd really better go back and check on Aunt Lute," I said, giving our house a concerned look so Shasta wouldn't think I was making excuses.

She frowned toward our driveway. "She could come with us."

"Aunt Lute's busy cleaning."

"I wan-go wit boys," Landon interjected, suddenly tuning in to the conversation. Jewel bounced in my arms, as if she understood, too.

Shasta bent over and smiled at Jewel, who reached for her. Aunt Lute's extremely politically incorrect nanny comment streaked across my conscience like a meteor looking for a place to land. The only similarities between Shasta and Barbie's last nanny were the dark hair and brownish skin, but that was enough for Aunt Lute. Typically, it would have been enough for me, too.

I felt the need to apologize. "Listen, I'm sorry about what Aunt Lute said the other day—about the nanny thing. Aunt Lute's . . . well, actually, she's kind of, like, nuts really. I mean, she's harmless, but she's just a little off. She moved in with us about six months ago, because her house was condemned. When the inspectors came in, the place was piled with stuff—food, and old pizza boxes, and scrapbooks, and clothes she'd bought and never even taken out of the bag, and paintings of all kinds—just about everything a person could hoard. She hadn't thrown a thing away since her brother died and left her alone in my grandparents' house ten years ago." If that didn't convince Shasta that we were normal people, I didn't know what would. Everyone has a crazy aunt somewhere in the family.

"Hey, I'm not one to talk." Shasta nudged me on the shoulder, like we were just girlfriend to girlfriend. I had a twinge of longing for Emity. "You should see *my* family. My folks are both mostly Choctaw—from southeastern Oklahoma. Everybody's related to everybody. We don't grow too many branches on the family tree, if you know what I mean." She nudged me again, and I laughed.

Shasta's son pointed out something in the creek, and she walked to the edge to look over. "A perch got my bread!" The older boy waved his arms excitedly. "A big ol' perch! Mama, can we come fish for it?"

Shasta rolled her eyes, turning to me. "They're just like their daddy. Cody'd sooner fish than eat."

I looked over the railing. The fish was swirling lazily through the water, its scales reflecting the sunlight in a metallic mixture of gold and pale blue. "My father loves to fish." As the words came out, I wanted to swallow them again. Landon turned to me, his eyes the iridescent blue of the fish.

"Where'sa Dad-dee?"

I rested a hand on his head, put a finger to my lips, whispered, "Ssshhh, we're talking." For days, the kids had been asking about my father, and Barbie had been telling them he was on a trip and he'd be back soon. I didn't want to lie to them, so I didn't say anything.

"Where'sa Daddy?" Landon blinked slowly, his forehead lined with little worries.

"Ssshhh, Landon. Don't interrupt when people are talking." I could feel the blood creeping into my face again.

Shasta's mouth curved to one side, and her eyelashes fanned upward, as if she were waiting for me to explain. I didn't, of course. I just guided Landon back to the bridge railing and said to Shasta, "It's complicated."

She shrugged, as if *complicated* weren't a problem for her. "Listen, if you were a fly on the wall in my family, you'd see complicated. My daddy left us when I was a kid, and there's still three of my uncles who'd, like, shoot him on sight. Actually, I think my mama probably would, too, but that's my family. There's always more people getting married, unmarried, remarried, and pregnant than you can shake a stick at. Just one big, crazy mess."

"Sounds familiar," I said, and we talked for a few minutes about her hometown and the fact that she and Cody had decided to move to the city so he could take a job with the Dallas Police Department.

"It was something we were always gonna do, anyway," she finished. "We just all of a sudden decided, now was the time. Of course, Cody's parents and my mama are waiting for us to screw everything up and come running back home. They don't even know we bought a house yet. When they find out, they'll freak, and I just don't want to hear it, ya know? Hel-lo-oh, we're, like, adults, after all."

"Sometimes they just don't get it," I agreed, thinking of my trip to Europe. I knew my father would never understand, but I had a feeling Shasta would. Except for the two kids leaning over the bridge railing, she seemed like a girlfriend my age.

"Exactly." Stroking a hand over her long, thick hair, she scissor-pinched the bottom and looked for split ends. "It stinks being the black sheep."

I chuckled. "I was always an only until the sibs came along, so I guess I've been the bad kid and the good kid."

Shasta looked me over. "You look like the good kid." It was hard to tell whether that was a compliment or not. "Your kind makes it hard on the rest of us."

"Thanks a lot."

We laughed together, and I decided I liked her. She was easy to talk to and irreverent enough to be fun.

"I guess we'd better go. I don't want to hold you guys up," I told her finally.

I reached for Landon's hand, but he twisted around and pulled away. "I wan-go da boys."

"Landon, now!" For a half second, I sounded mortifyingly like Barbie. Jewel whimpered and tried to crawl out of my arms, like she always did when Barbie went haywire. She leaned toward Shasta, her fingers extending and closing.

"Ssshhh," I whispered, bouncing her on my hip. "Landon, let's go." If I grabbed him now, he'd suddenly develop spaghetti legs and drop to the ground. I'd either have to leave him where he was or pick him up and lug him back in one arm, with Jewel in the other.

All of a sudden, I was sorry I'd brought them outside. It wasn't worth it. With the sibs, everything ended in chaos sooner or later.

Shasta cut in before I could say anything. "Hey, hey, hey," she soothed, bending close to Landon. "I'll tell you what. Why don't you go on back home right now and then we can all get together later and play?" She twisted to look at me. "Once Benji and Ty get up from a nap this afternoon, we can meet at the park. Maybe your stepmom and your aunt could come, too. Shoot, I'll even pack us some sandwiches and Kool-Aid and chips, and we can have a little picnic over there for supper. Cody's tied up this evening, so he won't be home. It gets lonely in the evenings."

It occurred to me that I had no idea when Barbie was coming home or what shape she would be in. "I'll probably have to see how the afternoon goes." With Barbie, there was no predicting. "I need to run to Walmart later for diapers and things."

Shasta's eyes widened. "Oh, man, if you're going to Walmart, can we ride along? I'm, like, running out of everything, and Cody'll have the truck at his night job all the rest of the week. If I don't come up with some Cap'n Crunch and Teddy Grahams soon, there's gonna be a mutiny at our house."

I laughed, because in the last week, I'd come to fully understand the value of bribery as a survival mechanism. "I'll probably go after lunch." An idea hit me unexpectedly, and given the fact that the alternative was to go home to the paint spills, Aunt Lute, and the sibs' usual warfare, it seemed like a good plan. "You know what—let me run back to the house, grab my purse and my keys, and we can go now. We've got extra booster seats that were for the nanny's car. I'll throw in a couple."

"Awesome. We never turn down a free ride to Walmart." Shasta peered speculatively down the street. "The guys and I'll walk on down to the church, check it out a little, and you can just pick us up there when you're ready."

"Sure," I replied, realizing that, whether I wanted to or not, I was going by the breadline for a visit.

Chapter 17

Sesay

Too many people in the Summer Kitchen today. Around me, the room is like the cane farm. It smells of sweat, and breath, and labor. The people watch you with quick, sideways glances, and you cannot know which ones might tell *him* something they've seen. Which ones might say, *I've seen her ill in the mornings; a baby is on the way,* or, *She tucked bread into her pocket. She wraps it in rags and dries it in the ropes under her bed. On the day the fields burn, when the rabbits run from the fire, she plans to take her pack and run away, too.*

You cannot know, with so many people around, which ones are loyal to *him*, or when *he* will come and take you back to the cane farm, or perhaps put you on the boat to drift out over the water again, or have the police throw you into prison. Any of these can happen to a thief, to someone who takes bread, who runs away when there is harvesting to be done, when she hasn't finished paying for her bed and her meals.

I am a thief, after all. All the people in the Summer Kitchen must see it. We are so close together, packed in among these tables, how can they miss knowing?

But MJ has asked me to come again today. She found me outside her bookstore as I watched the Indian chief paint a picture of a warrior kneeling. The warrior's head is tipped back, his face and hands open. I know without being told that he is praying. The sky has opened overhead, and he looks at the face of Father God.

MJ invited the Indian chief to come across the street to eat lunch with us, and he agreed. Now he sits opposite me, and he asks if I have animals in my pocket. Each day, he leaves paint by the door. Little tubes of paint, and I can choose any color I like. At night, when Teddy secretly leaves the shed behind the church unlocked, I slip inside. The shed has a light, and I can carve until my eyes grow so heavy there is only time to set down the knife and lay my head on my blanket. Straightaway, I am asleep, and there is no chance to wonder if tonight will be the night *he* finds me and takes me away. I do not think of the cane fields or smell burning, unless it comes to me in a dream. In the morning, I rise early and leave the shed before Pastor Al arrives to open the church. This morning, I saw him talking to Teddy by the shed. I think he knows someone has been in there.

There is a shed in the yard where Root and Berry play. I have noticed that it has no lock, and a light hangs inside. If Pastor Al locks the church shed, I will try Root and Berry's shed, instead. I can go in like smoke, as quietly as little Peter Rabbit into McGregor's cane field. I won't steal anything. I will only do my work, and then sleep, and leave before the sun rises.

As I go, I will look in the window and watch Root and Berry asleep in their beds, and then I will leave a little carving for them. A rabbit, perhaps.

I take the animals from my pocket and set them on the table, and the Indian chief turns them over in his hand, then holds a humming-bird up to the light. The wings are so thin, the light almost shines through them. To make this possible, the wood must be very wet. "I could sell these," he says. "They're very nice."

"Father sells them in the mission. Father Michael." I add his name at the last. Sometimes names fly in and out like sparrows.

The Indian chief turns over the hummingbird, touches its stomach with his fingertip. "You don't sign your work? You should always sign your work. And selling them in the mission store is one thing, but I have a friend with a folk art gallery." He looks up and catches my face, his eyes quick as a cat's paw. "Downtown, where people have real money to spend." He glances at MJ, and a conversation passes between them without words, and then I know it is not an accident that they have brought me to lunch today. They have taken me here to ask about my carvings. They have been talking about me while I am not around. This worries me. The more whispers in the air, the sooner *he* will hear. *Perhaps*, I think, *I should take my pack and travel on to another place. Perhaps it is time. . . .*

The idea presses hard in my chest, like a stone pushing my breath away. Another place, without a shed, without a light, without the Summer Kitchen where the woman will wash my clothing, and MJ's store with all the books.

It's hard to think about another place. I like this place.

"Do you ever work on anything larger?" the Indian chief asks, but I barely hear him. It's raining in my mind, all the rivers running dark and murky.

"Larger . . . do you ever work on anything larger?" he asks again.

"Larger things are heavy to carry," I tell him, and he laughs, as if he should have thought of that. Everything I have must be carried with me. You can try to hide your things, but the street people will find them.

"True enough," he says, then strokes his cedar-wood chin. The lines around his mouth and eyes are deep furrows, as if he has been frowning for a long time. He tosses his head, and hair flows over his shoulder like black liquid. He is beautiful. I know why MJ looks at him as she does. "You could leave them in my studio," he tells me. "Larger pieces, I mean. You could leave them there while you work on them. There's plenty of room."

He must be guessing that he has come too close to me all at once, because he eyes me for a moment and says, "Hey, no pressure, all right? It's just that . . . well, I know what it's like to be in a bad spot. When I got out of prison, someone helped me get off the streets. It made the difference, that's all. Just because a person's had a tough time doesn't mean they don't have something to contribute. I like your work. You create beautiful things." He admires the hummingbird while handing it back, and for a moment, I feel beautiful. I am as beautiful as a hummingbird, with its fine wings and green feathers that catch the sun.

"My grandfather taught me," I say. "A long time ago. In a far place across the water. The place I came from."

MJ rests a hand on her chin. "Where do you come from, Sesay? I don't think I've ever asked."

"The gallery would probably want to know that," the Indian chief says. "With folk art, the cultural tradition is important. Like with me, the fact that I'm Choctaw and I take on Native American subjects adds value, you know?"

Only some of his words make sense to me, but I nod anyway. Inside, the rock is so heavy in my chest, I can barely breathe. *If they know where you come from, they can send you back. Perhaps they work for* him. *Perhaps* he *is just around the corner.*

I stand partway, the bench pressing against my knees as I look around the room. No one is there except men, and women, and families, bent over their plates taking in food as if it might run away before they can eat it all. I put my animals back in my pocket anyway.

The Indian chief returns the hummingbird, but he seems to regret parting with it.

"I can bring a larger one for you," I say, and sit down again. Later, I will go to the creek, where tangles of branches have been left behind by the floods. I will sort out one that is perfect for a hummingbird. If I have a place to carve tonight, I will breathe life into the wood.

"Awesome," the Indian chief says. "I'll look forward to it." He stretches a hand across the table, the way men do when they have made a bargain. I am uncertain what to do. No one has ever held out a hand to me before. Even Michael at his Crossings Church is aware that people like me have learned to keep a distance. Yet, here is the Indian chief holding out his brown hand, open on the table with the palm up. I slide my fingers across and touch them to his, and his skin is warm. It feels strange. "It's a deal, then," he says, while still holding my hand. Then he lets go, as if he fears that too much of this will frighten me. He eyes me like I am a fish in a net, as he stands up and kicks one foot over the bench, then the other. "You know, you're welcome to come use my studio anytime."

I tell him I am grateful for the paint and the brush, and then he says he must go back to his work. He thanks me for the conversation, as if my conversation might be of value. I feel the stone lifting from my chest, air flowing in again. "You should tell your friends about the yellow houses," I say to him. "They should be told."

His face lengthens, and he nods. "MJ mentioned some things about Householders." There is a look of pain in his face.

"It is a bad thing, those houses. People come to them smiling, and they leave weeping." I have seen families in the mission who were in yellow houses. I have heard them curse those places.

The Indian chief nods again. "If Shasta and Cody would've given me some time, I could've asked around about Householders before they bought the place, but trying to hold Shasta back is like trying to stop a Mack truck with your bare hands, you know? She's a trip. Anyway, they're in the house now." He shrugs, as if it is not his business to tell. He says good-bye then, and MJ watches him leave. She has a fond look in her eye, a love look.

"I could carve a passion box," I say. "A passion box causes love to come about, if you put the hair of your desired one inside." I make the motion of tucking a bit of hair into a box, and her eyes fly wide, like a startled doe's.

"Are you talking about Terence and me?" She chokes as if she has swallowed the bag along with the tea. "He rents the back half of my building. That's it. He only came over here today because he wanted to talk to you about your carvings."

"I think he came because of you." I am certain this is true. Why would anyone walk across the street for me?

MJ tells me we should finish our plates and attend to story time on the porch, and so we do. But in my mind I am thinking about the passion boxes. I am trying to remember—what is the pattern my grandfather painted? My grandfather carved many such boxes. He traded them to the man who passed by with the cart, but the passion boxes never paid for enough food, so there were always more to carve.

I can see my grandfather's hands as we stand up. The girl with the beautiful hair, Cass, comes to take our plates. Today, she has a little girl trailing behind her, a mulatto girl with gray eyes. She hands a glass to the little girl and patiently says, "You can carry this, Opal." Then to us she adds, "Was it good?" She smiles at MJ, then at me.

"Yes, very," MJ tells her. "Are you coming outside for story time?"

"Who's telling today?" Her eyes dart from one of us to the other, as if she cannot decide which would be better.

"It is MJ's day to tell," I answer, and give a tiny bird to the little mulatto girl. Her mouth opens into a circle as she touches it. "I have already told the story of Peter, the muck rabbit. How he escaped the man's garden, but then he was almost lost when the cane fields burned. He ran with all the other muck rabbits. Everywhere there were men and boys with brooms and clubs and nets. But Peter was a clever rabbit. He ran back through the smoke and leaped the flames and escaped. Then he rushed home to his mother."

"Whoa," Cass whispers, her eyes bright with interest. "I must'a missed story time that day. How come they burned the cane fields?"

Beside her, the little girl, Opal, holds the bird very carefully and echoes Cass's words. "Come bun a cay-feel?"

I smile at her and answer, "Always the sugarcane fields are burned in the winter to clear the brush and the snakes before harvest, and the rabbits run from the fire." But then I wish I'd said nothing. I can hear the rabbits screaming in my mind. I can feel the black muck oozing over my feet. I can smell the blood.

Cass's mouth hangs open a moment, and then she says, "I saw a football dude on TV who said he learned to run so fast by chasing rabbits in the sugarcane. He makes, like, a bazillion dollars now. Are there sugarcane fields where you come from?" Like all children, Cass is filled with questions, like a jar filled with water. She pours them out in streams.

"I have lived in the cane fields."

"Where?" MJ asks.

"Far from here," I say, and I feel them chasing me into a corner. "I don't have a name of that place."

From outside, the children are peeking in the door. They are waiting for a storyteller.

"I guess we better go out. C'mon, Opal." Cass walks ahead of us to the door, talking yet. "Mrs. Kaye says if I keep getting all my summer-school work done, I can help in the child-care room when the literacy class starts. I'm gonna do storytelling. Opal and me have been makin' puppets at Holly's house."

"I think that's a great idea," MJ says, and we go out the door with Opal twirling her little bird on its string. On the porch, the children are waiting for us.

In the back of the crowd, I see Root and Berry.

Chapter 18

Shasta Reid-Williams

Tyler wouldn't stop pointing to what looked like a homeless woman on the Summer Kitchen porch and saying, "Dere da lady, Mommy. Dere da lady. Is a wed-dwess lady." For the life of me, I couldn't figure out why the boys were so into talking about people's clothes anymore. Next, I'd be having to tell them not to talk about the green-pants lady *or* the red-dress lady.

"Ssshhh," I whispered, pushing his hand down to get him to stop pointing at the woman in the red muumuu. Beside her, the other woman had just put on a chef's hat and coat to do story time. "Let's listen to the story, okay? The lady in the cook's hat is gonna read a book for us. Cool, huh?"

"But it da wed-dwess lady," Ty insisted again, his voice loud enough that the woman in the chef suit stopped dragging her chair across the porch and looked at us. Then everybody, including the lady in the muumuu, looked at us. Shaking her head, she slowly pressed a finger to her mouth, her long, gray dreadlocks falling over her eyes. She was kinda creepy-looking, actually.

Pastor Al stepped onto the porch with a platter full of cookies, and Ty hollered, "I wanna cookie!" And then every kid in the crowd was asking for cookies.

"All right, all right!" Pastor Al called out, holding the platter up high. "Now, Mrs. Kaye and Mrs. Holly did make us some cookies, but . . ." Whatever else he said was drowned out by squeals, bodies scooting forward, and cookie requests in both English and Spanish. The loudest ones in the bunch were my kids. Leave it to the Williams boys to show up and crash story hour.

I checked over my shoulder and Tam's Escalade was pulling up in the parking lot, and not a minute too soon. It was totally time to give up on story hour and make a break for it.

I grabbed the back of Ty's shirt just before he could dive into the cookie-crazed mosh pit; then I swung him onto my hip so hard he let out a big, "Ooof!"

"Cut it out!" I said, and then tried to weave my way forward to get ahold of Benji. I ended up grabbing the wrong arm, and a little African-American boy looked up at me like he was scared to death. The girl beside him grabbed his other arm and said, "Leggo my little brother!" Any minute now, some mad mommy would probably smack me upside the head. Tomorrow, I'd wind up in the paper: *Mom of Two Arrested in Story Hour Brawl.*

All of a sudden, a loud, warbling, shrieking sound shot over the crowd. The noise was so high and sharp, it sliced through the racket like a hog call at the county fair. Heads jerked, Tyler did a pretzel twist in my arms, and everyone froze, including me.

On the edge of the porch, the woman in the muumuu was crouched down like a warrior getting ready to heave a spear. She waved her palms over the frozen crowd the way a witch would if she was casting a spell. "A-i-i-i-i-i!" she shrieked again, and kids popped their hands over their ears. "Krik, Krik!"

"Krak!" the kids hollered back, bouncing up and down and bumping into one another.

"Krik, Krik!" the woman said again.

Ty hollered right along with the rest of them. "Krak!"

"Do ya hear de tale of Story Mouse?" the woman asked, her chin jutting out as she stared down the crowd with her dark, cloudy eyes, her accent making the story sound like it was from someplace far off. "Did'ja know about Story Mouse and her many little childs?"

"No!" the kids squealed.

The woman pointed for them to sit down, and, like magic, every little rear end found a space. Ty squirmed out of my arms and sat crisscross like everybody else. Benji'd worked his way to the front row, near the cookie platter and the story lady. No way I was gonna get him out of here now without a fight. I was ready to get to Walmart, but sometimes you've gotta pick your battles. I learned that from my mother. With Mama, everything was her way or no way. There wasn't any discussion and nobody got a vote. By the time Jace and me were teenagers, we sneaked around and did what we wanted. It wasn't worth trying to talk to Mama, because she wouldn't listen, anyway. I didn't want my kids to feel like that about me. Everything didn't have to go right on plan. Sometimes it was okay to stop in the middle of the day just to hear a story.

I turned toward the Escalade and waved for Tam to come on up. She poked her head out the window, like she wasn't one bit sure about that, but then she got the kids and walked up the sidewalk with them.

"It's story time," I whispered. "Let the boys scoot on in where they can hear. Benji's over there."

She moved a little farther, but it was pretty obvious this wasn't her scene. She was eyeballing a group of Mexican guys in work clothes over by the edge of the porch like she was afraid we were gonna get jumped any minute. They noticed her, too. She had on a cute little tank top and shorts, and she stuck out here like a really well-dressed sore thumb. I, on the other hand, blended right in.

Tam's little brother pointed at the storyteller and mumbled something, but Tam was too busy scoping out the crowd to pay attention.

"Ssshhh," I whispered, and the little brother hushed up before the creepy-looking muumuu lady started talking again.

"De grandmothers, they say all de stories come from de smallest creature. In de very old day, there been a time with no car, and no television box, and no radio to make music." While she talked, the woman acted out the words, her hands driving cars and turning on televisions in thin air, then cupping around her ear, like she was listening for radio music. The kids squiggled closer. I forgot about trying to sort out her accent, and I just listened to the story.

"The whole world been quiet then, and the people go around doing their work, but when their work been finished, the young, they sit at the feet of the old ones and listen to the stories. The stories make the young ones very happy in the long-ago time." She paused to look at the children. "How do you t'ink the young ones, they sit at the feet of the old people?" she asked, and the children straightened their little bodies, crisscrossing their legs and tucking their hands in their laps. The woman nodded. "But one day, there come a time when the children, they grow tired of the stories, and they do not sit and listen, and the old people tell their stories to the air."

The words came with a long, sad face, and the kids moaned and groaned. The storyteller waited a minute for the noise to die out. "Then nobody catch the stories, so they just float about in the air. And then one day come along a tiny mouse, and she go silently among all the people—into the rich homes, and into the poor homes. She capture the stories, and she make them her children, and they are so many. For each story child, she weave a beautiful dress of a good color—white, blue, red, green, and black. The story children, they live in her house and do all the work for her, then, and soon she is very jealous and she do not let them go out into the world. 'Why I give the stories back to the people?' she say in her own ear. 'The people have let them go float about. Why I give them back?' And she live in her house and she grow lazy and selfish and fat, like dis." Holding her muumuu puffed out in front, the woman waddled back and forth across the porch, and the kids giggled and squealed. By the corner of the building, the Mexican dudes elbowed and punched each other, pointing to their beer bellies and joking. They inched closer as the tale started up again.

"The story children, they are very much sad then. They remember the long-ago, when they travel like the wind and gather the young ones to the old ones, but now the world of the people go very quiet, so quiet, and the young boys and the girls only work, and the old grandmothers and grandfathers sit and look into the air with empty eyes." The woman made another long face. Her dreadlocks fell over her cheeks, so that she seemed like something out of a scary movie. "Oh, this be a sad, sad time. A very sad time. And long time. The story children know they must find a way back to the people, and so they decide that when the she-mouse is not looking, they gonna chew the door with their teeth, but the door is very thick, and heavy." Spreading out her feet, she pretended to push on the door; then she shook her head like there was no chance.

On the lawn, the kids whispered, "What happened? What did the people do? How'd the stories get away?"

Finally, the girl who'd yelled at me for grabbing her little brother half stood above the crowd and snapped, "If y'all shut up, she's gonna tell. Be quiet. Boo and me wanna know what comes next."

I wanted to hear, too. I'd heard parts of this story somewhere before, but I couldn't remember where. It seemed like I'd read it in a book . . .

with Benji, maybe. But we didn't read the whole thing. I knew the part about the colored clothes, but not the part about the door. . . .

I wanted to remember it this time, so I could tell it to the kiddos in our family the next time we went back to Oklahoma for a visit. Mama'd have a heart attack if I told her I learned it from a homeless lady at a free-lunch kitchen.

The storyteller lifted her chin, her eyes clear and sharp in skin the color of black dirt farmland. She looked like she could be a hundred years old, but she didn't move like an old person. She reminded me of my Nana Jo. Nana Jo gathered us up and told old stories about Choctaw history. I usually didn't listen like I should of. I wasn't that interested, and I couldn't see the point in all that old stuff. It seemed to me like we needed to get modern instead of hanging on to the way things'd always been.

Now I wished I'd paid more attention to Nana Jo, so I'd be able to tell those stories to Benji and Ty and this new baby. I'd let the stories float off into the air, just like the people in the Story Mouse tale.

I tuned in again when the lady moved down the steps and leaned toward the kids, until she was eye-to-eye with them. "You must listen, if you will know how the stories came back to the world. You must never again let the stories escape into the air." She shook her head slowly, like she was really sad, and the kids did the same. A breeze ruffled the grass and pulled her dress tight, outlining legs like toothpicks and a skinny body that couldn't've weighed more than ninety pounds.

I wondered if sometimes she didn't have enough to eat, and where she went when she left the Summer Kitchen.

"One day, the young men bring a herd of sheep through the village where Story Mouse, she live in her big house," she went on. "A ram break free, and he run against the door. The door, it so weak that it break down, and all the story children run into the sunlight, and the old ones reach into the air and find the stories again. They fill their eyes, and the young ones sit at their feet again. Now the story children run over the whole earth, and all the people can see the colors of their beautiful dresses. But the young ones, they must always hear the stories with their ears, and never allow them to go float about again, or Story Mouse, she gonna take back her children, and stories gonna be no more, forever."

She stretched out a hand and moved it slowly over the bunch of us. "Can you catch the story with your ears?" She snatched an invisible tale from the air and brought the fist to her ear, and listened to it like a tourist hearing the sea in a shell. "Can you catch it?" She walked back and forth, catching stories and listening, and pretty soon, story time looked more like playtime, with the kids grabbing stories and putting them in their ears.

When the kids settled in again, the lady in the chef suit read *If You Give a Mouse a Cookie.* Then she finished, and pointed across the street to the old gas station building with the glass bottles hanging in the tree and the Book Basket sign out front. She reminded the kids that they could come by for a book, and everyone's first book was free.

"We should do that," I whispered to Tam. "Cody's cousin's got the studio in the back of that building. If he's there, we can drop in and say hi, and the kids can pick out a book." Terence Clay wasn't the friendliest guy in the world, but he was the only family we had around here. Maybe I was trying to impress Tam a little, too. Terence was a real live artist, after all.

Tam nodded, but didn't look real enthusiastic. Holding the baby tighter against her, she checked out the junky building across the street. Her lip curled, as in, *Any book that comes out of there, I don't want to take home with me.*

I let the idea roll around in my mind while Pastor Al made a loop, handing out cookies. Tam watched her kid brother take the cookie off the plate, and her lip curled again. Even when Pastor Al stopped by to say hello, she wasn't too friendly.

"Seen any speeding cars lately?" he joked as he shook my hand.

"Nope. None." I wanted to crawl under a rock. The last thing I needed was for Tam to find out I'd called the police on them. I introduced her real quick, to throw the conversation off track; then I pointed out her brothers in the crowd, and showed off Jewel, just to give Pastor Al something else to talk about. Pastor Al seemed like the type who liked babies.

About a half second after Pastor Al finished shaking Jewel's hand and getting a smile from her, I was sorry I brought up the b-word. "So, how's that baby comin' along?" he asked, and stared straight at my stomach.

Tam looked confused at first, but she clued in quick enough. Her perfect mouth hung open a minute; then she gave a perfect smile, and she looked at my stomach, too.

I felt the hole I'd been digging get deeper by the minute. "Fine. Everything's fine." My mind fumbled for something else to talk about. Something other than me. "Story hour was neat. The kids really liked it." I glanced at the porch, but the woman in the red dress was gone, and the woman in the chef's hat was headed back across the street to her bookstore, her long black braids and beads catching the sunshine.

"Glad you enjoyed it." Pastor Al gave me a wise look, like he knew I was changing the subject on purpose. His round cheeks lifted, squeezing his eyes into a fan of wrinkles. "Sesay had them all going with her tale of Story Mouse, didn't she? Quite something to have all those tales stored up in the mind. No telling how far she's traveled, gathering them. Kind of remarkable to think about, isn't it? You never know what treasures live inside people until you sit down and listen. That's what I love about the Summer Kitchen." He gave the building a proud look.

Around us, the crowd was starting to leave. Moms and kids wandered down the sidewalk, the men beside the building lit cigarettes and headed off, and a homeless man trundled across the parking lot with his two-wheeled buggy and his dog. "You think any more about that literacy class?" Pastor Al asked, squinting against the sun. "Still need volunteers. If you're interested in stories, you'll hear some good ones there, and you'll get a chance to share some. You can't really imagine the friendships that come out of something like that."

I tried to picture what Cody would say about the boys and me coming up here in the evenings, but then again, it wasn't really like I needed his permission. "Well, I'm not sure . . . I mean, I thought about it, but my husband's going to be gone with the truck in the evenings now. He'd have a heart attack about us walking back home after dark, I think." Actually, if Cody's mother ever found out, she'd have me declared mental, and she'd take custody of my kids. Luckily, right now, Cody's mom wasn't speaking to us, which was why she hadn't called.

Pastor Al gave Tam's vehicle an astute look. "You two could volunteer together. We still need help. If you volunteer here just once, you'll be hooked, I promise." He glanced back toward the building as the cookie lady headed our way.

"Pastor Al, are you giving people the hard sell again?" she asked, then offered us cookies.

Adjusting his ball cap, Pastor Al cleared his throat. "No, ma'am, Mrs. Kaye. Just trying to drum up some more help for the literacy class."

"We'll take whatever assistance we can get." Mrs. Kaye pushed some stray curls off her forehead with the back of her wrist, then focused on us. "There's a meeting for mentors tomorrow night at six o'clock. You're welcome to come check it out."

A blond-headed girl who'd been helping on the porch turned our way and added, "It's real fun, and we're gonna do craft projects for the kids in the child-care room and stuff. And we're gonna have puppet shows, and . . ." The fact that Landon, Ty, Benji, and a little girl were playing tag in the flower bed caught her eye, and the blonde reached in to grab the little girl. "Opal, get outta there. You'll mess up Teddy's roses, and you'll poke your eye out."

Benji popped out from behind a bush, then ran by and tagged Opal on the elbow. She squealed and tried to tag him back. Ty trampled a plant on his way out of the flower bed, and right about then, I figured it was time to leave.

"We'll sure think about it," I told Pastor Al. We thanked him and Mrs. Kaye, and herded the boys to the car. I talked Tam into pulling over to Terence's studio for a minute, and I introduced them and showed off Terence's paintings, but he wasn't much on conversation, and the kids were getting restless in the car. Terence opened the back door and gave everybody gum from a pack in his pocket. I slipped around the front of the building and peeked in the bookstore windows, but it hadn't opened back up after lunch yet, so Tam and I headed for Walmart with all the boys smacking Doublemint in the backseat.

Benji started pouting on the way, because we didn't get to go in the bookstore. He didn't care that it was closed; he just wanted to pout. He kept it up all the way across the Walmart parking lot and all the while we were shopping, which was seriously embarrassing in front of our new friends. Of course, Tam's brothers were not a pack of peaches either, and by the time we'd done our shopping, the Walmart people were probably glad to see us go. A pack of Skittles at the Walmart checkout finally fixed Benji's problem, and by the time we loaded up in the car, I was tired, but it seemed like a pretty good day. It'd been a while since I'd been out shopping with a girl-friend, and it felt good. Tam was interesting to talk to, but nothing about her made much sense. I had a feeling there were a lot of things she wasn't saying. A girl who graduated from Highland Park, which meant she must've lived there, wouldn't all of a sudden be moving into our neighborhood, whether her parents were tied up in some messy divorce or not.

"It's kind of temporary," she said as we pulled out of Walmart and started down the street. "We're just living in this old house until we can work out something else." She flicked a glance my way, embarrassed, like she'd just clued in to the fact that she'd called my house *old*.

"Ohhh," I said. "Well, I hope y'all decide to stay. We're here for good. We just bought our place from Householders. They made everything real easy. No closing costs, and the monthly payment's super low, which is good, because we just found out the insurance on this new truck is a lot more than we expected, and the insurance on the house is higher than we thought, too. Cody spread the bills apart, so it'd work out better with the times his paychecks deposit. He's the math genius in the family. Actually, there's not a math genius in the family, and there's so much we want to do on the house, and it all costs money, which is why Cody's taking on a little night work at a parking garage downtown. It's quiet there, and he can study for his classes while he sits in the booth."

A monkey wrench turned in my stomach, torquing everything. I'd just gone out to Walmart and spent another twenty bucks. It was all stuff we needed—some more spackling and caulk, lightbulbs, a $3.99 rug for the bathroom, some more grout for around the tub— but when Cody found out, he'd have a fit. *I just gave you twenty bucks*, he'd say. *What'd you do with it?* It was probably the pregnancy hormones, but with the fun at Walmart over, I wanted to crawl into a corner and cry for absolutely no reason. Any minute now, I was gonna crack open like a watermelon. As soon as Tam pulled into our driveway, I grabbed the door handle and put on a happy face the best I could. "So, thanks for the ride, and for going to story time with us. Maybe we can give it a try again tomorrow, huh?"

"I'll check with Barbara."

"The thing about the reading class sounds cool. We could go tomorrow night and see what it's all about."

"Yeah. Maybe. I'll check. Everything's kind of, like, up in the air right now." Tam wiped the dust off the top of the steering wheel, and then seemed surprised to see that her fingers were dirty.

I felt myself sinking lower and lower. "So, I was thinking we ought to trade phone numbers, so we can get in touch easier."

"Sure." Tam pulled her phone out of her purse and checked it. "Mine's dead. There are, like, almost no plugs in that house that the Fearsome Foursome can't get to. I'll give you my number, and you can just ring me, so I'll have yours on my call log."

"Sounds good." I plugged her number into my phone and called it before we said good-bye. Then I unloaded Benji and Ty, who were definitely ready for a nap.

Inside the house, I went down for the count almost before the kids did. I meant to crash just for a minute, but by the time I woke up, it was past suppertime. Like usual, the kids weren't happy, because Daddy wasn't home, so instead of getting anything done on the house, I refereed fights and helped build a blanket tent in the bedroom, and then argued with Benji about a bath and bedtime, and then whether or not he could wear the dirty pajamas out of the laundry hamper.

While I was putting dirty stuff back in the laundry, Ty got the idea to make himself a glass of chocolate milk without asking. A gallon of milk and about a half bottle of chocolate syrup ended up on the floor, and by the time I cleaned that up and tried to keep from saying something to my kids that I'd be sorry for later, I felt like I'd hit a brick wall. Even though I usually hated going to sleep while Cody was gone, I was on the couch and out like a light ten minutes after the kids got in bed.

A charley horse woke me sometime later on. Since I was up, I staggered off to the kitchen in the dark for a cup of water. Just when I reached for the refrigerator, something caught my eye out the back door . . . some kind of . . . light. Yawning, I tried to clear my vision, then moved closer to the glass.

A creepy feeling crawled over my skin. Something wasn't right.

The glow was coming from . . .

The shed?

The door shifted in the wind, widening the dim wedge of light falling on the grass.

I moved closer to the back window. We hadn't even been in the yard today. *Maybe we left it open yester—*

A shadow passed through the light, blocked it for a sec, then disappeared. My heart launched against my chest.

Someone was out there. . . .

Chapter 19

Tam Lambert

The cell phone ringing snapped me upright. Swinging my legs around, I collided with something that shouldn't have been next to my bed. My mind groped for an explanation as I searched for the phone. A hazy memory floated by, out of focus like a minnow a few inches below the water, darting in and out of the light, clear for an instant, then gone. I went somewhere today. I drove Barbie's car. I took the sibs. . . .

The ring came again as I tried to put the memory together. Through the blur, I saw the phone lighting the table. The coffee table. I must have fallen asleep in the media room. That was probably Emity on the phone. . . .

I grabbed the phone and muttered drowsily, "Hey, what's up?"

"Somebody's outside in my shed." The voice was familiar, but I couldn't place it. It wasn't Emity.

"Wha . . . Who's this?"

"It's Shasta."

Shasta . . . Shasta . . . Shasta was the kind of name one of Barbie's friends would have. Shasta, like soda pop. Something sweet and bubbly.

"Across the street?" the voice whispered with an undertone of urgency. "We went to Walmart . . . and the church. Story time?"

The day came rushing back like a speeding train crashing headlong into the station. I knew why I wasn't in my father's house, why Shasta's name was familiar, why I'd hit my knee on the coffee table.

Our new reality snapped into focus—the white church, story time, Walmart, Barbie stumbling in when Fawn dropped her off. The sibs had barely noticed as she staggered through the living room on the way to her bed to pass out. Jewel was busy in her bouncy seat, and the boys were watching Aunt Lute. She'd picked up a palette and climbed onto a chair, then touched her brush to the wall, slowly drawing a long, brown line on the plaster.

I gasped, and she glanced over her shoulder, teetering as she smiled at me. "Look," she said, and pointed to this morning's paint spatters, now dry. Instead of cleaning the smudges off the walls, she'd turned them into butterflies. "They'll need a vine." Nodding at her own observation, she went back to work.

By bedtime, the living room had morphed into a forest. I'd lain awake looking at it and wondering what Uncle Boone would say. Finally I gave up and let sleep take over. . . .

Pulling the phone from my ear now, I looked at the time. A little after midnight. Why was Shasta calling? "There's somebody where?"

"Outside in my shed. The light's on, and I know this sounds crazy, but I think somebody's in there. I saw a shadow."

Pushing off the sofa, I stood up, crossed the room unsteadily, pulled up the queen-size sheet we'd tacked over the window, and peered out. Other than a single light in the kitchen, Shasta's house was dark. Along the creek, trees were blowing, casting shadows in the green-tinged glow of a lone streetlight. Underneath, a small brown dog sniffed at a pile of leaves, then trotted to the curb, seeming tranquil enough. "I don't see anyone. There's a dog wandering around out there. Maybe that's what you saw."

"I don't think a dog could turn on the lights in my shed," Shasta breathed. "I saw something go by the window."

A shiver ran down my back, raising gooseflesh underneath the old sweats I'd slept in. "Maybe you should call the police."

"Are you kidding? If a unit shows up out here, and I'm wrong, Cody'll have a fit, and, since he's not here, they'll figure out he took the night job. They're really picky about stuff like that. And besides, to be a police officer's wife, you've got to, like, be able to hold it together when he's on patrol and stuff. I'm gonna go out the carport door and sneak around there and see if I hear anything. I just didn't want to do it without somebody knowing what's going on, in case . . . Well, the boys are asleep in here."

My heart did a groggy barrel roll, fanning the sleep fog from my thoughts. I peered across the street again. "I'm coming over there, all right? Turn on your porch light and open your front door for me."

The porch light lit up, and I realized Shasta had wanted me to come over all along. "Hang on." I slipped my feet into my sandals, grabbed my house key, and checked the street once more. The stray dog was still sniffing around the bridge. If anyone was out there, he'd be barking, wouldn't he?

Turning on our porch light, I slipped out the door and whispered into the phone, "Here I come."

Shasta blinked her light. "I see you."

A rapid pulse fluttered in my neck as I ran across the yard. The night air was cool and damp, heavy with a coming storm. Dashing across the street, I smelled flowers, pavement, the fishy scent of the water in the creek. On the bridge, the dog started, turned my way, then tucked its tail and trotted off. Lightning flashed far away on the horizon, illuminating a distant line of thunderheads that would be moving in sometime later in the morning.

"Come on." Shasta's greeting quavered in a whisper as I crossed her porch, and the boards groaned underfoot. "Ssshhh," she breathed, then added an apologetic shrug. "Sorry. I feel like an idiot who's been watching too many horror movies. Like this is Elm Street, and Freddy Krueger's out in the shed."

"I'm not sure this is the best time to bring up *Nightmare on Elm Street*."

We shared a tense laugh that made me think of all the times I'd sneaked across the street to Emity's house when I was supposed to be studying in my room.

Shasta and I stood in her living room, the situation suddenly awkward. It felt strange to be here, visiting her house for the first time in the middle of the night.

"You probably think I'm an idiot, bugging you so late." Threading her arms over her stomach, she shivered, tugging the front of an old T-shirt she must have been sleeping in. "I couldn't think who else to call."

"It's all right. I don't mind." Oddly enough, that was true. It felt good to know that across the street, what had been just another house was now the house of a friend.

"I just didn't want to leave the boys alone in here, in case . . . well, you know, in case there really is someone out there."

Trepidation prickled over my skin and caused my shoulders to do an unintentional shimmy as we crossed the dimly lit living room, then slipped through a doorway into a parlor area furnished with a desk and bookshelves of the kind that come in a box from a discount store and start leaning the first time they're moved. Shasta snagged something from the shadows beside the bookshelf, and when we entered the kitchen, she was carrying a baseball bat.

"I really think we should call the police," I whispered. My heart was pounding like the raven tapping at Poe's chamber door.

Shaking her head, Shasta proceeded through the kitchen, her steps growing lighter, more careful, as if she were afraid someone might be right outside. "If I hear anyone in there, I'll come back, and we'll call nine-one-one."

"All right," I whispered, but this felt like one of those idiotic plans Emity was known for conjuring up. Typically, those plans landed us in trouble.

Shasta tiptoed closer to the door, and I found myself creeping behind her. I leaned over her shoulder as she inched the back curtain aside.

"There's probably no one in . . . Holy mackerel, the door's wide open!" Sweeping the curtain over, she jerked upward so suddenly that we collided. I staggered backward, tripped over a laundry basket, and landed against the washing machine.

Before I could regain my footing or argue, Shasta had opened the door, turned the lock on the burglar bars, flipped on the flood-light, and was headed outside. I followed without giving adequate consideration to whether or not it was a good idea, and by the time I reached the garden shed, Shasta was standing in the triangle of light, staring at the interior, the baseball bat slowly lowering until the barrel rested on the ground beside her.

"There's another one," she whispered, pointing into the shed and taking a stiff sidestep so that I could see. Among the gardening tools, rolled-up hoses, and workbenches that looked like they'd been there forever, a single lightbulb swung just slightly, as if someone had brushed by the pull chain. The shed smelled moist and earthy. Safe scents. Nothing dangerous.

Following the trajectory of Shasta's finger, I took in a bag of potting soil on the shed floor. The center of the bag was dented inward, as if someone had been sitting on it, and in front of the indentation lay a carved bird small enough to fit in the palm of a hand.

Shasta reached in and scooped it up. Her face paled, then hardened. "Someone keeps leaving these. Someone keeps coming here." Her dark eyes narrowed with a mix of fear and anger, her hair swirling around her, blue-black in the moonlight, as she backed several steps into the yard, tossing the bird into the dirt and raising the bat. "Go away! Leave my house alone or I'll call the police, do you hear me? Go away!"

Next door, a light came on.

"Let's go back inside." Touching Shasta's arm, I shivered, my pulse jittery with the sense of someone watching us—someone closer than the woman peering through a gap in the curtain next door. "Come on, all right?"

Shasta yielded to the pressure finally, and we turned off the light and closed the shed, then started toward the house. Inside, with the doors locked, I leaned against the counter and caught my breath as Shasta returned the baseball bat to the front room, then stood looking around the kitchen, as if she were suddenly afraid, even inside the house.

"The sibs found some of those carvings at our house, too," I said finally. "Maybe they're just around here, you know. Maybe someone who lived here before left them, or maybe kids in the neighborhood got them in an Easter-egg hunt, or painted them in school, you know?" The explanations didn't make a great deal of sense, but neither did the idea that inanimate objects could appear in strange places on their own. Anything was preferable to the thought that someone was sneaking around leaving behind little talismans where we would find them.

Shasta rubbed her forehead roughly, then combed her hair from her face, leaning against the refrigerator. "How did that *thing* show up on the floor of my shed?"

"It could have fallen from overhead. From the rafters. Maybe it was tucked up there, and you never noticed it before."

"Did it turn on the lights, too?" It was more a plea for an explanation than a question. Both of us had the sense that someone had been there just before we entered the shed, but neither of us wanted to admit it.

"Maybe you left the lights on earlier today, or even yesterday, and you didn't notice until you looked out there after dark."

Shasta's lips twisted to one side, and she let her arm fall, so that it slapped against her thigh, conveying frustration. "You sound like Cody. That's what he'll say if I bring it up."

"Sorry. It's the reporter in me—always looking for a logical explanation."

"Reporter?" One eyebrow lifted and one descended. "So you're, like, one of those disgustingly pretty girls who's also disgustingly smart and will be showing up on the evening news someday, ridding the world of evil and that kind of thing?"

My throat tightened, and I looked away. I didn't feel like one of those have-it-all girls anymore. I wasn't one. The broadcasting degree and the got-connections job I'd always been so sure would fall right into my lap now seemed a million miles away. "Not so much. It's just what I was going to major in—broadcast journalism." Who knew what would happen to the college plan now that there was no one to pay the bills? Even if the money were there, I couldn't leave the kids and Aunt Lute with Barbie—not the way things had been lately. With Uncle Boone making excuses to avoid us—everything from busy work schedules to out-of-town business trips—there was no one to look after things but me. I had no way of knowing when our situation would change, if ever.

The start of the fall semester was just a few weeks away. The truth, the reality, was that I wouldn't be going to college, or Europe, or anywhere.

"Pppffff!" From the corner of my eye I saw Shasta's hand flutter. "The boys think we've got Hannah Montana living across the street. Wait until they find out you're a future TV star. You'll be, like, their favorite celebrity."

"I'm not a celebrity." I didn't want to be anyone's celebrity. I just wanted to go back to life the way it had been.

Tears stung the back of my nose, the floor blurred, and I felt my mind and body coming in for a crash landing—vulnerable, out of alignment, none of the instruments reading correctly. I blinked hard, pretended to rub my eyes because they were tired. "I should go home." My voice broke. The words trembled.

I heard Shasta cross the floor, felt her touch my shoulder. "Hey, I'm sorry. Sometimes you've just got to ignore me the way you'd ignore one of those pocket poodles that barks too much. I've got a big mouth. I've always had a big mouth. Stay for a cup of cocoa, all right? I won't be able to sleep now, anyway. Cody'll be home in less than an hour, and he can walk you back across the street."

Shasta didn't wait for an answer, but opened a cabinet, took out two cups, and filled them with water. "Ummm . . . by the way. Cody doesn't exactly know about the baby yet, so don't say anything, all right? I'm kind of waiting for a good time to break the news." Frowning, she smoothed her T-shirt. "There's a lot of stress right now, with the house, and the police academy, and bills, and everything. It's complicated, sort of."

She slipped the cups into the microwave, and then stood drumming her fingers on the counter, watching the countdown on the microwave instead of looking at me.

After the cocoa was ready, we moved to the dining room and sat at an antique wooden table with climbing roses painted underneath a layer of varnish. When I complimented the artwork, Shasta ran a hand over it. "We picked the table up at a yard sale right before we moved in. I thought I could make it look a little better with a paint job—spruce it up before Cody's mom comes to visit. Lord knows she's never bought anything at a yard sale in her life."

I took a sip of cocoa, letting it soothe the lump in my throat. "Nothing wrong with recycling. In the pre-Barbie days, my mom loved to bring home flea-market finds, polish them, and use them in the house. She got a thrill when people came for parties and asked who her decorator was."

Shasta rested her chin on her hand. "Really? I never pictured y'all for the flea-market type."

"Barbie's a lot different from my mom."

"I kinda figured." Shasta poked at a marshmallow floating in her cocoa. "It's weird, the whole blended-family thing, huh? My dad left when I was eleven. Took off with the girl from the bank. I've got half sisters I haven't ever met. I don't miss it, really. I just don't, like, think of them as my sisters."

Something in the words struck a chord in me. I'd never thought of the sibs as anything more than a nuisance—a middle-aged whim my father had inflicted upon my life. The chance to move away and leave them behind couldn't come soon enough, as far as I was concerned. Until the past two weeks, I'd never felt a tie to them, never considered that they weren't just Barbie's little toys. They were my brothers and my sister, and they always would be. Whether I liked

Barbie or not, I did love them, and if Barbie wouldn't take care of them, I'd have to find a way to do it.

The possibility scared me to death.

Without intending to, I admitted that to Shasta, and we fell into a conversation about my life, her life, the reasons we'd moved to the neighborhood. Even though it felt good to finally open up and talk to someone, I knew better than to tell her too much. If she found out my father was the man on the Householders commercials, the one who was now frighteningly close to the center of the Rosburten financial scandal, our friendship would probably be over. I wondered if she'd even seen the reports about Rosburten, and if she knew that Householders was connected, but I wasn't about to ask. I settled for explaining that my father had some business troubles, and we'd lost our house. The economy being what it was, that seemed enough of an explanation.

"That's happening a lot of places." Shasta cast a sympathetic look across the table. "So where's your dad now?"

"Trying to work things out." The answer was intentionally vague, emotionless. I didn't know how to feel about my father. I hated him, and yet, I needed him. He'd left us twisting in the wind, but I wanted him to be our Superman again.

"Is he coming back?" Shasta seemed to have read my thoughts.

I shrugged. "I don't know."

Pushing her empty cocoa cup aside, Shasta turned an ear to the sound of a car in the driveway. "That must be hard," she said quietly, and we watched as the glow of headlights pressed through the doorway. I wondered what Shasta's husband would think when he walked in, tired after working two jobs, and saw me sitting in his dining room in the wee hours of the morning.

Standing up, I took my cup, and we walked to the kitchen.

"This was fun." Shasta smiled at me as we stood washing our cocoa cups. "So, we're on for the bookstore, lunch, and story time tomorrow?"

I considered the question. It seemed strange to be making plans after so many days of drifting in limbo, waiting for the pattern of life to suddenly morph into something that made sense. Adopting a schedule here, in this place, seemed like an admission that we were moving to a new kind of normal. On the other hand, the alternative was to continue wandering in denial, and with Barbie in the house, we had enough denial already. "Sure. All right. Come over about eleven, and we'll go to the bookstore first."

"Sounds good," she said. "What about the thing with the volunteer tutors—the info session tomorrow night? Volunteering might work out, if we did it together. I think I'm too chicken to go by myself."

"I'll give it some thought," I said, wondering if I was ready for a kind of normal that included homeless people and adults who couldn't read.

"I think you'd be good at it," Shasta said as we met her husband at the carport door.

"Shas, how come all the lights are . . ." Stumbling off the bottom step, he gave me a surprised look.

"We got caught up visiting," Shasta explained, and we smiled privately at each other, the secrets between us forming the first fragile bonds of a friendship.

I had a feeling she needed it as much as I did.

Chapter 20

Sesay

For seven days, I have stayed in the parking garage five streets from the Broadberry Mission. A whisper in my head tells me it is time to gather my pack and walk on, find a new place. When I close my eyes, I hear the mother in the yellow house shouting, *I'll call the police!* If she sends the police to find me, they'll tell *him*. So I must keep away from all the normal places. I should walk on, go to a new place, but I'm weary of all this coming and going. I like to be here. I like telling my stories at the Summer Kitchen, and getting my doughnut at the Book Basket, and painting with the Indian chief, and listening to Michael at his Crossings Church underneath the bridge.

But the police could be waiting in those places. *He* could be waiting there. If you run away without paying what you owe, *he* will find you. *And you always owe*, he says in my mind. *You people owe me for everything. You show up on a boat, half-starved, half-dead. I take you in, give you work, let you stay on my place. If it weren't for me, you'd all be dead. The police would put you on a boat and send you right back, and then what do you think would happen? If the ocean doesn't get you, the guerrillas will. I'm all you people've got. Your only friend in the world . . .*

Wretched, ungrateful scum . . .

Think you're too good to cut cane?

He talks in my head so often now. More than usual. I cannot stay here in the parking garage any longer, alone with him. And there is no food here. I had a bit in my pack, but it is gone. I must either walk on to a new place or go back to the places I know, so I gather up my pack and say a prayer before I step onto the street.

Does God answer the prayers of a thief, a wretched one like me?

He is always mindful of us, Father Michael promises in my mind. *He has done all these things so that we might look for him, and reach out, and one day find him. He is never far from any of us.*

Does God wish me to find Him?

Or will He find me?

I let my feet carry me into the sunlight, and I hope that Father God walks with me. *He is never far from any of us. Acts 17:27.* I have remembered it from one of Michael's many books.

Michael is surprised when he finds me standing in line at the Glory Wagon. "I was afraid you'd moved on." In his eyes, there is a soft sigh, as a man gives when a child he'd feared for comes walking along the path, safely home. He was not afraid I had walked on. He was afraid I lay dead somewhere. The streets down here are dangerous at night.

I tell him that I thought I might walk on, but I have walked here instead. "Father God led me this way. He is never far from any of us," I say, and Michael smiles, and this pleases me, and then I am worried again. I wonder if the mother of Root and Berry will bring the police and Michael will tell them I have been here.

"MJ from the bookstore came looking for you. She said she hadn't seen you in a week," Michael says. "The kids missed you during story time at the Summer Kitchen, too. Mrs. Kaye and Cass down there asked about you. They've gotten used to seeing you with the regulars."

They've gotten used to seeing you. It's dangerous, I know, but a bright feeling comes with it, like light shining in a window. Someone watches for me to come. No one has ever watched for me before. "Sometimes I go about in different places," I say. "Sometimes it's safer to be in a different place."

Michael only frowns and shakes his head, because he cannot understand the ones like me, the ones who must wander. "You got anything for me?" he asks. "I'm all out of your carvings in the mission store. A volunteer from Grand Prairie bought the whole stock to give to her Sunday-school kids."

"Just these," I say, and take two small Jesus crosses from my pocket and hold them out to him. They are on a green string from the barrier at the edge of a children's playing field in the park. "Only two."

"Only two?" Michael repeats. "After all this time?"

"Are two enough for my meal?" I ask, and look toward the wagon, where the line is growing smaller, like the tail of a snake disappearing through a hole in the wall.

Michael laughs and takes the crosses and admires them. "Of course two are enough."

"Then I have two," I say, but my pocket is heavy, and Michael can see this.

"So you're holding out on me now?"

"I must bring some to the Indian chief. The one who paints behind the Book Basket."

Michael's lips part, and his teeth are straight and white. His teeth are beautiful. "Oh, Terence," he says, and I tell him yes. "He's a good guy. He stayed with us at the mission for a while when he got out of prison. We used to sell his stuff in the mission store. That was years ago, and he's big-time now, of course."

I try to imagine that the Indian chief, with his large building and his many colors of paint, once stood in line at the mission. How can this be? "Have you gone to the Book Basket?" I ask. How long might the police look for me? I wonder. Will they find me if I visit the Indian chief? It troubles me that I have told him I will bring more carvings, but I haven't come. I am a thief, but I do not tell lies.

The voice inside continues to whisper that no place is safe. *You must gather your things and run*, the voice says. But when I am walking, there is no time to carve. There is only the walking. The journey is lonely, and it is more difficult now. My legs are not so young. The new places are difficult to learn.

I have hummingbirds, large ones, and other things in my pocket, and in a new place, there will be no paint for them.

"You should go down and see MJ today," Michael tells me, as if he knows I am walking in my mind. "Everyone's been asking about you. You're missed."

Missed? I think about the good thing to say now. If so many people know of me, *he* will surely hear. "Have men come around?" I ask, and Michael presses his lips together, so that the bottom one sticks out, as if he is a child confused by the middle of a story, so I explain, "New men? A different type of men?"

A bell rings on a church steeple somewhere out of sight, and Michael turns an ear toward the music, but he watches me, as if he would crack me open like a book and know my story. "Some new families, I think, but it's pretty much the same people around there. What kind of men are you worried about?"

"Bad men."

Michael laughs and lays a hand on my shoulder, and I feel the comfort, the holiness of him. It comes out of him and travels into me. "No worse than here." He steers me forward in the food line, then walks away, but he leaves a chain of words behind. "There are no bad men. Just the lost looking to be found, sister."

Near the Glory Wagon, a girl is handing out pieces of blue paper and talking about the reading class at the Summer Kitchen. "There's a beginning session tonight," she tells a woman with two children on her skirts.

I think about the cane fields burning.

Then I think that when the ashes cool and the hunters go away, even the rabbits must return.

Chapter 21

Shasta Reid-Williams

I hadn't ever pictured myself as a teacher. Honestly, I hadn't ever thought of myself as anything but Daddy's girl, and then the girl my daddy didn't want anymore. After that, all I could think about was getting a boyfriend to love me the way my daddy didn't, and then finally being in love with Cody, getting married, and starting my own family to replace the broken one I grew up in. All my life, I was part of somebody else—somebody's girl, because that's what I needed to be. Now I was Benji and Ty's mama and Cody's wife, but it never crossed my mind to wonder what else I could be—until the day we were supposed to start tutoring students in the reading class.

I stood looking at myself in the mirror—just stood there in my bra and panties with fifteen outfits piled on the bed. I'd tried every one of them on and yanked them back off, because I couldn't decide what somebody's reading tutor oughta wear. It didn't matter what I put on. I still looked like a total poser that nobody would want for a reading tutor. A week of training doesn't turn you into someone totally different, like Cinderella heading to the ball. The Literacy Here Group can put you in a class and show you how to use the curriculum materials and teach you ways to relate to adult learners and send you home with videos where other tutors talk about their experiences and their methods. They can try every way in the world to get you ready, but they can't give you confidence in yourself. Deep down, after all the training, you're still the same raggedy girl. Whoever ended up with me for a tutor was gonna take one look and laugh their head off.

The phone rang, and I knew it'd be Tam. She was probably out in the driveway waiting for me. She probably looked like Hannah Montana, headed to Beverly Hills 90210.

I picked up the phone and said, "Yeah, hey, I'm almost ready. I couldn't decide what to wear." As soon as I said it, I wished I wouldn't've. Someone like Tam probably never had trouble deciding what to wear.

She laughed on the other end of the phone. "T-shirt and jeans," she said. "Remember, they said not to show up in anything that looked too intimidating. By intimidating, I think they mean expensive."

"Do you *own* anything that doesn't look expensive?" I asked, and she scoffed.

"Just get dressed, all right? We'd better be going. Barbie took off with Fawn again, so I'm taking the sibs with me, and you know how that usually turns out. Prepare yourself."

"She's gone *again*?" For the past week, Tam's stepmother'd either been passed out in bed, or partying with her friend Fawn. We'd had to drag the kids along to training every single day. Barbie just walked out the door whenever she felt like it, and figured somebody was gonna look after her babies. I couldn't imagine doing that to kids, especially after their daddy'd just left them. When my daddy left, at least I had my mama, and Nana Jo, and Grandpa, and my aunts and uncles.

Even though I felt sorry for Tam's little brothers and Jewel, I really didn't want to mess with the wild bunch tonight, when my nerves were already shot. "You sure you can't, like, plug in a movie and leave them home with Aunt Lute? We'll just be gone a little over two hours." Moving those kids from place to place was like trying to take guppies for a walk. They just darted off whenever they felt like it. They made my boys look like angels.

"I think that would be child endangerment." Tam sounded beat, like it'd been a long day already, and she didn't feel like going anywhere.

"You need to kick your stepmother in the butt and tell her to watch after her kids, or else. She'll do it if she has to."

"I wish." Tam's voice trembled, and I was sorry I'd griped. I was being selfish because I was stressed about the reading class.

"Hey," I said. "Hang in there, all right? It's gonna be okay. This reading class'll give us something else to think about—like the video said, 'a higher calling.'"

Her sigh fluttered like laundry on a clothesline. "I shouldn't be starting this. Everything's so up in the air right now. . . ." Her voice faded at the end, and I knew she was trying to think of how to tell me she didn't want to do the reading tutoring thing at all.

"C'mon, don't whiff on me the first day. Think *free* child care."

She sighed again. "Yeah. Okay. I'll be there in a minute."

She was honking out front almost before I could dig a T-shirt and jeans out of the pile and get them on. I glanced one more time at the impostor in the mirror. She looked fat in the loose T-shirt, and her hair was hanging dark and stringy around her face. If Daddy's little princess or a reading tutor was in there anywhere, I couldn't see her.

By the time we got to the church, Tam'd picked up on the fact that something was wrong with me. In the parking lot, she turned off the car, but neither of us got out to unbuckle the kids. "All right, what's the matter with you?" She looked me over, and I didn't even want to think about what she was seeing.

"I'm just . . . I think I'm panicking. Maybe we should go home and play Candy Land."

Her perfect little nose crinkled on one side. She was probably thinking, *This whole thing was your idea in the first place. You made me come here, for heaven's sake.* "Why?"

A crush of bad feelings fell over me, and I was the used-to-be cheerleader walking down the high school halls, making plans to get married and have babies instead of going to college. The teachers who talked to me about academic competitions and college scholarships looked at me like I was pathetic. Even though I was getting exactly what I wanted, there wasn't any denying that going from being everyone's big hope to everyone's big disappointment hurt. "You know, I just can't quit thinking that on the video they were talking about how hard it is for people to admit they can't read and take the big step of signing up for a class. If I was somebody who finally got my guts up to go to an adult reading class, and I got me for a tutor, I'd be ticked."

Tam unbuckled her seat belt and pulled the keys out of the ignition. "Why?"

"Oh, I just . . ." Insecurity crawled over me like a nest of fire ants. Insecurity bites. Hard. "You're all glammy and sophisticated, and of course, anybody who got you for a reading tutor'd think they just won the lotto. But I'm just . . . me."

"You don't give yourself enough credit." Tam wagged her chin, like she was handing me a lecture. "You're going to be better at it than I am."

I shook my head. I doubted I'd ever be better than Tam at anything. "Everybody doesn't look at me and think I'm somebody, like they do with you. When we go out with the kids, people see you, and they think you're, like, the babysitter or the older sister. They see me, and they think I'm some kind of teenage-welfare-mom-immigrant. You don't know what it's like."

Tam looked at me for what seemed like forever, and then she stared out the window toward the church. "You know what, Shasta? You're right—I don't know what it's like to be you, but I do know what it's like to worry all the time about what everybody else thinks. When my dad . . . went broke, when we lost our house, all of a sudden all those people I was so worried about wouldn't even speak to me anymore. Even friends we went to church with didn't want anything to do with us. For a while, I thought that was God's fault—that He was using those people to punish us. But what I'm starting to realize is that I've been punishing myself. It's not God's fault that I care so much about what everyone thinks. It's mine. I've been letting them define me. I've been giving them all the control, but when you get right down to it, what should matter is whether or not you can live with who you are."

What should matter is whether or not you can live with who you are. Maybe that was the problem all along. Maybe all the things I'd thought I needed to be and do to fix my life—be pretty, be smart, be a cheerleader, a beauty queen, a Choctaw princess, find a boyfriend, get married, start a family of my own—were just patches on a suit of clothes that would never quit getting new holes. Something was always poking through from the inside. Until I quit beating myself up for my daddy leaving, until I quit letting that define me, I'd never be the person I wanted to be. Maybe he didn't leave because there was anything wrong with me. Maybe he left because there was something wrong with him.

"Let's go," Tam said again, and I realized I'd been sitting there with my hand on the door handle. Tam didn't wait for an answer. She opened her door, and I knew I'd better get ready, because in about two-point-five seconds, kids were going to come piling out in all directions.

I climbed out and swung the back door open. "I've got the baby," I said, and Ty gave me a pouty lip as his feet hit the pavement. He and Benji were tired of me making a fuss over the baby all the time. I hoped they'd feel different once "the baby" was their baby sister.

Ty was waving at somebody by the time I made it to the curb with Jewel. "Hieee!" he called. Across the street, the lady with the dreadlocks stood underneath the bottle tree in front of the bookstore. She had on a gray skirt and a raincoat, in spite of the fact that it was hot and dry. She was watching us, still as a statue, her face tipped to one side.

"She's baaa-ack." I gave a chin jerk toward the bookstore. "That lady just creeps me out."

Tam glanced that way while trying to hold four kids with two hands. "Come on, she's harmless." She started around the side of the building toward the nursery rooms in the back, and I followed.

"I don't like the way she watches the kids." I could feel her eyes following us as we passed the memorial garden, where the handicapped guy, Teddy, kept the roses blooming like something on a Miracle-Gro label. "I'm telling you, it's creepy. I hope she's gone when we finish class tonight. It's weird enough in the daytime, but after dark she'd be, like, Zombie Woman."

"You've got a wild imagination." Tam opened the door to the children's building, and Mark and Daniel ran through, knocking the handle against the wall so hard that the entire building vibrated. The boys took off down the hall, ruffling Sunday-school papers tacked to bulletin boards. Tam ran after them, hollering, "Wait a minute, you two. Mark! Stop it! Dan . . . Mark! Out of the kitchen, now!" By the time we handed the baby over in the nursery, Tam's little brothers had tried to break into a pack of Little Debbies, and three teenage helpers were out in the hall working to chase them down.

"Oh, no, you don't!" The girl we'd met before, Cass, caught Daniel and grabbed the Little Debbie box away. "These are for after our project and story time. If you guys wanna have snacks, you can just haul yourselves into the room and sit down at a table like you're supposed to."

Benji and Ty scooted into the room, and Tam's little brothers followed with major pouty lips. Tam caught a breath and looked at the ceiling. "Guess they've got it under control." She headed for the door like she couldn't get outta there fast enough.

My stomach knotted up again on the way to the fellowship hall, where the lights were on, and people were already gathering. I came in behind Tam, got my name badge, and stood there feeling like a fake. During the introductions, it didn't take me long to figure out that only a few of the mentors—four older ladies who'd gone through the training with Tam and me—were from the neighborhood. The rest were college kids bused over from SMU to get credit in some class. They were all in teaching school, which meant they already had way more training than us. When we huddled up to get last-minute directions, I felt like the odd man out. Tam fit right in, and the college guys couldn't stop flirting with her long enough to listen to what the class leader was saying.

While we were getting our marching orders in the front corner of the room, the students were coming in the back. They looked just as uncomfortable as I was. To make things worse, when I turned around, there was my grouchy next-door neighbor—the one who gave us dirty looks out the window—sitting at one of the tables. She turned her nose up, like she didn't see me heading to the back of the room to sit with the tutors. She probably didn't want me in her read-ing class any more than she wanted me living next door to her.

My palms started sweating during the greetings and intros. Pastor Al welcomed everyone to the church; Mrs. Kaye invited the students and the mentors to stop by the Summer Kitchen for lunch anytime, and then she said hi to some of the people she already knew. "And I see a few Summer Kitchen regulars here, too," she said. "Welcome." She waved at Tam and me as *regulars*, and the college kids checked us out, and I wanted to sink down through my seat and run like creek water.

Finally, Mrs. Kaye turned the class over to the literacy lady, and the lesson started. I couldn't focus on it. I couldn't think of anything but all the college kids sitting there, knowing I was a *regular* at the free-lunch café.

A few of the people at the tables were café regulars, too. It'd never crossed my mind that, while I was listening to story time with Benji and Ty, I might be sitting next to somebody, a grown person, who couldn't go home and read that same book to their own kids. Even after watching all the Literacy Here training videos, it didn't seem real. I wouldn't've thought there would be so many people like that, so close by. I guess when you've always known how to do something—like pick up a book and read it—it seems automatic that everybody else can, too. This was America, after all. How did anybody go through grade school and not come out knowing how to read?

I might not of made it to college, and every teacher in Hugo High School might of thought I turned out to be just another small-town loser, but at least I could read. Maybe I could handle this tutor-ing thing, after all. The lesson on the whiteboard up front was really simple—phonetic decoding, word patterns, and sight words you see every day on signs and restaurant menus. I was already teaching Benji that stuff.

I could do this. I really could.

I scanned the room, looking over each of the students, trying to picture what this person or that person would think if they got me for a tutor. My next-door neighbor'd probably laugh in my face. What was she doing here, anyway? She had to be at least seventy. How did a person get to be seventy, buy a house, drive a car, and do all the normal things without reading?

In the seat next to her, a Mexican guy, maybe about forty, was nodding and smiling. His clothes were dirty from work, his jeans green with a plaster of grass trimmings and clingy Bermuda seeds. The man next to him was young, maybe even a teenager, but they knew each other. Every so often, the younger guy pointed to the board and explained something to the older guy, and they both nodded. A dark-haired woman next to them slapped the younger man on the arm once, and put a finger to her lips. They were a family, I guessed. A whole family, at reading class together. The woman raised her hand and asked a question in Spanish. The teacher rattled off an answer as quick as you please, like she spoke Spanish every day.

The knot shimmied in my stomach. I couldn't speak two cents' worth of Spanish. If they tried to hook me up with somebody who didn't know much English, I'd look like a doofus.

The teacher finished answering, and most of the college kids, including Tam, laughed like they understood what she was saying. I felt like an idiot. An idiot who should of paid more attention in high school Spanish.

A couple African-American ladies on the left side of the room gave the Spanish talk a sneer and leaned back in their chairs, crossing their arms and sending tired looks toward the clock, like they weren't sure they belonged here, either. At least one of them had four kids. I'd watched her cross the parking lot after we left the children's building. The kids were quiet and shy, and they looked like their clothes hadn't been washed in a week. If my Nana Jo'd been there, she would of eagle-eyed the lady and whispered behind her hand, *It's one thing for folks to be poor, but soap and water don't cost much.*

The first thing you learn, growing up Choctaw, is that family's important. Nana Jo and Mama always looked down their noses at the hillbilly types who spent their money on beer, cigarettes, and weed, and went around town with their kids dirty and half-dressed. The women in my family believed in getting an education and being able to take care of yourself and your kids. If Mama'd been sitting in my seat right now, she would of turned her nose up at the people in these chairs, especially the moms. Maybe, when Mama came, if I could tell her I'd been tutoring people to read, she'd be impressed. . . .

The lecture part of the class ended, and Pastor Al, Mrs. Kaye, and the instructor, Lynne Barnes, started calling out students' names and pairing them up with instructors. After three pairs, they called Elsie Lowell, and my grouchy next-door neighbor raised her hand. Then, of course, Mrs. Kaye pointed to me and motioned. I dragged myself out of my chair, feeling two inches high. They couldn't give me somebody young and friendly, oh, no. I had to get the lady who shot dirty looks out the window whenever my kids made noise in the yard. "You two live next door to each other," Mrs. Kaye said, and smiled at my neighbor as I slid into the seat. "Elsie, did you know that?"

Elsie answered her with a constipated grunt.

Mrs. Kaye turned to me like she didn't even notice, and went right on. "Elsie used to come over and help with the Summer Kitchen when we were over on Red Bird. Did you know we started our little café in the house you're living in now? I didn't realize that until I looked at the address on your volunteer sheet. My uncle Poppy built your house. He lived there all his life. Sometime when you've got a minute, I'll tell you more about the house, if you like."

"That'd be great," I said. "When we bought it, they said they didn't have any background on its history."

Mrs. Kaye's eyebrows shot up and her chin pulled back into her neck. "Bought it? I thought those Householders homes were rentals." The strange look in her eye lifted me in my chair, made me lean closer to her, thinking she was about to say something really important. Then she didn't say anything.

Elsie grunted and turned her face toward the door, like she wanted to get up and head out.

"Well, it's a special kind of loan deal, but it's ours," I said. "Cody— my husband—knows more about that stuff than I do. I was busy trying to corral the boys when the guy was explaining everything." The picture of Benji and Ty running like wild men through the cubicles of the Householders office flashed through my mind. The loan guys couldn't get us out of there fast enough, which was probably why now Cody didn't really understand the paperwork, either. "Householders made it all real easy, though."

Elsie threaded her arms over her chest and muttered something that sounded like, "Hmph, those yellow houses."

Mrs. Kaye leaned across the table to pat Elsie's hand. "I'm glad you decided to come, Elsie. You know, we could use your help here during lunches anytime. Just because the Summer Kitchen isn't right next door anymore doesn't mean we wouldn't love to have you."

Elsie jerked her chin slightly. "Been busy lately."

I glanced sideways at her. As far as I could tell, Elsie sat in her house all day with the television going.

Mrs. Kaye smiled and slid a folder across the desk. "Oh, well, of course, but I want you to know you're always welcome. When you've lost a spouse, it's important to get out and spend time around people—you know, try something new, like this class."

"Heard you needed people." Elsie straightened in her seat. "Guess I can come fill a chair."

"We're glad you did."

I watched Mrs. Kaye walk away and thought, *Seriously, she has to be the nicest person in the world.* Maybe I wasn't cut out for tutoring, because the way Elsie acted irked me. I'd pictured getting paired up with somebody who was grateful I was there. Who actually *wanted* help. Instead, I got Elsie.

We sat there for a minute, watching while the rest of the folders were handed out, and tutor-student pairs took out the books and started working in them.

"Guess we oughta do somethin'." Elsie snorted so hard that nose hairs puffed out and then sucked back in. There were pasty rings of makeup around her eyes, two shades darker than her skin, like she'd bought it years before, when she actually got out of the house for more than just the daily trip to the mailbox.

"Guess so." I opened the folder and pages flew everywhere. I scrambled around, clumsily trying to catch them, but they fell off and slid under three different tables. I ended up crawling around everyone's feet, gathering them all back up.

When I put everything back on the table, Elsie snatched the stack out of my hand. "It's all catawampus now."

"Just a minute. I'll fix it." *I will be nice. I will be nice. . . .* I tried to picture how good it would feel to tell Mama I was a reading tutor.

"I know how to read. You think I can't tell number one from

number two?" Holding the papers close to her Coke-bottle glasses, Elsie checked the page numbers one at a time.

"Oh, okay."

"Just wasn't ever very good at it. Didn't like it much. Thought it was a waste of time."

Be nice, be nice, be nice. "Gosh, I love to read. My mama always said I was born making up stories."

"Thin line between makin' up stories and bein' a liar, my pap always said. I never had much time for books, anyhow. Had little brothers and sisters to tend. Then I had kids of my own. Nine."

"Nine kids?" I said it louder than I meant to, and the college girl mentoring next to us glanced my way. I mouthed, *Sorry*, then leaned closer to Elsie. "You had nine kids?" I whispered. So far, I hadn't seen anyone come to visit Elsie's house. Not even one person since we'd moved in.

Elsie took a long look down her nose at me and plunked the papers onto the desk. "Started early," she said, and I felt like, somehow, she was pointing a finger at me. "Once you're somebody's mama, you ain't got time to do what you want to do. You have a bunch of kids, you're tied down fer life. They just grow up and move off and say you never did enough for 'em. Used to be we gals didn't know any better, but you young gals, you can have your whole life, then have kids, if you got half a brain."

My mouth popped open, and I clamped it shut before something snippy fell out. Our table was right next to the exit, and for a millisecond, I pictured myself walking out the door. It was bad enough that I had to live next to this lady—I didn't have to come here and take lip off her, too.

But I didn't want to be a big failure at this. I didn't want to fail at one more thing.

Pulling in a deep breath, I straightened the papers and said, "I'm ready to start when you are."

She grunted and sat back in the chair with her arms crossed, like she wasn't gonna touch the papers, but I could if I wanted to.

"Then I guess we're ready," I said.

The door opened beside us, and I heard someone come in, and the rustle of clothes passing by. The person stopped by the back corner of our table.

I looked up, and the dreadlocks lady was standing there, leaning against the wall.

Watching.

Chapter 22

Tam Lambert

The third day of reading class was taking on the same strange framework as the first and the second. Shasta was trying to work with Elsie, Elsie was being obstinate, and the homeless woman was back again. As usual, she'd come in the door after the lesson had started and was standing against the wall by Shasta's table. In the same spot again today. When the lesson was over, Shasta would undoubtedly have a few choice words to say about tonight's foray into literacy. So far, the class wasn't what we'd expected.

My client, Demarla, was probably not even thirty, had four children ranging from fifteen to eight, and was in the literacy class because pursuing her GED was a condition of her probation. She wasn't convinced she had to get the GED, apparently, just pursue it.

"This place nasty," she complained, waving a hand vaguely toward the room, her brown eyes pale against a thick frame of iridescent blue eyeliner. "Let homeless people stand around in here, 'n' ching chongs, 'n' wetbacks, 'n' all that. If they're gonna keep doin' that, I ain't stayin'. Anyway, I can read. 'The cat run under the tree.' See? What I care 'bout all that for? That ain't my cat. He come runnin' up some tree in my neighborhood, he bes' look out. Somebody gonna grab a po-lice special and pop his butt. Them stray cats carry rabies 'n' all that mess, scream all night long outside the window.

Sound like somebody gettin' kilt out there. You probably don't got no stray cat outside your window. Where you live, anyway?"

"Just down the street," I answered, thinking, *Maybe literacy mentoring isn't for me.* Putting your time into someone who didn't want it was frustrating. Even though the tutor training materials had warned that adult students often had a difficult time adjusting to a classroom setting, it was difficult to remain upbeat and encouraging when you were faced with it in reality.

"Yeah, my butt, up the street. They brung you over here from the college, just like the resta' these little rich kids, so you can go sit in yo' big church on Sundey and say, 'I done taught some dumb gal to read. Ain't I good?'"

Whatever, I thought. I was tempted to grab my things and tell Demarla what she could do with the book and her GED, if she ever got it. If it hadn't been for Shasta, and the fact that our visits to the Summer Kitchen and the night literacy class were a chance to get all the kids out of the house at once and give Aunt Lute some peace, I would have already whiffed on the reading class.

I smacked my pencil down on the table. "You know what? I live about a block from here. Do you want to do the lesson or not?" After days of taking care of the kids while Barbie slept and partied, and Aunt Lute wandered the house in her own little world, I was at the breaking point where patience was concerned. It was starting to look like I was going to end up raising my siblings, and I had no clue what to do next. I wanted to lash out at somebody, and Demarla was a convenient target.

Jerking back, she pulled her chin into her neck. "Well, listen at you. You ain't such a sweet little thang after all."

I felt anything but *sweet* at the moment. "Do you want to do the lesson or not?" All of a sudden, I felt myself tearing up. I absolutely refused to lose it in front of Demarla.

"What'za matta wit' you?"

I closed my eyes, rubbed my forehead, opened my eyes again. "Nothing. I just have a headache." Lately, life was one constant headache. This class was supposed to be a chance to get away from all that.

The homeless woman was watching me from her spot by the wall. Our gazes met, and she tipped her head to one side, her cataract-clouded eyes thoughtful; then she turned away again, focusing on Shasta and Elsie, who were attempting to read a recipe off a cake box.

"I gotta do the lesson." Demarla sagged over the book, her elbows braced on the table. "I gotta work on my GED if I wanna keep my kids. That's what the judge say."

A lump formed in my chest. What if Barbie continued down the path she was on? What if I ended up in some court, trying to convince a judge to give me custody of the sibs? What if they ended up with no one but me?

I wasn't ready for that. I had no way to make a living, no permanent place to stay. I wanted a life of my own. . . .

"I ain't gonna let my kids end up in them foster homes again. Them people was mean to my babies," Demarla muttered.

I pictured the sibs in foster care with strangers who might be mean to them. No matter what, I couldn't let that happen.

My mind went into a tailspin, and for a moment I couldn't focus on anything. Demarla's voice seemed far away. "We gonna do the lesson thang? Hey? We gonna do this?"

I tried to shake off the cacophony of thought, to get focused. I was vaguely aware of Demarla leaning over, fishing something from her purse, and setting it on the table. "That bookstore lady send this book home with my kids yes'aday. I wanna know what it say. I tell them the wrong word, they gonna end up dumb as their mama." She turned to me, and for an instant, I felt a connection. "We read this book?"

Clearing my throat, I opened the reading folder. "Let's do the lesson on word decoding first. It'll help."

Demarla's lips twisted into a smirk-smile that, for once, wasn't unfriendly. "We gonna read my kids' book after?"

"Sure," I said.

"It's Jonah and the whale. I can figure that much."

"Yes, it is."

"Well, let's *decode* that crap about the cat run up the tree, then, if that's what we gotta do. Dumb cat." Demarla crossed her arms, and I chuckled. "Your headache get better?"

"Some," I said, and we started on the lesson. By the time class was over, we'd gone through *Jonah and the Whale* enough times that Demarla could read it with her kids.

As soon as the room began clearing out, Shasta found her way to my table. Her face was lined with concern, and she was chewing a fingernail. "The voodoo lady was here again. Did you see her? You saw her, right? She just stands there holding her stupid backpack, watching. I'm telling you, it's spooky. And then, as soon as we finish the lesson and close the book, she walks out the door. Not a word to anybody. Tell me you saw her, because otherwise I'll think I'm going nuts. It's just . . . weird. She's *so* weird."

"I saw her. I don't think she means any harm." Right now, even Shasta's upset couldn't dampen my enthusiasm. I'd arrived thinking that either Demarla or I would finally give it up and walk out today, but instead, we'd read *Jonah and the Whale*.

"Nobody says a word to her; have you noticed that? Not Mrs. Kaye, or the teacher, or Pastor Al. It's like she isn't even here." Shasta's gaze darted around the room, where students and other tutors were filing out. The college kids were in the usual hurry to get back to their own neighborhood, and the clients in a rush to gather kids from the nursery and walk home or catch the bus.

"They need to, like, tell her to move on or something, you know?" Shasta complained. "How're we supposed to do anything with some creepy lady hanging over our shoulders all the time? She makes me so nervous I can't even think about the lesson."

For once, I wasn't ready for Shasta's level of drama. I wanted to enjoy the leftover feelings of success instead of dealing with yet another problem. "Maybe she's just a little . . . I don't know, off or something. Maybe Pastor Al figures that if she watches for a while, she'll get interested in joining a class. Maybe that's her spot." I shrugged vaguely in the direction of the door. "When my grandfather was in the nursing home, there was a patient with dementia who sat in the same chair for hours every day. He'd get up and walk to the door, then go sit back down, then walk to the door, then sit back down. Always in the same chair. If somebody else sat in the chair, it really set him off."

Shasta's eyes widened as we went out the door. "Well, that's comforting. Thanks a lot."

I hip-butted her as we started down the sidewalk to the children's building. "You're welcome. Hey, just think, you're such a good tutor, they're standing in line."

"Pppffff!" Shasta rolled her eyes. "Right."

"You *are* good at it. It suits you. I think you're a natural-born teacher. You ought to look into it—you know, take some college classes toward a degree. You'd be great."

Shasta's lips twisted contemplatively, and her dark eyes glittered in the glow of a streetlamp beside the memory garden. "Yeah, right." She slid her hand over her stomach, and the smile faded.

As we gathered up the kids and headed home, I considered the mess Shasta was in. I'd thought Barbie's serial pregnancies were crazy, but at the time, Barbie had all the resources in the world to support the sibs financially and help raise them. Shasta had almost nothing— no one but herself and Cody, who was working at least fourteen hours a day to pay the bills. I wasn't much on finances myself—I'd never had to be—but my father had impressed upon me that life steps needed to be taken in the right order. Education. Job. Marriage. Savings plan. House.

Raising a family was difficult under the best of circumstances. . . .

Then again, the best of circumstances hadn't kept my parents together, or prevented my father and Barbie from making a mess of everything. The problems on this side of town weren't so different from problems on the other side; it just didn't make news when a family collapsed around here.

Shasta looked solemn as we pulled into her driveway. She sagged forward in the passenger seat after having been abnormally silent on the way home. In the back, the kids were yawning in their seats, but Shasta lingered for a moment before pulling the door handle and sliding wearily to her feet. Her purse spilled into the floorboard, and while she gathered the contents, I exited the car and helped Benjamin and Tyler climb out the back. Tyler wrapped himself around me, and I carried him to the carport door instead of handing him over to his mom. Shasta let the boys in and kicked her shoes off inside the door, then walked to the edge of the carport with me in her stocking feet.

"You haven't told Cody about the baby yet, huh?" I asked, guessing at the reason for her sudden change of mood. I was probably sticking my nose in where it didn't belong. Our friendship was still fragile, like a new bloom, filled with potential yet delicate.

She pushed her hands into her jeans pockets and kicked a pebble off the cement, keeping her voice hushed, as if she were afraid the boys could hear through the wall. "He's just so tired when he comes home every night, and between the truck and the new house and the credit cards, we've got so many bills . . . well . . . it's just that . . . Cody got it in his head that he didn't want another baby, you know, so it's a touchy subject. As soon as he can take a couple days off, he wants to go get a vasectomy—like, no matter what I say about it, or how I feel, and I just . . . panicked. I know it was stupid. It wasn't a good time, but I kept thinking, I want my baby girl. I always pictured that I'd have a daughter, and we'd be close and share secrets, and talk about hair and makeup and stuff. When Cody got so determined, I thought, If this is my only chance, I'm taking it, and so I got pregnant. I guess I told myself that wasn't any worse than him deciding we weren't gonna have any more kids, no matter what I said."

"It is different." I couldn't help thinking about my dad and Barbie, and the last two in vitros, which she had arranged largely on her own. He didn't want more kids. He didn't even really want the twins. It was all about what Barbie decided she needed, what she wanted. It wasn't about the children and what was best for them. "Kids deserve to have two parents who want them."

Shasta's eyes met mine, looked deep inside, and I knew she understood. "I think about that." Her voice was hoarse, ragged. "I'm afraid if Cody doesn't want this baby . . . if he blames the baby for what I did . . . I'd never want that for my kids, you know?"

I did know. I understood.

Something collided with the inside of the car windshield, then slid down and landed on the dash. A McDonald's toy. The Four wouldn't last much longer before mass destruction set in. They were tired. They needed baths, a story, and bedtime before things got out of hand. Across the street, the house was dark, except for the television flickering in the living room. Aunt Lute was probably already in bed, sound asleep with her earplugs in, as usual. For whatever reason, she always turned off the lights but left the TV playing a DVD.

Shasta reached out and hugged me. We clung to each other in the dim carport light until finally something heavier hit the car window. "You better go," she whispered. "Tomorrow's Saturday. No lunch at the Summer Kitchen. Want to take the kids down to the bookstore?"

"Sure. See you in the morning."

We parted ways, and I backed the Escalade across the street and into our driveway. The sibs were surprisingly docile getting out of the car and entering the house through the garage door. They followed me through the kitchen, no pushing or shoving as we threaded our way around fallen toys and stacks of boxes. On the other side of the wall, a DVD was playing on the TV, the sound blaring so loudly it was hard to believe Aunt Lute could be asleep, even in the back bedroom with earplugs in. As we rounded the corner into the dining room, the boys put their hands over their ears and Jewel twisted in my arms, trying to locate the source of the noise.

Through the doorway, I could see Barbie on the sofa—home early, for a change. Actually sitting up, rather than splayed across the sofa cushions, sleeping off her latest trip to the clubs on Lower Greenville with Fawn. She was wearing a slinky black minidress, skin-tight, but in an upscale way. Her shoes and purse lay scattered on the floor beside her, as if she'd dropped them in a hurry.

Daniel's foot caught one of the dining chairs, producing a loud scraping noise, audible even over the TV. Barbie's head snapped toward us, and before we'd crossed the threshold, she was through the living room, yanking Jewel out of my arms. Her eyes were wide, circled with black, her cheeks stained with tinted tears.

Fear shot through me, whipping the relaxed weariness of the evening into an ominous rush of adrenaline. "Barbara, what's the matter?"

Eyes flaring, she grabbed the boys with clumsy, aggressive movements, pulling them by their arms or their shirts, dragging them, stumbling, into the living room and backing them against the sofa. "You can't just *take* them," she growled, her voice low, guttural, unfocused, so that it was hard to tell whether she was talking to me, or just babbling incoherently. I could smell alcohol from across the room. "You can't just *go*."

"Barbara, what are you talking about? What's the matter? Is Aunt Lute all right?" Sidestepping, I checked the hall. The bedroom door was closed, the light turned off. Had Aunt Lute locked herself in her room to get away from Barbie?

On the sofa, the sibs sat wide-eyed, unmoving, their faces pinched, slowly turning pale. Landon's eyes welled, small blue pools reflecting the colored light of the TV.

"You guys go on back to your bedroom." I took a step toward Barbie, and she moved in front of me, spinning around so fast that Jewel's torso whipped outward, then back in, colliding with Barbie's breast. The baby's lips puckered and trembled. She turned a frightened expression toward me.

"Barbara, you're scaring her." I reached for Jewel, but Barbie yanked her away, twisting so that her shoulder was between the baby and me. "Stop it!" I yelled. "What's wrong with you?"

Jewel whimpered, and Barbie faced me with her teeth clenched and her eyes narrow slits under strings of hair that had lost their curl during another evening out. "You can't just *take off* with my *kids*!" she screamed. "You can't just *take off* with them!"

I stepped back, blindsided. "Wha . . . take off . . . what are you talking about? We went down to the church on the corner."

Barbie's fist shot toward me, the index finger pointed, stabbing my purse. "I called. I called over and over and over. No one answered. No one picked up." Her voice rose to a shriek, eclipsing the TV, piercing the air with sharp arrows of sound. On the sofa, the boys scooted backward, wedged themselves against the cushions. Landon pushed closer to Mark, and Mark wrapped slim arms around his brothers, a colored paper fish from craft time still clutched in his hand.

I blinked, trying to find a reality in which Barbie made sense. For weeks now, she'd been walking through the house in a fog, acting as if the kids didn't exist, as if they were anyone's responsibility but hers. Now she was accusing me of taking them without permission? Anger rose in me, boiled, spewed over, hot and bitter.

Daniel slid off the sofa and ran past Barbie, collided with me and held on, his arms locked around my waist. Barbie snatched at his T-shirt, and I moved him away. "Stop it, Barbie. Leave him alone!"

"They're mine. They're my kids!" She lunged at Daniel again, and my arm came up out of reflex, knocking her off balance so that she stumbled backward and collided with the coffee table. For a brief, horrifying moment, she was spinning sideways, falling, the baby's arms flailing in the air, her head snapping backward, then hitting Barbie's chest. Barbie gasped, caught herself on the sofa arm, stopped her fall, and clung to Jewel.

The baby wailed.

My heart hitched in my chest. "Stop it! Cut it out!" The words bounced around the room, crashing against objects like a bird trapped indoors, madly seeking escape. Everything, all the feelings I'd been tucking in silent corners, rushed to the surface. I wanted to hurt someone, anyone—Barbie, my father, my mother. "You're right, Barbie. They *are* your kids. *You're* their *mother*. Why don't you try taking care of them for a change? Why don't you get out of bed and stop feeling sorry for yourself and stop running off with Fawn and guzzling mixed drinks? Why don't you stop waiting for my dad to come back and fix things? Maybe he isn't coming—did you ever think of that?" Even as I said the words, part of me rebelled against them. Of course he would return. He had to. "Maybe you need to stop waiting and start figuring out how to take care of yourself . . . and them. You're their *mom*. Act like it."

"Shut up!" Barbie pushed off the sofa, backhanded the air in a quick, violent motion that caused Mark and Landon to shy away. They skittered to the end of the sofa, climbed over, and ran toward the hall. I saw Aunt Lute coming out of the darkness, pink chiffon floating like the veils of a ghost. Stopping at the edge of the light, she opened her robe and wrapped Landon inside. Mark clung to her sleeve. Through the diaphanous pink curtain, Landon's wide, fearful eyes tracked Barbie's flailing hand.

Jewel wailed louder, arched her body, and fell backward with a quick jerk that made me jump toward her, arms outstretched. Barbie caught the baby and wrapped her tightly, smothering the cries. "Don't you *touch* her," she hissed, twisting away. "You can't take my kids. I won't let you take my kids."

I clenched a fist, squeezed until the fingernails bit into my skin. My mind was racing out of control, running toward something that seemed too ominous to confront, especially tonight. The truth was that no matter how much I tried to normalize our situation by making friends with the neighbors, or volunteering at the church, or taking the kids to story hour, it was all a farce. We couldn't keep living like this. We couldn't stay in this borrowed house, with Barbie spending her nights on Lower Greenville, and Aunt Lute wandering in the backyard, and our supply of cash dwindling.

Barbie's eyes narrowed, and she swayed on her feet again. "You're trying to turn them against me. You and . . . and . . . her. I won't let anyone take them away. I know what that's like. I know how it feels to have someone . . . to have someone take your baby and. . . ." The sentence faded without an ending. I stood silent, waiting for more, wondering at the words. I knew almost nothing about Barbie's history. I had no means of understanding her, because she was a virtual stranger. I'd never tried to go beneath the surface. I knew my father had met her at a charity fashion show. He was the celebrity host; she was modeling swimsuits. When he brought her home, I told him he looked like a poster boy for midlife crisis. I said I couldn't wait to be old enough to move out, and as soon as I was, I'd go to a college as far away as possible. It never occurred to me to wonder if that hurt him, to wonder if he was lonely and if Barbie filled some need in him. I never cared whether the two of them loved each other, or why Barbie was willing to endure endless medical procedures and daily hormone shots to fill the house with kids. I thought it was idiotic, and I couldn't wait to leave it all behind.

Now, for just a moment, I saw something real in her. Desperation, need, pain, fear. Then anger, like clouds rushing over, covering everything.

"Don't you *ever* take them anywhere again."

"If you're here to watch them, I won't." My wild rush of emotions ebbed away, draining out to sea like a high tide, depositing me against the doorframe, clinging to Daniel, feeling beaten. A part of me wanted gratitude for having stepped up to the plate these past weeks. A part of me felt I deserved it. "But I'm not going to sit here and be your babysitter while you go out and party with Fawn, and come home wasted, and sleep it off."

"Fawn's the only friend I have left." Barbie's cheeks flamed red. Tiny beads of saliva dotted her lips and chin, and she swiped the back of a hand clumsily across her mouth, wiping them away, drawing leftover lipstick sideways onto her cheek.

"Fawn isn't your friend. If Fawn were your friend, she'd care whether you were looking after the kids. She'd care whether you were looking after yourself. She wouldn't be taking you out spending money when the bank account is low enough already. If Fawn were your friend, she'd be helping instead of hurting."

Barbie bounced the baby, awkwardly trying to quiet her. "You think you're right about everything. You think you're so smart. He left because of you. He left because he couldn't stand to tell you he'd lost the money, and he couldn't pay for that stupid college, and the stupid car you begged for, and your clothes, and all the things you want. You think that piddly little golf scholarship was going to pay for all that? Huh? Not even close. He left because *you* wanted too much. He left because of *you*."

I stepped back, momentarily stunned, then slowly feeling the sting of reality. Barbie was right, and not just about herself; she was right about me. My life had been all about the labels, all about having the right things and being seen in the right places. I never considered what my father did to acquire the money that provided the comforts. I just took them for granted. After he married Barbie, I'd made it clear that he couldn't possibly do enough to make it up to me. I'd taken all the gifts meant to buy my love, and cut the strings with such determination that, when life crashed down around us, there were no family ties left to bind.

Chapter 23

Sesay

The lines in the book draw a picture. Not a picture with colors and animals and houses you can see, but if someone should tell you what the line picture means, and you tuck the line picture into your memory, then when you see the line picture again, your mind will say, *This is a tree,* and you can see the tree behind your eyes. Mrs. Kaye has given me the book from the reading class, and in it, I can see *cat*, and *tree*, and *road*, and *sky*, and *bird*, and many others. I look at the lines, with their strange curves and crosses, and they are not only lines. They are pictures.

Some of them I knew. I understand this now. I have learned many of these lines all my life, but I did not know this. *Book*, I have seen on the sign at the Book Basket, *stop*, *speed*, *hospital*, *police*, *cleaners*, *restaurant*, *pharmacy*, *gas*. You will know these, because you have seen them many times. People have said them to you and pointed at them as long as you can remember. Your mind understands the line pictures, but you do not know this until someone shows you. I can read, after all, and I am learning more. I am learning faster than Elsie. For Elsie, the letters move on the page when she looks at them. *The letters won't be still*, she says, and she struggles with the words over and over and over again. Sometimes I wish to reach out and turn the page, and say, *Move along. I need to see more!*

But I must stand and wait and be silent. Mrs. Kaye smiles at me and tells me she would teach me, if I like. She points to an empty table, but to be in the class, I must write my name on the paper, the *form*, they call it. I am afraid of the paper. "No," I say, "I can watch here."

The mother of Root and Berry is patient. She smiles at Elsie even when the word pictures move around. "All right, let's decode it," she says. "Dol-lar. Dollar. It's not such a long word when you break it down."

Elsie does not smile in return. Elsie is an unhappy woman. This you can see in her face. Long lines travel downward from her mouth, and deep creases are like roads on her forehead, reaching to the places she has been. She has frowned for many, many years.

I watch her and think, *This woman owns a fine home, and a car, and flowers in her yard, and often I smell wonderful food cooking in her kitchen. What has she to be sad about?*

But I, of all people, know that sadness is an easy path to walk, once you set your foot on it. It travels down, and down, and down, and people tramp it with their possessions on their backs like a pack, the weight pushing them along faster and faster and faster, until they cannot stop. They cannot look up. They do not know that the secret is to lay down the pack, turn off the path, and go a better way.

Father God says, "Do not worry," Michael tells the people under the bridge. *"Look at the birds of the air, for they neither sow nor reap nor gather into barns; yet your heavenly Father feeds them. Are you not of more value than they?"*

I remember these words from my childhood, when I sat with Grandfather in the mission church, filled with people, the heat crowding in around us. *Is not life more than food and the body more than clothing?* When those words were spoken at the mission church, the people lifted their hands and cheered, and then they sang. Even as they went away, carrying on their heads heavy pots of water dipped from the river, they sang.

In my memory, they are the happiest people, even though the paths in that place are difficult to walk. There is no choice for them but to trust in Father God. They know no other way. They know nothing other than to be happy for breath in their bodies and food in a bowl and a place for a family to sleep, and wake, and keep together. They do not expect even these things, and so each is a gift.

I know this word, too, *gift*. I have watched Elsie try to read it in a string with other words. *I see a birthday gift.* If I can find a place with a light tonight, I will look at these words again, to be certain I remember them. I must not go to the shed behind Root and Berry's house again, and now the shed at the church is locked at night. Someone came in and stole a hoe, and a garden hose, and the Christmas lights. It was not me, but now Pastor Al checks the shed each night before he leaves, to be certain the door is locked. If I go to the reading class, it is too late to enter the mission. For a bed, you must arrive before supper and wait in the line. If you are late, the beds are full.

I have been sleeping behind the Book Basket. I have found a safe place there. MJ and the Indian chief do not know this. I am very clever at hiding my place so no one can find it.

The lights are on in the Indian chief's painting place when I leave the church with my book of line pictures to read. I am thinking about the string of line pictures, *I see a birthday gift*. I am trying to remember how the lines look, and I am so lost in it that at first I do not see the Indian chief standing outside, smoking a cigarette.

He crushes the cigarette and waves as I come closer, and I am aware of him there in the shadows. His hair is unbound again today, falling long and dark around his shoulders.

"I've been looking for you," he tells me.

"You were gone away," I say. For five days since I have come back to the Summer Kitchen, I have been watching his part of the building, but the doors have been closed and the lights dark. "I have some things."

"Some things you carved?" His eyes lift, and he smiles, as if he is pleased. This feels strange to me. I am accustomed to sad eyes, eyes that pity me. But the Indian chief looks at me with interest.

This concerns me, and I think, *Perhaps I should walk on, after all. It is not good to have others know your story. It is dangerous.*

"Come on in." The Indian chief—Terence, his name comes to me—opens the door, and the light spills onto the gravel. "I've been out of town for a few days. I've got to head out tomorrow for another art show, so I'm working late tonight. Need to catch up on some billing and get things crated for the next show."

These people run so fast downhill, I think. *They have so many things pushing them.* "The darkness is God's way of telling a man to quiet himself," I say as I pass through the door. "My grandfather told me this when I was very young." Far back in my mind, I remember Grandfather setting away his carving tools to sit in the moonlight with me. Overhead were so many stars, and far away, I could hear the ocean as the sun touched it. It was a peaceful sound, but I did not feel at peace. I was worried that the soldiers would come and take the little house Grandfather had found for us, as they had taken my father's big house. I was worried they would take Grandfather away, too. I told Grandfather this, and he only rested a hand on my head and said, *Ssshhh. Listen to the stars, how quietly they whisper. . . .*

"It's good advice," the Indian chief agrees. "But it doesn't pay the bills, unfortunately."

Unfortunate. I wonder how the lines look for this word. I imagine many lines, twisted together like chains. These fortunate people are unfortunate. Nights pass by, and they do not see the stars or hear the breezes whisper.

We enter the room, and the scent of paint surrounds us. The chief has started a new picture, only rough outlines in brown just now. I wonder what it will be. "Let me see what you've got for me." He pushes some rolled papers aside to create space on a table.

I take the carvings from my pocket. Three large birds and some smaller ones. There are also little boats, but those are not for him, so I put them back in my pocket, but then I pull one out again and hold it up. "Do you know the word for this?" I ask.

The Indian chief scratches his neck, looking confused. "It's a boat, isn't it? A canoe?"

"No, the way the paper would say it. Its line picture. The letter that makes it."

His lips part, and his teeth are not straight and white. "Oh, how to spell it, you mean?"

I do not know if he understands me. "How it is in a book. On a paper."

"How to write it?"

I nod. "I am learning the line pictures. The words. At the church."

"Oh, the reading class." He takes a book of empty paper, and then makes the word with a thick pencil he uses for his drawings. I think of the name for each letter, to try to decode the word, but the *a* causes trouble. It hides when you say the word. But I know that the lines say *boat*. I want to carve this on the bottom of my boats before I give them to Root and Berry and the boys in the blue house.

Boat is a small word, easy to make. I thought it would be larger.

Someday, perhaps, I will write the story of the boat that carried me here with Auntie.

I hold the paper book like something very precious. I look at the line picture.

The Indian chief laughs, a warm sound from deep in his throat. "You can have that art pad, if you like it so much. Here, take the pencil, too. As good as these carvings are, you might want to take up drawing." He lifts one of my birds, one I carved in the shed behind Root and Berry's house. He holds it lightly, as if it is real. He is careful with the wings. "You sure have an eye." His voice is only a whisper.

"I have two."

He laughs, and I do not know why. This is the difficult thing in people. They say things I do not understand.

"Sorry." The chief notices that he is laughing alone. "You have an eye—it means you have a skill for seeing things the way they really are."

"Everyone sees." It does not seem like such a gift.

He smiles and shakes his head. He is a good man, I think. A kind man. "No, not really. Not many people know how the feathers look on a hummingbird's wing. Most people go their whole lives and never even wonder about it."

I understand his words now. "They walk so fast." I wave a hand toward the street, then tuck the pencil and paper book into my pack. "The people always walk fast."

"True, that."

"The birds must have colors," I tell him. I have not painted the birds, because the building has been closed, the palette locked inside it. I need many colors for these birds.

Terence holds the carving up again. "No, you know what—let's just put a little wood stain on this one and see how it turns out." He moves across the room to another table, opens a can, and presses smooth, brown oil into the wood, then rubs it with a cloth until it shines like a round rock in the bed of a stream. "Beautiful, huh?" he asks, and I nod. I know I am smiling and he will see my teeth, but he does not seem to mind.

He lays the bird on a table to dry. "You can stay and work on the rest for a while, if you want. I'm not going anywhere," he says, and so I stay. He returns to his work and I color my carvings brown, and polish them until they shine. When those are finished, I color and polish some wooden things he is making—frames for his paintings, he tells me. We talk as he works and I work. He asks where I came from, and I tell him about the Broadberry Mission. "No," he says, "I mean where did you come from when you were little? You're not from here. I can tell by the way you talk."

I wonder what is the good thing to say. I wonder, if I say what is true, will he call the police? At the cane farm, they tell you, *If anyone comes, you must not mention the boat. You must say, "I come from Miami. I work here legal."* They teach you how to say the words *Mmm-eye-am-eee* and *lll-ee-gul*. You must know this, or the police will put you on the boat again.

"A far place from here. Near the water." I tell the Indian chief. "Mmm-eye-am-ee."

He laughs softly, as if something tickles his throat. "You didn't get that accent in Miami." Pausing as he wiggles a painting into a frame, he turns. "It's all right. You can tell me. I'm not gonna call the police or anything. Listen, I know what it's like to be on the run. I did some stupid things when I was young. Hurt some people I cared about, left behind a daughter I should've stayed to raise. I was in prison the whole time she was growing up, you know? I wanted to go hunt for her, but for a long while I just figured I didn't have anything she needed."

"Have you found her?" I look around us. It seems to me that the chief has much that could be given to a child, a daughter.

"She found me." He sets a tool in the tray, and his legs bounce nervously on the stool. "We've talked some these last three years. I've sent her a couple paintings I did from old pictures of her and her mama. It's a start. She's getting out of college soon—Juilliard—and trying to figure out what she wants to do next. She asked me what I thought, but I'm not sure I'm the one to be giving out advice, you know? She's got an adopted family, and I don't want to get in the way. I don't have any right to."

I watch him, and I think for a moment about this man. I gaze into him. He is like the porters who carry heavy packs atop their heads. You cannot *see* his burden, but you can feel the shadow of it. He struggles beneath the weight of the past. I can trust this man, I think. I can tell him my story.

I take a breath, and I let my mind go back, so that I am in my father's house again. For the first time in my life, I begin to tell what happened there. "When I am a young girl, I live in a big house with my father and my mother, and my grandfather and many brothers and sisters. My father is an important man in the city. He tells other men things to do, and when we walk with him on the street, men move out of his way. Even at a young age, I know he is a big man, a respected man.

"One day, while I am still young, the soldiers come to our house as everyone is sleeping. The noise awakens me, and I hear loud voices, and I run to hide. My mother finds me then, and she takes my hand and she whispers that I must not make a sound. We sneak away in the darkness, and she gives me to my grandfather, and we run in the shadow of the wall, where the soldiers cannot see. Behind, I hear terrible sounds, and I smell burning, and fire lights the sky, but Grandfather says I must not look, and so I do not.

I never see my mother, or my father, or my brothers and sisters again. My grandfather loves me very much, and we live in a small house then, but always, I watch the road, and I hope that one day my father and my mother and all the others will come walking home. I love Grandfather, and he teaches me to make carvings, but I do not stop looking for the others. My grandfather works very hard in the little house. He paints wooden beads, and the man comes to bring money to him, but the money is not enough. Some days there is no food, and then there is no house, and my grandfather walks with me across the burned country, all the way to the shore. He puts my hand into my auntie's, and she goes on a boat with me. I never see him again."

Terence's head tilts to one side, and he blinks slowly, his eyes large and dark and warm, like my grandfather's. "That's quite a story."

"It is my story," I say. Never have I told this story, but now it seems important that I tell it to him. "Perhaps your daughter has been watching the road for a very long time, as well."

He blinks again, surprised that my story has circled to touch his. "Maybe." He scratches paint from his fingers and watches the pieces fall to the floor. I polish the wood again. "Where were the soldiers?" he asks finally. "Soldiers don't come and take people away in Miami."

"A long distance from here," I say, and he laughs softly.

"Okay, I get it. You don't want to tell. It's all right. I wasn't trying to pry." He cleans his hands, and I take my pack, but I leave the birds, because the birds are for him.

"You know, you're welcome to sleep here, if you don't have a place," he tells me. "There's a bed and a bathroom in the office over there. I used to sleep here, before I got my loft."

A snake curls inside me, squeezing, and I move toward the door, shaking my head. *You sleep in a bed, you owe for it*, the man whispers in my mind. "If you sleep in a bed, you owe for it," I say.

The chief jerks away and eyes me. "Who told you that? The bed is free, just like the ones at the mission, all right? No strings."

I turn this in my mind. Outside the window, I see lightning in the distance. It is not a good night to be outside.

I stop, and set down my pack. Terence smiles as if he is pleased, and I think, *Perhaps not all men are the same.*

Perhaps some men are different.

Chapter 24

Shasta Reid-Williams

I woke up on Saturday with my mind made up that I'd tell Cody about the baby. Tam was right: I couldn't keep it secret forever. I was already getting queasy in the mornings, and pretty soon I'd be gaining weight. He'd figure it out soon enough, and besides that, I'd need to find a doctor and get going on prenatal visits.

I hadn't checked out the details of Cody's employee health insurance plan yet, but when Cody had insurance with the county sheriff's department back home, we'd figured out that the copay on a pregnancy wasn't cheap. Luckily, I could go to the Choctaw health clinic for free, but the Choctaw clinic was hours away now. When I made up my mind to get pregnant, I hadn't even thought about the fact that we'd probably have an insurance deductible to take care of and stuff. Where would we get the chunk of change for that?

My nerves were jumping like grasshoppers before I was even out of the shower. When I walked into the living room, all showered and dressed and ready to spill the baby beans to Cody, he was balancing our bank statement online, grumbling to himself, and shuffling papers around while watching ESPN. I stood in the doorway, feeling like someone was holding a blowtorch under my feet. "I need to talk to you a minute." If I didn't do it now, another day would go by, and probably two. Cody'd taken another temp job parking cars at a sports convention for the weekend, so he'd be gone before noon the whole weekend long, which meant that tomorrow I'd be getting the boys up and taking them down to the little white church for our first Sunday visit, all on my own. The boys were excited about going to kids' church, and it was time we stopped doing house chores on Sunday mornings and started showing up at service. I just hadn't figured on having to do it alone.

Cody kept one eye on ESPN and one on the computer, which didn't leave one for me. "Yeah, hey, later, all right? What are all these dadgum checks to Walmart for?" He pointed to the online bank statement with a sour look.

"Groceries and stuff for the house."

Sighing, he rubbed his forehead. "No more house stuff for a while, all right? Yesterday night, I was looking at things online, checking what else is gonna come due soon, and the payment Householders shows on our online statement doesn't match up with what they quoted us when we were in the office. It's the quote, plus a bunch of fees, but the statement doesn't say what the fees are for. I called the Householders office today, and they said the payment and fees are listed in our contract and we needed to read it. But I just dug out our copy of the contract, and there were whole pages missing. There's no fee schedule in there. I just e-mailed to tell them we needed a new copy. When my check goes into the account, and then the truck and credit card bills come due, if Householders drafts the payment for this amount, it won't go through. No more trips to Walmart until I get this Householders thing straightened out, all right? Keep watching the mail for the copy of the contract."

"'Kay," I muttered, walking over to his chair. So far, the breaking of the baby news wasn't going well. "Can you put that away for a minute?" I reached for the laptop, but Cody hung on.

"Cut it out, Shasta. I need to finish this before I go." Pulling the computer back into his lap, he leaned around me to check ESPN again and watch a replay of one of the Texas Rangers missing a fly ball. "Oh, dog! You idiot!"

My blood boiled up like bean soup in a pressure cooker on high, and all of a sudden I was mad all over. It was just a good thing the boys were in their bedroom, out of earshot. "You know what, Cody? You could leave off that stuff for a minute. I mean, it's like we never see you. You're always working or sleeping, and when you're not, you're watching ESPN, or sticking your nose in a book, or walking around the house mad. The boys never see you." All morning, Benji and Ty'd been asking Cody to take them over to the creek to try to catch the little perch, but he wouldn't get off his butt and go. What I really wanted to do was yank the computer out of his lap, turn off ESPN, and say, *Hey! I'm over here!* I wanted to get him talking about the reading class, the white church, the Summer Kitchen, and the bookstore. Then sometime in the conversation, I'd slip in, *Oh, by the way, I haven't started my period yet. Just so you know. There's an itty-bitty, teeny-weeny possibility Benji and Ty might be getting a little sister. Don't be mad, all right? I didn't mean for this to happen.*

But, of course, the truth was that I did, and there was more than a teeny possibility. When Cody thought about the timing, he'd know the pregnancy happened right after the vasectomy argument.

He jotted something on the outside of a file folder, and then slid a paper over it. "You know what, Shasta? If we don't get this house payment thing straightened out, we won't have any creek to fish in."

"We'll get it straightened out. They can't just . . . charge you more than they're supposed to. It's a mistake—a computer glitch or something. Mistakes happen, you know." Once the baby was here, he'd love it, just like he loved Benji and Ty. Wouldn't he? "We'll get it fixed." A tidal wave of tension traveled up my back, tying me in knots. Having Cody act so serious, so obsessed, felt wrong. Cody'd always been more likely to take off fishing than look at the checkbook. In fact, he could take off fishing when he was pretty sure the checkbook was overdrawn, and he'd never miss a beat. He knew Leonard at the bank would call Cody's mama, and she'd cover the check without ever telling Cody's dad, and everything would be okay. We'd get a lecture from her, and that'd be it.

Here in Dallas, there wasn't any safety net at the bank. Cody's folks were hanging back, waiting for us to fail, and maybe that was what had him so freaked out. If we messed this up, it'd prove everybody right.

Sighing, I sat on the arm of his chair and swirled a finger in the fuzz of his hair, short and thick, dark. "Come on, Cody, let's not borrow trouble. We'll make it work. We always get by. We'll get the extra fees taken off, and then we'll be fine. They can't just tack charges onto somebody's loan."

He rested his head against my arm, his shoulders deflating like a hot air balloon sinking back to earth. "Yeah, I hope not, but the way they acted when I called the office was . . . well, it's like the whole thing's part of a routine. Like they know exactly what to say and what kind of runaround to give you. Like they do this all the time." The ominous sound in his voice sent a chill through me, but the rounded shoulders bothered me more. He seemed so tired, like he couldn't figure out what to do next.

I looked at the computer screen. He had our bank account in one window and something about house payments in the other. There was no way Cody understood all those numbers. "Why would they sell houses so people can't make the payments? What good would that be? It's not like they're getting big down payments. I mean, there was that chunk of first-time home buyer grant money, but think of all the money Householders would have to spend kicking people out, repo-ing houses, and reselling them. It doesn't make a single bit of sense." One thing I'd learned from my Nana Jo was that dealing in houses was a serious hassle. Nana Jo'd had rental properties in downtown Hugo for years, and whenever people couldn't pay the rent, it cost her a fortune to get them out, then get the places cleaned up and ready to rent again. "If you're really worried about it, I could call Nana Jo and see what she thinks, maybe send her a copy of the contract when it gets here."

Cody jerked away, then caught the computer about to topple off his knees. "No. Don't call anybody."

"All right, all right." Sliding my hands over his shoulders, I started a massage. The muscles were tight under his skin, hard like curls of dried rawhide.

"I mean it, Shasta. I'll work twenty-four hours a day before we're asking for help from *anybody* back home. Especially not your mama or Nana Jo." He swiveled in the chair, so his eyes reflected the windows and the yard outside. Our yard. "Or my parents."

"Okay, okay." Cody was right. We had to take care of this ourselves. "I'll try to talk to Elsie when I see her, okay? The day Tam's family moved in across the street, Elsie acted like she knew something about Householders." Cody stiffened again, and I slid my hands over his chest, felt the round, solid curve of muscle there. The baby conversation could wait. This totally wasn't the time for it. "You know, you're really hot when you're all fired up about my mother."

He tilted his head back, his lips spreading slowly into a smile. "I'm not thinking about your mother."

"Hmmm . . . and I thought you were all fired up." One way or another, I was gonna get his mind off the house.

"I am." He shot a quick glance at the hallway. "What're the boys doing?"

"Watching *101 Dalmatians*."

"How long ago did they start?"

"Not too long ago."

Cody pulled me into his lap, and his body loosened and curved over mine. His mind definitely wasn't on the house. . . .

By the time Cody got ready to leave for his afternoon of parking cars, I almost forgave him for taking a job on the weekend. Sometimes my guy could be so sweet, he could get away with anything. Other times, I wanted to throw frying pans at him. Until he had one foot out the door, he didn't bother to mention that after he finished the job tonight, he was gonna ride out to Lake Ray Hubbard to try some night fishing with his new pals from his class. That's not what a woman wants to hear after sneaking off to make love in the morning.

"You have *got* to be kidding." I stood in the doorway, holding the door while he slid through like a snake. I had the urge to yank the burglar bars closed and knock him out. No one would blame me once they heard what he did.

He had the nerve to lean over and kiss me on the head, like I was his pet cow dog. "Just for a couple hours. I want to see if there's anything in that lake."

"Yeah, right." What did he think I was, an idiot? *Night fishing* was man code for, *Let's drive around on a boat and drink beer while the little woman takes care of the kids.* "You know, the kids are dying for you to take them fishing down in the creek . . . or anywhere, really. You could skip the night fishing, and when you get done at the convention, we could take a little picnic supper and go to the lake—watch the stars come out."

He turned and walked backward across the porch, gave me a big, stupid smile I immediately wanted to pinch off his face. "I won't be done till after their bedtime tonight. I can take them down to the creek tomorrow morning. We'll rig up a little perch pole."

Right then, Benji and Ty ran up the hallway, and I stepped out of the way to let them onto the porch, where Cody could see their pitiful little faces.

"Where Daddy goin'?" Ty asked, standing a few feet out the door, his blankie-dog crooked in his elbow and his belly sticking out the bottom of his shirt.

"Daddy's going to *work*."

"Man!" Benji complained, stopping halfway across the porch, letting his shoulders drop and his arms dangle forward, like someone'd just let the air out of his new ball. "Da-a-a-ddd!"

I hoped Cody felt guilty to the bone. Jerk.

"Sorry, buddy." Cody waved with that big, dumb smile still on his face. "Gotta work parking cars for a sports convention. I'll see if I can get you an autograph."

"Cool!" Benji cheered, lifting invisible pom-poms into the air.

"My mob-o-graph, too." Ty's voice was muffled by the blanket.

"You, too, buddy." Cody spun around and jumped down all three steps at once, and the boys giggled. Just like that, he was the coolest guy in the world, and I was stuck home with two kids who were gonna be bored today, because the Summer Kitchen was closed on Saturday.

All of a sudden, the day ahead stretched out in front of me like twenty miles of panhandle road—boring, lonely, and way too much of the same thing. In the distance, clouds blotted out the sun, making everything feel dingy and quiet. I felt the shadows closing in, and not just on the horizon. They were closing in on me, too. On a busy day, when the sun was out and there was plenty to do, I could walk right by a pile of worries and never give it a second thought. But on a day like today, if I didn't do something quick, I'd end up turning our problems over and over in my mind.

"Stay right here for a second, guys." I stepped inside and grabbed the cell phone and my purse, then stood on the porch and dialed while the boys trotted down the steps and crawled under the oleander bush that was still right where it'd always been.

Tam didn't answer her phone, which was strange, considering that it was after eleven. Surely they weren't still asleep over there. Their car was in the driveway.

I tried again, but the phone rolled over to voice mail.

The boys knocked on the porch floor from underneath. I stomped, my sandals making a hollow *rat-a-tat-tat* that gave the kids a giggle. "Who's under my bridge?" Bending close to the deck, I snorted and sniffed. "This is big Mr. Troll from 'Billy Goats Gruff.' I smell a human under my bridge. Two humans! Ohhhh, I like humans. I like to eat them all up. Yum!"

The boys shushed each other and giggled some more. Ty squealed.

I dug out my keys, closed up the house, and locked it. "If I find humans under my bridge, I'll tie them up and take them down the road to my secret place." The porch floor rattled as I crossed it, and underneath, little hands and feet scrambled toward the opening under the oleander. The boys bolted out, and I caught them at the corner, then toppled over with one in each arm.

"I think I'll take these boys down the street with me." I snuggled kisses under Benji's chin, then Ty's, and they pulled their necks in like turtles, their giggles traveling across the yard and bouncing off Elsie's house. I glanced over to see if Elsie was watching out her window, but the blinds were down and the place looked dark. Her car was in the driveway, like maybe she'd been somewhere already this morning. With my luck, she was probably tired out and taking a nap, and we were bothering her. Maybe later, if I could tell she was in the living room, I'd knock on her door and ask her what she knew about Householders. Elsie really wasn't so bad, once you got to know her. She still wasn't friendly. Mostly it seemed like she didn't want us bothering her, but she wasn't the worst neighbor you could have.

I wrestled with the boys, even though their rowdiness was starting to get out of control. It felt so good to hear them laughing and squealing, to hug their bodies close to mine. A warmth gushed over me like bathwater, filling me, driving away the bad feelings. This was my family. Mine. No one could take it away.

There was power in that, a completeness. No matter what, we were together—Cody, the boys, and me. This was all I'd ever wanted. Everything.

The boys wore down before we poked anyone's eye out, and I lay there with them piled on top of me. A squirrel ran across the branch overhead. "Look, look, look!"

They rolled onto their backs as I pointed.

"Is a sk-rul!"

"A squir-rel," Benji corrected, in his I-know-it-all, older-brother voice.

"Where him go?"

"Back to his house, with nuts." Benji's answer was matter-of-fact. Suddenly he was the nature expert. "Like in the book."

"Ohhhh. Where the sk-rul book, Mommy?" Ty climbed to his feet to look for the squirrel. "Where him go?"

"I didn't know we had a squirrel book." I stood up, dusting myself off, while Benji brushed the grass from his clothes. There was no telling what books we had around now. After a few visits to the Book Basket with Tam's brothers and the kids trading back and forth, we were loaded with reading material.

"It came from the green-pant—" Benji stopped in the middle of the sentence and popped his hand over his mouth, his eyes flying wide.

My good feelings scattered like rats in a grain bin. I'd thought we were past the pretend-people thing. It hadn't come up since I'd told them to quit talking about it. "Benjamin Williams, remember what we said? We're not going to tell that story anymore, and you're not supposed to be telling it to Ty, either. No more green-pants lady. We're not saying that name. That scares Mommy. Some people are just pretend."

Benjamin's sturdy shoulders lifted and then dropped, like it didn't matter to him either way. "Okay."

I checked Tam's house again, but there was still no sign of life over there. "Tell you what, guys. Why don't we walk down to the corner and see if the bookstore's open, or if Uncle Terence is in his studio?" I'd taught the boys to call Cody's cousin Uncle Terence, which I had a feeling Terence thought was weird, but they had to call him something. He was Uncle Terence whether he liked it or not.

"Yay!" Ty jumped, splitting his feet in the air like a mini cheerleader.

"I wanna go get my book in the house." Benji was up the steps and across the porch before I could stop him. He yanked impatiently at the burglar bars. "Ma-a-ohm! Lemme in! I wanna get my book."

"What book, Benji? I already locked up. Don't worry about it." Even we could afford books at the Book Basket. Everything there was used and smelled musty, but you could count on the prices being low. "We just won't take a trade-in this time."

"I wanna take the squirrel book back," Benji whined, throwing his weight against the doorknob. I sensed a fit coming on, and I didn't think I could handle it this morning.

"Benjamin Lucas Williams, you've got five seconds to get off that porch and march your little self over here. We didn't get any squirrel book from the Book Basket, and you know it. If we have one in there, it belongs to the Lambert boys." I *always* checked the books Benji and Ty picked out at the store, just to make sure there wasn't anything bad in them, and I knew for a fact we hadn't picked out any squirrel stories. The closest thing we owned was a nature book about reptiles. Squirrels are not reptiles.

Benji wasn't giving in. "I wanna get it. It's mine! She gave it to me."

Heat boiled slowly upward, under my shirt, into my chin, over my ears, like I was a hot pot about to blow. Sometimes Benjamin could be so much like his daddy. I was up the steps and across the porch before I even knew what was happening. Yanking Benjamin's hand off the door, I spun him around and pointed my finger in his face, and the tension I'd been tucking down all day flowed out with the power of water trapped behind a logjam. It pushed through me, swirling and foaming, a hot, murky mix of feelings I couldn't control. "Benjamin Lucas, what did I just tell you? Huh? Huh? What did I say? You *stop* this lying. I mean it. You stop it! I'm sick of it! I'm just trying to do something nice for you guys. I'm just trying to do something good, and you're being . . . you're being a . . . a little . . ." Snapping my lips closed, I threw my hand over them, a dozen harsh words trapped in my throat. They were meant to hurt, to dig at him so that he would know he was digging at me. Why did he keep doing this? Why was he so determined to keep some imaginary friend, some mystical lady lurking around our house, haunting our family? Was this imaginary friend his way of telling me his own mom and dad weren't good enough?

Doubts washed over me, sweeping up every thought, pouring tears into my throat, wetting my eyes. *Stop it. Stop this. It's not him you're mad at. It's not his fault. He's just being a kid.*

He doesn't love me. He doesn't. He wishes he had somebody else. Someone better.

This new baby won't want you either. Nobody does. Why would anybody want you? You never do anything right.

Stop. Stop it.

Benjamin's eyes filled up, two huge brown circles, so dark the centers were invisible. He blinked, and liquid matted his lashes.

Turning away, I pushed hard against my lips to stop the trembling, then blew out a breath. "Let's just go. Just come on." I started across the porch, Benji dragging from the circle of my fingers like a puppy on a leash. He didn't fight, but he didn't come easy, either. I ignored his glances back at the house. I had to, or else I was going to say or do something I'd regret later. I snagged Ty on the way past, and headed down the block with the boys jogging to keep up.

By the time we got to the corner, I'd slowed down and caught my breath. Benji was over his fit, and so was I, except for the leftover guilt for being a lousy mom. Every once in a while, even though I didn't want to, I understood why my mama was so grouchy and bossy all those years we were growing up, and why she was so down on me for getting married young and wanting kids right away.

It was so much harder having a family, making a life, than I'd ever thought it would be. It wasn't just playing with your kids, or changing their diapers, or making sure they had naps and food to eat. There were all the other things they needed—love, advice, understanding, patience. They needed you to set an example, to be good to them

even on the days you didn't feel like it, even on the days you wanted
to give up and have somebody take care of you for a change. Here
in Dallas, with no grandmas, and aunts and uncles and cousins to
watch the boys for a few hours, a day, a weekend, there wasn't any
ignoring the fact that they deserved a mom who had her act together
more than I did.

"There the bookstore!" Ty pointed ahead.

"Yup, there it is." I swung the boys' hands up and down, and Ty
jumped a crack in the sidewalk on an upswing. "Looks like it's open.
I see MJ's car out front and the lights are on."

"Yay!" Benji cheered, and all of a sudden I was the best mom in
the world. "Can I get two books?"

"Well, I'll tell you what." I let go of Benji's hand and fished in my
purse. "Mommy's going to stop in and talk to Uncle Terence for a few
minutes, and if you guys are real good, then I'll give you each a dollar,
and you can get as many books as that dollar'll buy."

"Awe-tum!" Ty's opinion was positive, as always. "I gonna get
five." Lately, since he'd learned his brother was five years old, everything with Ty was *five*.

"You can't get five for a dollar," Benji pointed out.

"Maybe." Everything with Ty was *maybe*, too. Never yes, never
no. Just maybe. "Maybe five."

Benji made a hard sound in his throat as we rounded the corner
into the parking lot. "You can't—"

"Benji, let him figure that out. It's his money."

Terence was busy cutting frames when we stepped into his shop.
I stood in the doorway holding the boys' hands until the noise of the
saw died down. Terence cut the power and pushed up his goggles,
snapping them over the tie-dyed bandanna on his head. "I didn't
see you guys there." One thing about Terence—you could never tell

whether he was glad to have company or not. Painting seemed to suit him because he couldn't think of what to say to real people. Luckily, I could usually talk enough for both of us, which made Terence like me a little, I thought.

"We sneaked in."

"Don't guess that was too hard."

"Yeah, you're lucky I wasn't a burglar or something."

That got a little smile out of him. "Nothing here worth stealing, unless you're into oil paints and wood stain. I don't think anybody'd take this table saw if I gave it to them."

"I bet Cody'd take it. Maybe he'd get some projects done around the house."

Snagging a towel from the workbench, Terence wiped the sweat and sawdust from his neck. He yawned, setting the towel aside, then hiking his jeans up on his waist, where there was a gap at the bottom of his T-shirt. I waited for him to make conversation, but he didn't, which was normal.

"You look wiped out," I said, although the truth was, Terence always looked tired. He looked like someone who was worn out by life and couldn't quite figure out why he was still here. In his paintings, the faces had a loneliness that made me wonder what he was thinking when he painted them. Back before Ty was born, I used to do some painting, so I knew you couldn't help putting a lot of yourself into what you created.

"Yeah, a little," he admitted. "I need to get a frame on this thing, and then I'm headed to another art show for a couple days." A chin jerk pointed out a painting on an easel turned away from us. A chair sat in front of the easel, near the door to the bookstore, like someone'd been posing for him.

I walked a few steps into the room, holding the boys' hands so they wouldn't touch anything. "What is it?" Once upon a time, I thought maybe I'd be an artist, so I loved seeing how Terence made his people seem real. I liked the fact that he talked to me like I knew something, and he was interested in my opinion.

"Take a look. You can let the kids come in here. They're not gonna hurt anything."

I turned loose of the boys' hands, and they wandered to the back corner to look at Terence's tools, while I walked around the worktable so that I could see what was on the easel. My mouth dropped open and a chill ran over my shoulders. "You painted the voodoo lady?"

"The what?" Terence laughed and coughed at the same time.

"The voodoo lady. She, like, stands by the wall and stares at me when we're doing the reading class. It's creepy."

"Maybe she's learning to read." Terence's smile was forgiving, almost tender. "She asked me to write out some words for her on a piece of paper."

"She did?"

He nodded. "She doesn't mean to bother anybody. She's just . . . a little afraid of people."

I rubbed my hands over the goose bumps on my arms. "If she wants to learn to read, she could sign up for class instead of lurking over everybody's shoulders."

He picked up a piece of wood, held it straight out, and squinted down it, like he was checking for straightness. "You don't know what it's like, living on the street, until you've been there. You get so far away from normal, you don't even know what normal is. Sesay has an interesting story, though. I was trying to capture that in the painting. I like to paint the street people sometimes—learn more about where they come from and how they ended up where they are." He pointed toward his work again. On the canvas he'd surrounded the woman with darkness. The red scarf tied over her dreadlocks floated into empty space. A faint reflection shone in her eyes. I moved closer to see what it was.

Water, maybe, and rocks and a shore? Behind me, Terence was telling me the woman didn't even know where she was from. An island somewhere. Someplace where soldiers came and took people away and burned down their houses—some kind of a military coup, he guessed. "I don't know where she's been all these years since. She wouldn't say," he finished. "I asked MJ about her. MJ didn't know much, either. Sesay just showed up here a few months ago. Probably came from another place where she was living on the street. Some of them move around a lot."

"Some of them?"

"The street people. Sounds like she works a little here and there, lives in shelters, does what she can. For them, it's about survival. Most of them are harmless. They're just afraid, you know? It's not easy when nobody wants you around."

I tried to imagine how it would be, wandering the streets, not knowing where you were going to sleep, or where your next meal would come from. "Do you think she's got a family someplace? Someone she could go to? She's kind of, well . . . old. She won't be able to live like this forever."

"I doubt she thinks about the future much. People on the street don't keep a calendar."

I looked at the portrait again, stared into the eyes, wondered what they'd seen. "It's kind of sad, though, to think . . . I mean, for somebody to end up that way." On the other side of the room, the boys were brushing sawdust off a workbench, watching it poof in the window light, and making a mess in the process. "Hey, you guys, quit that."

"She seems content."

"How could she be?" She couldn't read and she was homeless, after all.

Terence cast a sideways look at me, like I just didn't get it. "She had a message for you."

The goose bumps slid over my skin again. "For me?"

"About your house."

Chapter 25

Tam Lambert

I woke up on the sofa, the sun beating against the orange silk sheet over the living room window, turning the room a misty shade of mustard. I'd been alternately dozing and pacing the floors since the early hours of the morning, waiting for Barbie to wake up and wondering what would happen when she did. Last night's knock-down-drag-out seemed surreal—like a weird dream that should have faded now that it was almost noon. In the house, with the window coverings casting a pall over everything, it felt like morning still, as if the best idea would be to sleep until I woke in a better place.

I turned on my phone and multiple missed calls showed up— three from Shasta; one from Uncle Boone, apparently back from his latest business trip; and one from a blocked number. I stared at the blocked number and thought about my father. After all this time, could he be trying to call?

The phone rang again, and the screen flashed, *Shasta calling.* I answered, and her voice jingled into the room, loud, overly cheerful, out of place, like a bird singing at a funeral. "Hey, you up? I tried to call earlier, but no one answered."

"I was awake all night, so I didn't turn on my cell this morning. We had a major fight yesterday after I came home." I rubbed my head, my eyes burning. If Barbie was as messed-up today as she was last night, I couldn't let her stay here. What if she hurt one of the kids? What if she put them in the car and took off with them?

"You and the stepmonster?" Shasta's cheerful tone sobered.

"Yes. She was sitting here drunk or stoned or both when I walked in. She had it in her head that I'd tried to take off with her kids." A painful sensation rose in my throat. It mixed with anger and created something deeper. Despair. Helplessness.

Shasta gave an indignant snort. "Pa-lease! She's got some serious nerve. If it wasn't for you, the kids would be, like, gone already. They'd be running loose around the neighborhood while she's out partying, and somebody would of called social services already."

"I guess so." A breath shuddered in my chest, the air feeling heavy. "It seems like it's all for nothing. Maybe I'm just enabling. I don't know where we go from here. I can't let her be around the kids like this, but I can't take care of them. I can't . . . I can't do this. Sometimes I want to just . . . walk out the door and keep walking."

"Don't you even say that." Shasta's reply was quick and sharp. I pictured her eyes blazing, white rimmed around the dark centers, heated with righteous passion. "Don't you even think about it. I mean it, Tam. I'll come over there and tell the stepmonster what I think, if you want. I'll tell her I'll call social services if she doesn't get her act together. Those kids are just babies. They didn't ask for any of this. They need someone looking out for them. Their mom needs to step up and take care of them, but you're all they've got right now. I'm coming over there."

"All right, all right. Just slow down a minute." I stopped Shasta before the chaos in my head could become any worse. "I'm not packing up and calling a cab."

"You'd better not. So what happened last night, exactly?"

"I don't even know. It was just . . . bizarre. Barbie was waiting for me here. She was . . . nuts, and . . ." A blow-by-blow of the argument tumbled out of me—Barbie grabbing the baby from my arms, then dragging the other kids away, her almost falling with Jewel, her accusing me of attempting to take the kids, Daniel trying to get away, Barbie finally disappearing down the hall, bringing all four kids into one bedroom with her, then locking the door and refusing to open it. I could hear her inside, first playing a bizarre game of Candy Land with them, then sloppily reading books and singing lullabies until finally she passed out around three a.m., and Mark got up and unlocked the door.

I lay awake on the sofa all night, afraid Barbie would awaken and try to escape with the kids. If she came out of the bedroom, I was prepared to start a wrestling match, call the police—whatever it took—to keep her from leaving.

Finally, sometime close to morning, I fell asleep.

"I just don't know what to do next," I finished. "I'm afraid of what she'll be like this morning. I'm afraid of what will happen. When the kids finally wake up, I don't even know what to say to them."

"Why don't y'all come over to my house?" Shasta suggested. "I'll make you lunch and we'll figure something out."

"I don't think I'd better. If Barbie wakes up and we're gone, there's no telling what she'll do. What if she calls the police and has me hauled in for kidnapping?"

"Let her call the police. I'll tell them a thing or two. I'll get Cody in on it. He's seen your stepmom taking off all the time, coming home in the middle of the night. They'll take his word for it. The DPD listens to their own. He's gone working at a convention today, but I can try to get hold of him, and—"

"Wait, just settle down, okay? I don't want to do anything right now." Standing up, I stretched my back, feeling like my body was a twisted Slinky, the coils impossible to untangle. "I feel like I've been run over by a truck."

In the hall, a bedroom door was creaking slowly open. Mark peeked out, and then stepped into the shadows of the hallway. He was carrying Jewel. He came into the living room quietly, then stopped and stood in the doorway, as if he didn't know where to go next.

"Jewel's poopy."

I cast around the dim room, looking for the diaper bag. No telling where it had ended up. "Bring her in here. We've probably got some diapers in the bag."

"Who's that?" Shasta sounded as if she were ready for a fistfight.

"Just Mark. He got the baby up."

There was a quick exhale into the phone. "Oh, all right. I thought it was *her*. I thought she was, like, having the nerve to bring you the baby so you could change her. I'm coming over, all right?"

"You don't need to do that."

"I want to. The boys and I are already out and about, anyway. We walked up to the bookstore after Cody left this morning. Besides, I found out something about the voodoo lady, and . . . Did you know your aunt's in the front yard right now, like, doing karate or something?"

I walked to the window as Shasta hung up the phone. There in the yard was Aunt Lute, wearing flowered pajamas, performing what looked like a cross between karate, yoga, and some strange form of Asian dance.

By the time I'd changed Jewel's diaper, Shasta was on the porch with her boys. I opened the door, and we stood watching Aunt Lute. It was hard to believe that only a few weeks ago, we'd looked at this house and been afraid to get out of our car. Now Aunt Lute was calmly doing calisthenics on the front lawn, and, other than the pajamas, that seemed all right.

"What her doin'?" Tyler asked.

Shrugging, Mark lifted his hands, as in, *No telling.*

Shasta's eldest snickered behind his hand. "She's got her PJs on."

"Benjamin!" Shasta scolded. "Hush up. That's rude."

Aunt Lute continued with her routine, oblivious to the conversation.

I pushed the door open wider, and Shasta slipped through with her boys, who moved to the clutter of boxes and toys in the dining room. Shasta took Jewel. I pushed the sheet-curtain aside to let in some sunlight, and we sat on the sofa. Babbling, Jewel stretched out her arms, giving a two-toothed smile. I couldn't help comparing the joyous expression on her face to her confusion and fear last night when her mother took her.

I pushed the thought away because it was too hard to consider. I wasn't ready for it. "So, tell me about the bookstore. Let's talk about anything else, all right? Did you run into the voodoo lady at the bookstore?"

Shasta shook her head. "Not exactly. I saw Terence. He was in his studio working, so we stopped by. So he was, like, painting a portrait of her, if you can believe that. I asked him if he knew anything about her and whether she was dangerous, and should I be worried."

"What did he say?"

She leaned closer, as if we were sharing the dish. "Well, first of all, he said she told him to be careful about my house—something about a lot of people moving in and out of these yellow houses, and the color yellow being bad luck, but whatever. That wasn't really the interesting part. He said she asked him to write some words for her on paper. She's, like, trying to learn to read from watching the reading class. How cool is that? I mean, she still gives me the creeps, but I didn't really think about her actually learning to read, you know?

Now I feel kinda bad—like I should've asked her to sit down with Elsie and me."

"Maybe so." I tried to focus on the conversation, but my mind kept drifting toward Barbie's door. How much longer would she sleep?

Shasta's eyes widened with interest. "Terence said they got to talking last night as he was leaving. He said she comes from someplace where soldiers took her father away when she was, like, a little girl, and she's had a really hard life. He thinks she's been some kind of migrant worker part of the time, but she wouldn't even tell him where she's been exactly. He's pretty sure she's afraid to sign the papers for the reading class. Like she's afraid she'll get caught."

"Caught by whom?" My attention shifted away from the problem of what to do about Barbie to focus fully on Shasta's story. A tingle of intrigue tugged at me.

Shasta checked on the three boys in the dining room. "I don't know. Maybe she was, like, involved with some bad people, working for drug runners or something, and they're after her. So now I'm seriously curious about her. You know me—hopelessly nosy. When we go to the Summer Kitchen on Monday, I'm gonna talk to her, and see what I can find out."

"Are you sure you should get . . ." Before I could finish the sentence with *involved*, a door creaked in the hallway, and I jerked upright. Landon ran out and dashed toward the living room, followed by Daniel. The squeak of the mattress testified to the fact that Barbie wasn't far behind.

Shasta caught my gaze and mouthed, *Uh-oh*, then stood up and whispered, "Want me to take her on?"

I shook my head. "Let me see how things are this morning, first." No telling what shape Barbie was in now that she'd sobered up, or if she'd even remember yesterday's ridiculous rumble, but having a third party here, plus Shasta's kids, probably wouldn't help.

Shasta cocked her head to one side, watching as Barbie crossed the hall to the bathroom. After the door closed, Shasta whistled softly. "Someone looks seriously rough this morning."

I nodded, rubbing my eyes. As lousy as I felt, I could only imagine that Barbie was in significantly worse shape. "It's probably best if I talk to her by myself. I'll call you later."

Standing up, Shasta handed the baby to me, then caught a breath and lifted a finger as if a sudden idea had come to her. "You know what? I'll cook dinner for us. Cody's gonna be gone all night, and the kids'll be bored, and the house'll be too quiet. Plan on coming over, all right? We'll do hot dogs out back." As usual, Shasta rolled the day's schedule along without waiting for an answer. "I think I'll see if I can get Elsie to come, too. Cody's still obsessing about the house loan, and I told him I'd ask Elsie what she knows about Householders. She's been in this neighborhood a long time. I think she knows something about the yellow houses." Heading for the door, she tapped a finger against her temple, as if she were punching in tonight's menu. "Oh, hey, ask your aunt to come. Never mind. I'll ask her myself on the way out." Shasta called her boys, then let herself out the front door. Before closing it, she poked her head through the opening, her lips forming a sympathetic twist. "Call me if you need me. I'm two seconds away."

I lifted a hand in acknowledgment, and she gave me the high sign before leaving.

Down the hall, the bathroom door opened, and Barbie staggered to the living room, her nightgown hanging off one shoulder and her hair sticking out like straws on a broom that had been smashed against the floor. She crossed the room without speaking, headed toward the kitchen.

Shasta knocked softly on the window, then waved a fist in front of the glass. Jewel flailed her arms and babbled, "Ba ba-ee, ba ba-ee."

The sound halted Barbie in the dining room doorway. She stood frozen, swaying in place like a tower moving in the wind, leaning farther and farther off center until finally her shoulder came to rest against the wall. Her head lolled sideways, making a dull thud as she collapsed, her knees buckling, ankles softening, her body sagging to the floor in slow motion.

Mark looked up from playing with the pile of Duplo blocks under the dining table. "Mommy?"

"Barbara?" I stood and moved toward her. Was she passing out? Having some sort of seizure? Had she overmedicated already this morning?

"Momm-eee . . ." Landon crawled across the field of blocks, his eyes rimmed with white, the Duplos scattering.

Barbie's body slumped forward, her face falling into her hands, her arms trembling.

Mark and Daniel scrambled toward her, following Landon's lead. I crossed the room, setting Jewel in her bouncer seat on the way. By the time I reached Barbie, the boys were gathered in a semicircle around her, afraid to come closer. Fear took away the soft curves of their faces and created tight masks.

Nudging the boys out of the way, I knelt in front of Barbie, leaned close, tried to see her face, but it was covered with her hands, shielded by her hair. Long red fingernails dug in deep. She trembled wildly. "Barbara, what's wrong? Are you sick? What's the matter?"

Landon extended a hand and tentatively touched her knee, last night's chaos apparently forgotten or forgiven this morning. "Mom-eee?" he pleaded. "Mom-eee?"

"Move back, Landon." I elbowed him aside cautiously. "All three of you move back." If something was really wrong with Barbie, I didn't want any of them to get hurt. "Barbie, what's happening? Do I need to call an ambulance? Are you sick?" Gripping her wrists, I tried to pull her hands from her face. My fingers slid in the clammy moisture on her skin. "Barbie, do you need a doctor? Did you take something? Did you get something from Fawn?" My mind raced through the possibilities—everything from Barbie trying to commit suicide with an intentional overdose, to street drugs having been slipped into her drink last night.

"I'mmm . . . saaa . . ." she moaned. "I . . . ummmm . . . sooo . . . saaa."

"Barbie, talk to me. What's wrong?" I pulled harder on her hands, loosened her fingers, dragged them from her face, dislodging tangles of hair. She seemed oblivious to the pain.

"I'm soh, I'm soh, I'm soh . . ." she breathed, then pulled in a gasp that whistled and shuddered in her throat. "I'm soh-ryyy. I'm sorry. I'm sorry." The words were breathless, almost unintelligible.

Holding her wrists, I shook her. "Sorry for what? Barbie? What did you do?"

"I'm just . . . I'm just like her. I'm just like her."

I shook her again, and her head rattled like a ball on a tether. "Just like who? Barbie, stop this. You're scaring the boys. Tell me what's wrong." Behind me, Landon started to sob. Mark grabbed Landon's shirt and retreated backward over the pile of Duplos, taking Landon with him. Daniel tried once more to see his mother's face, then scooted away and crouched under the table with the others. In the living room, Jewel whimpered softly.

"I'm sorry." Barbie collapsed forward with the words, her head sliding slowly down my arms, as if she were pleading with me, begging for something.

I fumbled for a course of action. Yell for help? Call 911? Try to slap some sense into her?

Jerking upward, I bounced her head off my forearms like a volleyball. "Stop this! If you took something, tell me. Otherwise, go back to bed. Go somewhere. Do something. You're scaring the kids, and you're scaring me."

Her eyes met mine, and the fog slowly cleared. "I'm sorry," she whispered. "I'm sorry for . . . I did . . . I did everything wrong. I didn't ever want to be like her. I didn't ever want to do what she did."

I pushed her hair back, tucked it behind her shoulder. The gesture felt surprisingly intimate. For an instant, the woman on the floor wasn't Barbara, the queen of high heels and plastic surgery. She was just a human being, broken in front of me. "What . . . Who did, Barbara?"

"My mother." Barbara sniffled, wiping a hand across her nose, then pressing trembling fingers to her lips, the nails leaving reddened trails on her skin as she drew them downward, letting her eyes fall closed. "She let them take us away. She just . . . she just let them do it. She never even tried to get us back. She just . . . moved on." Her eyelids squeezed tighter, pressing tears from beneath her lashes. "I never wanted to be like her."

I felt the unexpected tug of compassion, a strange connection to Barbie that I'd never expected. My mother had moved on, too. She'd left me behind like I was a game she was tired of playing. "Barbie, I know you love your kids. They know you love them."

Her brows, blond and childlike in the absence of makeup, squeezed again. "They don't even want to come to me. Jewel likes that . . . that girl better than she likes me." She rolled her head toward Shasta's house. "Jewel wants *her*. Jewel wants you. The boys don't even care about me. They don't look for me. Everybody leaves." She collapsed again, sobbing. "I just wanted someone to love me."

I grabbed her shoulders again, holding her away from me, trying to force her to focus. "They're just kids, Barbara. They're just kids, and every time they turn around, something's changing. First, it's a different nanny every few months, and now there's no nanny, but you're here, except you're not really here. You're never the same twice. You're either passed out or taking off with Fawn, and every once in a while, you grab them and hold them so tightly they can't breathe. You're their mom. They need you to be their mom. They need to know they can count on you to . . . to take care of them and make them feel safe. All the time—not just once in a while. You can't just . . . check out whenever it gets to be too much."

Biting her lip, she sagged against the wall, pressed her forehead to it. "It's my fault. It's my fault we're here."

I held tightly to her hand. "No, it's not, Barbara. My father left us here. My father did this." As painful as it was to admit, it was true. Dad was the one who had run out, who'd left us to fend for ourselves. "I don't think he meant for this to happen, but he had to have known it was coming. He must have known it for quite a while, and he didn't tell anybody. He didn't tell us. He kept it hidden because he was too proud to admit it. He lied to us about it, and then he left."

"He loves us." The words ended in a stifled sob. "I need him. I can't do this without him."

I felt myself cracking inside, breaking open. I couldn't give in to it. I couldn't crumble, too. "He's not here. We have to take care of ourselves."

She swallowed hard, her chin bobbing with the effort. "I can't." Her lashes parted, damp and clumped, and she focused beyond me, on the boys. "I can't . . . I can't give them back their . . . house . . . the pool . . . their toys . . . their . . . They shouldn't be here . . . in this place. They shouldn't have to live like . . . in this . . . this. I know how it feels. I know how it feels to be treated like everybody's trash."

I caught her gaze through the veil of tears. "Barbie, they don't care. You're the one who cares about that. Have you looked at them lately? Haven't you noticed they're not fighting all the time anymore? They're fine here. They like it, even. They like it because we're all together, because we're all in the same space. They just need you to be in that space with the rest of us, that's all. They want their mom to *be* their mom." Barbie's hands held tightly to mine. Our gazes tangled, and she nodded. Where there had been only contempt and hatred, now I felt a bond.

Jewel let out a mewing cry in her bouncer seat, and I stood up to go after her. When I came back, the boys were curled in Barbie's lap. Her head was bowed over theirs, her hair falling around them like a shield. I took Jewel to the kitchen and left them there, clinging to one another.

The hours after Barbie's breakdown felt like the first time we'd spent together in the house as a family. We sat on the back porch with Jewel while Aunt Lute took the boys on what she called an *expedition.* She'd helped them put on baseball caps with scarves draped down the back to protect them from the desert sun. As they stalked off across the yard with Aunt Lute's colorful silk scarves fluttering on their shoulders, Barbie wiped her eyes again. She'd been crying off and on all day, as if our situation had suddenly come crashing down upon her in all its dismal reality. She'd cried off the last remnants of last night's makeup, and hadn't bothered to replace it today, and her hair now hung in a sloppy ponytail, not at all typical of her.

Pulling her knees to her chest, she hugged herself tightly, shivering under her T-shirt, even though the day was hot. In the muted afternoon light, without the free-flowing hair and makeup, she looked small and frightened. Vulnerable. Real.

She cupped a hand around her neck, as if she were feeling for the pulse there, or trying to steady it, then wrapped her arms over her knees again. "We'll have to do something. We can't stay here forever. Boone's going to need this house. You have to go to school. . . ." Blinking, she checked the yard, studied the trees overhead. "What time is it? What day?"

"The first of August."

"We've been here almost a month." It wasn't a statement or a question, more a thought left unfinished. Her eyes welled again. "The twins start at Bramler on August nineteenth. . . ." The sentence rose in the middle and fell at the end, as if she knew that Bramler Academy was now way out of reach. Her teeth clenched, drawing her cheeks tight. "It's not fair."

"I don't know what's fair anymore," I whispered. Living here, seeing the people at the Summer Kitchen and in the reading class, I found it hard to deny that we were still much better off than many. People who had been living just like us were now eating at the Summer Kitchen and subsisting in low-income apartments because they'd lost their jobs, lost their homes, made investments that went sour. Barbie and I could be so much worse off, and if we didn't do something soon, we would be. Our situation as it was couldn't last.

"I'm not going back to school in the fall," I said. "I'm going to start looking for a job."

Barbie's gaze flicked toward me. "You can't. Paul would be so upset. He wanted you to have that golf scholarship."

Her advocating for my father caused me to pull away. How could she defend him? If he cared so much, where was he? "I don't want to talk about him. I don't ever want to hear his name again."

I felt Barbie's touch on my hair. By instinct, I shifted away, and she withdrew her hand. "He loves you, you know. You should hear the way he talks about you, the way he talks about that scholarship. He's so proud of you."

"I didn't even want the scholarship. He never asked me what I wanted. He never listened."

The cat wandered across the porch, and Barbie scooped it up, held it in her lap, and stroked it. "I was always . . . jealous of the way he looked at you, like you were his little princess. He admired you so much. You were everything I could never be."

"Barbara, what are you talking about?" As far as I could tell, my father was mesmerized by Barbie. Why else would he have given her everything she wanted, including four kids, none of whom were his idea?

She laughed softly, ruefully. "You were perfect. His perfect little girl. I always wanted to be somebody's perfect anything. I wanted someone to love me that way."

"My father loved you." Even now, it was hard to admit. I'd always convinced myself that his attraction to Barbie was merely physical— the hormonal insanity of a man facing midlife. I'd told myself that the pretty young wife and the batch of in vitro kids were merely a form of denial—his way of pretending he was in his twenties instead of his fifties. I wondered if he'd ever considered that he'd be over seventy before Jewel graduated from high school.

Now she might never know him at all. Would she end up like Shasta someday—desperately trying to fill the gap created by a father who'd left her behind?

"He took care of me," Barbie said quietly, her expression hard and sad as she tracked something in the brush by the creek. "He liked the way I look. That's all there ever is."

"You let it be that way. You let it be just about the surface." Who was I to talk? Hadn't my life been mostly window dressing? In the weeks since the Rosburten crash, not one person, not even my so-called best friend, had called to check on me. I could be marked off like any other engagement that no longer fit into the social calendar. The worst of it was that I felt the same way. Other than the convenience, the ease of it, I didn't miss my old life, or the people who had filled it. Amazingly, this life, my life here, felt real, and raw, and important, close to the center. I'd dug down because I'd been forced to, excavated myself, and begun to discover someone I never knew existed.

Barbie's shoulders rose and fell with a sigh, thin lines of bone appearing through the T-shirt, and then disappearing again. "There's nothing else anyone would want to see. The inside's not always so pretty."

"The inside is what's real."

Her lips trembled, full, perfect, perfectly sad. "I'm not like you, Tam. I'm not strong."

"You must be." I felt the connection to Barbie again. Part of me wanted to reach out and take her hand, but I didn't. "You must be, or you wouldn't still be here."

Looking at her hands, she picked a rhinestone off the fingernail polish Fawn's spa had probably done for her, pro bono. "I always found someone to take care of me. You can always find someone who likes the way you look, if you're pretty. . . ." Her cell phone vibrated on the decking beside her, and she twisted to look at the screen. "It's Fawn," she muttered to no one in particular, then hit the button and silenced it. For a half second, I expected her to get up and take the phone into the house, but then she just slid it farther away, as if it were a temptation she didn't need right now.

Somewhere nearby, a car alarm started going off as we watched Aunt Lute and the boys patrol the edges of the yard and gaze over the fence into the creek. Aunt Lute plucked something from a bush and placed it carefully in the boys' hands. Running with newfound treasures cupped in their fingers, they hurried back to the porch to show us. Landon opened his hands, and a tiny canoe rocked back and forth, teetering on his fleshy index finger. "Is a boat!" Rolling the boat over, he displayed the bottom, where the letters *B-o-A-t* had been clumsily scratched into the wood.

"It sure is," I said. "Did Aunt Lute give that to you?"

"Her get it from a tree!" Landon's face was filled with the magical glow of toy-bearing trees—like wild blackberry vines, only better. Even the blaring of the car alarm couldn't dampen his enthusiasm. All three of the boys were so caught up in Aunt Lute's story, they seemed oblivious to the noise.

"The Lady of the Water has left them for us," Aunt Lute yelled over the racket as she crossed the yard, a paisley scarf fluttering on her shoulders like multicolored hair. "Aren't they lovely? We'll run a sink of water and sail them. Then tonight, we'll lay them by our beds so that in our dreams, we might sail off down the river like Hiawatha."

"The canoes were a great idea, Aunt Lute," I said. No telling where she had found the little boats—probably someplace in the boxes of junk she kept piled on the porch.

She laid a splay-fingered hand on her chest. "Oh, not mine— the Lady of the Water. The boats were hers. Perhaps her little fairies grew tired of rowing and left them there in the bushes." Sometimes it almost seemed as if Aunt Lute really believed her own stories. Other times, I knew she was crazy like a fox, and making up invisible ponies and the Lady of the Water was just her way of dealing with the kids and escaping the weirdness of our lives.

"It's really nice." Barbie fingered Mark's canoe, then set it back in his hands and smiled. I knew she was trying. Normally, Barbie didn't think anything Aunt Lute came up with was nice.

Aunt Lute drew back, her headscarf catching the breeze. "Why, thank you very much," she said, her surprise evident. "Perhaps one day the Lady of the Water will leave something for you, as well."

Barbie didn't sneer as she usually would have, but just nodded. "I don't have much imagination. Growing up, I didn't see much use for it."

Aunt Lute bent close to her, slowly extending a hand toward Barbie until her fingers cupped Barbie's chin and they were eye-to-eye. The noise of the car alarm suddenly seemed far away. "It's never too late," she whispered. "Don't let them tell you who you are. You know who you are." For a moment, they were frozen in that pose, an odd diorama—Aunt Lute in her sun hat with her scarf drifting on the breeze, and Barbie in her lopsided ponytail, still wearing the sloppy sweats she'd had on all day. They seemed as if they were transferring information without speaking, as if they understood each other for the first time. Aunt Lute took one of the Lady of the Water's wooden animals, which hung from a string around her neck, and slipped it over Barbie's hair, crowning her with it. "There you are," she whispered, as if Barbie had been lost and was suddenly found. "Welcome, Princess Andalusia."

Mark stepped back and pointed toward the side yard, where a long shadow was advancing. "Somebody's here!"

"Perhaps it's the Lady of the Water," Aunt Lute suggested.

Mark bolted toward the side yard and the other boys followed.

"Boys, wait!" I called after them, but they were already rounding the house. Barbie and I slid off the steps and followed, catching them at the gate as they were trying to let in Shasta and her kids.

"Hey, I meant to call you this . . ." I caught the look on Shasta's face, and my heart jumped. She was sweaty and wide-eyed, out of breath, her hair clinging to her cheeks in moist, dark strands.

"Something's wrong." She panted out the words, pointing toward the source of the alarm, somewhere on the other side of our house. "Oh, I'm so glad you're here! I didn't know what to do. I'm trying to get in, and the boys are following me around, and I'm trying to figure out how to get in, and I keep hollering and hollering, and no one's answering, but then I heard moaning. I know I heard someone."

"Where? What's going on?" I struggled to unhook the chain on the gate, but it was rusted shut.

Clasping a hand over her forehead, Shasta caught her breath. "At Elsie's. Something's wrong at Elsie's. Something's been weird all day. The place has been dark and the blinds have been down since morning. I noticed earlier that her car was in the driveway, but I didn't think anything about it. And then I heard a car alarm, and I walked outside to look, and the car door was open. Then I realized the car was there when Cody got off work last night. Elsie never leaves her car out all night. She always comes home from class, lets herself in through the front door, then goes around and opens the garage and puts her car in. She said her garage door remote quit working. I told her it wasn't safe for her to be leaving the car there and coming back out in the dark. What if somebody followed her in? What if someone did something to her? I tried to get into her house just now, but all the doors are locked."

"Okay, just a minute." Yanking the chain free, I opened the gate. "Leave the boys here, and I'll come with you to see what's going on."

Chapter 26

Sesay

The woman, Elsie, has trouble today, I think, and perhaps overnight as well. When I came this morning to leave tiny boats for Root and Berry and the other children, something was not right. I know the way the houses look. I know the rooms where they sleep, which spaces they enter in the mornings, which lights they use, when the curtains open. Elsie's house was dark this morning. I went away and came back again, and it remained so. I heard someone inside, faint, just a low moaning and moving, and the sound told me something was not as it should be.

I tried to think of the good thing to do. The best thing. If I told someone, and the police came, they would know I have been around her house. They would say I am a thief. *When you're living on the street, you feel like you can't trust anybody.* Terence said this last night, and I know it is true. *I understand, don't worry. But sooner or later, you have to come in out of the rain, Sesay. Sooner or later, you have to let yourself become human again.* He told me how to find the hidden key to his building, then. He showed me how to open the lock. He showed me the room where I could stay and the sink where I could wash. He said, *I'm leaving for an art festival in the morning. Look after the place a couple days for me, all right? You can stain those frames and sweep up the sawdust if you want. Be sure to lock up the place whenever you're gone.* We sat and talked a long time, and then he went to his home. He left me in his building with his things all around me, as if I were someone who could be trusted. As if I were *someone.*

I finished my boats early in the morning and went away. Everything was just as it had been before. I did not bother anything. I am not a thief. I am not a thief just because I watch the people. Just because I watch their houses. No one other than me has seen that it was wrong at Elsie's house this morning. But I left it. I left it as it was, because I must be careful. Elsie is not a kind woman. She would tell the police to send me back to *him.* She would tell them to put me on a boat.

But I could not stay away forever. A person, a person who is *someone,* wouldn't leave an old woman when there is trouble, and so I opened the car and caused it to wail, and then I hurried away.

I watch and wait as the young women run across the street and try to enter the house. I can see them from under the bridge, my hiding place. Sirens howl in the distance, coming closer. Someone has called the police. The good thing would be to travel down the creek to a safer place, but I feel as if I am bound here, my feet trapped in the sand. I want to know. I must know. The feeling is strange, after such a long time of being only myself.

Sooner or later, you have to come in out of the rain. . . . Terence is speaking in my chest, and I creep from under the bridge, move to the edge of the bushes, watch the police car and the fire truck race along the street. They work to open the garage door. They are quickly in. The young women run into the garage, and the firemen follow, and I can no longer hear their voices. I move out of the creek, slip along the front of the yellow house, hide behind the porch, but still the voices are too faint. There is only the noise of fast talking and clinking metal. I look around, creep across the front of the porch, slip behind the oleander bush. The police car is close. A breath pushes hard in my chest, trapped, and my heart pounds as if I am the muck rabbit in the cane patch. In my throat, a hummingbird flaps its wings.

I try to be still, to listen.

"Elsie? Elsie? Can you hear me? What happened?" a voice calls out, and Elsie answers in words that run together like drops of syrup on a plate.

Voices continue. I hear pieces.

". . . alert bracelet."

"Blood sugar or the heat. Give me a body temp. . . ."

"Elsie? Elsie? How long have you been here?"

"Okay, now calm down. It's all right. We're just going to check you out and . . ." An air conditioner wakes and roars between the houses, and I can no longer hear. I should go away, move farther from the police car, but I wait. I must know. Firemen walk to and from the garage with their medical boxes. A new police car comes, then drives away. I think of the line picture for this word *police*. I cannot sound it out letter by letter. I cannot decode it, but I know this word. I have seen it on their cars many times.

Finally, there are only the firemen. The air conditioner goes to sleep, and I hear them taking Elsie into her house. The firemen leave with concerned faces. The young women walk out and speak with them in the driveway. I crouch behind the oleander bush.

"I'll watch her," Shasta, my teacher, says. "I'll check through the night and make sure she's all right."

The fireman shakes his head. "We can't force her to go to the hospital, but she needs to understand that she had a close call. I know it's hard for an older person living alone to face that fact sometimes, but another hour or two locked in that garage, and this could've been much worse. Between the heat in there and her health problems, she could've easily slipped into a diabetic coma and been gone. I know she's upset and embarrassed now, but her family needs to address this issue with her. A fall like this, when an older person can't get up and get to the phone and, in her case, the medications needed to regulate her blood sugar, could easily turn deadly. She's extremely lucky someone was checking on her."

My teacher hugs herself and shivers, even though her skin has a sheen of sweat. "I wasn't checking on her. It was just . . . just a miracle that the car door fell open when it did, and the alarm went off. Thank God it did." She squints toward Elsie's car, her eyes narrow with thought, as if she is considering this miracle. *Did Father God bring me here this morning?* I wonder. And then I know that it is so. Father God has given a miracle to me in Terence, and now He has used me to make one. His was the voice speaking in my mind just now, telling me I must do the good thing. Telling me I can. I would not have found the courage to do such a thing on my own.

When their backs are turned, I slip from beneath the oleander bush and move to the bridge. They do not see me, but Father God sees. He smiles at me from heaven, and I feel it.

I sit in the cool sand underneath the bridge, where I have tucked my pack and my blanket. Leaning back against them, I close my eyes and let the hummingbird in my throat slowly beat its wings to a stop. All is well now. All is well. . . .

My mind drifts away on a sea of word pictures. *Bird, store, milk, the, dog, cat, run, jump, fly, sky, try, sun.* Such beautiful words. *Boat, water, God . . .*

I hear the creek passing by in a trickle.

I hear the ocean.

I feel the water.

I think of my grandfather. He is standing on the shore, beckoning me. I take his hand, and we walk long across the burned place, and I am a little girl again, hearing his stories. . . .

Children laugh somewhere nearby. "You ca-an't catch me!" one calls out.

I open my eyes to the long afternoon shadows. "You ca-an't catch me!" It is Root. I know his voice. "I wanna sail my boat!" He cheers. "Mommy, I wanna go down in the creek." They are on the side of the house, close to me. The chain rattles on the gate as the boy tries to open it.

I take my pack and move to the other end of the bridge.

"Not now, Ty," his mother says. "We need to stay here and get the hot dogs ready for everybody. We're gonna have a picnic, remember?"

"Yay! A picnic!"

She laughs at his words. "Tell you what—before the fire gets going too much, let's walk over and check on Elsie. If she's feeling better, maybe she'll come sit out with us while we grill the hot dogs."

"'Kay," the little boy says.

I can smell a fire starting. The smell carries my mind to the village when I am a child. I can see my grandfather bending over the small kettle that hangs above the fire outside our house. My mouth waters, and I think that if I hurry, I might walk to the mission before the line is long.

I listen as Root and Berry move away with their mother; then I climb from the creek and slip around the railing. The branches slap closed behind me, striking the railing, ringing it like a drum.

"Mommy! Wook! There a lady! Is a red-dress lady!"

I do not stop, but walk faster. The hummingbird flutters in my throat.

"Hey!" the mother calls. She is my teacher, but she has never spoken to me before. She has never *seen* me. "Hey, wait!"

I continue on, but she is coming. I can hear her running behind me, the boys running with her. She will be angry that I am here. She will say, *What are you doing near my house! Stay away!*

Their footsteps are hollow on the bridge. "Stop!" she says, panting.

I hope she will grow tired of chasing me, but she does not. Soon she is just behind me, close enough to touch. "Wait!"

Chapter 27

Shasta Reid-Williams

She stood on the sidewalk with her back to me, her shoulders hunched like she was hiding something, protecting it. I skidded to a stop, pulling Benji and Ty back by their hands. What if this woman was dangerous? I had the boys with me. If she got confrontational, it wasn't like I could run away.

Even Benji and Ty didn't seem sure of what we were doing. During story time at the Summer Kitchen, when she was telling tales, they smiled at the voodoo lady and scooted closer to the front, but they weren't smiling now. Benji had moved a step behind me, and Ty was tugging on his shorts like he had to go to the bathroom. Maybe they could tell I was afraid, or maybe they'd clued into the same thing I had—that even though she probably wasn't five foot tall, and her stooped-over body was so thin her hair was the biggest part of her, there was something intimidating about her up close.

"I can walk here," she said, keeping her back turned. Her voice bounced off the canopy of branches overhead and echoed under the bridge.

Benji cocked his head to one side, looking up at me. Ty fidgeted and crossed his legs. Whatever was going to happen here needed to happen quick, before we had a potty accident.

"It was you, wasn't it?" The question went from my mind to my lips before I had time to convert it into something that'd make sense. "You opened Elsie's car door, didn't you? You made the car alarm go off." Everything was coming together now. In all the excitement over Elsie's close call, I hadn't really thought about why a car door that'd been shut all night would suddenly come open. Even if it hadn't been latched all the way, something must of given it a push—something more than the wind. When I saw the voodoo lady hustling up the street, it all made sense. "You opened the car door, didn't you?"

She folded herself harder over whatever she was carrying. I leaned to one side to see, just in case it was a weapon or something I should be worried about. A backpack. It was only her backpack. The same one she kept with her during reading classes, like she was afraid someone would steal the nasty old thing, or she needed to be ready for a quick getaway.

"I can walk here," she said again. "The police, they know I can walk here." Her voice was rushed and breathless, nervous, her accent blending the words together in a smooth string.

"Who said anything about the police?" Did she think I was accusing her of doing something wrong? I remembered what Terence had said about the street people. *Most of them are harmless. They're just afraid, you know? It's not easy when nobody wants you around. You don't know what it's like, living on the street, until you've been there.*

"It was no harm to the car. No damage. I am not a thief." She swayed in place, like she was thinking about taking a step forward, wondering what I'd do if she tried to leave. The muscles in her thin, brown calves tensed and loosened under her leathery skin.

Ty held the front of his shorts tighter and whined, "Mommy, I ga go."

I squeezed his hand. If I took him to the bathroom now, the woman would disappear. No telling when I'd see her again—since she thought I was accusing her of something, probably never. "Look, I wasn't saying you did anything wrong. You probably saved Elsie's life. The paramedics told us if she'd been in there a couple more hours, it could've been seriously bad. I saw her car in the driveway this morning, and it seemed strange, but I just didn't think much about it. How'd you know something was wrong?"

She cut a quick glance over her shoulder, like she had a big dog behind her and she was trying to figure out whether it was friendly or not. "The houses tell things. And the clothes. You can hear them, if you listen."

Benji twisted to check out the houses behind us, like he was wondering why they never talked to him.

"Oh . . ." *Maybe she really is mental, after all.* "I just wondered how you knew, that's all."

She took two steps. One. Two. Slowly, in a circle toward me. Her eyes, cloudy black dots nearly hidden in folds of skin polished like shoe leather, checked me out from behind dreadlocks dusted gray and white. "It is quiet this morning when I am passing by. No television."

"At Elsie's house?"

She nodded. "The window is covered where she sits in her chair. No sun can come in, and she cannot see the street. She will always watch the street from her chair."

"Ohhh," I breathed, feeling like a horrible neighbor. The house *was* different this morning. There were no signs of Elsie's routine— TV on before seven, front window blind open by the time the sun hit the porch. I'd sort of noticed, but I had my mind on my own issues, and I never gave her another thought. It was weird to think that this homeless woman, this person who wandered our street, paid more attention than I did. If she hadn't been watching, Elsie could've died right there in her garage. "You did a good thing, you know."

She shifted another step, cocked her head, and looked at me curiously, like she was waiting for me to say something more.

Ty tugged my hand. "Momm-eee!"

I glanced over my shoulder toward my house, then Elsie's. The blind was up now. I could see a shadow figure of Elsie, still sitting in her chair where the paramedics left her. "Do you want to come eat a hot dog with us?" The question was out of my mouth and into the air before I knew it was coming. I felt the woman watching me as I turned around again. Her name popped into my mind. Sesay. I'd told Terence I wanted to find out about her. If I really did, here was my chance. "We're getting ready to have a picnic. . . ." I thumbed over my shoulder. "In the backyard." Her gaze flicked toward the yard. My mouth just kept right on sprinting ahead of my brain, which was nothing new. "We're not doing anything fancy. Just hot dogs, chips, and some cookies the boys and me baked earlier, but . . ."

"Momm-eee! I ga go." Ty was close to tears. It wasn't fair to make him wait any longer.

I let go of Benjamin's hand and scooped Ty up, so he wouldn't have to walk. "We'll be out back . . . in the yard. Give me a sec to go in and take him to the potty, and then we'll be there. Just come on around to the side gate, okay?" I didn't wait for an answer. Ty was working so hard to hold it, his face was turning red, and there wasn't much choice but to turn around, grab Benji, and make a run for it.

My brain caught up with me the minute I had Ty safely on the step stool with his shorts down and his body aimed in the right direction. *What in the world were you thinking, inviting some homeless woman to come share a picnic?* When Cody, Mr. Master-of-Gory-Police-Stories, heard about this, he'd have a cow. If my mother or Cody's parents ever heard about it, they'd ship me off and take my kids back to Oklahoma so fast Cody wouldn't even know what hit him.

She's harmless, though; Terence says she's harmless. . . . I could already picture myself defending this little stupid Shasta trick when Cody found out about it. *Geez, Shas, where does your brain go sometimes?* he'd say. Maybe I didn't need to be somebody's mother. I should've been thinking first about the kids and keeping them safe.

She probably won't come. I peeked out the front window, but I couldn't see anyone. *She probably thinks you're nuts, too.*

Just in case, I texted Tam and told her to hurry up and get over here. *Invited the voodoo lady*, I blurted out in rapid thumb strokes.

Tam was shocked textless, which just proved she had more brains than I did. All she could do was send a line of question marks.

Impulse, I sent back. *Explain later.*

K. All right if Barbie comes?

The stepmonster? I'd noticed that Barbie was actually in the yard with them when I ran over there during the Elsie incident, but this was too much. Barbie coming to the picnic instead of heading out with her party buddy?

Impulse, Tam texted back. *Aunt Lute coming, too.*

Full house, LOL. I wondered who was crazier—Aunt Lute, the voodoo lady, or me. It'd be a close contest.

Benjamin raced by with a plastic basket full of toy cars as I closed the phone and tucked it into my pocket. "I'm goin' outside!" I heard him trying to work the dead bolt to get out the back door.

"N' goin' outsigh!" Ty was a half step behind Benji, running bow-legged while trying to drag his shorts over his bare rear end.

"Hang on a minute!" The sharp edge of my voice froze them both in the laundry room. No way were they going out there without me. "Let's get the food and carry it to the picnic table. Then we'll worry about the toys."

The boys did an about-face. I handed out the supplies while they jittered and backed toward the door; then I went through the picnic checklist in my head before turning the lock and peeking into the yard.

It looked empty. Maybe Sesay was waiting at the gate. Part of me hoped she would come, and part of me hoped she wouldn't.

Benjamin plopped the tray of hot-dog buns and chips on the back porch table and took off as I was hip-butting the door out of the way so Ty could get out with the punch bottle he was hugging.

"I'm gonna go let the lady in!" Benji called back.

"No, Benji, wait!" I swiveled, and the weenies rolled to one side of the platter, almost tumbling off before I could catch them.

Ty dropped the punch bottle like a hot potato and took off after his brother.

The weenies rolled to the other side of the platter while I rescued the punch bottle. The phone rang in my pocket.

By the time I'd stopped the weenie roll, set down the platter, and grabbed the phone, my boys were leading the voodoo lady into the yard like she was the Easter bunny dropping by for a visit.

I answered the phone and, of all people, it was my mother. Talk about bad timing. After "Hello," she went right into, "Well, I thought I'd better call, since we haven't heard your voice in weeks now. I know you don't want to use up your cell minutes, but once in a while, Shasta, you could pick up the phone and call. If it weren't for an e-mail every once in a while I'd think you had dropped off the face of the earth."

"No, Mama, we're fine." Of all the times for her to decide to end the war of who was going to call first, she had to pick now. "We've just been busy, that's all." I knew I should start out by telling her about the house, but if I did, I'd get a full-blown lecture, and I didn't have time for it. If I didn't tell her, the boys would spill it as soon as I put them on the phone. "Mama, can we call you back later on? We've got some neighbors over and we're about to grill hot dogs."

"Neighbors?" Mama repeated suspiciously. Right after we'd moved to Dallas, I'd let it slip that the boys didn't need to be hanging around anybody who lived in those nasty apartments. "I'll be at work later. Night shift tonight. Let me talk to my babies real quick."

I watched the boys lead Sesay to the shed to show her their dirt pile. She picked up a stick and drew something in the sand. If I put either of them on the phone, who knew what they'd blab. In three-point-five hours, Mama would show up at my doorstep, ready to see what kind of a mess we'd gotten ourselves into. She'd be sure this was just like when we jumped into getting the trailer. "They're all the way at the other end of the yard."

"Yard?"

Shoot! Wake up, Shasta. "I mean the park. We're at the park. With some other . . . families . . . from Cody's class." There's something really pitiful when you have kids of your own and you're still lying to your parents. "It's a long story, Mama. I'll tell you later, okay? I don't think either of the boys could stand still and talk on the phone right now. They're busy having fun." That came out exactly wrong, and Mama made a throaty sound that let me know it right away.

"I didn't realize talking to their *grandma* was such a burden." When she was in a mood like this, nothing I could say would be right. This was totally not the time to tell her about the house.

"I didn't mean it like that, Mama. Of course they want to talk to you. They ask about you all the time."

"Then you'd think you could call once in a while."

I sighed, frustrated, trying to keep an eye on things as Sesay and the boys headed around the side of the house. Tam's brothers were making a racket at the gate. "I've been trying not to run up the cell minutes, remember? Cody's after me to save money."

"Well, I told you everything in Dallas would cost more than you thought. Those ads make it sound like the jobs bring big money up there, but when you get to paying for things, it's all gone quicker than you can say *flat broke*. Honestly, Shasta, Cody'd be so much better off back here at the Push County Sheriff's Department. Y'all could maybe even get into a house here. Luanne Wright has hers for sale. She's moving into the nursing home. I dropped by and looked at the place yesterday, and . . ." Mama went on as Tam's brothers bolted into the yard, then scattered, all giggles and squeals while they whipped each other with long stalks of grass they'd picked from the fence. Sesay stepped out of their way, watching as Tam rounded the corner. Aunt Lute was behind her, along with, major surprise, the stepmother, who was carrying my favorite baby girl.

"Mama"—I jumped into Mama's description of Luanne's house for sale. Three bedrooms, and the cutest little bathroom, all redone— "Mama . . . I should probably go, okay? I'll call you later on."

Mama answered with a loud huff. "You'd better, Shasta Marie, and if you don't, my feelings are going to be hurt. I know there's a lot going on here, with your cousin building that new house and having a big church wedding, but that's no excuse for you to sulk."

"I'm not sulking, Mama."

Setting a plate of carrot sticks and dip on the table, Tam raised an eyebrow at me. Beside her, the stepmonster pretended not to hear me arguing with Mama on the phone.

"Well, it sure seems like it." Mama's voice quavered, close to tears. No matter how much I wanted to, it seemed like I'd never find a way to break free without hurting her. "Used to be there wasn't a day went by, you didn't call two or three times, and that was when y'all were living right down the road, for heaven's sake."

I'm trying to grow up. "There just hasn't been much to call about. Things've been pretty tame, and besides, like I said, we're trying to save the cell minutes. E-mail's free."

"Do you two need money? Is that the problem? Because if you need money for the phone bill, Shasta Marie, I can . . ."

"We don't need money, Mama." I felt myself being reeled in like a pet puppy on a string, pulled to a place that was easy and familiar, where someone would pat me on the head and feed me Milk-Bones. If I let myself, I'd end up right back where I started from, a kid having kids, letting my mama raise us all when she should of been doing what she wanted. If she hadn't been putting her time and money into us, she could of traveled, or fixed up her place, or bought that convertible Ford Mustang she always wanted. She could put the top down and drive around town with the wind in her hair, and give all the other ladies at the hospital something to talk about. "Don't worry about us, okay? We're gonna do this ourselves." Blood prickled into my cheeks, and I felt everyone listening while they politely arranged picnic food and pretended not to hear.

Tam thumbed toward Elsie's house and whispered, "I'll run over and see about Elsie, 'kay?"

I nodded and Tam disappeared, seeming glad to escape the Mama conversation. Tam's aunt and stepmother walked a few steps away and pretended to admire the hollyhocks.

"There's just no point in being too proud, Shasta." Mama knew there was a secret I wasn't telling her. Sometimes it was like she had ears in my brain.

I want to be proud. I want to be proud of something I've done. "We're fine, Mama. Really. I promise we'll come down for a visit once Cody's not working so much. He's been doing some temp jobs."

"Because you need money."

"Mama, I told you, we're fine."

She huffed again—the same sound she used to make when some teacher sent a test home with a note saying, *Shasta is capable of more, but she just doesn't apply herself.* "Why do you have to be so stubborn?"

"Because I'm like my mama."

I could picture her rolling her eyes and shaking her head as she said good-bye and hung up the phone.

Tam came back with Elsie just about the time I was moving to the sand pile to make what would probably be some highly weird introductions. Tam walked slowly beside Elsie, her elbow held out like she was trying to help Elsie walk, but Elsie wasn't having any of it.

They stopped at the porch, and Elsie plunked herself into a lawn chair, looking like she was here to get a cavity drilled or pay her taxes instead of share a hot dog and a little company. By the sand pile, Sesay retreated into the shadow of the bushes, watching the boys sail little wooden boats on a pretend lake. Meanwhile, Tam's stepmother was keeping her distance with the baby, and the crazy aunt was talking, but it was hard to tell who she was talking to. She looked like an actor in a play, sending a monologue into thin air.

"I'm fine," Elsie grumbled. "You didn't need to come bring me over here, and . . ." She squinted across the yard then and figured out who was in the shadows beside the shed. "What'n the name of blazes is *that* doin' here?"

I took a breath. So far, my neighborhood picnic was a bomb. "I asked her to come eat a hot dog with us."

"You joinin' the mission service?" Elsie wasn't in one of her better moods, although her moods were usually bad, or at least that's what showed on the outside. I had a feeling that, on the inside, Elsie was lonely and scared. It couldn't be easy at her age, living all by yourself.

"I thought you might want to tell her thank you," I said, still feeling pretty snippy after talking with Mama.

Tam's head swiveled, and her eyes went wide. She'd never seen my bratty side. Normally, it took Mama, my brother, Jace, or one of my know-it-all cousins to bring that out.

Elsie pulled back, sitting ramrod straight in her chair, her chin disappearing into the folds of skin hanging underneath. "What'n the world for? For hangin' around lookin' over my shoulder all the time in that class? Just standin' there like some kind of vagrant, gettin' in the way of normal folk?"

Something in me snapped, then. I was sick of people being hard on each other, being hateful and critical when there wasn't any need for it. I was sick of mortgage companies sending bills you didn't sign up for, and Mama acting like I'd always be a screwup, and working but never seeming to have enough money, and the world just taking one look and sticking you in a box and trying to keep you there. Maybe people, even people like Sesay, were more than what showed on the surface.

I turned to Elsie and blurted out the first thing that came to mind. "Well, you know what? Maybe you might want to thank Sesay for saving your life, because she did."

Chapter 28

Tam Lambert

The picnic in Shasta's backyard was like one of those somewhat unwanted presents you end up with at the holiday gift exchange: It
seems like a disappointment at first, but over time, it grows on you.
Our gathering started off on shaky ground, none of us knowing what
to talk about or where to be. Elsie sat on the porch giving everyone
unpleasant looks, Sesay hid in the shadows by the garden shed, Shasta
fussed over the food like Martha Stewart, and Barbie hovered by the
sandbox, holding Jewel and nervously fingering a heart-shaped neck-
lace my father had given her. She looked as if she regretted having
come.

Fortunately no gathering could remain quiet with five young boys
present. After they'd finished in the sand pile, Shasta's kids wanted to
pull out a croquet set they'd found in the shed. Shasta told them no at
first, and I leaned close to her and whispered, "Why not? It'll give us
something to do." We shared the slightly desperate silent exchange of
people whose party was flopping, and then she set down the hot-dog
platter and turned off the grill.

"Good idea," she said. "Let's have a little fun before we eat."

Mark, Landon, and Aunt Lute passed out the mallets, while
Shasta, Tyler, and Benjamin pushed wire hoops into the ground. Tyler
handed a mallet to Sesay, and she held it close to her face, smoothing

a finger over the cracks in the old wood. When Mark took a mallet to Elsie, she frowned and pushed it away.

"I'm just gonna watch," she grumbled. "I ain't up for game playin'."

Standing by the porch step with her arms crossed, Barbie seemed to echo those sentiments. She checked her watch, probably counting the minutes until we could go home. When Mark tried to hand her a mallet, she smiled indulgently, but didn't reach for it. "I don't need one, honey. You go ahead and play."

Mark's smile faded and his shoulders drooped, the mallet hanging loose at his side. He was used to being told that Mommy didn't have time.

I was tempted to walk across the yard and smack Barbie. Couldn't she see that all the kids really wanted was her attention? Would it kill her to play croquet?

Aunt Lute handed Landon a mallet and sent him back to Elsie's chair. "Oh, but everyone must play," she insisted. "The Queen of Hearts has decreed it. The game isn't the least bit strenuous. You won't muss your hair." With a pointed look at Barbie, she motioned for Mark to return to the porch with the unwanted mallet. "Unless, of course, your hedgehog should run away, and then it's off with your head! Hedgehogs are such mischievous little things. Alice's hedgehog wouldn't cooperate at all. And the mallet kissed her. Good heavens, what a sight that was!"

Barbie and Elsie grudgingly took possession of their croquet equipment. Aunt Lute explained the rules in terms of flamingos and hedgehogs, and the game of queen's croquet began. After a few shots, Elsie was granted a reprieve from play, when she stumbled over an uneven spot in the yard. "I ain't a invalid," she argued, then laid a hand on Daniel's shoulder. "Go get my chair, there, little fella, and bring it out here where I can sit in it while I wait for my turn." She reached for Jewel, whom Barbie had been carrying in one arm. "Here, let me hold that baby while you take your shot. You're gonna need both hands to outplay me. I got that hedgehog goin' right where I want it."

The game continued from there, Aunt Lute directing the queen's men, Jewel watching from Elsie's lap, Sesay tucking her hair into the collar of her dress to keep it out of the way, and Barbie purposely missing shots, so as not to get ahead of the boys. Landon and Tyler, too young to navigate the game very well, eventually resorted to rolling their hedgehogs like bowling balls. Aunt Lute decreed a foul, pronounced a sentence of "Off with their heads!" and she and Barbie chased the boys around the yard.

While Shasta cooked the hot dogs after the croquet game, Sesay helped the boys find rocks from the flower bed and a small ball from the sandbox toys. "I will show you a game my mother teaches me when I am very young," she said, moving to the porch with Aunt Lute following curiously behind. "The game is called *oo-slay*. When I am young, the children play this game everywhere they go."

As Sesay explained the game, Elsie peered over the boys' shoulders. "Well, that's like jacks, except usin' a ball and pebbles," Elsie observed, scooting forward in her chair. "I used to win all the time at jacks. Let me see that ball."

Barbie squatted down to watch, and Landon snuggled in beside her, his fingers toying with her hair. Giving him a tender look, she took his hand and kissed it. "You want to give it a try, Landon?" she asked. "Tell you what, I'll bounce the ball and you grab the rocks. Get ready now. . . ."

From her post behind the hot-dog grill, Shasta caught my gaze, winked, and gave me the thumbs-up. Even she knew that this game of mother-son jacks was long overdue.

After supper, we sat together on Shasta's back porch while the boys chased fireflies. Shasta flipped on the porch lights, and Sesay pulled out an art pad Terence had given her. On the pad, she'd drawn familiar objects—a paintbrush, a leaf, a flower, a lizard, a toad, a hummingbird, and dozens of others. She'd planned to have Terence help her write the words, the *line pictures*, she called them, but we sat at Shasta's picnic table and filled in the blanks instead. When the yard grew too dark, the boys wandered to the porch and sounded out the letters as we wrote. Even Elsie participated, leaning forward and tapping a finger to the pad. "That ain't a flower; it's an iris," she said, pointing to Sesay's drawing. "You oughta write *iris*, not flower."

"Let's make both kind," Mark suggested, and Barbie tousled his hair.

"Good idea," she agreed. "They're both nice words to know."

By the end of the evening, we'd achieved a strange but comfortable group harmony, in which we ignored the difficult issues—Elsie's fall in the garage, Barbie's recent behavior, the fact that Sesay was homeless—and we focused on reading instead.

Our time together was quiet, pleasant, relaxing.

"That was nice," Barbie said, as we walked home. Shifting Jewel's droopy body from one shoulder to the other, she turned to watch Sesay disappear down the street. Sesay hadn't said good-bye. She'd simply tucked her pad into her backpack and walked away as we were picking up the dishes. "Where do you think she's going?"

"I think she stays at the mission some." The truth was that I'd tried not to consider it in too much detail. Sesay's life was hard to imagine.

A shiver ran across Barbie's shoulders. "That must be awful."

"Shasta said she's working for the guy who has the studio behind Book Basket, and she might be staying there some. To tell you the truth, she seems more worried about learning words than she does about where she's living."

Barbie sighed, cuddling Jewel under her chin as the boys ran ahead to catch up with Aunt Lute. "I can't imagine what that would be like—to be so old and not know how to read."

"Me, either," I admitted. Watching Sesay struggle over words tonight, I'd tried to imagine being surrounded by words whose meanings were a mystery. Suddenly I realized that the reading class was more than a way for me to pass time. It gave purpose to my stay here on Red Bird Lane. It was something important for which I didn't need money, or nice clothes, or a big house, or a golf scholarship. All I needed was time. Time, I had.

Barbie climbed our porch steps with a resolute sigh, as if she had to steel herself to go inside. "I guess I shouldn't be complaining." It was hard to tell whether she was talking to herself or to me. "At least we have a place."

"Yeah," I agreed, but the words were halfhearted. Even though I knew I should be grateful, it was hard to properly appreciate our overstuffed mess of a house. Right now, the boys were climbing the burglar bars on the front windows, making monkey sounds, and Aunt Lute was pretending to be a zookeeper. Getting them bathed and in bed would be insane tonight, as usual.

Barbie slipped around them and stuck the key in the dead bolt. "I still hate this house, though."

"Me, too," I admitted, and both of us laughed. For once Barbie and I were on the same page, and there wasn't any point trying to hide it. This house was too small for lies, anyway.

Pausing with her hand on the door, Barbie squinted toward the street. "Tomorrow's Sunday," she said out of the blue. "Maybe we should get up and go to church. Not our old one—the little white one where you do the reading class."

I backed up a step, surprised. Shasta had been after me to go to service with her this Sunday, but I'd been putting her off. Attending seemed pointless when it felt like our family was totally off God's radar right now. "Maybe," I muttered.

Barbie shrugged as she pushed open the door. "I guess we can see how we feel tomorrow."

"I guess," I agreed, secure in the knowledge that after such a busy night, Barbie and the kids would sleep way too late to make it to the service at ten a.m. Whenever I saw Shasta tomorrow, I'd apologize and say we overslept. I just wasn't ready to sit in church and sing all the same old songs, and pray the same old prayers. If God hadn't answered by now, He wasn't going to. I was better off not focusing my hopes on divine intervention.

My plan would have worked nicely if Shasta hadn't shown up at eight a.m. with a tray of homemade cinnamon rolls. "We were up early," she chirped, as I answered our door with a serious case of bed head. "We baked." She gave me a big, sheepish smile that was as transparent as a Caribbean sea. She was just making sure we were up. With Cody going to work again today, she didn't want to attend church alone. "See you in a bit." She headed back across the street with an annoying little finger wave. I could already hear Barbie and the kids beginning to stir in the bedrooms. Sunday was off and running, whether I wanted it to be or not.

As it turned out, though, Sunday wasn't all that bad. The congregation members at the old white church were welcoming enough. Elsie greeted us with a curt wave as we came in. Pastor Al acted as if we were visiting celebrities. The choir sang off-key. A homeless man wandered through the door ten minutes into the service and sat in the back among the empty pews. I caught myself looking around for Sesay, but there was no sign of her.

The service was traditional and quiet—no giant projection screens or Christian rock bands like our old church. No call for anyone to come down front and offer up dramatic testimony. Just a simple sermon, a few songs, and a short time of meditation while ushers collected the offering. Barbie dropped a fifty in the basket, and I watched in shock. Not only did the fifty stand out amid the ones and fives, but we couldn't afford it.

When we left, Barbie was in a good mood, and if the fifty-dollar donation bothered her at all, she hid it well. She offered to buy Happy Meals all the way around, and we ended up driving down to McDonald's in the Escalade and Elsie's car. While we ate and talked, the kids played on the playscape, and then we headed home and spent the afternoon trying to figure out how to hook the television to the TV antenna on our roof, so the kids could watch PBS. By the time we were finished, we'd been down to Walmart three times and over to Elsie's twice to look at her television attachment, and then finally concluded that we needed a digital converter box. After it was all said and done, the group of us ended up in our living room, cheering as *Antiques Roadshow* came on the screen. It seemed as if someone were missing from the gathering, and as I glanced out the window, it occurred to me that I was looking for Sesay.

By Monday night, we still hadn't seen her. Shasta and I dropped Shasta's boys at the children's building early and walked to reading class with a sense of anticipation.

"What if something happened to her?" Shasta asked, as we entered from the back.

"It's early still," I whispered, motioning to the room, which was empty except for Elsie and an elderly Hispanic man. "There's hardly anybody here yet."

"Where do you think she was yesterday?"

"No idea, I . . ." I let the sentence trail off as the side entrance creaked open, the gap empty at first, then filled as Sesay shuffled silently through and took her place against the wall.

"She's here early," Shasta whispered, and then cracked a sideways smile.

In her seat up front, Elsie straightened. "If you're gonna be here, you oughta sit down like a normal person," she barked, without looking at Sesay. Reaching under the table, Elsie pushed a chair outward. "There's empty seats here." It wasn't a soft, friendly invitation, but it was an invitation—as close as Elsie was likely to come to repaying Sesay for saving her life.

Sesay moved toward the chair, her gaze darting around the room, her backpack clutched in front of her as if she were sheltering it, or it was sheltering her.

"You got as much right here as anybody. You can set that bag down." Elsie motioned to the floor, the gesture more of a command than a request. Tapping the table with a stiff finger, she added, "Let me see what you got in that drawin' pad of yours today. I might know some of them words. I been workin' with my book. If it kills me and if it don't, I'm gonna get where I can read my Bible for my own self before I meet the author."

The rest of the class and finally our instructor filed in while Sesay and Elsie were studying the notepad. I sat watching, thinking that two days ago I would never have believed they would be huddled together, sounding out words. But you couldn't tell what was possible on the inside just by looking at the outside. These past weeks with Barbie had taught me that much. I'd never imagined she would descend into madness with Fawn, or come out again and take on the Four. But she was trying. We'd sat up talking after the TV fiasco, and I was coming to understand who Barbie really was. She knew what it was like to be a kid bounced in and out of her parents' homes, and farmed out to relatives, and when it came right down to it, she was willing to do whatever it took to keep history from repeating itself. Tonight, she and Aunt Lute were home alone with the Four. "Baby steps," she'd said when I was getting ready to go. "I'm trying."

"I know." I felt a seed of tenderness toward Barbie, which in itself was a minor miracle, considering where we'd started. It occurred to me that if my father could see it, he'd be amazed. I banished the thought as quickly as it came. He wasn't here. He'd left both of us behind, and perhaps Barbie's finally facing that fact was what had created the newfound bond between us.

We were both angry with him. We were both hurt. We were both alone. All we had left was each other and a too-small house that wasn't even ours.

I had no idea where we should go from here. I turned over the problem in my mind as the instructional part of the class proceeded. When we partnered with our clients for tutorials, Demarla had another children's book with her. "They keep givin' my kids these things in the stinkin' children's building here while I'm sittin' in class," she complained. "Soon's I get where I can read one, the kids've got another. I don' know where them people get off, tryin' to make me look dumb in front'a my kids. Like I got time for all this. That judge oughta have his kid bring . . ."

As usual, I waited while Demarla ranted on. Eventually, she gave me a dirty look, smacked the book down on the table, and grumbled, "You gonna help me read this thang, or not, Hannah Montana? That's who you look like, you know? Daggum Hannah Montana."

"Somebody told me that once," I muttered. "Let's do the lesson first, and then we'll read the book."

"We ain't got time for all that."

"We'll make it."

"It's fifteen after already."

"If we'd started right in, instead of you complaining about the judge, we'd have more time."

"Ffff!" Demarla rolled her eyes, and we proceeded with the lesson. When we were done, the college tutors were gone, and the classroom had emptied except for Elsie, Shasta, and Sesay in the front. Demarla beelined through the back door as I gathered my things and moved to the corner of Shasta's table, listening as they finished the lesson. Sesay looked ahead at tomorrow's lesson, while Elsie and Shasta leaned close together, engaged in a conversation I couldn't quite hear. I scooted closer to Sesay to help her with some of the words.

"You're doing really well," I said, when she finally closed the book.

Her eyes lifted from the page, slowly met mine, and she smiled at the compliment. One of her front teeth was rotted or cracked halfway off, and the rest were brown around the edges. She seemed to realize that I'd noticed, and quickly hid her smile behind a wrinkled hand, the knuckles knobby and calloused from some sort of repetitive labor. Obviously, she hadn't always been homeless. "I have known these words before, some of them. My mother teaches me when I am very young, I think."

"Maybe that's why you're doing so well," I suggested. "Maybe you're remembering."

Sesay considered the idea, her eyes cloudy behind a haze of cataracts. "My mother, she is dead when I am very young. I do not know the way she looked, but she is a good mother, I think."

I slid from the table into a chair, trying to imagine not knowing what your mother looked like, not knowing your family. "Where did you come from before you were here, Sesay?"

She studied me intently, as if deciding whether or not she should answer. "This is not good to speak."

Elsie abruptly tuned in to our conversation and scooted away from Shasta. "Why? It a secret?"

Checking the room, Sesay leaned closer, her hand slipping under the table, settling on her backpack. "If *he* finds you, *he* tells the police to bring you back again."

Apprehension tingled under my skin, like gooseflesh rising. Maybe she was running from an abusive husband. Maybe Shasta and I were inadvertently involving ourselves in something that could become dangerous. "Who does?" Around us, the old building creaked and settled, making the conversation seem more ominous.

"*Him.* He brings you back to work if he finds you."

My mind grasped for possibilities—sweatshop employee, prostitute, shill in some kind of illegal drug trade. . . .

"Can't nobody force you to work. It's a free country." Elsie jumped into the discussion again. Beside her, Shasta had turned away, her head in her hand, as if she wasn't feeling well.

Sesay's gaze darted back and forth between Elsie and me. "You must pay for your bed and the food you have eaten," she whispered. "Or the police will take you away and lock you in a room, or send you over the water in a boat."

Elsie snorted, her lips pressed into a thin line. "Where's this?"

"In Mmm-eye-amm-eee."

Scoffing, Elsie hammered a stubby fist against the tabletop, causing a pencil to hop sideways. "Listen here. I don't know what kind of hogwash you been told, but I do know that Miami's in the United

States of America, and I sure as heck got far enough in school to learn the dadgum Declaration of Independence in the fifth grade. 'We hold them truths to be self-evident, that all men been created equal, and their creator give them the right to life, liberty, and the pursuit a' happiness.' This ain't the Soviet States of the Union. There ain't no king here. Nobody can *make* you work for them, nor drag you off to jail if you don't. Nobody can get throwed in jail unless they done somethin' illegal. It ain't illegal not to work—just look at all them folks sittin' around collectin' welfare, and livin' on the street down by the mission. There ain't *a man* throwin' them in jail." She punctuated the sentence by pushing her chair back, sending an ear-piercing squeal through the room. Shasta didn't even notice. She was staring at the floor, scrubbing her forehead with her fingertips, her face pale.

"Are you all right?" I tossed a pencil down the table to get her attention. As interested as she'd been in Sesay, it was hard to believe she wasn't tuning in to the conversation.

"That's my fault, I reckon," Elsie said bluntly, while fishing under the table for her purse. "She's been askin' me about her house, and I didn't figure it was my place to serve up bad news, but somethin' like that'll eat away at you, so I just now told her the truth. I ain't trying to be an unfriendly neighbor, keepin' to myself, but the fact is that folks don't stay long in them yellow houses. Ever. They move in, they're there for a little while; then they're out, and the house goes up for sale, and the whole thing happens again. I been watching them places for a couple years now. After a while, when Householders gets the whole street, they'll kick everybody out, doze it all under, and put in more of them dadgum condominiums. You don't believe me, you just drive up Blue Sky Hill a few blocks. You'll see." With a disgusted snort, she tossed her head, then yanked her purse off the floor and set it in her lap.

Behind her, Shasta was ashen. I'd never seen an expression like that on her face.

Oblivious, Elsie went on, "There's a lot of places where all the old houses are gone and there's nothin' but condos with nice cars parked out front and high fences all around. They're workin' their way toward Red Bird, you mark my words, but I ain't sellin'. That's been my house most of my life, and they can have it over my dead body." Wrapping her purse over her elbow, she stood up, taking out her keys and gripping them as if she were fending off an attacker. "I may be a hateful old woman, but I got salt, and nobody pushes me around." Pointing the fistful of metal at me, she narrowed one eye. "You and yer stepmom better watch out, too. They was on the way to paintin' your house yellow before you moved into it. If you put your money in that place, you better look out. It's a Householders home, sure as a toad's got warts." The chair squealed as she scooted it out of the way, started to leave, but then stopped without turning around. "I ain't tryin' to be hateful. I thank y'all for what you done for me the other day." She exited without another word. Shasta and I sat shell-shocked in her wake, listening as her bulky black shoes clacked away down the sidewalk.

"Do you think she's right?" I asked finally, but I was afraid of the answer. My father was the face of Householders. Superman on their commercials. . . .

Shasta's lips pressed together, her jaw tightening as she swallowed. "I don't know. First of all, Cody found these weird fees tacked onto our first statement, and then every time he calls the office, they give him the runaround. We told them we wanted a copy of our contract, and so far, it hasn't shown up in the mail. Cody thinks they're doing all this on purpose, like it's some kind of scam or something, but I told him, why would a company sell houses to people just to have to take them back? My nana had some rental houses, and geez, every time she had to kick people out, it cost her a fortune. Why would a company want to do that?"

"I don't know," I admitted, but the truth was undeniable. Ross Burten was under indictment for criminal misdealings in one company, why not two? Why not all of them?

Did my father know? Was he involved, too?

Uncle Boone . . . Uncle Boone refitted homes for Householders. He profited from their construction contracts to refurbish old neighborhoods and provide low-income housing. Would he knowingly get involved in something so cruel and unethical? Would he and my father intentionally cheat families who could never afford to recover?

Had we been living on profits gained from broken lives, from the destruction of families like Shasta's?

I felt a catch in my chest, a cramp that hurt with every breath. "We'd better go get your boys," I muttered. "The children's building is probably empty by now."

Shasta blinked, confused. No doubt she was wondering why I wasn't as passionate about the houses as she was. "Did y'all buy your house from Householders?"

The muscles tightened in my throat. My mouth turned cottony. "We're just living there . . . for a while. Renting." The lie slipped out easily, so much simpler than the truth.

"From Householders?" Shasta pressed.

"I don't know. My uncle set it up." One lie, now two. How would Shasta feel if she found out who we were?

She gave me a sympathetic look, unaware that we were hardly in the same boat. "You know, if your place *isn't* a Householders property, then maybe Elsie's all wet about this, or about some of it, anyway.

Maybe she's just sitting around her place dreaming up issues to get hostile about."

"I don't know, Shasta! Why would I know?" The words bit the air sharply. Sesay drew back, a surprised look beneath the tangles of hair, and Shasta blinked and craned away from me, shocked by the outburst.

I stood up from my chair, feeling disoriented and dizzy, as if I'd just stepped off a ride at Six Flags and couldn't quite find the ground. I had to get out of the room, away from her, away from the musty smell of Sesay's backpack, to someplace where I could breathe fresh air. "I'll go grab the boys and meet you out front, whenever you and Sesay are done."

I skirted the corner of the table and hurried from the room without waiting for an answer. In the darkness outside, I leaned against the wall, shut my eyes, tried to breathe. The night air was heavy with humidity, and a fine mist had started to fall. I felt it coating my skin, dampening my hair, chilling my body.

I thought of people like Sesay, sleeping under plastic bags and cardboard boxes on nights like this. I thought of the families who came to the Summer Kitchen for free lunches and story time, and the ones who shopped across the street at the Book Basket.

The playroom in our Highland Park house had been full of books—so many books they lay scattered on the floor like loose tiles. The kids walked on them, threw them, used them to build forts and launch toys across the room. There was so much space there, such a clutter of stuff we never really saw.

Were those books stolen property?

It couldn't be true. It couldn't be. My father wasn't an evil man. If anything, he was guilty of being too softhearted, too much of a push-over for friends asking favors, school groups requesting donations and autographed footballs, kids in need of expensive medical care, people wanting him to speak at charity luncheons and act as emcee for fund-raiser fashion shows.

He wouldn't do something that he knew was hurting people. He wouldn't.

But he'd hurt us. He'd left us. All he cared about was protecting himself. . . .

The fellowship hall door opened, and I pushed off the wall, wiped my eyes, and tried to scoop my emotions into a ball as I walked to the children's building and retrieved Shasta's boys.

She was on the sidewalk with Sesay when I came out. Even in shadow under the streetlights, the body language of their conversation had a sense of intensity that caused my pulse to quicken again. Sesay was pointing down the street, while Shasta shook her head, her hands lifting into the air, as if she couldn't believe what she was hearing. I passed by them, opened the car door, and let the boys in, hoping Shasta would follow. Right now, I just wanted to go home, get away from Shasta, and try to think things through, maybe ask Barbie if she knew anything about Householders. The answer would be no. Barbie never kept up with my father's business dealings.

Shasta met me at the driver's-side door, and Sesay waited on the sidewalk. "Can you take us down to the Broadberry Mission?"

"The mission . . . What?" I stammered.

Shasta pointed. "The homeless mission. It's only a couple miles."

My head throbbed, the ache rebounding off the noise of Shasta's boys jockeying for position inside the car. I was tired of taking care of people. I just wanted to lock myself in a room and lick my own wounds. "I really need to get home. Barbie's alone with the sibs, and . . ."

Shasta gripped the car door. "Tam, please. It's important. It won't take long."

Behind Shasta, Sesay stood on the curb watching us, clearly waiting for my answer.

"What's going on?" I asked finally.

Shasta's nostrils flared as she exhaled a breath and pushed the door closed, shutting the boys' racket inside the car. "Sesay says there are people living in the homeless shelter who came from Householders homes. She knows of a family that was living just a few blocks from us until about a month ago. If we go down there right now, she thinks she can get me in to talk to them."

Chapter 29

Sesay

You cannot enter or leave the Broadberry Mission after the evening meal. To enter, you must be in line before the meal, and if too many are in line, you may not go inside. These are the rules. I know the rules, but Michael is here, and I hope he will let me enter. He frowns at me as I tell him the reason and point to the young woman, Shasta, standing at the door.

"She only asks to speak with them," I say. "She will not stay here for the night. She wants to know about the yellow houses. She lives in a yellow house."

Michael looks at me, his lashes thick and low over his eyes. He has heard many reasons why a person must come in when they have not followed the rules. If you break the rules for one person, the others become angry.

By the door, Shasta paces anxiously, murmuring to herself and chewing a fingernail. She looks like a person you could find on the street, the mind busy with things that are not there. This worries Michael. He can see that she is angry and afraid. Her anger travels in the air, like the scent of something dangerous that could ignite at any moment.

Father Michael does not want to allow this into the mission. The mission is a place of peace, of shelter. I can see the concern in his face.

"Wait here a minute," he says finally. "I'll check with them and see if they're willing to come out and talk." By now, the church service is over, and the families will be keeping to themselves. For the families, there are small rooms separate from the areas where the street people sleep.

In a short time, Michael returns. He pokes his head through the metal doors that lead down the hallway to the family rooms. Through the small square of glass, I can see the family, the husband and wife only, waiting in the hallway. Their little children will be in the room by now, tucked in the bunk beds, fighting for sleep against the clanging of trays in the kitchen.

"She can come on in and talk to them in the hall," Michael says. "I can't let you stay tonight, though, Sesay. It's against the rules."

"I have a place," I tell him. "I polish frames for the Indian chief at night. There is a bed there for me, and a sink to wash in." I can even wash my own clothing now. The Indian chief allows me to hang it in the back of his building. He says, *It isn't hurting anything. Make yourself at home.*

Home. This is a word I have never considered. For so long, my homes have been the places I laid my pack. My homes have been crowded with other people. The studio is my home now. No one sleeps there other than me. The Indian chief has been gone away for two days, but still I can sleep in his place. He knows I am not a thief. I will not take anything. *It's good to have someone watching the studio while I'm traveling,* he says.

Michael's face softens. "Good. I'm glad. How was the reading class tonight?" He watches as Shasta crosses the room, her strides uncertain, her arms stiff at her sides. Turning the corner, she cocks her head and looks through the doors, as if she fears what she will find beyond. Inside, the mother and father wait with equal uncertainty, their faces tight with worry, yet curious. The mother is young, with red hair and the round, mottled face of a child. Her eyes are puffy and pink-rimmed, sad and weary. Not like a child's. She cries as they sit in Michael's services at night. She weeps as she prays. I have seen her.

"It was a good class," I say, as Shasta passes through the doors. "I am making my own book now. Of things I know, and the line pictures. I am learning to read them."

Michael's reply is a quiet, tender laugh that is out of place here. "It's about time. Won't be long before you'll be teaching, I bet."

"We all have much to teach and much to learn," I tell him, and Shasta regards me over her shoulder for an instant, as if she is wishing for me to come along. "I am going to my place now." I do not wait for her to answer, but just turn and walk out. This talk of houses means nothing to me, and I do not want an understanding of it. *Remember the lilies of the field and the birds of the air*, Michael says in his church, and I do remember. The people in these houses are filled with worry and fear. What they possess, they fear losing, and what they do not possess, they fear not gaining. The fears chase them from both sides, breathing fire so that the people cannot lay down their heads and rest. They only catch a breath between two dragons.

Chapter 30

Shasta Reid-Williams

Waiting for Cody to get home from his night job was agony. I felt like someone had poured gasoline on our life, and I was holding my breath until a spark came along and blew everything to bits. The family that Sesay'd taken me to meet at the shelter was so much like ours, it was like staring at a postcard from the future, except the picture wasn't pretty. A year ago, the Farleys had been right where we were now—new home, thanks to a Householders easy-in loan, and then when their first bill came, it was higher than what they expected. They went round and round with the financing people until finally they found out all kinds of unexpected fees had been tacked onto their loan, and that Householders had added a huge credit life insurance policy to the loan. It was all in the contract, if you had a law degree and knew how to read the fine print, and if you actually read it, instead of just listening to the double-talking salespeople at Householders. While the Farleys were arguing about the fees and trying to scrape up the extra cash, they were late paying the bill. The next thing they knew, they were getting hit with late fees and big charges for drive-by property inspections. Then they found out that their loan interest rate was readjusting, and the extra interest was being added onto the loan, too.

Once the Farleys' mortgage problems were reported, their credit score went down, all their credit card companies raised their rates, and pretty soon the Farley family was tanked. Householders had the house back in less than a year, and there wasn't anything the Farleys could do about it. They couldn't afford a lawyer to fight it, and they'd spent every bit of savings they had and gone way into debt trying to hang on to their house. Then Mr. Farley lost his job, and they went from buying a home to living in the shelter in less than twelve months. They weren't the only ones. In the two months they'd been there, they'd met other families with similar stories. In this neighborhood, Householders was the common thread. Elsie and Sesay were right: Terrible things happened to Householders families. The yellow houses weren't a blessing. They were a curse.

At first, I thought about calling Mama for money. If we just could keep the bills paid until Cody got through the academy, then we could take the graduation bonus and use it to either get ourselves out of this loan or get a lawyer. Right now, what we had to do was keep ahead of the loan, so Householders couldn't start tacking on late fees and drive-by inspections. That would keep disaster from happening, at least for now. In three days, Dell would be here for her visit. The cat was about to be out of the bag anyway. . . .

I stuffed the idea away as soon as it crossed my mind. I couldn't call home. Whether Dell would tell Mama and Jace about the house wasn't the point. Cody and I'd promised each other, promised ourselves, that this time we were standing our own two feet. We got ourselves into this mess, and we had to find our own way out. There had to be a way. . . .

Without wanting to, I imagined spending nights in the shelter with Cody, the boys, and me living in one tiny room, our clothes in trash bags we'd carry around each day when we left the shelter to hang out in places like the Summer Kitchen, passing the time until the shelter opened for the night again.

Mrs. Farley was pregnant. Six months. They were hoping the pregnancy would help them get into more permanent housing.

I pictured myself having this baby, our little girl, on the street.

That wouldn't be us.

If I had to comb the Internet, look up laws and legal cases until my eyes crossed, go to work scrubbing some lawyer's floors and cleaning toilets to pay for legal help, search to the ends of the earth for someone to take on a Goliath like Householders, I would do it, because this house was *our* house. *Our* place.

By the time Cody drove in, my head was pounding and my stomach was achy and cramping. I felt light-headed, but I was too nervous to eat, so I'd spent the time on the Internet, searching anywhere I might find information. I'd learned more about mortgage fraud, predatory lending, broker price opinion inspections, late fees, negative amortizations, and property-flipping scams than I ever wanted to know. What I needed was that copy of our contract, so I could try to figure out whether any of that stuff was in there.

Cody was surprised to find me sitting awake at two a.m. with the computer in my lap.

"Hey. What're you doing up?" he whispered, yawning, then leaning over to kiss me on the head. I closed my eyes, felt them burn and sting. His chin rested on my hair for a minute, and he sagged over the chair. He was so tired. After spending all day at the police academy, and then going to the parking booth job, and trying to study, he didn't have any energy left. He was working so hard. He didn't deserve this.

I didn't have any choice but to tell him. He had to know.

"I couldn't sleep." My stomach shifted lower, grumbled and clenched. "Something happened at reading class tonight."

Cody's elbow pressed the back cushion of the chair as he rested his head on his fist. "Oh, well, hey, you'll work it out." He drooped against the cushion, his body jerking as his eyes fell closed. His arm lurched forward and bumped the back of my head. "Sorry." Pushing off the chair, he stood up. "I've gotta hit the shower and get to bed."

I grabbed his arm, and suddenly he was awake. "You could come with me," he offered, and raised an eyebrow. No matter how tired he was, Cody was never too tired to try to get me into bed.

"Cody, there's something I need to tell you."

"You could tell me in the shower." He reached for me, and I pulled away, the anger that'd been simmering in me all evening boiling over. "Stop it, all right?"

He huffed a breath, on a short fuse tonight. "Fine." Pulling his shirt off, he started toward the bathroom.

"Wait!" The word shot across the room, stopping him with the shirt hanging from one arm.

"What's your problem?" His voice was sharp, a little louder than mine. In a minute we'd be waking up the kids. "You want to be left alone, I'm leaving you alone. I don't have time to play games."

An answer blasted toward my lips like a cannonball. *You never have time. You're never here. I have to do everything—everything for the boys, everything with the house. . . .*

All of a sudden, the words I normally would of said, the words that would of spiraled us into a fight, seemed pointless and immature. Most of our fights were pointless and immature. Cody was working just as hard as I was. He was working to pay the bills on our house, the house I'd wanted to buy. Now that I had it and the problems that went with it, it was time for me to grow up, time for *us* to grow up and act like a team instead of poking holes in each other because we were too stressed to think. "Listen, I don't want to fight, okay? I found out some things about the house tonight, and I need to tell you. We've got to figure out what to do."

He let his eyes fall closed, swiped a hand across his forehead, stretching the angry line in the center. "It can't wait?"

"No, it can't wait. Really, Cody, it can't." I took a breath and started in on everything I'd learned about Householders. By the time I'd finished, Cody was wide-awake and looked like he was ready to put a fist through the wall. His anger choked the room like smoke as he paced from the door to the hallway and back again. "They can't do that," he growled, pointing a finger out the window, toward *they*, whoever they were. "They can't tell people one thing to their face and put something else in the paperwork. It's fraud."

My stomach squeezed and clenched, and I slid my hand across it, rubbing hard. "Well, it looks like they've been getting away with it. We shoulda read the papers. We shouldn't've signed until we had it looked at by a lawyer or something. We shouldn't've trusted that salesman, no matter how nice he was. He *works* for Householders. Of course he's going to make it sound like one big picnic." *Never sign anything you haven't read.* It was one of those grown-up rules I hadn't really thought about until now.

Cody lifted his hands, then let them fall to his sides. His shoulders, normally square and strong, fell forward with his hands. His face melted. "Why can't we ever just do something right for once? Why is it always one screwup after another?" Punching a fist in the air, he kicked a toy police car one of the boys'd left on the floor. It skittered across the room and hit the wall. In another thirty seconds, he'd be doing actual damage, storming around like a kid throwing a fit.

"Listen to me, all right? It isn't going to help to tear things up."

"If they take this house back, they're gonna get it in pieces." The muscles flexed in his arms, ready for a fight.

"They're not getting this house back. This is our house. We have to think about what we're going to do. I've been reading on the Internet. There's an article about a lady in New Jersey who took a mortgage company to court for tacking junk fees and credit life insurance onto her loan without telling her, and she won."

Cody's lips parted and air hissed through. "How're we going to take Householders to court? Where're we gonna get the money for that? You know what kind of lawyers those companies can pay? They'll just tie it up in court until we run out of money. They know they can do whatever they want. They're not afraid of us."

I stood up from the chair and felt light-headed, like I was dreaming all of this and it wasn't really happening. "We'll figure it out. We'll get some lawyer to take it on contingency, or maybe find other people they've cheated and start a class-action suit. Lawyers take those on percentages. I read an article about . . ."

Cody rocked slowly backward and landed against the wall, then stayed there like he needed support to keep on his feet. "Geez, Shasta, reading it on the Internet doesn't make you a lawyer. We don't know squat about this kind of thing. How in the world are we gonna do all that stuff—start a court case, get people to join some kind of class-action suit, talk to lawyers and stuff?"

"I can do this, Cody. Remember back in sophomore English when we had to do all those debates about Supreme Court decisions? Mrs. Lindoll always wanted me to go on and be a lawyer. She said I'd be good at it, and she should know, considering that almost everyone in her family is either a lawyer or a judge." While I was searching the Internet all night, I was thinking of Mrs. Lindoll. *You know, Shasta,* she'd said, *with your kind of passion and people skills, you could go a long way—college, law school, you name it. If you'll just apply yourself, there's no limit to what you could accomplish. All these things you believe are*

wrong in the world, you could have a hand in changing them—put that
fire to good use. . . .

Maybe when all of this was over, someday when there was more
time, more money, I'd do it. Maybe I'd take some classes and start
working toward Mrs. Lindoll's vision of me.

Cody gave me a tired look. "What we need to do is figure out
how to cover the payments. That's how we're gonna stop them from
digging us in deeper with the late charges and the—what did you
call them—broker price inspections." In Cody's world, things were
always black-and-white.

"Cody, we . . ." I stopped myself just short of arguing some more.
It wouldn't do any good. Cody was falling asleep on his feet. "We can
talk about it more tomorrow. If the copy of the contract doesn't show
up in the mail, I'll call the Householders office and tell them I'm
coming over there to get one. I'm sure I can get Tam to drive me after
lunch, or the boys and I can catch the city bus. I figured out how the
route works; I just haven't tried it yet."

"Yeah, all right." Cody rubbed his eyes, yawning. "I'll check with
the hotel and see if there's any way I can get my check for the parking
garage job early. That would help. Householders can't take this place
if we meet the payments."

I thought of the Farleys and my stomach clenched. They'd probably had this same discussion a year ago. "We have to fight this, Cody.
What they're doing is wrong. We shouldn't have to pay those fees. We
can't just sit back and let them walk all over us. What about all the
other people they've hurt?"

Letting out a long sigh, Cody rested his head against the wall,
his eyes closing. "We're just regular people, Shasta. Ordinary folks.
We can pay the fees cheaper than we can pay a lawyer. You can bet
Householders knows that."

"Sometimes ordinary people end up in extraordinary situations."
Mrs. Lindoll had said that when she was talking about *The Diary of
Anne Frank*.

"Geez. You sound like Lindoll."

"She was right."

Sliding his hands into his pockets, he opened his eyes and shifted
off the wall. "Maybe," he said quietly. "Let's go on to bed, all right? I
can't talk any more tonight. I'm dead."

I rubbed my stomach, feeling like I was about to be sick. "Go
ahead. This whole business has me tied up in knots. I think I'll sit up
awhile and . . ." I stopped just short of saying, *search the Internet some
more and look for lawyers who've taken on cases like ours.* That would
only make Cody feel like I was ramrodding him. If he had a little
time to think about it on his own, he'd know I was right. ". . . wait
until I feel a little better."

"Okay." His answer came out in a sigh as he headed down the
hall. Right now, he didn't care if I showed up in bed or not. He
wanted to get away from everything, including me. After he turned
on the water in the bathroom, he came back up the hall long enough
to break the news that there was a chance the department might send
him out of town for a couple days.

"Out of town? When? Where?" I choked out.

"D.C., the day after tomorrow. But it probably won't happen.
They're doing some kind of a pitch for federal money to bring in
minority officers. They need faces. They just mentioned it was a possibility, that's all."

A supportive wife probably would have been proud of him, but
all I could think was that if Cody left me here by myself right now, I'd
never be able to handle it. On top of all the trouble with Householders, Dell was coming in three days. The house wasn't anywhere close

to being ready for company, and the yard was a mess, not to even mention that stupid oleander bush. "Tell them you have a family emergency, and they'll have to send somebody else."

He rolled his eyes, like I was crazy for asking. "Yeah, right. I tell them that, I won't be the kind of guy the department wants. You've got to be able to keep your personal crap together, Shasta. You can't let it interfere with the performance of your duty."

"But, Cody . . ." I moaned, and he crossed the room and kissed me on the head, like that was supposed to somehow make it better.

"Like I said, don't worry about it. I'm sure it won't happen." But he didn't sound sure. He sounded like he was prepping me. He squeezed my shoulder just before he headed off to the shower. "Whatever you find out tomorrow, don't get in touch with your mom or Nana Jo about this."

"I won't," I promised, thinking that maybe he'd read my mind. A little voice was whispering that if Cody left me alone with this mess, I was going to break down and call Mama. The wimpy little girl in me wanted someone, anyone to bail us out of this hole.

By the next day, I was sorry I'd made that promise to Cody. Tam wasn't feeling good, so the boys and I went to the Summer Kitchen by ourselves. When we walked back up the street, the mailman was just turning the corner. I held my breath as I opened the box, and I wasn't even sure what I was hoping for.

The contract was in there, finally. I took it inside and put the boys down for a nap and spent the afternoon reading through legal mumbo jumbo and trying to understand it. The stuff that might be about fees was so confusing you really did need a lawyer to figure it out. I wanted to call home and see if Nana Jo could help me, since she'd seen a lot of house contracts over the years. I couldn't call, of course. Cody and I were on our own with this one.

I settled for typing some of the contract clauses into a couple of legal advice sites on the Internet, and then reading more information about predatory lending. The news there wasn't good. Articles were filled with warnings like, *Unexpected and unexplained charges can be added to a borrower's account as soon as they are late in making a single payment. Homeowners then find themselves in an unfortunate legal gray area. If and when they are able to obtain legal documents from their mortgage companies, the documents can be almost impossible for the average homeowners to decipher.*

That much was true. If Cody and I were average homeowners, then that paragraph sounded like our situation exactly. It also fit with the story the Farleys had told me about their Householders disaster.

After feeding the kids supper and getting them to bed for the night, I found another paragraph that fit even better and answered the question of why a company would want to sell homes they'd just have to repossess later on: . . . *property-flipping scams, which have become a common occurrence in a number of cities. Property flipping begins with the purchase of distressed properties at a low price, and then, after limited or no repairs, the property is resold at prices inflated beyond the actual value, frequently with the intent of later repossession. The victims of property flipping are often unsuspecting low-income, minority first-time home buyers. Residents of surrounding properties often become secondary victims of such a scam, as property valuations and tax bases for the area increase. . . .*

By the time Cody came home, I was convinced there was more happening on Red Bird Lane than just bad loans with unexpected fees tacked on. There was something bigger going on, and without knowing it, Cody and me had landed right in the middle of it.

He was tired again when he walked in the door, and I hated to spring my bag of suspicions on him. I picked up the paper about property-flipping scams and handed it to him. "Read this," I said. "I'm not sure yet . . . I mean, I don't have any proof, but I think this might be what's going on in this neighborhood."

He just shook his head and set the paper on the coffee table with a sour look. For whatever reason, he was really in a mood tonight. "I can't, Shas. I've got to pack. I'm leaving for D.C. tomorrow."

Chapter 31

Tam Lambert

I jerked awake from a fitful sleep and lay staring at the ceiling. Something felt wrong, but the living room was dark, the house silent except for the faint sound of Aunt Lute snoring at the end of the hall. Towers of boxes cast odd shadows in the muted, mustard-colored light pressing through the window covering. The glow caught my attention as I blinked away sleep. There were two points of light . . . a car . . . someone was outside in a car. Sitting up, I looked down the hall, my pulse fluttering. Maybe Barbie had decided to take the kids and run away, after all. Maybe these last few days since our big fight, she'd only been playing along. Maybe Fawn was outside, poised to help them make a quick getaway. . . .

The hallway was quiet, the doors still closed. Barbie's purse and cell phone were on the coffee table, her shoes underneath it. I checked the time on the phone. Five thirty in the morning. The sun wasn't even up yet.

The lights died outside. Car doors opened and closed. There were voices. Men's voices.

Grabbing Barbie's phone, I stood up, moved unsteadily across the room, slipped close to the narrow crack at the corner of the window covering, tried to see the driveway, but the gap revealed only a slice of yard. Across the street, Shasta's outside lights were off, which meant Cody was home. I could call Shasta. . . .

Outside, the lock clicked on the security bars, the sound startlingly loud against the early-morning silence. I jumped, dropped the phone, felt it bounce off my foot, then heard it skitter away and hit a box. Who was there? Uncle Boone was out of town on a business trip again. Who else had a key to this house? I hit the switch for the porch light, dropped to my knees, and scrambled for the phone. Someone knocked softly on the door.

A rapid pulse thrummed in my ears as I stood up and tried to see through the peephole. The glass was cloudy. I couldn't make out anyone on the other side. My hands pressing on the wood caused the door to rattle.

"It's me." A voice came through the door, and another soft knock. "It's Uncle Boone."

Relief washed over me in a warm wave, then drained away, leaving brackish tide pools of apprehension. Why would Uncle Boone be here so early in the morning? Did he have news about Dad?

Catching a breath, I turned the dead bolt. "Uncle Boone, what are you . . ." The remainder died in my throat. Uncle Boone wasn't alone.

I stood staring at my father, my mind silent momentarily, then racing so fast the thoughts flashed by in fragments, a blur, like the view from a roller coaster speeding around a curve. I blinked once, twice, searched for words, but none came. My father's presence here made no sense. Perhaps he wasn't here. Perhaps I was only dreaming.

The stray dog was sniffing around the curb near Shasta's house again. I watched it as if it were proof of something.

Dad didn't speak, but stood on the porch, his hands clenched over each other, his fingers kneading, his uncertainty obvious. He looked pale, thinner. His hair had grown frosty gray around the temples—something he normally attended to each week at the barbershop. The skin beneath his eyes sagged in a weary half-moon, and his chin was dark with stubble, his trademark mustache now just a shadow.

Uncle Boone laid a hand on my father's shoulder, ushering him closer to the door. "Hi, Tam," Boone said quietly, his tone seeming to indicate that this visit in the dark hours of the morning was perfectly normal. "Everyone else asleep still?" He cocked his head, his gaze darting toward the interior, his face tight and apprehensive, as if he were afraid Barbie might rush from the shadows with a weapon in hand.

"They're . . . still in bed," I whispered, taking an unsteady step backward. "What are you doing here?" My father was wanted by the federal government. By coming here, he surely risked being apprehended. Had he decided to give himself up? If he did, what would happen to him? To us?

"Let's talk inside," Uncle Boone whispered. "Paul's not well."

I felt a rush of concern that was both unexpected and unwanted. The anger, the bitterness I'd thought I would experience were slow in coming—like armor that wouldn't fall into place now that I needed it. There was only a suspicion, and a murky uncertainty of what would come next. Now that Barbie and I finally had things on an even keel, was he here to upend our lives again?

Boone guided him into the room. Dad's steps were unsteady, his legs seeming to drag in slow motion.

"What's wrong?" I wanted to take the question back as soon as I asked it. Why should I care? He didn't deserve it.

"Paul had a slight heart attack in Mexico," Uncle Boone answered.

I watched my father, but he wasn't looking at me. Instead, he studied Aunt Lute's painted butterflies as he moved through the room, passing from the dim light by the door into the shadows beyond. I took in my father's silhouette—stooped, thin, unfamiliar.

"How long ago?" My question sounded clinical, emotionless, just the way I wanted it to be.

"Two weeks. The doctors just cleared him to travel home." The two of them crossed the room together, Uncle Boone with his hand between my father's shoulder blades, positioning him like a stick puppet. Dad sank into the armchair and Uncle Boone stood between it and the door.

I turned on a lamp. "You two have been in touch for *two weeks*, and didn't tell us?" Suddenly Uncle Boone's recent business trip made sense. He was in Mexico with my father . . . but the business trips had been going on for longer than two weeks. Uncle Boone had been coming and going since the day after we moved into this house. Fury burned hot in my face, and Boone lifted a hand, glancing down the hall as if he didn't want me to wake the others yet.

He backed away a step. "I haven't been in touch with him for very long. His lawyer called me after he had the heart attack, and . . ."

Turning to my father, I cut into Uncle Boone's explanation. "You can call your *lawyer*, but you can't call us? Did it even cross your mind what *we* were going through? What Barbie and the kids and Aunt Lute were going through?" I didn't add myself to the list. I couldn't admit to him that I still cared about him, still needed him. "The boys asked for you every day. What were we supposed to tell them? We didn't know whether you were alive or dead."

Uncle Boone laid a hand on my arm, trying to quiet me again, but I pushed him away, my emotions spinning beyond reason, beyond compassion for my father's medical condition, or the fact that he'd apparently been traveling all night. How dare he think he could drop back into our lives now! He had no right to show up when we were finally moving ahead, when we were finally building a day-to-day existence that was something other than chaotic.

Sagging forward, he rested his elbows on his knees, looked through the pyramid of his arms, and studied the floor, his face wearily impassive. "I didn't want you to get caught up in this. I never wanted you and Barbie and the kids involved." His voice was hoarse, a thin thread floating through the stillness in the room.

"Not involved?" I hissed, the sound ricocheting against the painted butterflies and vines, disappearing down the hall. I swallowed hard, clenched my fists, grabbed a breath, and tried to calm myself. I didn't want the kids to wake up now. I didn't want them to see him until I knew what would happen next. "How could we not be involved? Do you have any idea what's been going on around here? Any clue what we've been through?"

"I wanted to keep you out of it." He straightened in the chair, and for an instant he became the strong, determined man I remembered. The man who had everything under control, who was a competitor in every way, a winner, powerful enough to hold off all threats and dominate the opposing team. He faced me, his steel blue eyes hard and determined, self-righteous. "I didn't want . . . this." His gaze strafed the room, indicating the house, me, the boxes, the mess our lives had become.

Air solidified in my throat, as if I were choking on his explanation. "What did you think was going to happen? You've been lying to us for months—about our house, the bank accounts, everything. How could you do that? What were you going to do when they came to take our home—barricade the door and fight off the constable?"

"I thought . . ." The gaunt-faced man in the chair cratered, sinking inward, shaking his head, and coughing softly into his hand. "I thought I had it . . . worked out."

Uncle Boone touched my arm. "He's not supposed to do this now. He's not up to it. He just came out of the hospital." Despite everything, Boone regarded my father with compassion, the long ties of friendship still strong between them. How could he feel that way? How could he find the forgiveness to bring my father back here, to guide him tenderly across the room, protect him even now? Was it habit, a sense of duty, grace of a sort I couldn't find within myself?

I looked at my father—pale and shrunken, broken—and all I felt was anger. I wanted payback. I wanted explanations. I wanted him to know how terrible the past weeks had been.

I didn't want peace. I wanted to win at war.

"Let him rest a bit before everyone else wakes up," Boone suggested, his voice soft, tender. "There'll be time for this later."

"Let him rest?" I protested. "Do the feds know he's back? Won't they be coming for him?"

Boone pulled his lips inside his mouth, parted them with a smack. "The lawyers made a deal before he came back from Mexico. He's co-operating fully, but to be honest with you, the feds are having a tough time building a case against Ross Burten. He's slick, and he's got good lawyers. With a little luck, this whole thing'll go away."

This whole thing'll go away. I should have been grateful. Life for us could continue on in some form, although it was hard to imagine what the picture would look like. "What about all the people Rosburten cheated? They're just out of luck, and we go on with our lives? Ross Burten goes on with his, because his slimy lawyers help him slide out of a conviction? Is that how it works?"

"One issue at a time." Boone rubbed his forehead, his fingers stroking back and forth over a bright patch where the lamp reflected off his dark skin in a tiny orb of light. "Let's take it one issue at a time, all right? Let him rest. I'll come back in a while."

"I'm fine." My father lifted his body, chin first, as if he were being pulled upright in sections like a Jacob's ladder.

Both of us watched Boone open the door, step through, and close it. Boone's shadow grew smaller and smaller against the window sheet, receding until it melted into the noise of his footsteps descending from the porch, then his vehicle starting.

The room felt smaller once we were alone in it. Emotion filled the corners like carbon monoxide, traveling along the ceiling, moving inward. Dad sank in the chair, wheezed out a sigh, feeling the heaviness in the air. I watched him for a moment, compared him to the man who'd sat in the living room of our big house in Highland Park, still wearing his Superman disguise, still convinced he could stop the speeding bullet before it destroyed us.

He couldn't. The bullet had hit its mark.

I crossed the room and sat on the edge of the sofa, trying to decide how this should play out. At some point, Barbie would awaken and find him here. "You shouldn't lie to Barbie. You shouldn't lie to her about what's going to happen next."

His chest rose, shuddered, lowered in a rhythmic motion, as if his heart were visible, thrumming beneath the surface. "I don't know what happens next. Even if the case falls through, I come out looking like a con man. Nobody wants to do business with a failure, with someone they can't trust. I don't know where we go from here. Barbie doesn't need to hear that. She doesn't want to hear that."

"She's stronger than you think." The sentence was out before I had time to consider the fact that I actually believed it. Like the rest of us, Barbie was changing, reinventing herself.

My father blinked and drew back, surprised; then he sighed and let his head roll sideways. His jaw twitched, his mouth and cheeks pulling tight. "The legal people will handle it. The feds know that Ross pays good money for lawyers to cover his tracks. If you want my opinion, this whole thing with them turning the case into a media circus is all about politicians getting press ops. There's an election coming up, after all, and this gives the mayor and the district attorney and even that moron of a senator the chance to shake their fists and rail on about corporate corruption. Bringing my name into it makes it big news. For heaven's sake, if I'd known Ross's financial guys were jockeying the accounting and paying off city councilmen, I wouldn't have sunk my own money into Rosburten, would I? I wouldn't have put my name and my face on it, especially on this last deal with the athletic park. If I'd known Ross was funneling money out of it, I never would have talked everyone I knew into investing."

"But you did."

He winced again. "If something sounds too good to be true, it usually is. But you get to the point where you need to gamble big, and you don't really analyze it the way you should. You need the money. You want it to be true, so you let it be. I'd seen investors come and go, and I'd seen them come out with big gains. How was I supposed to know the money wasn't really coming from profits? How was I supposed to know Ross was using the money from new investors to pay gains to old investors, and to line his own pockets? I took Ross at his word. I did my job, and my job was to sell his ideas to people. In a time when the economics aren't good, the moneymen are looking for a sure thing. It's easy to get them to buy into an investment that looks like it's going to pay off big. Ross knew that. He made this athletic park deal look like a gold mine. He needed big money to make it go, and he needed city councilmen on his side. The quickest way to get city councilmen is to give them something they want, and the quickest way to bring in the big moneymen is to make it look like you've already got big money on the books. Ross is a risk taker. He lives by his own rules. Deep down, I think I knew that the projects we had out there couldn't possibly be paying the kinds of returns Ross was claiming, and he promised even bigger returns once the athletic park came online. I knew the fundamentals weren't there."

"If you knew, then why did you keep working for him? Why didn't you quit?"

He focused on me, his eyes a narrow slice between lowered lashes, his expression patronizing. "The economy's not what it used to be, Tam. Investments fail; endorsement opportunities dry up. I needed this athletic park deal as much as anybody. I couldn't just sit there and watch us go down the tubes—lose the house, the cars. Everything."

"We lost the house. We're still here." The truth of that struck me. Despite all that I'd thought and felt a few weeks ago, it wasn't the house that mattered. "We're still a family."

A soft, rueful laugh pressed past his lips. "In this place?"

His answer heated my anger again. How could he still believe that the house, the business, his reputation were all that mattered? Was what he'd lost worth more than what remained? "Yes. Here. In this dinky house with Aunt Lute's stupid paintings on the walls and boxes everywhere. We're a family here. We don't have any choice. The kids can't shuffle off to some playroom with the nanny and Barbie can't hang out at the spa and the country club all day. We have to actually live here together."

He answered with a tolerant smile. "You're young and idealistic, Tam. I've done my years in places like this. It's no picnic."

The conversation fell mute. I sank into the sofa, feeling as if he'd slapped me without lifting a hand. We didn't matter to him. Even after everything that had happened, we were just a line item in his life—a box on a spreadsheet of necessary possessions.

A noise—a small, strangled gasp—bisected the thought. Both my father and I swiveled toward the sound. Barbie stood at the hallway entrance in shorts and a cutoff T-shirt, her mouth hanging slack, her arms loose at her sides. She blinked. Her lips moved but produced no sound.

I felt as if the room were in suspended animation, as still as the painted butterflies on the wall. Barbie stared at my father, her hand rising slowly, her fingertips touching her lips as if to move them. The tiny rhinestones from her last manicure glittered in the lamplight. Her eyes welled, then spilled over, crystal blue pools of emotion. I wondered at the thoughts behind them—was she glad he was here, shocked, relieved? Was she angry for what he'd done, or would she simply forgive and slip back into the usual pattern?

Wasn't this what she'd been waiting for all along—for him to come back and save the day? To take care of everything?

"You're h . . ." she whispered, stretching a hand behind herself and touching the corner of the wall, as if she needed to confirm vertical and horizontal. "You came home." She stepped forward, stopped again, scanned his body from head to toe, seeming to notice the changes in him—the gray hair, the gaunt cheeks, the absence of his mustache. For a moment, I thought she'd say something, but then she only crossed the room, leaned over the chair, and took my father's face in her hands. Fingers trembling against his cheeks, she studied him, then finally slid her arms around his neck and collapsed against him, weeping. I stood up and left the room, uncertain of how I felt about their reunion.

In the boys' room, I curled up in the bed next to Landon and wrapped my arms around his tiny body, felt his heart beating against my forearm and tried to imagine our future. The boys were just getting comfortable here, just settling into a pattern with Shasta's kids, and story time, and life in this little house. Now my father was back, and things would change again. He would never be content with the quiet, uneventful life here. He would feel the need for more. More space, more money, more deals. More . . . everything.

More than just us.

He'd be mortified at the idea of our spending time at the Summer Kitchen and the reading class. *Show some sense*, he'd say. *Anything can happen in a place like that, around those kinds of people. I didn't give you the best education so you could hang around derelicts. . . .*

He would never understand life here. He'd never be willing to try.

I closed my eyes and listened to the boys' breathing, and tried not to think about it—tried to pretend today was just another day, an ordinary day on Red Bird Lane. . . .

When I awoke, the kids were gone. The bedroom door hung ajar, and I could hear my father in the living room. He was on the phone, but his voice was hushed, as if he didn't want anyone to listen in.

The floor creaked as I stood up and started toward the door. In the living room, the conversation stopped abruptly. When I stepped into the hall, my father was on the sofa, looking my way. He watched me while he listened to someone on the phone; then he stood up and started toward the front door. "That's fine," he said. "We'll talk tomorrow."

As Dad hung up, Barbie announced that breakfast was ready, her voice fluttering through the house in a joyous singsong. "C'mon, Tam," she chirped when she saw me in the hall. "Sleepyhead. We made pancakes." I stopped, and she focused on me with a hopeful half smile that said, *Please don't mess this up. He's back.*

I headed for the bathroom. "Just a minute." Locking them outside the door, I splashed water on my face, took a deep breath, and tried to get my head together. I swallowed the urge to storm out and tell my father how I felt about his leaving, and his coming back, and the idea of Ross Burten potentially emerging from this scandal unscathed.

When I reached the dining room, the scene was surreal, like a domestic ad from an old magazine—overly colorized, unreasonably bright. My father sat at the head of the table, and the sibs were lined up along one side, waiting expectantly with forks in their hands. Barbie whirled from the kitchen like a short-order waitress, holding a platter of bacon and toast in the air. My father was sitting close to Jewel, feeding her bits of a pancake he must have stolen from the kitchen early. For an instant I watched, caught off guard. Jewel's face was alive with light, and my father laughed as she navigated the difficult task of pinching tiny bits of dough between her fingers.

"Paul, don't give her that," Barbie admonished, playfully batting a hand at him.

He returned an indulgent look as Barbie set down the platter. "It won't hurt her. I gave pancakes to Tam when she was even smaller than this." Glancing up at me, he smiled. "Remember that, Tam? Remember all those times we ended up at the Waffle House at midnight after a game?"

I stood staring at him, at Barbie. What was the matter with them? Didn't anything about this day bother them? How could they sit at the breakfast table chatting about pancakes as if nothing were wrong?

Aunt Lute emerged from the kitchen carrying a plate stacked high with pancakes. She was wearing a wide sun hat, flip-flops, and a long, loose cotton dress, as if she were prepared for combing the beach. A tiny carved dolphin dangled from her neck on a leather thong. "Why, of course she doesn't remember. She was only a wee one. Just a sprite. How could she remember such a thing?" She waved the platter toward Jewel. "This one won't remember the pancakes, either." Right now, Aunt Lute seemed to be the most lucid person in the room. "She won't remember the butterflies, or the Lady of the Water. The big boys, my princes, they might remember, but the wee one won't recall this tiny castle. She'll pass right by it and never know the difference."

I slid into a chair as Aunt Lute dealt out pancakes, Barbie poured milk into sippy cups, and Mark and Daniel started a fight over the butter tub. "What's she talking about?" I asked, watching Aunt Lute load up my father's plate while Barbie handed out the cups. "What does she mean, Jewel won't remember this house?"

Barbie's lips lifted into a wide smile that looked glamorous again with a fresh application of makeup. "Paul thinks he's found a place for us." Slipping into the chair next to him, she laid a hand on his knee, her face filled with a trust and adoration that made me feel betrayed. Apparently, the fact that he'd run out on us didn't matter, as long as he could fix everything now. "He's taking care of it."

"How?" I asked blandly. "We don't have any money."

My father gave the syrup bottle a tired look, and then reached for it. "I still have a few aces up my sleeve. I'll work it out." Handing the syrup to Barbie, he forced a smile, but when she leaned over the table to reach the sibs' plates, he rested a forearm on the edge and sagged over it, as if the weight of her expectations were almost too great a burden.

Mark tipped his head to one side, taking my father in, seeming to struggle to match the picture of the gaunt, stoop-shouldered, gray-haired man with that of the stranger who'd come and gone from our house in Highland Park. Mark's frown appeared to question whether they were one and the same. "Daddy, did you gimme pancakes when I'm a baby, like Jewee? D'we go to the Waffle House?"

The question surprised my father. He turned to Mark as if he'd suddenly realized the boys were in the room, too.

Barbie paused with the syrup bottle and glanced over her shoulder, her expression a silent plea to my father. Aunt Lute stood with the pancake platter, hovering above the table as if she, too, were wait-ing for the answer. We all knew that Dad had never torn up little pancake pieces for any of the sibs.

My father gave Mark the Superman wink—the one that sold cars, and energy-efficient replacement windows, and houses that would eventually leave unsuspecting families on the street. "'Course I did, buddy," he said, then tore a bit of pancake from his plate and pitched it across the table. Mark clapped it between his palms, gig-gling, and my father was Superman again. What was one more well-intentioned lie on top of all the others?

The remainder of the day went by in a mishmash of Let's Pretend and clandestine calls on my father's cell phone. An FBI agent from the local field office came by to talk to him. During their meeting, Barbie, Aunt Lute, and I spirited the kids off to McDonald's to get them out of the way.

"How can you do this?" I asked Barbie, as we ordered food and the boys followed Aunt Lute to the playscape. "How can you pretend things are normal, after what he's done?"

Some stray emotion—regret, perhaps—lowered her eyes, but it was quickly masked. "He's back," she said quietly. "That's all that matters now."

"It's not all that matters. Are you just going to forget about what he did to us—all the lies he told? Are you going to forget what he did to other people? Just because Ross Burten might skate out on some kind of plea deal, that makes it okay?"

There was a flash of emotion again—something deeper; then she turned to the counter to order Happy Meals, a salad, and two com-bos. "That sound all right?" she questioned, pointing to the menu board. "I can get you a salad, if you'd rather."

"I don't care." I didn't want a salad or anything else. I wanted this day to end.

Sighing, Barbie turned her back to the counter as we waited for the clerk to make our drinks. She looked at her shoes—high heels in place of the sandals and sneakers she'd been wearing since she gave up partying with Fawn. "Listen, Tam, I'm not like you, all right?" Her gaze rose slowly. I saw myself reflected in her eyes, saw my anger. "I don't have . . . all these . . . these big ideas floating around in my head. I'm not the type who wants to teach everybody to read, or go help out at some soup kitchen, or make sure the old lady across the street is safe in her bed at night. I'm not trying to . . . fix everything that's wrong in the world. I just want to take care of my kids. I don't want them to wonder why Santa didn't show up on Christmas, or to walk into school and have other kids make fun of their clothes, or have to stand outside the fence and watch everybody else play soccer because nobody wants them on their team. They need Paul. *I* need him. I just want them to have it good, you know?" Stretching out a hand, she touched my shoulder. "It's best for you, too, Tam. You should have college, and your golfing, and hanging out at the country club, and going to the mall with your friends. All the good things."

College, the mall, the country club . . . I tried to imagine slipping back into the shoes of the girl whose overriding concern had been whether to take a scholarship or spend a year bumming around Europe. If my father moved us back to Highland Park, if he managed to clean up his image, would all those things be waiting? Would Emity be ready for a trip to the mall or a night of hanging out with rented movies and a quart of ice cream?

"I don't want those things anymore," I whispered. That life seemed artificial, shallow, pointless. It was empty, even while I was living it, which was why I'd wanted to take off for the far side of the world. I was searching for something, and somehow, in the house on Red Bird Lane, I'd found it. I'd found a purpose that was bigger than just me pleasing myself. Now they wanted me to leave it behind—as soon as Barbie and my father could make the arrangements.

She touched my hair in a gesture that felt oddly parental—strange, considering where we'd been these past weeks. "You're so young, Tam. You don't know what you want."

Frustration welled inside me. "It doesn't *bother* you . . . everything that's happened? You don't feel wrong about letting some sleaze win out, just because he can afford good lawyers?"

She shook her head, her mouth pressing into a downward curve. "Like I said, Tam, I'm not you." The clerk slid our tray across the counter, and Barbie turned to receive it. "Let's go eat, all right?"

We shared lunch and let the kids play until they were exhausted. Barbie wanted them to wear down for a nap, so my father could rest. "He's under a lot of stress," she pointed out.

"What a shame," Aunt Lute chimed in, but it was hard to tell whether she was following the conversation or not.

By the time we got to the house, Landon and Jewel were asleep. The federal investigator was gone, and Dad was lying on the sofa asleep as we put everyone to bed for a nap. Barbie lay down with the kids, and Aunt Lute and I tiptoed around the house until finally a knock on the door disturbed the silence. Aunt Lute jumped, as if, in spite of my father's reassurances, she was expecting bad news.

I answered the door, and Shasta was waiting on the other side with her boys. Seeing her there felt like having someone from a long-lost past drop in without warning. "Hey!" She looked at her watch. "You ready? We're gonna be late for class. Cody's gone to D.C. for a few days, so I've got the truck. I can dri . . ." She paused, craning to see past me as my father swung his feet around and sat up on the sofa, scratching his head. Her eyes narrowed, as if she were trying to remember where she'd seen him before.

I stretched a hand across the doorway, like a security bar. "My father's here." I was conscious of him surveying me from behind, trying to figure out who was visiting.

Blinking, Shasta stepped back. "Ohhh," she breathed, concern evident in her face. "Ohhh . . ." Taking one last look into the room, she stepped out of his line of sight, and mouthed, *Are you okay?* Then she waited, her gaze darting suspiciously, anticipating some clandestine sign that we needed to be rescued.

"It's fine." I moved onto the porch, pulling the door closed behind me. "I'm not going to make class tonight, though. Can you ask Mrs. Kaye or someone to sit in for me? Tell them we've had a . . . a family emergency."

Shasta's disappointment was evident, and I immediately felt guilty—guilty for lying to her, guilty that my father was making arrangements to move us out of the neighborhood and I couldn't say anything, guilty that Householders' Superman was right around the corner, and Shasta didn't even know it.

She leaned over and spied him through the window. "You sure you're all right?" she whispered, rubbing her stomach and frowning. Clearly the situation made her nervous. "How's Barbie?"

"Happy." I wanted to slip away with Shasta and tell her the whole, bizarre story of my father's homecoming. I couldn't, of course. "She's happy."

"Whoa." Shasta frowned, cocking her head and studying me. "You don't look happy."

"I don't know how I feel about it," I admitted.

Shasta sighed. "You want me to hang out? We could go over to my place. I can call up to the church. They could get a few tutors to double up in class."

"No." Just looking at Shasta, seeing her house behind her, brought everything into focus. My father was her nemesis—the face of the evil that was trying to take away her home, slowly stealing this neighborhood and causing people to end up in the shelter down the road. "I'd better stay here. Besides, Sesay would be disappointed if you didn't make it. Who would she show her new picture words to?" I forced a half smile, thinking of Sesay and her art pad filled with drawings and the words that Terence and MJ had helped her write.

"'Kay," Shasta took another step back, pulling the boys with her. "You call if you need me. I mean it. Whether it's during class or not."

"I will."

"Promise?"

"Sure." The lie seemed almost natural. My entire friendship with Shasta was built on lies. The minute she learned the truth, she wouldn't want anything to do with me.

She waved behind herself as she walked away with the boys, and a heaviness, a sense of ending, settled in my chest.

When I came back inside, my father was trying to figure out why the TV wouldn't get CNN. "There's no cable," I told him. "We didn't have the money for it."

He sighed, his chin hardening, as if he were tired of being confronted with our current reality. No doubt in Mexico he'd been living in a place with cable. "Well, it won't be for much longer. A couple days, max. As soon as I can get something arranged, we'll be out of here."

We'll be out of here . . . soon . . . The words pulled and tugged, twisted painfully. He said them with a sense of abandon, indicating that this place meant nothing. To him, it didn't.

"I want you to tell me something, and I want the truth," I said finally.

"I'll try." He was already looking away, focusing on something else, thinking through the process of making a deal for our new living quarters, perhaps.

"How much do you know about Householders?"

His chin pulled inward, his mouth forming a bemused curve, the way a parent might look at a child who'd suddenly popped out a question like, *Why is the world round,* or *How many stars are in the sky?* "Householders?"

"Yes." Even while composing the question, I was afraid of the answer. "Is it another deal like the sports theme park? Do you actually know what Householders does?"

Frowning, he pinched his chin between his thumb and one knuckle, stroked contemplatively. "Householders is legitimate. It's actually just a sideline—not even under the Rosburten umbrella. They redevelop neighborhoods. Neighborhoods like this one, where the real estate is undervalued based on surrounding locations. You take a neighborhood like this one, with this kind of proximity to downtown, buy up the old houses, eventually clean them off the lots, construct something more . . . upscale. The tax base goes up, crime goes down, uptown workers get something close in with almost no commute. It's a win-win."

"*Who* wins?" Had he never considered the people who were here first? The people for whom upscale wasn't an option?

His shoulders lifted, then lowered, as if the answer were elementary. "Everyone."

I thought of Shasta and the family she'd met in the shelter, of Elsie and the people who came to the Summer Kitchen. I didn't want to find out that my father knew what was happening to them, that he didn't care, but I could see the truth without his even admitting to it. "What if people don't want to move? What if they want to keep their homes the way they are?"

He shrugged again. "Once the properties around them are bought and sold at higher prices a few times, they don't have much choice. The values go up, taxes increase, and the holdouts turn loose eventually. The investment company finally clears ownership of a block of properties, the neighborhood advances, and redevelopment goes on. In the right circumstances, it yields some handsome incentives for the development company—tax abatements and such. It's a simple process."

A simple process. The words rang in my ears. A simple process. Something clinical, with no human attachments, no complications. "So they sell the houses with no intention that people will be able to keep them, in the long term? It's all part of a financial game?"

He coughed indignantly. "I wouldn't characterize it that way."

"How *would* you characterize it? This company is stealing people's homes. They're taking advantage of families who have no way to fight back, and *you're* helping them." I sucked in a breath. I'd never, ever talked to my father that way. Few people had.

He drew back, seeming offended. Then slowly the shadow of guilt turned his gaze downward, and I knew why he cringed every time those Superman commercials came on. Whether he wanted to admit it or not, he knew exactly what Householders was doing, and no matter what flowery technical terms he used to describe it, he knew it was wrong.

"How *would* you characterize it?" I demanded, the words harsh, sharp edged. "I'd like to know, because to me it looks like Householders is taking advantage of people who don't have the resources to defend themselves."

"Fff!" He tipped his head back and looked down his nose at me. "Don't be so idealistic, Tam. It's business. Everything Householders does is legal. It's all in their contracts."

"These people don't understand the contracts!" The words exploded from my mouth and bounced around the room. Aunt Lute came running from the kitchen, her eyes wide as she skidded to a stop in the doorway. "They're not lawyers. They can't even afford lawyers. They believe what the salesmen tell them. Only the salesmen don't *tell* them everything, do they?"

Dad's hands flew upward, came down hard, slapping the leather covering of the sofa. In the doorway, Aunt Lute was suspended midstride. She pulled her foot back and settled it behind her, then froze again.

"How would I know?" Dad's voice rose to meet mine. Craning his head away, he leaned on the opposite arm of the sofa, like a man trying to maintain distance from something distasteful. "It's not my department. I don't keep track of the particulars. I do the commercials. I helped Boone's company get the construction contracts. That's as far as I go with Householders. I don't run the company. I don't make the policy. I don't formulate the loans or write the legal jargon."

"You own part of the company."

"I had stock. Stock I received in return for doing my job. I sold it back to Ross months ago to raise some cash. Householders isn't my problem. It isn't my responsibility." He washed his hands in the air, the clapping disturbing the dust floating in the window light.

I stared at him, stunned. How could he sit there and claim absolution? How could he, with a face that seemed filled with conviction, defend what Householders was doing? Was he so unlike the hero everyone believed him to be? Did I not know my father at all? "You put your name on it. You put your face on it. You endorsed it. People trust it because they trust you, because they know who you are."

He sank against the cushions, his energy suddenly spent. "I can't be responsible for everyone, Tam. We've got problems of our own. It's business. People need to look out for themselves."

"It's not just business. There are people living down in the homeless shelter because they lost everything in a Householders home. Entire families. Do you realize that? You and Ross Burten didn't advertise that on your commercials. This isn't *just business* to them. We're talking about people's lives, their dreams. You can't just turn your back and say it's not your responsibility."

My father's gaze tangled with mine, held it, and I felt myself pleading, hoping, holding my breath. If he wasn't Superman, then who was he? If he wouldn't do the right thing now, then where did we go from here?

"Tam . . ." His voice was soft, conciliatory. I felt hope creep upward inside me. "I have to think of our future. You get on the wrong side of a giant like Ross Burten, you lose. I can't . . ."

The sound of one of the boys coughing amputated the sentence, left it bleeding onto the floor. We turned, my father, Aunt Lute, and I, in unison to find Barbie in the hallway. Landon was curled against her chest, his blond head nestled under her chin, his blue eyes blinking slowly, taking in the scene in the living room with a concern that caused something inside me to twist painfully. His lips trembled, and Barbie cupped a hand around his head, cradling him. "Paul," she said flatly, her gaze settling on my father. "Tam's right."

Dropping his hands slowly to the chair arms, my father gaped at Barbie as if he'd never seen her before. "It's not that simple."

Barbie's lips pursed, her eyes hardening to a cool blue. "What's so complicated about it, Paul? While you were out there selling Householders, they were cheating people."

"You don't understand the position I'm in here." The finality of the sentence seemed to say that Barbie and I were hardly capable of grasping the difficulties involved, that there was no point in his trying to explain them to us. Turning away from the conversation, he switched the channel on the television, indicating that he was tuning out. "I have to do what's best for us."

Barbie's nostrils flared, and she set Landon down, whispered in his ear, and sent him to the bedroom. Padding off down the hall, he cast a worried look over his shoulder. Barbie waited until he was gone before she spoke again. "You can't ignore me, Paul. Stop using us as an excuse for doing what you want to do." She moved between him and the television, insisting she be heard. "How could you be involved in something like that? How can you defend it? You and I both know what it's like to live in a place like this, to have your family slide headlong into disaster. We're the lucky ones. We got out. But these people could be you and me. What if that football coach who plucked you off the street hadn't bothered? What if he'd decided it was 'too complicated'?" Her face pleaded for him to be the man she believed him to be. "Come on, Paul, nothing's ever going to be good for us until we make this right. Don't you see? These people down here need help."

Ramrod straight in the chair, my father shook his head. "We're not in a position to help!" he roared, frustrated with her, with me, probably with his own conscience. "Look around you. We're in the same boat they are."

We're in the same boat. . . . Did he really believe that?

In the bedroom, Jewel woke and started crying. Barbie flailed a hand toward the sound. "Great! Now you woke the baby. Why don't you think about how you're going to explain this to her in a few years? I wonder if she'll be proud of you." In a swirl of blond hair, she turned and strode off down the hall.

Dad raked his wallet off the table and slid forward in the chair. "Where are the car keys?" Pushing to his feet, he took a wobbly step toward the door. His gaze flicked down the hallway, as if he wanted to know whether Barbie was watching. Perhaps he was counting on her to come running in and apologize for upsetting him. "I can't talk to her when she's like this. I need to get out of here for a minute."

"Good," I said, grabbing my purse, "I'll drive. There's something I want you to see." I hoped that when we got to the Broadberry Mission, my father would finally understand the real cost of a House-holders mortgage.

Chapter 32

Sesay

When reading ends, I go to my new place. The door is open, and Terence is there. He has returned from his travels again. He is smiling tonight, happy. "Well, hello, Sesay," he says. "You been to reading class across the street?"

I tell him, "We learned new line pictures. Colors and . . . acting words."

"Action words?" he asks. "Verbs?"

I nod and open my pad, where my words and pictures stay. *Verbs*, I think. It sounds like a thing that would grow in a garden. *Grow* is a verb. A thing you do. I can see the line picture for *grow* in my mind. My mind is *growing* very fast. The words and pictures spin like dust. *Spin* is a verb, something you do. I have not seen its line picture. *Ssss*. It begins with *S*, like *store* and *stop*. I know the line pictures for those. I have always known them, but no one told me this. "I have new drawings. Perhaps you can make the line pictures for them?"

"What? Shasta didn't do it with you?" His mouth crooks like a branch reaching for sunlight.

"She is weary tonight." I consider telling him that I wonder if I did a wrong thing when I brought her to the mission to meet the family there, the yellow house family. I do not think Shasta is tired tonight. I think she is unwell, unhappy. But Terence is joyous. He smiles as if something is bursting inside him, so I do not tell him about the mission. I decide that perhaps I will walk down Red Bird early in the morning. I have the book about Peter Rabbit, and I have the fluffy toy rabbit, and two little muck rabbits I carved for Root and Berry. I can leave them outside the window where Root sits to read. He will look there when first he opens his eyes in his bed.

Terence presses together the corners of a frame, holds it up, and looks at it.

"You are very happy tonight," I say. "Your travels were good?"

"Not bad." He smiles. "Not a bad couple days at Art Fest, and then I did a gallery opening."

"But you are *very* happy." Something about him is different tonight. Something is new.

He laughs softly. He lays down the frame, and his eyes light. *Light* is a verb, sometimes. "You don't miss much. My daughter called a while ago. She's flying in tonight, late. She wants to come by and visit in the morning—see the studio, my paintings, maybe get a late breakfast before she heads over to Shasta's place. Dell hasn't ever called like that before—just to come visit, you know?"

"Dell is a good name," I say, trying to imagine the line picture, to decode it. *D*, like *doll*. "It has a good sound."

His happiness fades for an instant. He looks away. "It's about the only thing I ever gave her. I didn't do much right when I was young." I feel the pain in him, and I think I should stretch across the table and lay my hand over his, but then I know I should not. If you touch people, they pull away and rub their hands on their clothing.

I only sit and wait until he looks my way. He seems to wonder what I am thinking. "You are young yet," I say. "And she is young. The path behind is only the path ahead, if you walk backward. Do not let yesterday use up too much of today."

His eyes pinch as he considers this. "Good point." The sadness fades from him, and his face brightens again. "I've got something for you." From his pocket, he takes an envelope and slaps it onto the table. "Sold your birds. All three of them. Didn't even make it to the folk art gallery with them. All three sold right out of the booth at Art Fest. You're a hit, Sesay." He slides the envelope across the table toward me. "Here you go. This is yours."

"I have never seen it before." There are dollars in the envelope. A small stack of them. It is not mine.

"For your hummingbirds." He pushes the envelope closer. "I sold them."

"But I gave them to you. For my room. For my bed."

He laughs, his smile lovely in his cedar-wood face. "The room is free. No one's using it, and you've paid for it by staining the frames and sweeping, anyway. This place hasn't ever been so clean. I'll teach you how to use the saw, and you can help cut frames if you want to do more. But I'm not keeping the money from the birds." He slides the envelope farther, so that it teeters on the edge of the table and will fall if I do not catch it. "Come on. Take it. Buy something you want."

I watch the envelope quiver in the breeze of the fan. If it topples to the ground, the money will spill out, but if I take it, with it will come the worry of where to hide it, and who might try to take it from me when I set down my pack or fall asleep on the benches along the street. "The Lord says, 'I shall not want.'"

Terence clicks his tongue on his teeth. "You've been hanging out at the mission with Michael too much."

"To want is to choose to be unhappy with what is." My grandfather told this to me long ago, and now, when I say it to Terence, I remember a story my grandfather told, a story about want.

Terence taps a finger to his ear. "You've got a point there, but it's your money. I'm not keeping it."

"It can remain here." I cannot think of reasons for the money, and it seems useless to try. I have a bed, and the sink to wash in, and work making frames and creating my carvings. I am learning to know the line pictures in the book, and this costs nothing. In the bookstore, the books cost nothing, and if I go to the right places each day, there is food enough.

Terence stretches across the table and takes the envelope, then moves a few steps to his workbench. "Tell you what. We'll keep it under the tray with the drill bits for now. Nobody'll think to look for it there. Want to count it or anything?"

I shake my head.

"You don't even want to know how much it is?"

I shake my head again. The amount would mean nothing to me.

He closes the drawer, and I can see that I have disappointed him. The money was a gift, and I have refused it. "I will tell you a story my grandfather says to me when I am a little girl."

Terence puts a leg over a stool and rests his hands on the table. "Why do I have the feeling there's a lesson coming here?" He nods toward a rusted chair that is used around the shop, sometimes as a seat, sometimes as a ladder, sometimes as a table for his paints. The chair is splattered with colors, like a rainbow that has dried in place.

I sit in the chair and slide my pack under the table. "All good stories contain a lesson."

"Your grandfather probably said that, too." He laughs, the way a friend laughs when he knows you. Terence has learned that many of my stories are from my grandfather. I have learned much about him, as well. It is strange to have this young man know me. Strange and wonderful. Wonderfully strange.

"Perhaps this is a Grandfather lesson. You can decide when you hear it." I close my eyes, and I smell the damp, heavy soil of my grandfather's home. Sand squeezes between my toes, and overhead, the sun pushes through the high, thick roof of leaves. I tell the story as my grandfather told it. In my mind, I hear his voice:

"Many, many years ago, there lives a king. This king, he is very rich and has many wives and children, but he is not happy. He think to himself: I have everything, but that does not make me happy. What must I do to be happy?

"One day, Mr. King, he shout angrily to his servants: 'Why can I not be happy? What must I do to be happy?'

"One of the servants, he say to the king, 'Oh, my king! Look at the sky! How beautiful the moon and the stars are! Look at them, and you will see how good life is. That will make you happy.'

"'Oh, no, no, no!' answers the king. 'When I look at the moon and the stars, I am angry, because I know they are beyond my reach and I cannot have them.'

"Then another servant, he say, 'Oh, my king! What about music? Music makes a man happy. We shall play to you from dawn until darkness, and music will make you happy.'

"The king's face, it grow fierce wit' anger. 'Oh, no, no, no, no!' he cry. 'What a silly idea. Music is most fine, but to listen to music from morning until evening, day after day? Never! No, never!'

"So the servants, they go away, and the king sit angry in his rich room until one of the servants come and bow to him, and say, 'Oh, my king. I t'ink I know something that will bring you much great happiness. It is very easily done.'

"'What is it?' ask the king.

"Says the servant, 'You must find a happy man, and then you must take off his shirt and put it on. His happiness, it will go into your body and then you gonna be as happy as he!'

"The king, he like this idea greatly, so he send his soldier men all over the country to look for a happy man. They go on and on, but it is not easy to find a happy man in the king's country. They are afraid to return to the castle without a happy man.

"One day then, the soldier men come to the smallest village in the farthest part of the Mr. King's country. There, they find a man who say, 'I am the happiest man in the world!' He is poor, but he always smile and laugh and sing. Everyone know this about him.

"The soldier men, they don't waste any time bringing the happy man to the king, and the king is so much excited. 'At last I gonna be a happy man!' he say, and he take off his golden shirt and throw it aside. 'Bring him in!'

"The doorkeepers open the door to the king's room, and the king, he stand in front of his throne. 'Come here, my friend!' he call down the long aisle. 'Please take off your shirt and give it to me!'

"The little smiling man, he come slowly in the door, but when he step into the light, do you know what the king see? The king, he look at the man and see . . . what does he see? He see that he cannot take the happy man's shirt, because the happy man, the happiest man in the world, he has no shirt!"

I throw my hands open at the last words, and Terence tips his stool back on two legs and laughs.

He slaps the tabletop and says, "Now, that is a great story."

"Yes, a good story," I tell him. "A good story to know."

Terence nods, as if he agrees with this. "True enough. Your grandfather must've been a wise man." He looks around the room, considering the many things within it; then he shakes his head and looks toward the envelope. "All right, I get your point, but, Sesay, there must be something you'd like to do with that money besides keep it under the drill bits. There must be something you'd like to have. Something you wish for."

I touch my mouth and laugh at myself. I do want something, after all. I am not so unlike the king. "I wish for a smile. A beautiful white smile, like the happy man."

Terence allows the stool to settle onto all four legs. He rests his elbows on the table and studies me as if I am a book filled with line pictures. "Sesay," he says softly. "You keep carving those birds, and I promise you, I'll find someone who can give you that smile."

I watch him, and I know he is true about this.

I feel as though I have just put on the happy man's shirt.

Chapter 33

Shasta Reid-Williams

When I got home from reading class, Dell called to say she was coming into town early to hang out before her conference, and maybe spend a little time with Terence. She was flying in on a red-eye, which normally would of been good news, especially with Cody out of town and the house feeling lonely, but all my house projects were taking longer than I thought they would, especially now that I was burning up time digging into the Householders problem. I'd called their office three times today and sat on hold for over an hour total, and all I got was the runaround. Meanwhile, the house was a mess, the painting wasn't finished, and the pictures that were supposed to be hanging in the hall were still on the floor. I hadn't even finished decorating the red wall because I couldn't decide if I liked it or not. Dell picked the worst time in the world to come early.

I didn't argue with her when she said she'd get a hotel near the airport tonight and be here tomorrow after she visited with Terence. At least that'd give me a little time to do damage control on the house and try to get it looking respectable.

As soon as I hung up, I gave the boys their baths, put them to bed with a movie, and went to work like a madwoman, scooping laundry off the floors and finishing some of the spackling and painting. There wasn't any hope for the cracked plaster in the boys' bedroom. That was a bigger project than I could get done in one night. It didn't help that I'd been feeling lousy since yesterday. My stomach was in curlicues over the Householders mess, and now with Cody gone and Tam tied up with her family, I didn't have anybody to vent to. All I could do was stew and worry, and walk around the house feeling queasy and too nervous to eat. Just like with the other two pregnancies, the upset stomach kept hitting me at the worst possible time. As soon as Cody came home from D.C., I'd have to tell him about the baby. It'd be obvious once he saw me nursing glasses of Sprite and nibbling on dry toast. He knew what that meant.

By one in the morning, I felt too lousy to keep working. I was light-headed from not eating, but too sick to eat, so I gave up and climbed into bed with my body achy and my stomach gurgling. Then I lay there flopping around like a fish onshore, until finally I got out of bed again and settled in the living room with a glass of Sprite and the laptop. If I couldn't do anything else, maybe I could figure out a way to keep us afloat until we solved this Householders mess. I started out by looking through page after page of short-term loan ads, trying to figure out if we could get a loan against the truck, and ended up looking at articles and printing pages about real estate fraud and development companies like Householders. Somewhere in the swamp of Internet information on loan companies and home fore-closures, I fell asleep.

I woke up kinked sideways in the chair with the laptop balancing on one knee, and the clock on the VCR telling me it was five in the morning. An Internet page came on the screen as I set the laptop on the table. I couldn't remember why the page was there, at first, but then everything came back to me. Around my feet, the floor was lit-tered with printouts of notes and articles about Householders and home foreclosures. Sometime while I was sleeping, they'd slid off the chair arm and scattered.

While the computer shut down, I gathered up the papers, leaning on the coffee table to grab the sheets that'd slid under the sofa. A sharp twinge pinched in my lower back, and I rocked forward onto my knees, then sucked in a breath and waited for the muscle cramp to pass before I stretched a hand under the couch. It was dusty and disgusting under there, a minefield of Matchbox cars and something slimy that felt like it might of been food in a former life. Yuck. Before Dell got here, I needed to . . .

A paper came into view, trailing from my finger—a sideways headline and pictures mixed with a column of words that'd printed almost too small to read. *From Householders Hero to Homeless*. The headline was hard to ignore, even at five in the morning, with a stomachache and sore muscles. Lifting the paper into the light, I slid to the floor with my back pressing into the chair and my knees crunched against the coffee table. I blinked hard, tried to get my eyes to focus on the picture of a man giving a speech at a banquet. His face was familiar, like I'd met him somewhere. Not likely, though. The caption read, *Ascher Arts Center*—not the kind of place where I'd be hanging out, for sure. I blinked again, trying to read the rest of the photo description. *Pictured here at a 2009 luncheon benefiting the Ascher Arts Center, former quarterback Paul Lambert has not been seen since Wednesday, when he fled town amid a storm of controversy and a federal investigation regarding Rosburten Company, which touted high returns via real estate investments, including numerous housing developments and most recently a planned athletic theme park featuring miniature replicas of major-league baseball diamonds, a pro-level training facility, a wax museum showcasing sports greats, and dozens of elaborate athletic-themed rides. In the face of several deals gone sour and a declining real estate market, Rosburten allegedly employed fraudulent tactics, including channeling money in the form of a Ponzi scheme, using capital from new investors to supply returns to existing investors, as well as to fund generous bonus packages and lavish vacations for its executives, including Lambert. Questionable monetary compensations were allegedly also delivered to one or more city councilmen in return for favorable zoning clearances and tax abatements to benefit Rosburten's ongoing development projects. Federal investigators are seeking Lambert, known in his professional sports days as the Postman. . . .*

Pictures had printed over some of the type there, and even holding it to the light, I could only make out one more sentence . . . *also known for providing on-screen celebrity sales appeals for several local car dealerships, Dallas-based Willie's restaurants, and several smaller companies owned by Ross Burten, including Householders Corporation . . .*

I looked back at the picture. That was where I knew him from. The commercials. *Hey, that's Paul Lambert. The Postman,* Cody'd said, when he caught one of the ads during some fishing show. *Dadgum, he got old. Man, I remember when my dad thought the Postman was gonna win the Super Bowl single-handed. He was a beast, big-time. Guess that's where you end up after six consecutive losing seasons and a knee injury— wearing a Superman suit and hocking houses.*

I didn't think a thing about it at the time, but now the story seemed like it mattered. Grabbing the stack of printer papers, I flipped through them, looking for the second page, but it wasn't there.

I found it under the sofa, mounded over a toy police car. Snatching the paper, I held it to the light.

. . . now wish to question Lambert in regard to his involvement with Rosburten and his personal financial stake in the floundering theme park. At the time of Lambert's disappearance, his Highland Park home, valued at over $4 million, was in the final stages of foreclosure. Prior to recent

events, Lambert, years past his football career, remained a darling of Dal-
las events and charity gatherings. Along with daughter Tamara, Lambert
won last year's Celebrity Scramble Golf Tournament, but apparently, for
Lambert, the good life turned sour. Currently, he is suspected of having fled
the country. Sources at the DA's office declined further comment. . . .

I set down the paper, my head reeling. *Tamara . . . Tam . . . Tam*
Lambert. Paul Lambert wasn't out of the country; he was right across
the street from my house. All this time, I thought Tam was like me.
I thought we were friends, but she was lying about everything. Even
when the questions about Householders came up, she never said a
word. She never told me her father was involved. How could she keep
that secret, especially after the visit to the mission, after we talked
about the families who'd lost their houses? How could she sit there
and quietly listen while I blabbered on about Householders?

Why would she do that? Why wouldn't she tell me who she was?
Why wouldn't she say something?

Because she knew. Because she knew the truth about Householders.
She'd been pretending the whole time—pretending to be just like us,
pretending to be interested in the reading class, pretending to be my
friend. She was using us the same way she was using Red Bird Lane.
This was a place to hide out—the last spot anyone would think to
look for her and her family. She was a rich girl, Daddy's little princess,
slummin' in the low-rent district until Daddy figured out how to buy
his way out of his problems, like rich people always did. They didn't
have a clue what it was like for the rest of us, how it'd feel to lose your
house and have no place left to go. For them, there was always a soft
spot to land.

The truth tasted hot and sour in my throat. I wanted to walk across
the street right now, even though it wasn't even five thirty in the morning. I wanted to pound on the door, grab Tam, Barbie, and Paul, "the

Postman," and make them tell me what they knew. Until I'd pulled the article from under the couch, Householders'd been just some giant in the fog, huge and greedy and hard to make out. Now Householders was living right across the street. Now it had a face, and a name.

I stood up and crossed the room, my legs stiff as ax handles. Little sparks of light swirled in front of my eyes as I yanked open the door and reached for the key to unlock the burglar bars. I stopped without turning it, stood with my fingers wrapped around the bars, squeezing tighter and tighter. The twisted metal felt cool under my palm, sharp and hard. I laid my forehead against the bars, let my eyes close for a minute as the morning dew dripped onto my skin. I'd stood up too quick. That was all it was.

My stomach cramped and gurgled up my throat. Something wasn't right. Something didn't feel . . .

There was a sound outside, a rustle in the bushes, then mulch crunching in the flower bed. A muffled cough drifted on the air.

Someone was out there.

Backing away from the door, I pushed it silently closed, turned the lock, stood with my heart hammering and my hand pushed against the wood. What now? What next? Was someone trying to break into the boys' bedroom?

Grabbing the phone, I moved silently down the hall, listening for the normal sounds, for anything that didn't belong. Benji was moving in his sleep, making the bedsprings squeak, whispering to the people in his dreams. *Ssshhh*, I thought. *Ssshhh*. Ahead, the glow from the porch lights shone through the boys' bedroom, into the hall. A shadow moved in the corner of the light, then backed away. Who was there?

A weapon. I needed something to protect the boys if an intruder was already in the house.

My mind spun, floundered, hesitated. *Cody's guns. I could get one of Cody's guns.* But the guns were hidden on the top shelf of the closet, secured with trigger guards, unloaded. The baseball bat was in the front room. There wasn't time. I had to think of something quick. *Think. Think of something.*

Rushing into our bedroom, I tripped over the rug and landed against the bed. Something metal slid underneath. Cody's golf club—the old pitching wedge he used for knocking the heads off dandelions in the yard. Grabbing it, I stood up. My head reeled, and I reached for the dresser, steadied myself. Moving through the darkness, I tried to shake off another shower of floating sparks. I had to get to the boys' room.

Blood pounded in my ears. Above the noise, I heard Benji whispering, then the light groan of a loose floorboard, the click of something springing loose—the window lock? I ran the last few feet, burst from the darkness of the hall into the boys' room.

Kneeling in the window seat in his pajamas, Benji gasped, then jerked upright, his hands letting go of the wooden frame, leaving the window open several inches. In the dim light, his eyes were round and black and afraid—not afraid of what was outside. Afraid of me.

"Benji, what are you . . ." My gaze went past him to a movement outside, a swirl of gray hair, a face that was just a shadow, a hand yanking back through the torn corner of the screen, leaving something behind. "Wha . . . Sesay?" Swallowing the bomb blast of adrenaline inside me, I crossed the room. "What are you do . . ." I stopped a few feet from the window seat, my eyes adjusting until I could make out the items on the sill. A book, a stuffed bunny from Benji's Easter basket last year. Something was dangling from Benji's hand—a piece of red string. A carved rabbit lay huddled in his palm like it was hiding.

I'd never seen it before. It hadn't been anywhere in the house before this moment.

This one was larger than the others. . . .

"It was you!" I exploded. Shaking the golf club at the shadow person in the window, I yanked Benji away, spun him around, and dropped him on the bed, out of reach.

"Mamaaa!" he sobbed. In the other bed, Ty jerked in his sleep and started to awaken.

"Be quiet! Don't move!" I hissed, turning toward the window again. Lights whirled around my head as I raised the club and shook it. My voice felt far away. "It was you all along! Stalking our house, spying on us, giving things to my kids. Sneaking around our yard like a . . . like a . . . a . . ." I lowered the club, gripped the wall. Something was wrong. Something was very wrong. "You can't . . . You're not supposed to be here; do you hear me? I'm calling the police. Don't you *ever* come back here. You *stay away* from my kids. You stay away from my . . . my . . ." I felt myself sinking, falling, felt something stab inside me, a white-hot searing pain. Suddenly there was no air in the room. I couldn't breathe. Everything was spinning. I gripped the wall tighter, gasped, heard air leave my mouth in a soft cry. Pain shot through me as my head collided with the window seat, and then I felt myself drifting, leaving the room, then coming back, then leaving the room again.

I heard voices but they seemed far away—too far off to bother with. I closed my eyes tighter and tried not to listen. I was so tired. My body felt like someone had filled it with lead.

Foggy realities came and went, swam in my mind like pieces of a movie playing out of focus—sharp pain, Benjamin yelling my name . . . Tam was there, and Elsie. "Don't worry, hon. The paramedics are here," Elsie said, and stroked my hair.

"She's in here!" I heard Tam's voice, and then Ty crying. He was on the bed, Sesay holding his hand.

There was a paramedic—a man with soft brown eyes. He lowered a mask over my face. *My boys*, I tried to say. *I can't leave my boys.*

Something stabbed me in the stomach again, and I heard a sharp cry, felt it inside my head.

Then the quiet swelled and swallowed me, peaceful, painless, dark. It seemed like a long time before the voices came back. They were louder now. They were asking me to wake up. They were calling my name. Calling me over and over and over. I wanted to tell them to stop.

I opened my eyes, and everything spun. A room. A hospital room. The kind with just a curtain around it. A recovery room. White and stainless steel. I could hear other people nearby.

"Hey, there. Welcome back." Tam leaned close. I dimly felt her holding my hand, rubbing it between hers.

I closed my eyes again, too out of it to care.

"Come on, now. Wake up," a deeper voice insisted. I blinked once, twice, three times, making out the image of a nurse. "Come on, now. Come on, Shasta. It's all over, hon. It's okay. You need to wake up for me now."

I nodded slowly, tried to say, *I'm awake*, but my lips dragged on my teeth and my throat felt like someone had packed it in cotton. "What happened?" came out a little better—well enough that the nurse understood, or else she guessed.

"You had a close call." Her voice was sympathetic, kind yet clinical. "Your doctor will be here in a little while."

An ache tugged somewhere deep inside me. I remembered the pain earlier, the way it was sharp and sudden. "The baby?" I whispered. My throat tightened around the words.

"Ssshhh," Tam whispered.

"The doctor'll be here in a little while," the nurse promised again. They looked at each other over the top of me, their mouths sad, narrow, grim.

Tears pushed into my eyes. "I need . . . I need to. . . ." The sentence cracked open. I swallowed the ragged edges of it. ". . . to know."

The nurse's nostrils flared and contracted. She took my other hand, her fingers a sticky latex cage. "The pregnancy was ectopic, sweetie. Tubal? You might have heard it said that way before. Dr. Naduna was able to take care of it laparoscopically. You're very fortunate to have been brought in when you were. You came close to a rupture of the Fallopian tube, and those can be fatal. You'll have some soreness for a few days, but you're going to be as good as new. Dr. Naduna can answer any other questions you might have."

Tam's head tilted to one side. She touched my shoulder, massaging in the bad news.

"But the baby," I whispered, trying to sort things out in my mind. Nothing made sense.

The nurse rubbed my fingers between her latex hands. "I know it's hard. I can send a counselor in, if you want."

"The baby," I whispered again. My daughter. My baby girl. *Brenna*. In my mind, she already had a name.

The nurse's face blurred, her eyes and nose running together behind a sea of moisture. "Honey, the pregnancy wasn't viable. It never was. A tubal pregnancy doesn't have room to develop. It's just a . . . mistake nature makes sometimes. In cases when it's caught early, it's likely not to adversely affect fertility in the future. . . ."

I closed my eyes, tried to shut out her words, felt tears drip down my cheeks, heard someone pull a Kleenex from a box, felt it touch my cheek.

Brenna, my daughter. Our baby girl.

Just a mistake nature makes sometimes . . .

I cried until the darkness swallowed me again, until my mind was quiet. When I woke, someone was sitting by the bed. My throat hurt, and she offered me a sip of water from a cup on the nightstand. I lay there thinking, remembering, hearing the nurse's words all over again until my vision cleared, and I saw who was sitting with me.

"Dell?" I whispered, wondering if I was dreaming or if she was really there. Homesickness crashed over me. Seeing her made me think of my brother, and Mama. Did they know what'd happened last night? Was Mama here? I looked around the room, but Dell and I were alone.

"Hey." Smiling, she touched my cheek with the backs of her fingers. "I just got here. Your friend stepped out."

"The . . . boys?" I croaked, still trying to string together more than two words at a time.

Dell set the cup back on the table, her dark, silky hair falling over her shoulder and brushing the sheet. She was still beautiful. She looked more grown-up than I remembered. "Benji and Ty are at home. Your neighbors are watching them. When I got to your house, they told me what had happened." Her lips pursed and trembled. "I'm sorry I didn't come on straight from the airport yesterday. I could've been there last night. You had a close call."

I swallowed hard, nodded, blinked. My eyelids felt like sandpaper. Mama wasn't here. If she was here, she'd've either been with the boys or in the room with me. She wouldn't let Dell or anybody else take charge.

"The doctor came by. He said they'd discharge you around two. We need a phone number to get in touch with Cody, all right? He should be here with you." She gave me a concerned look that let me know Tam had told her I was keeping the pregnancy a secret.

My mind raced ahead, clumsy and sluggish, tripping over itself. Maybe it was better that this had happened while Cody was gone.

Nobody would ever have to know. . . .

I wished Dell didn't know either. . . .

Would she be willing to keep the secret?

I swallowed hard, croaked out, "I don't want to call Cody. I don't want to call anybody."

Dell's eyes went wide—dark circles surrounded by white until her eyebrows came down over them. Her head tilted to one side. "We have to call him, Shasta. He needs to know."

"I'm fine. The nurse said it's . . . no big deal." I swallowed hard, *no big deal* burning on the way down.

"Shas," Dell said softly, stroking my hair in a way that reminded me of Mama. I wanted my mother so bad it hurt. I wanted Mama to promise me that everything would be all right. "You can't keep it a secret." She fussed with the sheet, and I noticed there was a ring on her finger—an engagement ring.

I grabbed the chance to change the subject to something less painful. I didn't want to talk about the baby, or Cody, or what'd happened. I couldn't. "Is that what I think it is?" I pointed to the ring, and Dell nodded. All of a sudden, her visit and my brother's traveling to Juilliard to help her with her project made sense. He wasn't there to help her with a project—he was giving her a ring. She was headed to Oklahoma after her conference so they could tell everyone they were engaged. She'd probably planned to spring the news on me when she came to my house. I'd screwed that up along with everything else.

Dell's lips twitched, like she thought it'd be wrong to look too happy right now. I stared at the ring and tried to smile, and had the fleeting thought that, when Cody saw that ring, he'd feel bad. He'd always wanted to buy me a ring like that one. "It's really pretty," I choked out. "When did you guys decide?"

Dell stared at her hand, her face glowing. "A couple months ago, when Jace flew up for our spring concert. We wanted to keep it a secret until I could come down, so we could tell Jace's kids first."

"They'll be thrilled out of their minds." Who wouldn't be? For a stepmother, my niece and nephew were getting a girl who did everything right—college, dating, marriage, maybe a baby or two sometime in the future. All in the right order. Completely unlike Aunt Shasta's screwed-up life.

At that moment I hated Dell, my future sister-in-law, even though I loved her.

But I knew it wasn't her I hated; it was myself. I couldn't do anything the way it was supposed to be done. Now I couldn't even get pregnant right.

I let my head sink against the pillow. "Give Willie and Autumn a kiss for me when you see them." My voice was scratchy, the words warped by the lump in my throat. "Tell my brother I said he did a good job."

Dell's smile fell flat. "Shasta, your mom and Jace are probably on their way here by now." She shot a guilty look at the door, like she expected my mother to show up any minute.

The pulse monitor did a rapid-fire leap. The fog burned from my mind and a desperate feeling replaced it. "Mama knows what happened?" Suddenly, everything was crashing down at once, and I couldn't stop it.

Dell's forehead knotted. "I had to call somebody. Your neighbors didn't have any phone numbers for your family. They'd left messages trying to track Cody down through the police department, but it's a big place, and only the night shift people were there. I thought your mom or Jace might know a faster way of getting in touch with Cody."

A fresh batch of tears stung my eyes. "Tell them not to come. I don't want them here."

Dell's mouth hung open. "Shasta, why in the world not?"

The tangle of emotions inside me broke loose and threads ran everywhere. "It's just . . . the house is . . . Everything is . . . It's wrong. I messed up everything. I don't want Mama to see the house the way it is, and the . . . the plaster's all cracked in the boys' room. . . and the pictures are on the . . . on the floor. . . . and I didn't get the quilts . . . on the red wall. I don't want everyone to see it . . . to see it like . . . this way. I don't want them to see my house like this, and . . ." I threw my hands over my face. I wasn't making any sense.

Dell slipped her arms around me, her head resting over mine. "Shasta, they don't care what your house looks like. They just want to be here for you." I heard Tam come back into the room and ask what was wrong. Dell's chin moved as she mouthed something. I didn't want to guess what they might be saying without saying anything. I was too tired to care. My mind and body and soul were worn to the core.

I couldn't do anything but close my eyes and mourn for the baby girl who was real whether the doctors called her *viable* or not. I couldn't imagine why, when we were in danger of losing everything else, God would take her away from us, too. I'd always been taught to believe that He had a plan, that He knew what was best, that everything worked out for our good.

But none of this was good. Nothing so painful could possibly be good. I closed my eyes and let sleep take me for a while.

When I woke, everything passed in a fog. The talk with the doctor, the paperwork for the billing, waiting forever to finally be discharged, the nurse helping me into a wheelchair, Tam picking me up in her car, Dell saying she'd go get some food and bring it over to the house—it all felt like it wasn't real. Even the drive home seemed to be happening to somebody else. We passed the church and the Summer Kitchen. I thought about the reading class, but it didn't matter anymore.

I wondered where Sesay was now. I remembered chasing her away from my house.

Was she the one who went for help? Was it her, or was it Benjamin?

I let my head fall against the window, imagining how scared the boys must of been. What might of happened to them if I'd passed out sooner? What might of happened to me if I'd lain there until morning? *You're a lucky girl*, the doctor'd said. *An ectopic pregnancy can lead to a fatal hemorrhage.*

Lucky.

I watched the church pass by. Teddy was outside with Pastor Al, trimming rosebushes in the memorial garden.

Memorial . . . I wanted a memorial for my baby girl. Nobody would understand that.

She wasn't really a baby. She never was meant to be. She was only a dream I had.

"You okay?" Tam asked softly.

I shook my head, asked, "Who called the paramedics?"

"Sesay went to Elsie's house for help. Benjamin let them in the door. You would have been proud of him. He kept his little brother calm and helped the paramedics find your information in your purse. He was a real little man."

"Benji." Pride and pain mixed inside me until I didn't know how to feel. My son was taking care of me when I should of been taking care of him. "Who's with the boys now?"

Tam glanced sideways with a half smile. "Elsie and Aunt Lute . . . oh, and Barbie. Now, there's a combination. Barbie left the kids home with my dad. That's a first, too."

The night came back to me. I remembered what I'd discovered right before I heard Sesay outside the window. "I saw you and your father on the Internet. There was an article about Householders." From the corner of my eye, I saw Tam stiffen. I didn't even turn toward her. I didn't want to.

"I know. The article was on your coffee table." Her voice was flat, hard to read. "I should have told you sooner. I'm sorry."

A laugh pushed past my lips. It tasted bitter. If she knew I'd found out the truth, then why was she here? Why were we still pretending? "I thought you were my friend."

She pulled away like I'd slapped her. "I am your friend."

"Yeah, right," I spat. "What does it matter now, anyway? What's done is done." I wanted to hurt somebody. I wanted to hurt her. "Y'all can just move back to wherever you came from—go play tennis and do whatever you people do."

She leaned forward over the steering wheel, tried to see my face. I felt her watching me as we turned onto Red Bird Lane. "It's not like that, Shasta. I know that's maybe what you think, but it's not like that. Barbie and I talked to my father for a long time yesterday. I took him by the Broadberry Mission. I wanted him to see where some of the families from this neighborhood were ending up. I really don't think he knew what kind of damage Householders was doing. But he understands now. He watched his own family bottom out when he was nine years old. He knows what that feels like. He wants to help make things right here in Blue Sky Hill, and he has some ideas. There are ways to work against Householders—a class-action suit about the predatory nature of the loans, for one thing. Dad knows some lawyers

who lost money with Rosburten, and they might be interested in ex-
acting a little revenge. But lawsuits require time, and even if you win,
that only takes care of Householders. While you're tied up in court,
they can sell their assets off to another developer, and the same thing
happens all over again. But you can—"

"What does it matter now?" I turned further away, curled into the
space between the seat and the door. My stomach ached. My heart
ached. I was hurting everywhere.

"Come on, Shasta. It matters, and you know it. My dad said
that in the past, Rosburten had some development projects stopped
cold by neighborhood associations. You get a big group of property
owners and community members together, and organize and form
a coalition. The coalition looks after the interests of the neighborhood. They oppose bad projects and support projects that are good
for the neighborhood. If the coalition is vocal enough to the press
and to city council members, they can make it almost impossible
for developers to get the approvals they need at city hall. City council members are elected, for one thing. Public opinion counts. If it
looks like they're supporting development corporations at the ex-
pense of the people . . . well, like I said, they have elections to worry
about."

I didn't answer, just watched the creek pass by as Tam's car pulled
up to the curb in front of my house.

"We can talk about it later." She put the Escalade in park, then
reached over and popped my seat belt. "When you're feeling better."

I'll never be feeling better. This will never get better. . . .

I turned, and Mama's car was in the driveway. She and Jace were
on the porch before Tam and I could make our way there. Jace smiled,
kissed me on the cheek, and whispered, "Hey, sis."

Mama shook her head and spread her hands wide, and without

even meaning to, I fell into her arms, just the way I had with a hundred skinned knees and hard knocks and broken hearts before. In spite of all the ways we drove each other crazy, I should of known that Mama would always be there to patch me up. "Shasta Marie," she whispered against my ear. "Why didn't you call me? What in the world am I gonna do with you?"

I shook my head, blubbering on her shoulder like a little kid. Mama just patted my back, and rocked me from side to side, and whispered, "Ssshhh, now, don't cry, baby girl. Don't cry. It's gonna be all right. Mama's here."

By the time I finally got my head together, I'd soaked her shirt clean through, and Dell was back with a box of fried chicken from the grocery store. She handed it to my brother, and he kissed her, and they looked at each other like they'd forgotten there was anyone else within a mile.

Mama put her arm around me, and we walked through the door. Except for a LEGO tower on the coffee table, the living room was spotless as could be. Someone'd finished hanging the Choctaw baby quilt on the red wall, and laid a woven blanket over the torn spot in the back of the sofa, and put a vase of cut flowers on one of the end tables. Hollyhocks from the backyard. The room looked beautiful.

I stared at it with my mouth hanging open, wondering if I was still back in the hospital, dreaming. This wasn't my house. My house was a disaster area.

Tam gave me a private little smile, and from the sofa, Barbie winked. Beside her, Elsie nodded and Aunt Lute put two thumbs up. For some reason, her thumbs were baby blue and spring green.

Mama took my purse and set it on the back of Cody's favorite chair. "You want to lie down in your bed, or sit here awhile?" she asked, fussing over a wrinkle in the neck of my shirt and smoothing my hair behind my shoulder. "I could fix you a little cocoa, or some tea."

"I don't want anything." I forced what I hoped looked like a smile. "Thanks for coming, Mama."

"Where else would I be?" That sounded more like Mama. Inside that sentence, like the filling in a burrito, was, *Why didn't you tell me about this house, Shasta Marie?*

I turned toward the sofa, toward Barbie, Aunt Lute, Elsie, and Tam, to keep from looking at Mama. "Thanks for helping me last night. Thanks for looking after the boys."

Elsie batted a hand. "Why, a'course. You're my neighbor, after all, and my teacher. Who's gonna teach me if you're laid up?"

"The little knights have gone to the land of Nod for a nap, I'm afraid," Aunt Lute chimed in, with a flourish toward the hall. The boys' door was closed. "They had a long night last night."

I felt my chin tremble with leftover emotions. My boys. This house would only have two boys in it, at least for now, but I was so lucky they were here. Some people wanted babies and never got them at all. "I need to see the boys, okay?"

I started toward the hall, and Mama followed, catching up and holding me around the waist, like I shouldn't make the trip on my own. "Cody called," she said quietly. "He's flying home."

I bit my lip, stopping next to a grouping of family pictures that had magically found their way onto the wall. I glanced back toward the living room, and everyone was clustered around the sofa, watching me look at the photos. While Dell was at the hospital waiting with me and helping me slog through all the paperwork, Tam must of come home and gotten everybody busy on fixing up the place, so I wouldn't be embarrassed when Mama got here. Only real friends would do that for you.

Mama didn't have a clue about all that, of course. "Cody wants you to call him back," she said. "As soon as you feel up to it."

"Is Cody mad?" I scratched my forehead, wishing I could claw through to my brain and root out all the worries racing through it.

Mama sidestepped and held me by both shoulders. "Mad about what? He just wanted to know that you're all right. That boy loves you, Shasta Marie."

"I know." Of course Cody loved me. Nobody'd ever loved me like Cody did. I didn't deserve that love. I wasn't honest with it. "But I did it on purpose, Mama. I meant to get pregnant. Cody said he didn't want—"

Mama lifted a finger and pressed it to my lips. Her jaw went stiff, and she shook her head. "Don't," she said, and I felt a twinge in my heart. "That's *your* private business. Yours and Cody's. You need to talk about it with him. You're a grown woman, Shasta Marie."

You're a grown woman. . . . I looked into my mama's eyes, and I felt the two of us turning a corner. "I guess I am," I whispered, and we started down the hall again, Mama wrapping her arm around me, and me resting my head on her shoulder. Grown or not, I felt good having her here. Sometimes you need your mama, no matter how old you are. "I didn't think I'd ever hear you say it, though."

Mama laid her head over on mine. "We're all growing up a little, I guess. Just remember we're here when you need us, all right? You and Cody don't have to do everything on your own."

"I know."

"Guess you heard that you're going to have a new sister-in-law," she said. I nodded, and she ponytailed my hair between her fingers. "You and Cody and the boys are coming home for the wedding, no matter what. You hear me?"

"We will." When Mama took that tone, I knew better than to argue.

She gave my shoulder a squeeze. "See? I can still boss you around when I need to."

I nodded, swiping my eyes with my fingertips. I wanted to tell her how good it felt to have her with me, but I couldn't. Sentimental words didn't come easy between Mama and me. "I know you can. I probably need it."

"Oh, shush." Mama wouldn't stand for anybody criticizing her baby girl, even me. I realized we'd made it to the end of the hall and were stalled out in front of the boys' door. "I love what you've done with this house," she said, and I felt myself swelling inside. "I can't wait to see the boys' room." She reached for the door handle, and I cringed. The boys' room was a plaster disaster.

"I hadn't quite gotten to . . ." The door creaked open, and I stopped in the middle of the sentence. Where there had been cracks and chips of missing plaster, and water stains in the paint, now the walls were alive with vines, and flowers, and thumbprint butterflies in all colors and sizes. In their beds, the boys were sound asleep, their rainbow-colored fingers splayed against the covers.

Above Benjamin's bed, in the corner where the headboard had been pulled away from the wall, a little brown rabbit crouched among cane stalks, his coat so freshly painted it glistened, his small blue sweater and mittens perfectly matched to the storybook sitting on Benjamin's night table. In case there was any question, underneath the painted rabbit, the name was written. *P-E-t-E-r*, in the careful, round print of someone who was new to letters, but who had put them there very carefully. Dangling from the boys' bedposts, Sesay had left tiny carved rabbits as companions for little Peter.

"Seems like you've got some real nice neighbors here too—the way they took care of you and the boys last night," Mama said quietly, and Benji stirred in his bed, then drifted off again.

"We do," I agreed. "We really do."

"Don't get neighbors who look after each other, just everywhere in the big city," Mama pointed out. "You and Cody found a nice little spot here."

"It found us." The darkness inside me lifted as I took in the boys' newly painted room—the front bedroom of our first real house. The house where my dreams had changed, and I had changed. Without this place, without all the baggage that came with it—the neighbors, and the Summer Kitchen, and the challenges that were behind us and those still ahead of us—I wasn't sure who I'd be. I wouldn't be the person I was now. I wouldn't be Shasta Marie Reid-Williams, who could paint, and fix plaster, and repair tiles, and teach someone to read, and build a life for her boys, and face the giants, if she had a mind to.

In spite of all that had gone wrong, or maybe because of it, Red Bird Lane had grown me in ways I never knew I could grow—taken away the little girl who was waiting for her daddy to come home and replaced her with a woman who could build a home of her own and keep the people she loved safe inside it.

It happened because of a house, but not just any house.

A special house.

The little yellow house where my family lived.

Chapter 34

Tam Lambert

The formative meeting of the Blue Sky Hill Neighborhood Coalition was held one week after Shasta came home from the hospital. The crowd of interested residents, business owners, and community activists filled the Summer Kitchen and spilled onto the porch, where Teddy and Pastor Al were handing out questionnaires and proposed bylaws.

My father, Barbie, and I drove over from Highland Park. My father had managed to move us into a house belonging to a friend who could afford to keep houses he wasn't living in at the moment. Now that Dad was becoming the force that turned the tide in the growing corruption case surrounding Ross Burten and several city councilmen, Paul "the Postman" Lambert was an odd sort of folk hero—someone willing to speak out against the rampant executive greed and reckless speculation that had led to widespread economic meltdown. Overnight, the image makers and the spin doctors had redrawn my father, morphing him from an example of abuse of power into a symbol of repentance and retribution—an honest man who was willing to come forward, admit his mistakes, take his lumps, and help in the government's efforts to unearth Ross Burten's hidden millions, so that the money could be redistributed to his victims.

As quickly as a media image can be destroyed, it can be rebuilt, and Dad was rising from the ashes. As for Ross Burten, he'd fled to Europe, where he and his wife were reportedly living the high life in a comfortable chalet in Switzerland. His Swiss bank accounts would keep him well supplied for the long term. The future of Ross Burten's other corporations, including Householders, was uncertain, but as my father addressed the crowd, he warned them that this was only a temporary reprieve.

"Rest assured that the properties in Householders' cache represent valuable assets intended to come together as part of a future development plan," he told the crowd, his gaze sweeping sternly from one side of the room to the other, taking in money-strapped residents from streets like Red Bird Lane and wealthy homeowners of historic estate properties on Blue Sky Hill. "This is an issue that affects all of you, regardless of location, or property value, or financial resources. If you want the neighborhood to resist an overabundance of new multifamily housing complexes and retain its historic look and character, then existing residents must take action while there is still time. There are numerous avenues through which current residents can retain a voice in how the area changes, and exert power over new development. In general, these processes begin with the formation of a neighborhood coalition of homeowners, small business owners, and groups with vested interests in the preservation and quality of life in the area. The coalition should be organized with a clear mission statement, governing officers and/or a council, and bylaws. Property owner signatures must be gathered on letters of support. Typically, this sort of effort begins with door-to-door footwork, but the results can be powerful. The neighborhood coalition can accomplish many things individual homeowners cannot, including petitioning to have the area declared a historic district, fighting zoning changes, soliciting press coverage, making the city planning and zoning commissions aware of residents' interests and quality-of-life issues, such as lot sizes, traffic congestion, and other questions of environmental impact. Currently, Householders' stake in the neighborhood is approximately twenty-five percent, so gathering the majority of the remaining independent property owners into one force is essential."

Elsie half stood in her chair. "I'll sure as heck do whatever it takes. My husband and I built our house with GI money when he came home from the war. Put our blood, sweat, and tears into it. The whole street was built by GIs. We all worked together to put up them homes, back when folks had some morals and neighbors looked out for one another. Somebody like Householders is gonna tear the place down over my dead body."

"Edward's father built our home," Teddy's mother, Hannah Beth, added from the back of the room, where she was leaning on a walker. "Blue Sky Hill had row after row of lovely old homes, and now we have condominiums right around the corner from us on Vista Street. Our daughter, Rebecca, and her husband are lawyers. They'll help us draw up the legal paperwork for this coalition. They'll pitch in any way they can."

"My sister gone come take 'way them con'amimums! No more con-a-minamums!" Teddy added, striking a fist in the air and receiving a round of applause. A murmur of agreement circled the group.

"Nobody's getting our house without a fight," Shasta piped up. "We might be new here, but we're not leaving. This is our place. Our neighborhood. If we have to sell everything we own, we're not letting Householders take over our house and force us out. We're going to figure out how to bring a class-action suit against them for the way they do their contracts. In fact, if there's anybody else here who's in a Householders home, we've got a list by the door, and you need to sign it, so we can get in touch with you. I'm still looking for a lawyer to take the case, but I'll find one. What Householders does to people is wrong, and we need to stand against it." Beside her, Cody nodded and slipped his hand into hers.

"I agree," Mrs. Kaye offered from the kitchen, where she, MJ from the bookstore, and Cass were putting out coffee and cups. "My uncle Poppy lived in this neighborhood all of his adult life, and while it may have its issues, the solution isn't to take advantage of existing residents, tear down the houses, and destroy the historic character of the neighborhood. If downtown workers want to move to this area to be close to their jobs, let them buy the existing houses and reno-vate them. There are empty commercial buildings and warehouses all around here. If developers want to put in multifamily housing, let them rehab those properties. Part of what always made this neighbor-hood special was its sense of identity. People were proud that they lived in Blue Sky Hill. This neighborhood has always been diverse. Within a few blocks, you could find small single-family homes like the one my uncle built, and then just uphill, the estates of doctors and lawyers. There's still enough room here for everyone, but new construction needs to be planned and controlled, so that it doesn't displace existing residents or destroy their quality of life."

"Exactly," my father agreed, taking command of the crowd the way he once took command of a football team. "And I can promise that none of you, on your own, have the resources to fight off devel-opers like Householders. Your defense, your ability to preserve this neighborhood lies in banding together"—to illustrate, he linked his fingers, forming a double fist—"in creating a neighborhood coali-tion to prevent wholesale rezoning and rebuilding. Developers, quite frankly, recognize the power and political pull of an active, vocal, united neighborhood. As a coalition, residents have the power to negotiate such things as community benefits agreements, in which community groups have a voice in shaping development projects, and are able to press for benefits tailored to the community's needs. Developers use this community support to help in getting the permit approvals, rezoning, and abatements necessary to go forward with a project. For many projects, the amount of community support or opposition determines whether the project makes it through city hall. Developers and the neighborhood coalition working together can provide a win-win . . ."

I let my mind drift as the conversation and the planning of the Blue Sky Hill Neighborhood Coalition went on, the hammering out of details, drafting of a mission statement, and election of officers lasting well into the evening. For her part, Shasta had done her homework, both on the Internet looking up bylaws and organizational structures, and through speaking with my father and a lawyer friend of his. The necessary paperwork for the formation of the coalition was typed, copied, collated, and ready to be handed out, which may have been why Shasta was unanimously elected to the office of secretary, serving beneath MJ, who'd been elected president, and several board members hailing from various portions of the Blue Sky Hill area.

By the time the meeting ended, it was dark outside. As residents finished paperwork and wandered to their cars, Shasta and I stood on the sidewalk next to the memory garden, watching my father and Barbie walk to the children's building to pick up the kids.

"They may have to wrestle Benji and Ty to get your brothers out of there," Shasta commented, smoothing her T-shirt self-consciously as she watched Barbie and my father cross under the streetlight. "My guys sure miss having friends across the street."

"The sibs miss them, too—even Jewel," I said, but my mind was still back in the meeting. My father had taken a bold step tonight—

one worthy of the Superman suit on the commercials. "We'll get them all together to play soon."

Shasta flashed a doubtful frown, staring glumly at the memory garden.

"Sure." The word was flat, open to interpretation. She crossed her arms and bent forward, seeming cold despite the balmy night air.

The conversation faded. The lack of things to say felt awkward and strange, given all the times we'd sat in the car after driving somewhere and talked until pandemonium finally broke out in the backseat. Those conversations seemed distant now, as if too much had happened for them to be relevant anymore.

"We miss you at reading class." Shasta flicked a glance at me, curious about my reaction.

I wondered what she was thinking—if she was looking at the Summer Kitchen, like I was, and realizing that the two girls who first visited here were vastly different from the women who stood here now. "I'll be back. I just needed to take a few days to . . . well, help get everything moved into the new house in Highland Park. I want to come back and finish out the reading class."

Shasta's head rolled loosely to one side. "Yeah, right." She wagged her chin, her skepticism visible even in the flickering glow of the church windows. "You're going to drive all the way up here from the University of Texas?"

"Who told you I was going to UT?"

Shasta shrugged, tossing her long, dark hair over her shoulder. "Barbie told me the day we helped y'all load the moving truck. She said you had a golf scholarship there."

I shook my head, surprised that Barbie had been discussing my future, or that she cared what it might be. Then again, Barbie wasn't the person she once was, either. This summer had changed us all.

Blue Sky Hill had transformed everything I thought, and felt, and wanted. "On the way over here I told them I wasn't going to UT."

Shasta coughed softly, rocking back on her heels. "Why? I mean, I figured you'd be, like, dying to, like . . . move on with your plans, get on with your normal life."

Tipping my head back, I drank in the night air, looked up at the dome of stars twinkling overhead. "I guess the old normal doesn't seem normal anymore." Emity had left a dozen messages on my phone in the past few days, and I hadn't bothered to answer her. She wanted to know about Europe, but drifting around Europe was as far from my plans as the moon from the earth. "I don't want to play golf—not competitively, anyway. It was just something I did . . . I'm not even sure why. I guess . . . because I thought my father would like it. I want to do things that . . . matter, you know? I told my dad I'm going to stay here in Dallas and go to SMU, work toward law school."

"Whoa," Shasta breathed. "Too bad you're not further along. You could help us slay the Householders' Army of Death. You and me could be like Xena the Warrior Princess, times two."

I giggled at the picture. "Yeah, well, you can wear the leather Xena suit. I'll just be me."

"Pppffff!" Shasta braced her hands on her hips, her face jutting toward me. "You're the one with all the cute clothes, Hannah Montana."

We laughed together, and for a moment it felt like old times. "You know, we really could," I said finally, watching as Sesay crossed the street and met Terence in the doorway of his studio. The collection of colored glass bottles hanging in the tree outside chimed softly in the breeze from passing cars, the sound coming and going as attendees from the meeting started their vehicles and pulled out of the church parking lot.

"We really could what?"

"Be like Xena times two," I said absently. "You'll have Benjamin in kindergarten this year, and Tyler going to Head Start. You could come take some classes with me."

Shasta scoffed. "College classes?"

"Sure, why not?"

"Ffff! And do what? Be a lawyer?"

I paused, thinking that perhaps I should have found a more subtle way to bring up the idea. As I was making my plans to tell my father about SMU, it had occurred to me that the college wasn't far from Shasta's house. A city bus would take her right to campus. I could stop by and pick her up any day she needed a ride. "I think you'd be a great lawyer. We could be partners—defend truth, justice, and the American dream."

Chewing her bottom lip, she squinted at me, her eyes narrowing as she considered it. Finally, she sighed and shook her head. "Yeah, I'll be able to pay college tuition with all the money that's left over after we get through paying off all our dumb bills."

Barbie and my father emerged from the children's building with Aunt Lute, who had elected to spend her evening with "the courtiers," as she called them, rather than attending the meeting in the Summer Kitchen. Shasta and I tabled our conversation, watching my strange jumble of family come up the walk. As always, the Lambert clan didn't go quietly. Dad had Landon tugging on one arm, Daniel trying to tackle him from behind, and Mark darting in and out like a wild banshee. In Barbie's arms, Jewel waved her hands and squealed.

"Let's get a move on," my father ordered as they passed by.

"Guess that's your cue." Shasta thumbed toward the children's building. "I better go get my kids. Cody's probably out there in the truck having a rigor, wondering what's taking so long."

Checking the parking lot, she vacillated in place, as if she wanted to say something more. "Well, anyway, hug for luck." She opened her arms, and I wrapped mine around her, and I rocked back and forth in the arms of the only friend I'd ever had who didn't care who I was, or what I looked like, or what kind of car I drove, or how well I played golf. Shasta was my friend just because she wanted to be.

"Don't be a stranger." She sniffed and swallowed hard. "Come over for lunch and stuff, when you're down there taking those college classes."

Emotion swelled in my throat. "I will." We let go and hovered on the sidewalk, the conversation still seeming unfinished. "You know, they have scholarships and grants and things." The words tumbled from my mouth sounding clumsy and unplanned, even though they weren't.

"What?" Shasta's head cocked to one side as if I were speaking in gibberish. "Who does?"

I swallowed the rest of my apprehension and plunged in. "SMU. I printed off some information sheets last night. They're in the car." I nodded toward the Escalade, where Barbie and Dad were getting the kids into their seats, and Aunt Lute was standing on the sidewalk with her arms high in the air, a diaphanous scarf catching the night breeze and streaming from her fingertips like a paper-thin flag. "My dad's got connections there, like everyplace else. If he can get me on the golf team at UT, he can help you find some financial help for SMU."

Shasta's hands hitched onto her hips, and she gave my idea a sassy lip smack. "Tamara Lambert, you are so pushy."

"Look who's talking, Miss Neighborhood Coalition Secretary." I was wearing Shasta down, I could tell. She'd give in, eventually.

"I have two kids to take care of."

"Who are going to be in school all morning, every morning."

Exasperated, she flipped her hands into the air. "I haven't cracked a book in five years, Tam. I'd be, like, the dumbest college student ever."

"No, you wouldn't. You should see some of the people I graduated high school with. They're idiots, and they're going to college."

"Well, that's comforting." Swatting at a moth investigating her face, she snorted. "Are you, like, afraid to go by yourself, or what?"

"Uh, no," I shot back, even though there might have been a grain of truth in her assessment. College seemed a long way from where I'd been this summer. "I just think you got potential, kid."

"Geez." She walked a few steps toward the children's building, then turned around and continued walking backward. "Let me go get my kids before Cass locks them up in the closet for the night, and then you can give me your stupid papers."

"Okay." Checking the parking lot, where my father was in the process of trying to capture Daniel, I trotted after Shasta, and we headed down the sidewalk, as we had so often. This time, it felt as if we were moving toward something.

"It's a really dumb idea, though." Shasta hip-butted me, and I stumbled off the edge of the sidewalk. She didn't bother to apologize. "Me being a lawyer."

"Or a teacher. You'd make a great teacher."

Grabbing the door handle, she rolled her eyes. "Lawyers get paid more. So then you'll always have cuter clothes than me. That's part of your plan, right?"

"You decide," I said, and she threw her chin up and strode into the hallway. I didn't follow—just let the door close behind her and wandered back to Teddy's memorial garden. Standing in the moon shadows, I took in the scent of roses and night-blooming jasmine. Overhead, the pecan leaves rustled their summer-dry branches, and the moon rocked on its back, bright and full of promise, balancing just above the cross on the steeple of the old white church. Here, in this place that was like nothing I'd ever imagined, suddenly nothing seemed impossible. Here, away from the labels, and the expectations, and the rules I'd allowed to define me, I was free to find out who I really was.

In the parking lot, Daniel giggled as my father scooped him up. I watched them in silhouette, as Dad juggled my little brother under his arm like a football. In the farthest reaches of my mind, a memory stirred, now tender in its return and beautiful to look at, like last season's birds coming back to nest. Somewhere between the Waffle House years and the summer of unanswered prayers, I knew the rise and fall of my father's footsteps, the strong circle of his fingers, the feel of his arm holding me suspended above the ground. I remembered how it felt to fly, safely snuggled on Superman's hip.

The memory seeped through me, warming cold spaces as I watched my father tuck Daniel into the car, and Aunt Lute gather her silky banner, and the residents of Blue Sky Hill disappear into the darkness. Above the parking lot, the church marquee flickered, the old bulb undecided between yellow and white, between light and shadow. Sometime in the past week, Pastor Al had taken down the invitation to the Summer Kitchen and replaced it with a simple quote from George Meredith. A sense of rightness filled me as I read the words and listened to Pastor Al moving across the hollow floors of the old church, turning out the lights, one by one. As the glow dimmed, I knew that my prayers hadn't gone unanswered this summer. The answers had only gone unrecognized.

Blue Sky Hill was the answer to a prayer I'd never known was inside me. A question I hadn't the words to ask. No matter what came after, this would always be the place that broke me and remade me, and gave me to understand the words on Pastor Al's sign.

Who rises from prayer a better man, his prayer is answered.

Beyond Summer

Lisa Wingate

This Conversation Guide is intended to enrich the
individual reading experience, as well as encourage us
to explore these topics together—because books,
and life, are meant for sharing.

A CONVERSATION
WITH LISA WINGATE

NAL Accent sat down with Lisa Wingate, Tam Lambert, and Shasta Williams in the Summer Kitchen of Dallas, Texas.

NAL Accent: First, I'd like to thank all of you for joining me. Tam and Shasta, I'm especially pleased that you could participate.

Shasta Williams: Hey, I still can't believe you asked me. Since the Blue Sky Hill neighborhood association started up, I've been on TV, like, three times, but it still feels weird that people want to know what I have to say. For Lisa and Hannah Montana over there, it probably seems like no big deal to do interviews, but for me it's a major change.

Tam Lambert: I don't know why she keeps calling me Hannah Montana. She's the one who's Miss Big Deal. You should have seen her at the last city council meeting.

Lisa Wingate: To tell you the truth, I'm afraid to get in the middle of these two, but I always enjoy spending time with my characters.

NAL Accent: Lisa, my first question is for you. Home foreclosure, financial scandal, mortgage fraud—in some ways *Beyond Summer* seems inspired by recent news headlines. Why did you particularly want to tackle these current subjects?

Lisa: As with many of my novels, *Beyond Summer* grew from the story that came before it. After *The Summer Kitchen* hit the shelves, I began receiving e-mails asking what would happen next to the Blue Sky Hill neighborhood, and in particular what would become of Poppy's little pink house. One reader said, "I hope the developers don't tear it down. I hope the house goes to someone who will love it." I realized I harbored those hopes for Poppy's house, too. I began searching for someone who would not only love the little house, but have the gumption to fight for the survival of the neighborhood. Shasta was exactly the right person for the job. As she and Cody were closing the deal on their new home, a new question came to mind. What if the very people who were profiting from shady real estate deals in the Blue Sky Hill neighborhood were suddenly forced to move into the neighborhood themselves? What if they moved in right across the street from Shasta and Cody? In an economic era when many families find themselves living on the edge financially and reversals of fortune are not uncommon, it seemed entirely plausible. I wondered how someone like Tam, who has been living what most of us would consider the good life, would deal with such an experience. What would she learn about life in those little houses across town? What would she learn about herself?

NAL Accent: How would this experience change her?

CONVERSATION GUIDE

Tam: You know, looking back, I don't think of our old lives as the good life. I know from the outside, everything probably looked perfect. We had the things other people want—big house, nice cars, clothes, nannies, housekeepers, huge birthday parties for the kids. But we were just a bunch of people living in a house together, going through the motions. We weren't a family. I think the most important thing I learned in the little house on Blue Sky Hill is that possessions aren't a substitute for relationships.

Shasta: Pppfff! Relationships are great, but I think I could deal with the swimming pool, the country club, and the cute clothes, too.

NAL Accent: Lisa, you took on a real challenge in writing about Sesay, a homeless woman, yet we at NAL Accent think you really pulled it off. What inspired you to tell Sesay's story?

Lisa: In spending time at various mission projects, in particular the Gospel Café in Waco, Texas, I've crossed paths with so many interesting people—both among the volunteers and among those who are served. What you realize, if you take a little time to listen, is that each person who comes through the doors has a story. Each story is unique.

Each story is valuable. The fact that someone is homeless, or illiterate, or poor doesn't make the story any less valuable. We each have lessons to teach and lessons to learn.

Years ago, I interviewed a woman who'd come from Haiti and worked in the sugarcane fields in Florida, under terrible conditions. Eventually, due to a fire that forced the sugarcane company to temporarily shut down in that area, she left the cane fields and became homeless. Years later, when I met her, she had found her way into a program designed to help the homeless get off the streets. She told me the story of the rabbits running when the cane fields burned. I always thought that story, and her story, should be shared.

NAL Accent: Shasta and Tam, I'm curious to know whether meeting Sesay has changed the way you look at homeless people, and what you would like readers to take away from your experience.

Shasta: I think, mostly, it's made me see that you can't tell what's inside somebody from looking at the outside. Putting people into categories just comes natural, I guess—even to someone like me, who gets tired of being judged by the way I look. I think, by getting to know Sesay, I've learned to look deeper. At least, I hope I have.

Tam: Shasta's right. I think I'd like readers to take away the belief that we each have the power to make a difference. While not all of us have the resources to start something like the Summer Kitchen, we can all find places to give our time and talents. Even just a few hours a week can be the beginning of something life changing.

NAL Accent: Shasta, through you and other characters such as Dell and Terence in *Beyond Summer*, Lisa weaves characters from the Tending Roses series into the Blue Sky Hill series. How does it feel to be part of both series?

Shasta: Well, what can I say? As cool as Dell is, and as much as I'm going to love having her for a sister-in-law, I always knew I had my own story to tell. My Nana Jo used to say we all wander the world until we find our feet. I think that's what I was doing when I first met Dell, back in the Tending Roses series. Now, here in Blue Sky Hill, I think I've finally found my feet.

NAL Accent: Lisa, did you feel a particular satisfaction from merging these two worlds?

Lisa: It is incredibly satisfying to see these two series come together. Dell's story actually began in my first novel, *Tending Roses*, and throughout the Tending Roses series, she was growing up and discovering herself. In a way, she became the daughter I never had. When her story ended in *A Thousand Voices*, readers began asking what would happen next—would she choose to go to Juilliard to pursue her music, or would she choose to marry Jace and move to southeastern Oklahoma? I've been waiting to answer that question, and waiting to discover what Dell's friend, Shasta, would decide to do with her life. Watching both of these characters come into their own has been like reaching the finish line of a marathon with two sister-friends running alongside.

NAL Accent: Lisa, many of the characters in the novel act foolishly, sometimes even go a little crazy. There are a number of "meltdowns" or threatened or imminent meltdowns. Do any of the characters stand out for you as particularly challenging or interesting to write about?

Lisa: Even though Barbie has a smaller role in the novel, she was one of the most challenging characters to write about. At the beginning of the novel, she appears to be fairly plastic and hollow, but I didn't want her to end up that way. I wanted to understand, and to help Tam understand, why Barbie felt the drive to have so many children so quickly, and why material possessions were so important to her. I wanted her to be a whole person, and in the end to recognize her own motivations and to experience a shift in her priorities. I hoped Blue Sky Hill would grow her and change her, even if she didn't want it to.

Shasta: Well, yeah, okay, I guess anything's possible. Barbie is a trip, but I would've thought Aunt Lute would be the hardest one to write about, since she's nuts, anyway.

Tam: I think I knew all along that Barbie was teetering on the brink. I kept hoping that she would pull herself together and be a mom to the sibs, but to tell you the truth I didn't think she had it in her. She surprised me.

NAL Accent: Lisa, is there a character in *Beyond Summer* that you have a hankering to write about in another book?

Lisa: I think it would be interesting to know more about MJ, the woman who owns the bookstore. She lived in the Blue Sky Hill neighborhood when she was a child, then moved away, but felt the pull to return and start the Book Basket. She is obviously well educated, either in the traditional sense or self-educated. I've always wondered what happened to her during the years she was away from Blue Sky Hill, and what motivated her to return.

Shasta: Oh, I think you should write about Aunt Lute. I wonder where she got all the things that are in her head.

Tam: No, not Aunt Lute. I say you should explore the family that ended up in the shelter after losing their house on Blue Sky Hill. Where did they have their baby? Were they able to rebuild their lives? Did they sue Householders?

NAL Accent: Shasta, I understand that in addition to being active in the Blue Sky Hill Neighborhood Coalition and tutoring at the Summer Kitchen, you've signed up for some college classes. How's that going for you?

Shasta: Not so bad, but I should've studied harder in high school. Geez. My English teacher was right. I should've been paying attention.

NAL Accent: And, Tam, now that you're closer to your original upscale neighborhood, are you tempted to slip back into your old ways of hanging out at the country club and the mall? Have you been in touch with Emity?

Tam: Really, my mind's on school, and working with the literacy program, and volunteering at the Summer Kitchen when I get a little time. Mrs. Kaye's son, Christopher, is hot, for one thing, and he works down at the Summer Kitchen a couple days a week. There's also a program in Dallas that teaches inner-city kids to play golf. My dad and I have been getting involved there, so I guess all that time at the country club wasn't wasted, after all.

Emity called once from Europe. She was having a good time, but after we talked about the basic tourist stuff, we really couldn't find much to say. She never called back after that, and I haven't called her. I guess sometimes people just grow in two different directions.

NAL Accent: One message I took away from the novel is that we're all connected. Decisions that one of us makes affect the rest of us, often in ways that profoundly alter our lives. This is certainly true within families, but it extends well beyond families. Shasta and Tam, would you agree with that? And, Lisa, is this a message you think we particularly need to hear these days?

Shasta: That's one of those things you understand, growing up Choctaw. Even in these modern times, Choctaw kids are still taught that we're part of the Tribe. What hurts any member hurts the Tribe, and what hurts the Tribe hurts every member. We understand it in a way that a lot of folks don't.

Tam: I think the interdependence of people was one of the biggest revelations for me during my time on Blue Sky Hill. In today's society, we value independence above almost everything else. We work toward it. We crave it. We think that success is in not having to depend on anyone, and not having anyone depend on us, but the truth is that we're not meant to go along the path alone. We're meant to lean on each other and to support each other. Success is in having the grace to give when you can and the humility to take when you need to.

Lisa: I think Tam stole my answer.

NAL Accent: I'm curious to know what each of you thinks will happen to the Blue Sky Hill neighborhood in the years to come.

Tam: I think the neighborhood will grow, change, and develop naturally. As current residents age and leave their homes, new residents will move in, remodel and redevelop the historic properties, allowing those properties to retain their character. Blue Sky Hill will be a place where cultures meet and people of different backgrounds and income levels mix.

Lisa: I imagine that Blue Sky Hill will become a place with its own identity. Like many neighborhoods in Dallas, it will be nurtured and regulated by a coalition of residents who value the character of the neighborhood, but who also value each other. I imagine that as the neighborhood grows, more services, like the literacy class, will be available to existing residents.

Shasta: It'll be home, of course, and in the future, outfits like Householders will know not to mess with folks in Blue Sky Hill.

NAL Accent: Lisa, in what ways is the fictional Summer Kitchen similar to and different from the Gospel Café, which you say in your acknowledgments helped to inspire *Beyond Summer*? And is there a real-life counterpart to the Blue Sky Hill neighborhood?

Lisa: There are many neighborhoods in Dallas that are similar to Blue Sky Hill. The neighborhood is roughly in the area of Lakewood, and shares some similarities, including the streets of grand old mansions, like those on Blue Sky Hill, and more modest houses only blocks away, like those on Red Bird Lane.

The Summer Kitchen is in many ways similar to the real-life Gospel Café. While in the story, the Summer Kitchen operates from the church building, the real Gospel Café still operates from its original location, a blue Victorian house in the Kate Ross neighborhood of Waco, Texas. Like the Summer Kitchen, the Gospel Café was started by a very small group of people. It proves that a few people can step out and make a difference in the larger community. The café now offers meals, care and concern, and services such as medical help and substance abuse classes for residents and homeless men, women, and families who would have nowhere else to turn. So much more than food is delivered through the kitchen window. When people have become invisible, like Sesay, the mere experience of being valued, of having a choice of menu items, of having someone look you in the eye, of being offered space at a table set with real plates and silverware, of finding a place where people greet you and remember your name, can be life altering. Often, the contact that begins with a lunch at the café becomes the first link in a chain of events that changes lives. There's really no way to describe the experience of looking across the kitchen counter and seeing a customer in tears over a kind word and a plate of food.

QUESTIONS
FOR DISCUSSION

1. There are a lot of characters in this book. Who are your favorites and why? Who don't you like?

2. Most the characters are deeply flawed, yet we care about them anyway. How does Lisa Wingate achieve that?

3. The Lambert family members find their lives turning upside down almost overnight. Tam ends up in a place she can hardly conceive of being. Yet most of us experience at some point some sense of disconnect between what we thought our lives would be and what they really are. Has that happened to you? How did that experience change you?

4. Why do you think Lisa Wingate chose to include the stories that Sesay tells the children at the Summer Kitchen story hour? What insights did you receive from them?

5. Did you notice that Lisa Wingate narrates Tam's and Shasta's chapters using verbs in the past tense while she narrates Sesay's chapters using verbs in the present tense? Why do you think she

made this choice? Do you have any thoughts about other ways in which the novel is structured?

6. Barbie experiences an emotional turning point that offers some insights into her background, and might suggest she has tried to satisfy an emotional loss by surrounding herself with material possessions. Is that how you read Barbie? Do you think our culture is too obsessed with acquiring things, and if so, what are some of the reasons for that?

7. Shasta has made some impulsive decisions in her life, and is suffering the consequences. Perhaps the worst consequence is the bruising of her own self-image. Discuss how she sees herself, how she thinks others see her, and whether her self-criticism is deserved.

8. What do you think of Aunt Lute? In what ways is she truly crazy? In what ways is she crazy like a fox—in other words, smarter in her handling of a situation than either Tam or Barbie?

9. Several characters experience major insights or turning points during the course of the novel that suggest they will make different choices in the future—Tam, her father, Barbie, Shasta, Sesay, to name a few. Did you find these transformations believable? Why or why not?

10. What would you like the Blue Sky Hill neighborhood to be like in five years? Fifteen years? Fifty years? How much responsibil-

ity do you think you have for helping to shape the places where you live and work?

11. Simple acts of kindness can go a long way in helping someone get through the day, or in knitting together an entire community. What are some acts of kindness that stand out for you in the book?

12. Is there a need for a Summer Kitchen or a neighborhood association near where you live? If you were to start something like that, what needs might it try to fulfill and what form might it take? What resistance might you encounter? What joys might you experience?